Tomorrow's First Light

Texas Promise Book 1

Naomi Rawlings

Cover Design: © Clarissa Yeo 2017

Cover Photographs: Shutterstock.com

Editors: Natalie Hanemann; Melissa Jagears

Formatting: Polgarus Studio

To Melissa,

For the countless hours you've spent helping and encouraging me both as a writer and as a friend. Can you believe we've known each other for almost a decade? In some ways the time seems so short, and in other ways it feels so very long considering the countless valleys and hills through which both of us have helped each other. I value our friendship and wish you many happy tomorrows filled with light, hope, and grace…

And strawberries. Many, many strawberries.

Prologue

Twin Rivers, Texas; September, 1869

"They're kissing." Sam Owens tried to keep his voice to a whisper as he peered around the canyon wall at the couple standing near the entrance, wrapped in each other's arms twenty feet away. He glanced back at the shallow crevice where his four friends sat with poker cards held tight to their chests. "Don't the preacher know he ain't allowed to do that?"

"The preacher's kissing someone?" Harrison scrambled up, his cards forgotten on the rocky ground.

"Who's he kissing?" This from Daniel, who set his cards aside and came to join him and Harrison. "Oh, that's Miss Emmaline. He's been sweet on her ever since he showed up in town."

"Reckon they'll get married?" Wes asked as he came up behind them to take a peek.

"Never can tell." Cain was the last one to put down his cards and join them. "Sometimes men just like to kiss women."

"Nuh-uh." Sam peeked back around the corner, where Preacher Russell had now tilted Miss Emmaline's chin to the side and wrapped his arms tight around her. "A man kisses a lady like that, and they've got to get hitched. It's in the Bible."

Cain scratched the back of his head. "I don't never remember reading no Bible verse like that. My ma says…"

"Don't reckon your ma counts." Daniel muttered the words to himself, but they rang through their nook of the canyon like a shout.

Sam winced and looked back over his shoulder. "Sorry Cain, Daniel didn't mean—"

"Y'all best get your hides back here, unless you're wanting to forfeit." Cain was already sitting back in the crevice, poker cards in hand.

"I don't know. I still don't think it's right for the preacher to be kissing a woman like that." Sam pushed away from the cool rock, shielded from the sun by the towering sandstone walls jutting up toward the sky.

"It's fine iffin he's going to marry her, you mule." Harrison gave him a little shove.

"But they ain't married yet, and that ain't no quick kind of kiss like Ma gives me before bed." Daniel sank to the ground and took up his cards.

"Still don't think he should be doing it." Sam sat and crossed his legs in front of him, snatching his cards off the loose earth. "Should we tell Deacon Sutherland come Sunday?"

"Don't look like Miss Emmaline minded it too much. Probably best to keep your mouth shut." Cain scowled down at his card hand. He'd not bothered to look up once since Daniel had said Cain's ma didn't count.

Sam shifted away from the hard rock poking his thigh. Was Daniel right, did Cain's ma not count? She was a woman, sure 'nuff. But she wasn't a married woman. Lots of folks around Twin Rivers said…

Well, he wasn't sure what all they said, but whatever it was, it meant Cain's ma didn't count the way a married woman did.

"Pa used to kiss Ma like that, and no one ever said there was nothing wrong with it." Wes sat beside Sam and blinked, a tear streaking down his dusty face and plopped into the patch of sand between his legs.

"Don't cry." Sam reached for his friend's shoulder.

"I'm not." Wes shrugged away from him, then swiped at the wet streak on his face and grabbed his cards.

Sam hunched his shoulders and looked at his friends. It was the first time the five of them all managed to sneak off since Wes's ma died a month ago, and they were supposed to be having an afternoon of poker and fun, like cowhands on Wes's ranch. But here they'd somehow managed to get Wes crying and Cain scowling.

"All I know is, I'm never going to get tangled up with some stupid woman like Preacher is. All they do is ruin things." Cain jutted his chin out and gave a firm nod. "Now let's play poker."

"Maybe your ma ruins things but mine didn't." Wes tossed his cards onto the sandy dirt. "My ma was one of the finest women to ever walk Texas soil."

"Then how come you're crying over her like some ninny? My pa says crying makes a man weak. Don't reckon he ever cries over my ma neither."

"Reckon your ma's cried a whole river full of tears over your pa, seeing how he's only ever around for a few days before he up and leaves you." Daniel's voice was as hard as the sandstone surrounding them, his eyes as sharp as a knife's blade.

Cain's lips twisted into a sneer. "Which just proves kissing and love and marriage only make you stupid."

Wes shot to his feet, his hands clenched into fists. "My ma wasn't stupid, and neither is my pa."

Sam scratched behind his ear. He didn't rightly know about love and kissing and marriage, but he'd seen Wes's ma and pa together.

They were always smiling at each other, always hugging on Wes and his sisters.

The only thing Mrs. Codwittle gave him was a switching on the hand for taking too much porridge at the orphanage.

"My parents aren't stupid either." Daniel stood up next to Wes.

Sam pushed himself up to stand beside Wes and Daniel, which only left Cain and Harrison sitting. "I don't think getting hitched is stupid. I think the stupid people are the ones who spend their lives all alone."

"As if you know anything about it." Cain tossed his cards on the ground and rose to stare him down. "You're an orphan."

"True, I ain't never had a ma, but anyone's got to be better than Mrs. Codwittle. Besides, if Wes and Daniel say mas are worth having around, then I believe them."

"I plan to get myself hitched just as soon as I have a place of my own. Then we'll see which one of us is happy." Wes's voice trembled as he spoke, but he thrust his jaw up all hard and angry as he glared at Cain. "You'll be the stupid one, all alone."

"I ain't stupid neither." Cain dug his heel into the ground and swiped away a strand of dark blond hair—hair that was much longer than the hair of any other boy their age. "You're stupid for wanting to get yourself married to some woman who's going to yell at you when you track dirt into the house, complain when you get your clothes dirty, and cry every time you leave."

"My ma didn't do that." Wes crossed his arms over his chest. "And I'll find me a woman who'll take care of my house without complaining."

"So will I." Daniel leaned closer to Cain, bringing their noses so close they nearly touched. "'*Two are better than one.*' Means a man is better off getting married than being alone. That's in the Bible."

"It is not," Cain spat.

"Is so. In the book of Ecclesiastes." Daniel scratched his head. "Or maybe it's Lamentations. Or Song of Solomon. Anyway, it's in there. And if God says it's so, then I'm going to get married just as soon as I get me a house. Or you can… can… can shave my head."

"Blood swear?" Cain took his knife from the sheath strapped to his belt and shoved it at Wes.

Blood swear? Sam gulped. "Wes, no, think about…"

But Wes grabbed the knife and slit his hand, his dark eyes never leaving Cain's. "If I had any money, I'd wager you end up getting hitched too."

Cain spit. "I ain't never gonna get hitched."

"Yeah?" Daniel sneered. "Then maybe you should swear it too. Unless you're too yellow-bellied to stand by your word. I'm going to swear here and now that I'll get myself a wife one day." Daniel took the blade from Wes.

Sam stared at the knife. What was Daniel thinking? Wes could be goaded into just about anything if he was mad enough—and he'd been in a mood ever since his ma died—but Daniel had no business making a blood oath alongside him.

Daniel gave the blade a quick slice down the center of his palm, then thrust the knife back toward Cain. "Your turn to swear. And if you do get married, we get to shave your head."

"Fine." Cain's eyes flashed as they met Daniel's. Cain didn't even wince as he sliced the blade of the knife against his palm.

"Well, what about you two?" Wes jutted his chin toward where Sam stood. Harrison had set his cards down at some point and now stood between him and Cain in a misshapen sort of circle. "You both gotta swear too. Are you going to get yourself a wife one day or not?"

"By the time you're thirty," Cain growled. "You don't get to live as no bachelor all your life and then find a wife right before you die. And if you're not married by the time you're thirty, then you better believe I'll tie you down and shave your head."

"Harrison?" Sam turned to his friend. Surely Harrison had enough sense not to go cutting up his hand over some silly marriage pact.

Harrison bit the side of his lip, his forehead wrinkled in thought. Then he took the knife from Cain's hand. "My pa's gotten along just fine without a wife. Guess I'll do the same."

No! The word burned on Sam's tongue, but he held it in as Harrison ran the blade down his palm, then held it out for Sam.

The leather hilt felt warm from being held by four others before him. His hands were already bruised enough from Mrs. Codwittle's switch. Did he really have to go cutting one of them on purpose?

"Sam?" Wes's voice had turned deep and raspy. "Are you with Daniel and me, or with them?"

Did he want to get married one day?

Maybe with a wife, he'd be as normal as Wes and Daniel. He could get himself some land too, a regular place that belonged to him with a regular wife and little ones running around. That sure seemed a heap better than staying an orphan all his life. "I'll get me a wife before I'm thirty. And Cain and Harrison can't get married until after they're thirty."

"I won't need no wife after I'm thirty." Cain's lips twisted into a scowl. "I won't need no wife ever."

"I'm keeping the thirty part."

Cain glared at Harrison.

Harrison just shrugged. "What? Could be I change my mind, if I find a nice enough woman anyway."

"Chicken liver," Cain muttered.

More like fools, the whole lot of them. Wasn't it foolish to decide when they'd get married at twelve years old? And to seal it with a blood swear, no less? But Cain was determined to prove women were useless, and Wes wasn't about to let anyone insult his ma's memory while fresh dirt still covered her grave. And the rest of them… well, they were probably all chicken livers and fools for getting caught up in the argument.

A bead of sweat trickled down Sam's cheek. But of everyone here, he was the only one truly alone. Cain might say he wanted to be alone one day, that he didn't care if he had no one to love him. But he didn't know what that truly felt like.

Sam looked at the silver blade in his hand, then at the swell of blood rising from everyone's palms. His friends didn't make a family, but they were the only people in the world who'd care if he up and disappeared tomorrow or died in the night. And if the rest of them were swearing…

"Before I'm thirty." Sam looked away as the sharp blade bit into the soft skin of his palm. "Reckon it's settled now."

Chapter One

Sixteen Years Later; May, 1885

How much did it cost a man to build a future for himself?

Sam Owens stood in the center of his future and looked around at the thick adobe walls and the handful of furnishings. Some might say it was just a house—a house that had only been finished for two days, at that. But it was his future too. And by the end of the day, he'd have the two things he'd spent his entire life wanting.

A family and a home.

Provided the woman he'd been writing for over a year didn't take one look at the yellow, barren landscape of the Chihuahuan Desert and decide to go back to Michigan.

Sam stared down at the flower in his hand, the orangish-red petals flaming amid the brown hues of the adobe walls and packed-dirt floor, then headed into the house's single bedroom.

He set the prickly pear flower on the bed beside the pillow. The petals looked even bolder against the brown linen blanket covering the bed than they had in his hand. Would Ellie think it was too bright?

Or maybe the problem was that he didn't have enough flowers. Did he have time to pick a couple more before he had to meet the stage? His house might be sturdy, the kind of building meant to last five or six generations, but mud walls weren't exactly pretty to look at.

What had made him think one flower would be enough to brighten up a room with brown walls and a brown floor?

Sam grabbed the bandana tied around his neck and pulled the end up to rub at the sweat trickling down his temple. Instead of riding out to check the cattle earlier, he should have headed into town and gotten a different blanket to spread over the bed. Something blue or red or green—any color besides brown.

Maybe if he left now, he'd have time to buy a new blanket before the stage arrived. He didn't have much money to spare, but he could manage a dollar or two on a blanket if it would make his new wife feel at home. He turned and stepped through the door into the house's main room but stopped short when he saw the table, plain and brown just like the walls and floor. Why hadn't he thought to fancy up this room too?

Perhaps instead of buying a blanket, he should gather more cacti flowers and put them in a mug at the center of the table. Or he could buy a can of paint to brighten the entire place.

But what if Ellie didn't like the table no matter how many flowers he put on it? What if it was too small to fit him and her plus the three siblings she was bringing? He didn't have room for a bigger table unless he got rid of the bunkbed crammed against the wall. If he did that, then her two brothers would have to sleep in the barn, though the one-year-old could probably still sleep in the small bed he'd tucked into the corner.

Sweat slicked his palms, and not because of the midday heat. What if Ellie thought the entire house was too small? What if she took one look at his land and decided she'd be better off marrying someone with more than a hundred head of cattle and fifty dollars in the bank? What if…?

"Hello, the house."

Sam jolted, the sound of the familiar male voice jarring against the desolate silence of the desert.

"Sam, you in there?" Wes's voice rang out again.

Sam took a final glance around the house that suddenly seemed too small—never mind that he'd spent the past six months building it—and walked out the door.

"Howdy, Wes." Sam pulled his hat lower on his head to shield his eyes from the bright Texas sun. "You finished with spring round up?"

"Got back last night. There's a handful of calves still needing branded, but the hands can handle that. Thought I'd stop by, see how your house was coming." Wes slid off his horse in that easy manner he had, the manner that spoke of a man who'd been raised on one of the largest ranches in West Texas. "Looks like you finished it."

"Told you I would."

"Don't reckon I believed you." A small smile quirked the side of Wes's mouth.

Sam rubbed the back of his neck. He didn't have much choice about getting the house finished, not with Ellie and her siblings due to arrive today, but the notion of telling Wes he had a mail-order bride coming caused his throat to grow drier than the desert beneath his feet.

Wes sauntered toward the paddock holding the handful of longhorns that still needed branding. Most people who stopped by to look at a house would probably, well, go inside and have a gander. But Wes had four generations' worth of rancher's blood running through his veins. Like a fly drawn to honey, the man couldn't keep himself away from a cow.

"I was thinking..." Wes settled a foot on the paddock's bottom rail and leaned his arms on the top. "Might bring Minos over for a few days at the end of May. If you don't mind breeding a little early, that is."

Sam's heart gave a solid thunk against his breastbone. Did Wes truly mean to let him breed his cows with the A Bar W's prize bull?

No, he couldn't afford it. He needed the money he'd saved to see him and his new family through until fall. Besides, studding Minos was probably worth four times what he had in his bank account.

But he couldn't let a chance to breed a few of his cows with the A Bar W's prize bull slip by.

"How much do you want to stud him?" What were the chances the bank would give him a loan?

"You come along on the cattle drive with us in the fall, and we'll call it even."

Sam met his friend's eyes. Wes was being too generous. Breeding a bull like Bernard to his heifers was worth two decades of eating trail dust, not a single cattle drive.

Silence lingered, leaving only the empty quiet of the desert to fill the space between them. Wes didn't move his gaze, but his dark brown eyes gave away nothing, which said just about everything.

"You don't plan on telling your pa," Sam muttered the words on a rush.

"Pa can't keep track of every last cow, not when we've got fifty thousand head."

"No, but he keeps track of that prize bull."

"Look, Sam, I want to help, and short of giving you cattle, this is probably the best way for me to do it." Wes hooked a thumb on his gun belt and stared out over the craggy peaks of the Bofecillos Mountains. "Accept my offer and let me worry about the rest."

"All right." Sam nodded, his throat growing tight.

"Good. Now let's go see this house of yours."

Sam narrowed his eyes toward the cloud of dust that appeared at the crest of the next hill. Riders, two of them, by the look of it. "I've got company."

Wes studied the duo, his jaw set in its familiar firm line beneath the black stubble that told of two weeks spent on roundup. "Want me to ride out with you?"

"Naw, this shouldn't take more than a minute, and I've got to get my hide into town soon." Sam headed to where he'd tied Long Arrow's reins to the post of the paddock. "Go inside and look around the house before I go, if you'd like."

Wes headed toward the house as Sam swung into the saddle, then he dug his heels into Long Arrow's side. The beast's muscles bunched beneath him, long and fluid as they sped across the top of the hill. Hot Texas air rushed past, threatening to tug the hat from his head. He looked out over the land, his land, and a smile crept across his face. To the untrained eye, his rolling patch of the Chihuahuan Desert might not be much to look at. The desert grass, cacti, yucca, and candelilla all blended together in varying shades of brown, rubbing out the brightness of the yellow rocks that filled the rest of the landscape. But when a man owned the land he rode across and a hundred head of cattle to go with it… well, the possibilities seemed endless.

Sam dropped into the valley between the two hills, then Long Arrow started up the second incline. He didn't find strangers on his land too often, not with the road lying directly west of his property and the mountains bordering his land on the east.

When he reached the top of the second hill, the men ahead of him slowed and angled their horses to meet his.

Sam reined in Long Arrow and straightened himself in the saddle. "Can I help you?"

Dust covered the two men, from the tops of their wide-brimmed hats to the boots resting on their stirrups, and their horses hadn't fared any better.

The larger of the pair, with dark eyes and hair that matched the black shade of his hat, answered. "Naw, just doing some surveying."

"Surveying?" Sam raised his eyebrows.

"For the railroad." The shorter, blond-haired man pulled back on his horse to keep him from eating a clump of mesquite.

"The railroad's going in sixty miles north of here, so that doesn't explain what you're doing on my land."

The shorter man sent the taller one a puzzled look.

"Don't think this is your land," the tall man growled. "It belongs to the Southern Pacific Railroad, signed over by the State of Texas itself."

The Southern Pacific Railroad? Sam leaned forward. "That's news to me, seeing how I have the deed to the property. It'll be news to our courthouse as well, since they have a copy of the deed on file there."

"You're wrong, mister. This here land belongs to the Southern Pacific Railroad." The blond man straightened in his saddle, his eyes taking on a challenging gleam. "If you don't believe us, maybe you should go down to the courthouse and see for yourself."

"Maybe *you* should, because I know who's going to win this argument." Sam's shoulder muscles tightened, his hand only a breath away from the pistol strapped to his side.

"Is that your place?" The taller man nodded toward the top of the next hill, then glanced at where Sam's hand hovered near his gun. "That house over yonder?"

He couldn't quite name what irked him about these men, but something set the hairs on the back of his neck to bristling, and his fingers itch for the feel of his revolver. Maybe it was the way the men kept exchanging looks with each other, or the way neither of them had a pencil or paper in sight though they claimed to be surveyors. Either way, he'd had enough.

"It is, just like this is my land. I want you off it, now. The road lies about a half mile west of here, and if you don't stick to it, I'll haul you into the sheriff's office myself." Sam jutted his chin toward the road.

Hoofbeats sounded behind him, but he didn't need to turn to recognize the familiar canter of Wes's prize stallion, Ares.

"Now get." Sam settled his palm firmly on the butt of his gun.

The tall man looked in Wes's direction, then flicked the reins on his horse, taking off at a gallop and leaving the shorter man scrambling to kick his horse into motion. The man shot off down the hill just as Wes pulled to a stop.

"What was that about?" Wes narrowed his eyes at the strangers.

"I'm not sure." Sam stared after the men, but they headed due west toward the road, just as he'd instructed. "Claimed they were surveying for the railroad."

"Weren't dressed like any surveyors I've ever seen."

No, they were dressed like cowhands who'd been eating trail dust for a week or better. "They said this land belongs to the railroad, awarded by the state."

"That's ridiculous." Wes squinted into the sun as the men disappeared over the next hill. "Old man Griggs owned this land back when it belonged to Mexico, and seeing how he hired some highfalutin' lawyer and gave it to you when he died, it's yours."

"I told them to go check at the courthouse if they think otherwise."

"I heard of similar trouble a ways north of here." Wes rubbed his jaw. "Something got mixed up in Austin, and the state gave land that already belonged to a farmer to the railroad."

"If those men were from the railroad, then I'm a dancehall girl."

"Probably rustlers or bandits with a handy story then. We better keep an eye out for missing cattle or anything else suspicious. I'll alert the cowhands at home."

Sam shivered despite the glare of the sun beating down on him. The Rio Grande was only a quarter mile south, and his land ran clear up to it. Were those men dusty because they'd been moving cattle into Mexico? His herd was too small to grab their attention, but a ranch like the Westins' made prime picking for a couple of men looking to steal cattle and move it out of the country before the law could be called in.

"When I get to town, I'll..." *Town. Ellie. The stage.*

Sam pulled his watch out of his breast pocket. "I'm late, and I still have to hitch up the wagon."

He dug his heels into Long Arrow's sides and flicked the reins. He should have left a quarter hour ago. What kind of impression was he going to make on his fiancée if he was late to meet her the very first time?

Sam swung down from his saddle in front of the long lean-to he used as a barn, but when Long Arrow spied the wagon and Bella, the sturdy paint mare, waiting in her stall, he whinnied and pawed at the ground. Long Arrow hated being harnessed with Bella, but the wagon would probably be laden with enough trunks that he'd need both horses to pull it on the way back.

"Thought you said you were going to town." Wes reined Ares in beside the lean-to but stayed atop his mount.

"I am."

"With the wagon?"

"Yup." Sam unfastened the cinch from around Long Arrow's belly and then hefted the saddle off his horse.

"What are you in such an all-fired hurry for?" Wes frowned. "The mercantile doesn't close until five, and if you've a mind to report those men to Daniel, he ain't going to close down the sheriff's office before eight, and even then he'll have a deputy on patrol until the saloon closes."

Sam slid the collar over Long Arrow's head then drew in a breath. He'd put this off long enough. It was time to tell his best friend.

Trouble was, Wes would be furious.

But probably not as furious as he'd be if he found out through the scuttlebutt around town.

Sam unhooked Bella's bridle from where it hung on the wall then moved to open the door of the mare's stall.

"I'm going to meet my wife," he mumbled, keeping his back to Wes while he fit the brown leather straps over Bella's head and led her out of the stall.

"Your *what*?" Wes's brows drew down beneath his hat brim. "You don't have a wife."

"I will in about an hour." Provided she hadn't changed her mind about marrying him at some point on the long journey from northern Michigan to Twin Rivers. "She should be on today's stage, and I already have an appointment with Preacher Russell."

"On the stage? An appointment with the preacher?" Wes jumped down from his horse and grabbed the collar intended for Bella, then held it away, his dark eyes narrowed. "You're not talking about a mail-order bride, are you?"

Sam pursed his lips together.

"You can't be serious." Wes threw his hands in the air, loosening his grip on the collar just enough for Sam to snatch it from him. "Since when do you need a wife?"

"You know the verse as well as I do. 'Two are better than one.'" Sam didn't look up at his friend as he guided the collar over Bella's head, then fastened the traces.

"I don't like this," Wes muttered as he stalked in front of the horses. "Of all the crazy, harebrained things. How much do you know about this woman?"

"I know enough." Sam hooked the harnesses to the pole, then attached the traces to the wagon. "And you're in no position to criticize me, not when you've got your sister, your pa, and ranch hands to help around your place. Besides, you liked being married well enough, once."

Wes stopped pacing, his jaw turning as hard as an armadillo's shell.

Sam winced. What had he been thinking? He knew better than to bring up Abigail around Wes.

Silence filled the lean-to for a full minute. Sam focused on attaching the traces to the wagon, the heat of Wes's eyes boring into him, while the cattle from the paddock lowed in the distance.

"Abigail was different. I'd known her my whole life." When Wes finally spoke, his voice was as gritty as the earth beneath their boots. "You don't know anything about this woman coming on the stage."

"We've been writing for over a year now." Though it did feel strange speaking of Ellie aloud. That would change after they were wed, wouldn't it? "Reckon that's about as well as any man ever knows a woman before they marry."

Wes gave a hard, rough laugh. "Spoken like a man who knows nothing about women. This isn't about that bargain, is it? That pact we made all those years ago?"

Sam sighed. It had been a foolish pact made only to cheer up Wes when Cain started harassing him after his ma died. But still, a man couldn't rightly go back on a blood oath. "No. It's just… I'm twenty-eight and tired of being alone. Reckon I'd be looking for a wife about now even if we'd never made that pact."

Though having a wife would also save him from getting a shaved head, because he had no doubt Cain would come back into Twin Rivers just to see him bald.

Wes shook his head. "I still don't like it."

"I didn't ask whether you liked it." Sam spit the words into the dry desert air. "I've spent my whole life not knowing where I came from. And now that I've finally figured out where I'm going, now that I have land and cattle and a place to call home, you're going to criticize me about getting a wife?"

"Not about getting one, about how you're going about it. You've been writing her for a year but haven't mentioned her to me. That right there tells me you know advertising for a woman in a newspaper is no way to find yourself a wife."

"I need to go." Sam climbed the wheel up to the wagon's seat.

"You've got enough land that you could sell it and be half rich." Wes kept right on rambling as though he hadn't said a word. "Why tie yourself to a stranger who'll inherit it all if something happens to you? Women have poisoned their husbands for less."

The muscles in his shoulder bunched into a hard, solid knot. "I should knock you flat for that, Agamemnon Westin."

He flicked the reins, and the horses started forward with a small lurch.

Wes stepped out of the lean-to and swung up onto Ares.

Good. Let Wes go home and rant to his sister or pa. He'd had enough scolding for one day.

Sam gave the reins another flick. The noise of a horse galloping sounded behind the wagon, but instead of the commotion disappearing into the distance, it grew louder. A moment later Wes reined in Ares to trot beside the wagon.

Sam glared at his friend. "Your ranch is in the other direction."

"I want to meet this bride of yours for myself. And if I don't like her, she can find herself another husband. I don't care if I have to pay to send her back to wherever she came from either."

Sam ground his teeth together. This was precisely why he hadn't told Wes more about Ellie coming. Precisely why he'd hoped to be good and hitched by the time Wes got back from spring roundup.

"I want to be alone when I meet my wife, and I'd appreciate it if you'd respect that."

"Last I knew, the road in front of the mercantile where the stage parks is open to anyone who shows up." Wes kept his gaze pinned to the road, his voice flat and emotionless.

Sam set his jaw and stared at the road ahead. It was going to be a long ride into town.

But what if Wes was right, and marrying a woman he'd never met turned out to be the biggest mistake of his life?

~.~.~.~.~

The life she headed toward seemed too good to be true.

Twisting her free hand in her crumpled skirt, Ellie Spritzer looked down at the sweaty face of six-year-old Janey asleep on her lap. While it might be common enough for a man to take a wife purely because he needed someone to cook and keep house, most men didn't agree to that wife bringing along eight siblings.

Across the stage, Suzanna, Lynnette, Joe, Leroy, and Martin all squished into the seat. Every one of them had a red face, sweaty forehead, and shirt plastered to their chest.

What if Sam Owens took one look at them all filing out of the carriage and changed his mind?

What if he took one look at her, in her crumpled, sweaty dress, and decided she wouldn't make a good wife after all? What if…?

No, she'd wouldn't work herself into a panic. She needed to trust God would provide. A verse somewhere in the Bible probably said something about God providing for His children's needs. She was just too hot and tired to remember it.

But what if God failed them?

Again.

Like God had failed them when He let their mother die last fall.

And when their father had finally returned to Eagle Harbor and said none of them could live with him.

And when Aunt Maude changed her mind and refused to take in five of her siblings.

Ellie leaned away from the seat, sending a fresh bit of air down her back. But the movement also allowed the sweat beading at the top of her shoulders to run down, further dampening her shirtwaist where it pressed against the worn cushion.

The stage hit a small bump, and she fell back against the seat. Could a stranger truly be God's provision after all their relatives had failed them?

"Scoot over." Eight-year-old Henry wiggled on the seat beside her. "You're squishing me."

"Sorry." Ellie scooted a smidgen to her right, but that nearly put her on top of a sleeping Christopher.

They'd taken the train as far south and west as the railroad track had been laid, then the man behind the ticket counter in San Antonio had said he could sell her nine tickets for the same stage, but the little ones would need to sit on laps. But she hadn't quite understood how small the stage would be. After being wedged between one or another of her eight siblings for four hundred miles from San Antonio to Twin Rivers, she'd never again call the bunkroom in the cargo ship they'd boarded in Eagle Harbor or the seating on the train they'd changed to in Chicago cramped.

"How much longer until we get there?" Henry absently twirled the string of a yo-yo. "I'm hot."

"Not that much longer." *Please, God, don't let it be much longer.* She looked out the open window, not that having it open did much good when the air outside was so hot and dry.

Was there a town on the horizon? They should be coming into Twin

Rivers soon. She shifted again, arching her head around Christopher so she could better see. Nothing but yellow and brown greeted her. Flat yellow open spaces, scrubby bushes with leaves more brown than green, and an occasional cluster of rockfaces that jutted up in the distance. The rockfaces weren't big enough to be called mountains. Hills, perhaps? But these bald, craggy hills looked nothing like the hills in Eagle Harbor, which were filled with dense, green forest.

Did her fiancé truly own a ranch somewhere near here? Where did the cattle graze? Certainly not in the lush green fields she'd imagined. But what cow would want to eat the scrubby bushes dotting the land?

"She's supposed to be on your lap, not mine." On the other side of the carriage, Martin scowled at Suzanna, who was holding one-year-old Lynnette while she slept.

"Maybe you should take a turn holding her." Suzanna scowled right back at her older brother, her pert little nose tilted up in the air. "She's getting heavy."

"And maybe you should keep her on your lap instead of mine." Martin slouched against the side of the carriage, his lips turned down into the frown he'd worn ever since their ma died last fall.

Ellie sighed. "Just hold her for a few minutes, Martin. Suzanna's done more than her share of caring for Lynnette."

"Give her to Leroy." Martin crossed his arms, as though that would somehow prevent him from helping. "She cries whenever I hold her."

Leroy rolled his eyes. "Maybe try treating her like a little sister and not a racoon you're trying to scare off, and she won't cry."

"Shove off."

"Martin, take your sister." Ellie swiped a strand of sweaty hair away from her face and tucked it behind her ear. "Leroy is already holding Joe."

Though Joe was technically sitting on his own, his small body had somehow ended up sprawled over Leroy's lap, and unlike Martin, Leroy didn't seem to mind.

"Fine." Martin grabbed Lynnette and yanked her onto his lap so quickly the child woke and let out a scream. "See, told you she doesn't like me."

"Someone make her be quiet." Janey squirmed against Ellie's lap, her eyes blinking open for a moment before she closed them again.

"How can she be crying again?" Christopher stretched and yawned, his own drowsy eyes opening. "Isn't she tired of that?"

Ellie glared at Martin with a look that clearly said *See-the-trouble-you-caused?*

He turned his head away and ignored her, just like he ignored Lynnette's screaming. He kept Lynnette on his lap, but that was all he did. The boy didn't even try patting her on the back or jostling her to see if she would quiet.

"I'm hungry." Henry patted her free hand.

When *wasn't* the boy hungry these days? Given how quickly he'd been growing of late, she'd need to let out the hem on his trousers when they reached Twin Rivers. Ellie reached for the handbag at her feet where the biscuits were stashed.

"I'm hungry, too." Joe yawned and straightened into a sitting position beside Leroy.

Ellie pulled out a couple biscuits that had long gone stale and held one out for Henry.

"Not another one of those." He wrinkled his nose.

She really couldn't blame him. The owner of the bakery where she'd worked in Eagle Harbor had insisted she take a plethora of biscuits and cookies and bread to tide them over on their trip. But after a month of traveling, the food looked about as moist and appetizing as the misshapen yellow rocks that covered the ground outside.

"I'll take one." Joe leaned forward and snatched a biscuit from her hand.

"Joe's awake and Leroy's lap is free." Martin scowled at his older brother. "It's his turn to hold Lynnette."

"My lap wouldn't be free if you hadn't woken her up," Leroy snapped.

"Boys," Ellie breathed, but the word was swallowed by Lynnette's next bout of screaming.

"Will there be food when we get to Twin Rivers?" Henry eyed the stale biscuit on her lap.

"How much longer?" Christopher asked from her other side.

"Ellie, tell Leroy he needs to take Lynnette, now!" Martin demanded.

"Ellie, tell Martin to stop hogging the seat." Suzanna gave her brother a shove, which caused Lynnette to shriek even louder.

"When's the next stop?" Joe's voice turned into a high-pitched whine. "I have to use the privy."

Ellie sank back and closed her eyes against the endless stream of voices. But that didn't stop a bout of hot tears from scalding her eyes. What stranger in his right mind would open his home to a group of loud, complaining, sweaty children? When they got off the stage, Sam was going to take one look at them and change his mind about letting them stay.

And then what was she going to do?

Chapter Two

"You're really planning to get married?"

Sam pulled his gaze away from the empty road leading into town and slanted a glance at Daniel. Blue eyes looked back at him, blue eyes that were probably too kind for the tin star pinned to the front of Daniel's dark brown hat and the other star pinned to the lapel of his duster.

"Don't tell me you have a problem with me getting hitched too." Sam crossed his arms and scowled over his shoulder at Wes, who stood a few feet away, leaning against the porch beam in front of the general store.

Wes had ridden ahead into town, but only to get Daniel. They'd both been waiting in front of the store when he'd pulled the wagon up a few minutes ago.

"You should see his house. It's swept and dusted." Wes's eyes were as dark as the black hat shading his eyes, his jaw as hard as the wooden beam he leaned against. "He's even got a flower on the bed."

"Isn't it time for you to leave?" Sam muttered.

"I already told you, I intend to meet this woman." Wes shoved away from the porch.

"Why? What good will come of it?"

"Probably none, which is why I'm staying. This might not be the first mess you've gotten yourself into, but it's gotta be the biggest." Wes shoved a finger into his chest. "Someone needs to get you out of it before you sign your life away to a stranger."

"She's not a stranger!" Sam threw up his hands.

Mrs. Munson emerged from the general store, her baskets full of foodstuffs. She raised her brows at them. "Gentlemen?"

"Sorry, ma'am." Sam dipped his head toward her and stepped away from the stairs, which brought him closer to Wes. "I already told you, I've been writing Ellie for over a year."

"Before you inherited the land?" Wes's brows drew down into a frown, as though he couldn't quite believe Ellie would have wanted anything to do with him without his land.

"Yes, I started writing her a few months after I made foreman on your ranch." He could still recall the ad he'd seen in the paper, claiming that women from out east were looking to move west and marry upstanding men. "I didn't have any land yet, but I was living in the foreman's house and was earning enough money to save for buying my own spread. Figured it was time to start looking for a wife too. If two of us were working and putting money by, then I'd be able to start my own ranch sooner."

Daniel scratched the side of his head. "If you know this woman so well, why didn't you tell us about her?"

"And how do you know her letters aren't lies?" Wes snapped.

Sam balled his hands into fists.

Before he had a chance to do anything with those fists, Daniel stepped between them. "Simmer down, the both of you. You start a brawl on the street in broad daylight, and I'll lock you up for disorderly conduct."

Sam unclenched his fingers, but his shoulder muscles were as taut and prickly as barbed wire. "Leave, Wes. This isn't any of your business."

"Not my business." Wes yanked his hat off his head, fury radiating from his dark brown eyes. "We've known each other for two decades. You were there when my ma died. You lived on our ranch and worked as a cowhand for ten years. You stood next to me the day I married Abigail, and the day I buried her and our baby girl. Don't tell me who you marry is none of my business."

"He has a point." Daniel repositioned his hat on his head and looked back at the dusty road leading into Twin Rivers—a road that was still empty of the coming stage. "Who you marry is a mighty important decision, and considering how long the three of us have known each other, it seems strange you'd up and get married without saying a word about it."

"I tried telling the both of you," Sam mumbled.

Daniel's eyebrows disappeared into his hat. "Then maybe you better remind us, because I don't exactly recall that conversation."

"It was last spring. We were at your house, and I told you I'd started writing a lady through a mail-order-bride service."

Wes rolled his eyes. "And I said you were crazy."

"No, you yelled I was crazy, then stumbled out of Daniel's house in the dead of night, shouting about me being crazy so loud you woke up half the town."

"I was drunk." Wes crossed his arms over his chest and looked away from them.

"And you almost got locked up for your antics," Daniel muttered.

Sam leveled a glare at Wes. "Don't pretend like you'd have been any different sober." Wes had been deep in mourning right about then, having just lost Abigail and his stillborn daughter.

"This is the same woman?"

Sam pressed his mouth into a firm line.

"I'll be." Wes settled back against the porch beam for a moment, then shook his head. "I still don't like it. Was the marriage arranged before you inherited all that land last fall? If not, then I still think she means to poison you and then sell your land."

"You wonder why I didn't tell anyone Ellie was coming?" Sam turned to Daniel. "Maybe because I didn't want to deal with Wes trying to control my life."

"I'm not trying to control it, just stop you from ruining it." Wes shoved a hand in Daniel's direction. "Talk some sense into him before he makes a mistake he'll spend decades regretting."

Daniel looked between the two of them, his expressive blue eyes carrying so much compassion Sam looked away. "Are you sure about this? Wes has a point about you never having met her and not being sure if you can trust her."

Neither Wes nor Daniel were being fair. They both knew what having a family was like. Wes even knew what being married was like. What was so wrong with him marrying a woman who also had a hankering to have a family? And if he got himself some children to start off the marriage, then they'd be a true family right from the get-go.

"'Two are better than one; because they have a good reward for their labour. For if they fall, the one will lift up his fellow: but woe to him that is alone when he falleth; for he hath not another to help him up.'" Sam looked up and met Daniel's gaze. "I learned those verses from you, so you're not in any position to argue now that I've found a woman willing to come alongside me and help with the ranch."

"I'm not saying you shouldn't have a wife." Daniel rubbed the back of his neck. "But you're not exactly getting one in a way that guarantees you can depend on her to lift you up if you fall."

"She's more likely to run off with the deed to your ranch, if you ask me," Wes quipped.

Sam scowled. "That's precisely why I didn't ask."

The clomping of approaching horses grew louder behind him, and Sam turned to find the stage rolling into town behind a team of four.

Wes stepped out into the road, right about where the stage usually stopped. There was no point in telling him to leave again. The man was determined not to listen, as if Ellie was some sort of spectacle for gawkers.

Sam sent Wes another scowl, not that Wes seemed to care. Still, the first time a man met the woman he was going to marry, it should be… it should be… well…

He rubbed a hand over his chin. He didn't rightly know how it should be, but something told him a controlling friend opposed to the lady shouldn't be a part of it.

The stage stopped directly in front of the general store. Before the driver could climb down or Wes could reach for the stage door, it burst open, and two boys with sandy-red hair tumbled out.

Sam blinked. Were those Leroy and Martin? Ellie said they were fourteen and fifteen, but these two boys looked to be around ten.

"Henry, that was my foot!" A child's screech emanated from inside the stage.

"Be careful." A weary feminine voice this time. "We made it this far with no injuries, don't kill yourself now that we're finally here."

"Children?" Wes's dark eyes met his over the tops of the two boys' heads. "Don't tell me you agreed to take in children too."

A small redheaded little boy came to the opening, stared at the ground for a second, then jumped onto the dusty road.

An older girl with blonder hair than the boys came out next. She turned to pick up a small girl from the doorway and set her down beside the boy that had jumped.

Sam took a step back. These couldn't all be Ellie's brothers and sisters.

Except they could, because she had eight of them. But five were staying in Michigan. She was only supposed to bring three to Texas.

Were the younger ones Ellie's twin siblings? Janey and Joe? They were supposed to be staying with her aunt.

Daniel stepped beside him and bent his head close. "Is your fiancée supposed to be on this stage, or just a bunch of young'uns?"

"Maybe I got the date wrong?" Sam croaked. Except the children matched the siblings Ellie had spent the past year describing to him, which meant…

Sam scratched the side of his head beneath his hat brim. No, his future wife had not brought all eight brothers and sisters with her. She simply couldn't have.

"So you don't have any clue what these children are doing here?" Daniel kept his voice low, though given the commotion the children were making, he could have shouted without anyone noticing.

Two older boys came next, one with sandy-blond hair and the other with hair a full-out red. They at least looked like how Ellie had described Martin and Leroy, the brothers she said could work on the ranch.

"Three of them." Sam stuck a finger in his collar and tugged. "Three of them were supposed to come with Ellie."

"Something else you forgot to mention. Just how many siblings does Ellie have all together?"

"Eight." He nearly choked on the word. He could feel the heat from Wes's eyes boring into him. He forced himself to step forward and extend his hand to the taller of the two youths. "Howdy, I'm Sam. You must be Leroy."

"I'm Martin." The boy scowled and crossed his arms over his chest.

Sam sighed. Looked like he was going to have his work cut out training this ranch hand.

"I'm Leroy, sir." The second boy held out his hand for Sam to shake. "I know Martin's taller, but I'm the oldest."

Ellie must have forgotten to put that in her list of the children's names and descriptions.

A young child's cries sounded from the stage, then a woman with hair the color of carrots peeked her head out the door and stepped outside, a small child wedged onto her hip. She was thin, so very thin it was almost painful to look at her, and the child she held—little Lynnette, most likely—looked no different.

The woman's faded dress was crumpled and streaked with road dust. She scanned her surroundings with wide eyes, and he could almost see her mentally counting the children to make sure everyone was accounted for.

Sam took a step closer. "Ellie." But the scratchy sound in his voice nearly swallowed the name. He cleared his throat and tried again. "Ellie? You must be Ellie."

Hazel eyes flew up to meet his from beneath eyelashes as red as her hair. Freckles sprinkled a nose and cheeks that were otherwise as pale as a moonbeam on a clear night.

"Yes, I'm Ellie." A soft smile tilted lips that were a downright pretty shade of pink. "Are you Sam?"

"I am." He should probably smile at her, but he couldn't quite force his lips to tilt upward.

Wes moved to stand beside them, the expression on his mouth nowhere close to a smile.

Before Wes had a chance to start yammering, Sam pulled Ellie aside. "Can I have a word with you? In private?"

"Oh, um… of course." She glanced over her shoulder at where the children had started playing catch with a ball. "Leroy and Martin, please see that the trunk gets unloaded. And Christopher, you watch the younger ones. Suzanna, take Lynnette for a minute."

The girl who looked to be about ten or eleven tossed the ball to one of her brothers and came over to take the small child. Suzanna peeked up at him, revealing more pale skin covered by freckles, but she didn't say a word before spinning around and heading back to her brothers with Lynnette in tow.

"We can talk over here." Sam took Ellie by the elbow and tugged her around the side of the general store. He could already imagine the questions Wes would demand he answer later. But first, he had some questions of his own. "Why are they here?"

"Who?" Ellie looked back around the corner, probably to make sure the older children were watching the younger ones.

"Everyone, all of them." He waved his hand in the direction of her siblings.

"Because you said they could come… remember?" Her last word was no more than a whisper, and instead of smiling at him like before, wariness crept into her eyes.

"I said three of them could come. The two brothers old enough to help on the ranch, and the baby. Put together with you, that makes four people all together. You said the others were staying with an aunt."

"She changed her mind."

"She what?" He stared over Ellie's shoulder at where the children played. Boy howdy, there were a whole heap of them. So many, in fact, he couldn't quite blame Ellie's aunt for not taking them in. But what was he going to do with everyone?

"You at least should have told me." Were the young'uns even his problem? "It's not fair, you showing up with all your brothers and sisters and not saying a word about it."

"But I wrote you." Mere inches separated them, but her voice was so soft, he had to bend closer to catch all her words. "And you said we could come."

"Don't lie to me." He spat the words like arrows from an Apache warrior's bow. Was this the kind of woman he'd agreed to marry? Her letters from northern Michigan had always sounded so honest and authentic, but maybe Wes was right. Maybe he couldn't trust her. "I never once got a letter asking if you could bring all eight of your siblings to Texas."

"But… but I sent it, and you wrote back. It was the very last letter I got before we left. You said you were looking forward to seeing everyone and sent an extra five dollars for our trip." She blinked at him, her brow furrowing into a mess of confused lines. Then she dug in the pocket of her thin dress and pulled out three bills and a quarter. "We didn't use all of it. Here's the extra."

He stared at the money in her slender hand. How had she managed to feed nine people on the trip down with only a dollar and seventy-five cents?

But he knew how, because the Codwittles at the orphanage would have done the same. The taste of the porridge he'd eaten every day for both breakfast and supper lingered in his mouth to this day.

He swallowed away the bland, mushy flavor and tried to meet Ellie's eyes, but instead his gaze fell to the way her threadbare dress hung on her bony shoulders. If he looked closely at the others, he'd wager they'd be just as thin, their clothes just as worn.

"Well? Don't you want it back?" Ellie pushed her hand closer.

"Keep it." He held his palm straight up in a stopping motion.

"But…"

"Just keep it. I'm sure you'll have need of it at some point. And I was talking about the four of you in the letter. When I said I was looking forward to everyone coming, I meant all the people we'd already written about, not your entire family. I never got a letter from you saying that your aunt couldn't take in the rest of your siblings."

"I sent you one. I suppose you don't have much reason to believe me, but maybe the letter got lost or delivered to the wrong home. Maybe I addressed it wrong or didn't quite make it clear I meant all of us. I was upset when I wrote it, and I probably…" She drew in a shaky breath and took a step back from him, causing her to bump against the wall of the general store. "We'll leave, of course. I'm sure we can go somewhere that—"

"I can't exactly marry you if you leave."

"You still want to marry me? Even though I showed up with all my brothers and sisters?"

Did he? He'd no interest in marrying a lying, manipulative woman. But everything about Ellie said there'd been an honest mistake—the sad tilt to her mouth, the hope that had been in her eyes when she'd stepped off the stage, the closed wariness that had replaced that hope the longer they spoke, the way she twisted her hands in her skirt as though she were trying to wring out a wet rag.

"I can't send them away. There's nowhere for them to go. That's why when I got your letter, I thought you…" She shook her head and swallowed, the muscles in her throat working so hard his hand itched to reach out and stroke the tenseness away. "I should have known it was too easy. I should have known all of us coming here was too good to be true. We'll have to go—"

"Now hold on. You're getting ahead of yourself."

She pressed a hand to her mouth and sniffled.

She wasn't going to cry, was she? What was he supposed to do with a crying woman? He peered around the corner, where Daniel and Wes stood talking while also watching the young'uns. Maybe Daniel would know what to do with Ellie's tears. He had himself a ma and sister and was a heap kinder than Wes.

Confound it. Wes was right. He didn't have the first clue about women, other than that he had to stop this one from crying right quick. "If you leave instead of marrying me, where will you go?"

"Um, is anyone in town hiring?" Her sniffling ceased, but a single tear spilled over her eyelashes and streaked her face. "I can bake and sew and take in wash. Or if there's not a place for us to stay in Twin Rivers, we can try the next town over."

The next town was forty miles away and wasn't somewhere Ellie and her siblings were going tonight. And did she really think she could house and feed and clothe nine people by baking and sewing?

He leaned back against the wall of the haberdasher's, which gave him a full view of the young'uns. Most of the children were still playing with that ball, running and whooping and hollering as though they'd just gained their freedom after spending a month behind bars.

Ellie might be telling herself she'd find a way to keep them together, but he'd spent the first thirteen years of his life watching siblings come through the orphanage doors. The children always had an aunt or uncle who was supposed to take them in but hadn't. Boys on the cusp of adulthood like Leroy and Martin were farmed out right away to households that needed workers. The littlest ones might be adopted by a family who just plain wanted children, but the ones in the middle would languish on two servings of porridge a day and get their hands switched for taking an extra spoonful without asking.

The one thing he could absolutely guarantee? They'd not stay together. Families never did at an orphanage.

Sam rubbed a hand over his jaw, still studying the children. His house wasn't big enough to sleep ten people, he'd do well to fit five around the table, and he didn't have much money saved. Could he afford to feed everyone until he drove his cattle to market in the fall?

He'd been younger than Lynnette when he'd been dropped off at the orphanage. What if he'd had an older sister like Ellie? What if there'd been someone, anyone, willing to take him in? He didn't even know if he had brothers or sisters, but he might, both older and younger. Had they known his parents at least for a time? Had they lived as many different places as he had?

He closed his eyes against the sudden, gritty sensation flooding them. *But if any provide not for his own, and specially for those of his own house, he hath denied the faith, and is worse than an infidel.*

Mr. Griggs had shared that verse with him years ago, before he'd gone off to Austin and left Sam the ranchland in his will.

"You can stay, all of you." He blew out a breath. Ellie was only trying to provide for her family, and if he was going to marry her, he had a duty to provide for her siblings as well.

"You're willing to marry me even if it means keeping my brothers and sisters?" She twisted her hands in the folds of her dusty dress.

He pushed himself off the wall. He couldn't let the children go to an orphanage. As for the marriage bit, he still needed a wife to cook and clean while he worked the ranch. And he still wanted to put down roots, start a family. It just looked like now his wife would be cleaning for a whole heap of people, and he was marrying into a ready-made family. A really big one.

"I wasn't planning on so many young'uns, and my house isn't very big, but if you're willing—"

"Thank you." She threw herself against him and squeezed his middle. "Just thank you."

Her smile was so big, his own lips curved up in response. He wrapped one arm around her, then another, hugging her back as tightly as she hugged him. Boy howdy, she might be thin as a rail, but she had some womanly curves hidden beneath her loose dress.

Curves that were pressed clear up against him.

As her husband, he'd be expected to do something with those womanly curves later that night. He swallowed. Maybe he should ask Wes for advice about that, provided Wes pulled out of his temper sometime soon.

But for now, he had other matters to attend. He set Ellie back a pace and flashed her a smile. "Let's go find the preacher and get ourselves hitched."

He'd worry about the rest once he and Ellie had been married right and proper.

Chapter Three

Ellie kept her chin high and back straight as she balanced Lynnette on her hip and herded the rest of her siblings down the dusty road toward the white church at the far end of town. Sam had been serious when he said it was time to find the preacher. Had he not gotten the letter from Miss Julia at the matchmaking service that had paired their letters together? The one about how a betrothed couple should spend at least two weeks living in the same town and getting to know each other before they wed?

But if he wanted to marry today, she'd go through with it. Better that than wait for two weeks and have him change his mind the way Aunt Maude had. And if having the wedding that afternoon meant getting married in a ratty old dress rather than the new one she'd sewn before coming to Texas, then so be it.

Everything still seemed too good to be true. Something was sure to go wrong any moment, then Sam would refuse to marry her, and she and her siblings would be stuck in a strange town and an unfamiliar state with no one to help them.

"That man doesn't like you." Leroy leaned close enough so as not to be heard while they shuffled their way toward the church. "Not the sheriff, but the one with the black hat."

Ellie glanced behind her. Sure enough, the man that had scowled at her when she disembarked from the stage was still wearing the same dark expression. He walked with Sam and the sheriff a whole train car length behind her family too. "He was probably only expecting four people to arrive and isn't quite sure what to make of all of us."

"Sure hope that's all it is."

Ellie straightened her shoulders and forced herself to face forward. She couldn't make out every word the men behind her said, but his tone of voice told her enough.

"I'm hot." Christopher turned to her and fanned his face with his hand.

So was she. The sun beating down on her head was causing a fresh bout of sweat to form on her brow.

"I'm hot too." This from Joe, who pranced a few paces ahead of the group before running back to them. "Where's the beach? I want to go swimming."

Martin snorted. "Don't you know nothing? Texas ain't by the ocean."

"Anything," she corrected. "Don't you know *anything*. And Texas is by the ocean, just not this part of Texas." Which was a shame, because it was so hot she was ready to dive into some cool water, sweaty dress and all.

"Where's Lake Superior?" Janey reached up and tucked her hand inside Ellie's free one.

"Far, far away." But oh, how she wished it wasn't. And not just because of the fresh breeze that blew across the lake all summer or the cold, turquoise waters that offered coolness on days such as this. Had she made the right choice in coming to Texas? What if she was wrong and marrying Sam would be an even bigger mistake than putting the children into an orphanage? What if—

"I want to go back to Eagle Harbor," Joe whined.

"So do I." Martin kicked at a rock in the road. "Why'd you have to drag us all the way here? I'm so hot I could be one of the cookies baking in the oven at the bakery back in Eagle Harbor."

"It was the only choice we had." She eyed her second-oldest brother. He was just sullen and moody enough to run off and find trouble, never mind how many times she'd warned him to be on his best behavior in Twin Rivers. "Unless you'd rather go to an orphanage?"

"I'd rather be in Eagle Harbor." Martin kicked at another rock.

"I don't want to go to an orphanage." Janey's grip tightened on her hand.

"We should have stayed in Eagle Harbor and found a way to make do on our own." Leroy grabbed Joe's arm before the six-year-old could dart across the road toward a store with candy sticks in the window. "Just because Ma died didn't mean we all had to come here."

"But Ma wasn't…" No, she wasn't going to tell Leroy that. She wasn't going to tell anyone, not ever. Though surely if the children knew the whole story, they'd understand why they had to leave Eagle Harbor, especially without Ma around to guard their secret anymore.

"Do you want everyone to go in?" Leroy asked.

She looked up to find herself staring up at a white clapboard church.

"I want to go inside." Suzanna clapped her hands beneath her chin. "Don't you want to see Ellie get married? This is so exciting!"

Exciting. Right. She was marrying a man she'd never met before, wearing a dress that reeked of sweat and travel dust.

But not a man she was completely unfamiliar with. After all, she had every last one of the letters he'd sent her stored in the trunk they'd brought.

I'd love nothing more than to share my land and share my life with you, if you'll have me.

You strike me as a kind woman, Ellie.

I'm so sorry to hear of your ma's loss. I know this probably seems like a trite offer, considering I'm two thousand miles away, but if there's anything I can do to help, let me know.

Even though we've never met, I feel like I know you.

She'd felt the same too, until she'd arrived and he'd looked at her with cold eyes, then asked why she'd brought her entire family to Twin Rivers.

But his eyes hadn't stayed cold when he'd realized there'd been a mix-up, though he hadn't exactly shown kindness either. What had she hoped for? That he'd whisk her off her feet and kiss her senseless?

She wasn't pretty enough for a man to consider kissing senseless. He was letting the children stay, and that would be enough for her.

"Well, do you want us all to go in or not?" Leroy asked again.

"Please say we can, please." Suzanna rocked up onto her tiptoes, her hands still clasped together beneath her chin.

Sam pulled away from his two friends and walked past her and up the church steps. He didn't so much as look at her as he passed, let alone wave the children inside. Instead, he opened one of the double wooden doors and disappeared behind it.

"If Sam doesn't want a whole passel of children in there, then I won't force it." And at the moment, it didn't seem as though he wanted anyone in the building, not even her. She twisted her hands together. She already didn't have a pa to walk her down the aisle or a ma to sit in the front pew. Was she asking too much by wanting her siblings to be at the wedding?

"You know the twins and Henry aren't going to sit still." Leroy glanced at where Janey and Joe had started chasing each other up and down the steps.

"And Martin will probably object in the middle of the wedding." Suzanna glowered at her older brother, who'd stopped kicking rocks and now leaned against the side of the church with his arms crossed and a scowl plastered across his face.

"Here, hold Lynnette." She handed the child to Leroy, but before she could drag Martin over to rejoin the family, the church door opened.

Sam stepped onto the small wooden platform, as did a man with brown hair and a fancy white collar around his neck. For a preacher, he was on the young side, with a few age lines around his eyes and mouth, but no gray hair.

"Sam? You said you were getting married?" The man surveyed the group while a frown worked his way across his lips.

"I am. To Ellie there." Sam pointed toward her.

"And these children are?"

"Ellie's brothers and sisters."

The preacher's brow furrowed.

A flicker of worry ignited in her belly. God hadn't allowed her to come this far only to have a man of the cloth refuse to marry her, had He? She started up the church steps. Surely once she explained that she had nowhere else to go, the preacher would agree to marry her and Sam.

The minister bent his head and muttered something to Sam, then Sam turned to her. "I need to talk to the preacher for a minute. Everyone come inside and get out of the sun."

The children needed no further invitation. They raced up the steps and followed the men indoors, leaving only Leroy to enter the church at a reasonable pace and Martin to straggle up the steps behind them.

Indeed, the church was cooler than standing on the street, but Janey, Joe, and Henry were still of a mind to chase each other, only now they had pews to dart between and crawl under.

Ellie studied the door to the side of the pulpit where Sam and the preacher had disappeared. Sam had seemed so certain when he'd said everyone could stay, but what if the preacher talked him out of the wedding? It sure wasn't common for a man to take in a mail-order bride *and* eight children.

Trust in the Lord with all thine heart, and lean not unto thine own understanding. In all thy ways acknowledge Him, and He shall direct thy paths. There. That was the verse she couldn't remember in the carriage. If she just trusted God, then everything would fall into place.

But trusting God hadn't done her any good in Eagle Harbor. Why would trusting Him do her any good in Twin Rivers?

Then again, standing here and worrying wouldn't do her any good either. If the preacher talked Sam out of marrying her, she'd find another way to carry on. But until then, she'd go about her business as though today was her wedding day.

She ran a hand over her dress and tried to smooth away one of the wrinkles on her stomach. She probably didn't have time to retrieve her wedding gown, but if she had a basin of water, she could freshen up. The strand of hair that kept falling beside her cheek meant her updo was likely in disarray, and wiping the sweat from her brow surely wasn't asking too much.

A man came up beside her and offered a smile. He had kind eyes, their clear blue color bringing to mind the water in the shallows of Eagle Harbor on a sunny day. "Howdy, I'm Daniel Harding, Sheriff of Twin Rivers, and one of Sam's long-time friends."

Smiling back at him wasn't hard. There was something quiet and patient about him despite the tin star pinned to the lapel of his duster. "It's good to meet you, Sheriff Harding. I'm Ellie Spritzer."

"Soon to be Ellie Owens, from what I understand. Do you need something?"

She blinked at him. Besides a perfect marriage to a man who loved her and wanted to adopt her siblings? Or a God who sent blessings her way rather than a constant string of hardships and sorrow?

"You were looking around like you were trying to find something." Sheriff Harding waved his hand toward the front of the church.

"No, ah, it's just…" She scanned the small wooden church again, but still only saw the one door where Sam and the preacher had gone. "Maybe there's somewhere to freshen up?"

"Why are you helping her?" The man with the constant scowl came up beside them. He'd taken his hat off along with the sheriff, probably because they were in a house of worship, but the hair atop this man's head was almost as black as his hat. A thin layer of stubble covered his jaw, as though he usually shaved but hadn't bothered for the past week. And unlike the sheriff, his lips held no smile for her.

Sheriff Harding smacked him in the back of the head. "This here is Wes. You'll have to forgive him. He has trouble being kind and hospitable most days."

"Mr. Westin." The other man's jaw turned even harder, which should have been impossible considering it already looked as though it had been chiseled from one of the rockfaces the stage had passed on the way here.

"Don't mind him. You can go on calling him Wes. Everyone does. Mr. Westin is his pa."

"For her, it's Mr. Westin." The scowling man took two steps forward, bringing himself closer. "Why do you want to marry Sam?"

"I've about had enough of you today," Sheriff Harding muttered.

Mr. Westin just looked at her with dark eyes that promised she'd not be able to evade his question.

But how to answer? Should she say that Sam was one of the first men to show her kindness, even if only through letters? That he was the first man to ever act as though she was desirable? She'd warned him of her bright hair and atrocious freckles, and he'd written back that he liked freckles and red hair. She could still recall the warmth that had spiraled through her as she'd sat by the fire reading those words for the first time.

"Sam's in need of a wife, and I'm in need of a husband. Seems like we should suit well enough." She peeked up at Mr. Westin.

He leaned down until his breath puffed hot into her face. "A husband who owns twelve thousand acres of ranchland?"

Was that how much land Sam owned? He'd never said, and she'd never thought to ask. But that sure sounded like a lot, like enough land not for a mere ranch, but for a cattle empire.

"No, a husband who will help me care for my siblings." And maybe a husband to love her. She glanced down at her wrinkled, dusty dress, at the spot where water had spilled before she'd been able to wipe away the crumbs from Janey's biscuit. The water had long dried, but the fine white biscuit dust had ground itself into the fabric, leaving a white smear that would only come out with laundering.

What man would love a woman who couldn't even manage to look presentable on their wedding day?

Clapping sounded from the front of the church. "All right, let's marry these two off."

The preacher stood behind the pulpit, and Sam stood in front of it with a lopsided smile directed her way.

She reached a hand up to touch her cheek, which was damp with perspiration, then swiped that dratted lock of hair behind her ear again and looked back down at the spilled food on her dress. Too late to worry about being a presentable bride.

The sheriff's gaze followed hers down the skirt of her dress. "I believe Miss Spritzer wanted to—"

"No, I'm ready." If she went to freshen up, that Wes character just might talk Sam out of marrying her.

Sheriff Harding scratched behind his ear. "I thought you said—"

"I'm fine, thank you."

"Then come up here," the preacher called. "Daniel and Wes, I'm assuming you two can serve as witnesses."

"Sure thing," the sheriff answered.

"No way am I taking part in this." Wes gave his head a hard shake.

"That's how you're going to be?" Sheriff Harding crossed his arms but kept his voice low enough Sam and the preacher likely couldn't hear him. "You're going to tell Sam no after all he did when you lost Abigail?"

"I'm not going to stand by and watch him throw his life away on this freeloading stranger, let alone help him do it." Mr. Westin turned and stalked outside.

Ellie stared at the double wooden doors swinging shut behind him. She'd not been in Twin Rivers an hour, and she was already causing trouble for Sam.

What a way to thank him for taking in her siblings.

Chapter Four

I'm not going to watch him throw his life away on this freeloading stranger.

Ellie spun on the heel of her bare foot, causing her thin, lacey nightgown to slap against her calves as she paced across the confines of the bedroom. The words had haunted her all through the wedding ceremony and trip to Sam's ranch. They'd followed her through dinner and baths and settling the children into bed. Even now, as she waited for Sam in the small room with a bed big enough to fit both of them, she couldn't get the words out of her mind.

Did Sam think so poorly of her too? If so, why had he married her?

Ellie twisted her hands together, her fingers crushing the delicate lace fabric that her friend had given her so she'd have something special to wear on her wedding night. Stalking over to the far wall, she peeked out the window that faced the open-style barn where Sam had gone to check on the boys. She'd put them to bed about a quarter hour ago, then come inside and settled the girls in for the night. But no sooner had Lynnette drifted off to sleep than Sam had pushed himself back from the table, tugged on the collar of his shirt, and said he wanted to check on the boys.

The window was open to the night, without a pane of glass or a stitch of tarpaper to cover it, just like every other window in the house. She'd never seen such a thing before. Were all the windows in West Texas like this, square holes cut into the wall without any coverings? She wrapped her arms around herself and shivered, not because of the hot, dry heat surrounding her, but because she could almost imagine the sharp Lake Superior wind whipping through a window such as this in Eagle Harbor.

No dim light of a lantern flickered inside the lean-to. What if Sam had decided to sleep with the boys? He never said he was coming back.

She sank onto the bed and smoothed a hand over the cover. She should probably just go to sleep herself and stop worrying. If Sam came, he came. And if he stayed in the barn…

A creaking sounded from the direction of the door, and she looked up. Sam was there, standing right before her in his dusty clothes.

She shot off the bed, and Sam's eyes traveled down her, long and slow.

His eyes were a warm brown color, like coffee with a dollop of cream. He'd removed his hat to reveal hair a similar shade to his eyes. His jaw was firm and defined, and coupled with his long, lean face and a strong nose, he had an air of rugged strength about him.

His shirt held the outline of both shoulders and a chest well-muscled from hard work, and even without his hat on, the top of his head came within an inch of touching the doorway. She wasn't sure how she'd done it, but she'd landed herself a handsome husband.

Which somehow made things worse. Was she daft for suddenly wishing her new husband had a balding head, an overly large nose, and a belly that sagged over the waistband of his trousers?

Sam did nothing but stare with those unreadable brown eyes, his throat working. What was he thinking? Did he like the lacy nightgown she'd donned? The way she'd brushed her hair until it shimmered in the lantern light?

Maybe he wasn't thinking of her appearance at all, but of what his friend said before storming out of the church.

An ache started somewhere in her chest. *I'm not a freeloader.* She nearly blurted the words, but something told her they wouldn't make the situation any better. And while she wasn't here to take advantage of him, she hadn't yet told him the full reason why her siblings couldn't stay with friends in Eagle Harbor.

Still, one of them had to say something. They couldn't just stand here staring at each other all night. She took a step forward, then gripped her hands together at her waist. "Thank you for the flower on the bed. It's pretty."

"I... ah... was just in here to..." He scanned the room, though it held nothing besides a plain bed and old dresser. "That is, I forgot... my shirt."

She blinked. He was already wearing a shirt, and if he wanted fresh clothes for the morning, wouldn't he be after trousers too?

He took a step nearer, bringing them so close the tips of his boots almost touched her bare toes. "Um, maybe I should... Or rather, we should..."

He reached out and grabbed her shoulders, pulled her forward, and set his mouth on hers.

She stiffened. She couldn't help it with the sudden way he yanked her to him and then planted his hard, firm lips on hers. His lips stayed hard and firm too, though he was insistent on moving them over her mouth. Why, she couldn't say, because she kept her own lips pressed tightly together.

This was nothing like the gentle peck on her cheek he'd given her at the end of their wedding. Nothing like the soft, sweeping kiss she'd barged in on last month at the Eagle Harbor sheriff's office between her friend Aileen and Aileen's husband, Isaac. No, this was awkward and clumsy and stilted.

Just as suddenly as Sam had started kissing her, he dropped his hands from her shoulders and lifted his head.

"I, uh… I'll sleep in the barn with the boys, just to make sure there isn't any trouble." Rather than meet her eyes, he focused on the wall behind her. Then he grabbed a shirt hanging on one of the pegs by the door and spun on his heel, stalking from the house without even a glance over his shoulder.

Ellie sank down onto the bed and wrapped her arms around herself. Why had she gone stiff on him? She was supposed to wrap her arms around him and draw his head down closer, let him lead her to the bed.

Oh, what a fool she was. Had she really thought marriage would suddenly make her life easy? If how her life had gone in Eagle Harbor was any indication, things would probably get worse now that she was in Texas.

God, can You please just let us all stay together here? Can You please keep everyone happy? I know I haven't asked for much, but if You could please do this for us.

She fell back onto the bed and stared up at the ceiling, where her prayer seemed to stop and bounce back at her, rather than floating up to the ears of God. Was she doing something wrong? Was that why God never answered her prayers? Or maybe she wasn't good enough for God to bother with and not worthy of the same blessings He gave others.

Yes, that had to be her problem. And if Sam knew her secret, he'd probably agree.

~.~.~.~.~

"I'm not selling." Muscles tense, Sam stood across from where Agamemnon Westin V sat behind his grand desk, polished to the point it shone. He'd been

offered a seat in one of the cushioned, highbacked chairs positioned in Mr. Westin's office but had bolted out of the chair after only a half-minute of conversation.

"This is three times what that land is worth." Mr. Westin scooted the banknote closer on the top of the desk, so near that no one could mistake the overwhelming number of zeros in the sum.

"I said I'm not selling." If he'd told the man once, he'd said it a hundred times. This was hardly the first time Wes's pa had presented him with a check for the land he'd inherited, though this check was certainly larger than the previous four.

Sam blew out a breath and looked around the office—the one room in the Westin home where he'd never felt comfortable. From the fancy dueling pistols hanging behind Mr. Westin's desk, to the series of exotic stuffed birds that had come from various places around the world, to the mounted whitetail buck's head and ram's head with curly long horns, it reeked of ancestry and money. Of a family that knew exactly where it came from, right down to giving all its firstborn sons the same name for six generations.

"What do you want?" Mr. Westin sat back, his arms crossed over his chest.

Sam blinked at him. What did he want? Truly? He wanted to feel like he belonged in the fancy office where he stood. Or maybe to hear that the wizened rancher was proud of him, or to be treated with respect. He had a land deed with his name on it, after all, a small but growing cattle herd. Maybe he wanted Mr. Westin to invite him into this office to discuss breeding one of the A Bar W's bulls with some of his cows, just like Mr. Westin would discuss with any other rancher.

"Another fifteen hundred dollars?" Mr. Westin pulled another bank draft from his desk drawer and dabbed the tip of his pen in the inkwell. "Is that what this will take?"

Sam set his jaw and met the older man's gaze.

Mr. Westin twisted his lips into a sneer and dropped his pen back into its holder. "You're a fool, Sam Owens."

Oh, he was. Absolutely. But not because he was keeping his land. He was a fool for hoping Agamemnon Westin V might be proud of him, might actually treat him as an equal—or even more, as a son. He'd spent ten years of his life living and working on the A Bar W and knew Mr. Westin's cattle better than the man himself did, probably better than Wes too. But evidently that wasn't enough to earn the man's good favor. Only blood relations could do that, and as far as Mr. Westin was concerned, he'd only ever be an orphan.

Agamemnon Westin humphed, his jaw turning hard beneath his scruffy gray stubble, and his eyes sparking like the flintlocks on the dueling pistols displayed behind his desk would when cocked. "You'll never make anything of that land."

"You're wrong."

"What good will twelve thousand acres of ranchland do you when you can't even afford to buy cattle?"

"You're wrong again."

"Those hundred head you bought at auction aren't enough to make you a real rancher." Mr. Westin leaned back and took his cigar from the tray.

Sam clenched his teeth together. He reckoned there was a time when the Westin family had only owned a hundred head of cattle, though that was probably clear back when Texas had belonged to Mexico. There'd never been a day in Agamemnon Westin V's life where he hadn't owned at least five thousand head, which was why he needed more land. Or more particularly, land that had water access—like a spread that ran clear along the Rio Grande for miles.

The man puffed on his cigar. "If a disease passes through or rustlers move in, you're finished."

Sam swallowed the bitter taste filling his mouth, a taste that had little to do with the cloying smoke from Mr. Westin's cigar. He'd spent most of his savings on his cattle, true, but he'd picked prime ones, yearlings that would be ready for market this fall and pregnant cows that had given him upwards of thirty-five new calves this spring. Breeding time was only two months away, and he hoped to get another third of his stock pregnant. Sure, it would be a few years before he had a sizable amount of money in the bank, but his plan was solid, and he'd set himself up to make a profit his first year of ranching. Most new cattlemen had to wait two full years before they saw a dime for their efforts.

But if something happened to his cattle…

He had no savings to replace his herd, and while being on the Rio Grande meant he didn't need to worry about water, it also meant his ranch was just across the river from Mexico. Many a beast had disappeared into the arid, rugged terrain over the years.

"Go on now. Take the banknote." Mr. Westin picked up the flimsy paper and held it out.

"I'm not changing my mind, so you may as well stop asking. Now if you'll excuse me, I need to see Wes."

"This is enough money that you can leave Twin Rivers and go anywhere you wish." Mr. Westin's chair screeched across the stone-tiled floor, and he stood. "You could make something of yourself."

Sam turned at the door and met the dark brown gaze that nearly matched Wes's.

"I plan to make something of myself right here in Twin Rivers." And he would do that with or without Mr. Westin's approval.

"Do you know how many times I offered to buy that land from Griggs?" Mr. Westin slammed his hand on his desk, rattling the coffee mug sitting to his left. "He was just as stubborn as you. And after he finally died, he wasted it on a worthless orphan. You got three days to consider this deal. I won't offer you such a high price for the land again."

He didn't need three days. He didn't even need three minutes. "I gave you my answer."

"What do you plan to do with all that land?"

"The same thing I've planned to do since I was twelve years old." Sam raised his chin a notch. "Get me a wife to settle down with and grow my herd."

The old man's cracked lips twisted. "As if anyone around these parts will marry a no-account orphan."

Sam sucked in a breath and dropped his hand from the door latch. Mr. Westin was wrong, for sure and for certain. Ellie was already on her way to Texas. And if her ma hadn't died last fall, he'd have been a married man of six months by now.

But Mr. Westin was also right about one thing: Ellie wasn't from these parts.

He'd told her he was an orphan, sure enough. But if Ellie had grown up in Twin Rivers, would she still want to marry him?

Sam found the door handle again and yanked open the heavy wooden door, then strode through, heaving it shut behind him.

"You're going to fail, Sam Owens." Mr. Westin's shout filtered into the hallway behind him. "And when you do, I'll give you a third of this price for your land."

Oomph! *Something knocked him in the stomach. Sam spun around, but the door to Mr. Westin's office was still closed, and neither Wes nor his sister were in the hall.*

Oomph!

Another knock to his stomach. Sam's eyes flew open, his hand reaching in the darkness to where he's stashed his sidearm beneath his pillow. His palm closed around the butt of his pistol just as a shadowed form kneeled over him.

A very small shadowed form holding a thin blanket.

Sam released his pistol and scrubbed a hand over his face.

"Did I wake you up?" The little boy snuggled down against his stomach. "I would have gone to Ellie, but she's clear across the yard and…"

A pack of coyotes yipped in the distance, and the boy curled into a ball, hugging the blanket against his chest rather than using it to cover himself. "C-can I lay here with you?"

The coyotes yipped again, and the boy snuggled so close the child might just end up inside his shirt.

"Sure." It wasn't as though the boy had given him much choice, never mind the four other bodies sleeping on the pile of hay. "You don't have coyotes in Michigan?"

The child wriggled closer yet, and a tuft of feathery hair brushed against Sam's cheek. He wrapped his arm around the small form. Joe, was it? The youngest boy and the one who had a twin sister. He was maybe five or six.

"We had coyotes, but we had a house to... sleep in...in Michigan." Joe yawned and nestled his head right up in the crook of Sam's shoulder. Joe blinked once, then twice, before his eyes closed, the look on his face blissfully peaceful despite the coyotes still making a ruckus.

Sam shifted the boy a little lower, then tucked the child's head beneath his chin.

Own his own land and house, put down roots, have a family. He'd wanted those things for as long as he could remember.

But what if Wes's pa was right? What if something happened to his cattle, and he failed at being a rancher? He looked down into the serene face of the child that had no trouble trusting him to protect his family from a pack of coyotes. It would be one thing to fail by himself, but now he had eight young'uns and a wife to care for—and only fifty dollars in the bank.

What if he'd already made Mr. Westin's predictions come true and destined himself to fail the moment he'd told Ellie he'd take in all her siblings?

Chapter Five

Sam woke to the warm, soft feeling of a woman in his arms.

A rather small, squiggly woman?

He opened his eyes only to find a mess of short, red-blond hair just beneath his nose.

So maybe he'd woken to the feeling of a certain woman's brother in his arms, not the woman herself.

Sam groaned at the memory of Ellie standing in the bedroom the night before. He'd written her for over a year, had felt like he knew just about everything there was to know about her. When he'd thought about bringing her home for the first time, taking her into his arms, kissing her, leading her to the bed… he'd never imagined the night would end with her turning as hard as sandstone in his arms.

Maybe the two of them needed some time to themselves so they could feel more comfortable with each other. He'd barely been able to say two words to her yesterday without being interrupted by one of the children. He would talk to Ellie more this morning and see if she wanted to go to the river for a picnic, just the two of them. Or maybe they could go to town together and…

Town. The courthouse. How had he forgotten?

He jolted upright. Joe was still curled up, sleeping away with his blanket tucked against his chest, but everyone else was gone. Bright yellow light flooded the yard, telling him the sun itself had already crested the mountains to the east.

How had he slept so late? But then, when a man laid awake for half the night trying to figure out how ten people could live five months on fifty dollars, he was apt to oversleep in the morning.

Good thing he hadn't remembered the men who'd claimed to be railroad surveyors, or he wouldn't have gotten a lick of sleep.

Sam rose and stretched. The other boys had all folded their blankets and left them on the hay, and noise emanated from the house. Should he leave Joe, or wake him? The child looked so peaceful sleeping, but what if a rattler slithered inside, and Joe jerked awake to find the poisonous snake in bed with him?

Sam crouched and gave the boy's shoulder a shake. "Howdy, cowboy."

Red lashes fluttered open, and the boy blinked.

"Time to get up."

Joe sighed and closed his eyes again.

Now what was he supposed to do? The little guy was probably exhausted after weeks of travel.

He bent and swept the child up in his arms. A warm sensation unfurled itself as he cradled Joe to his chest. And to think, he'd not even known this boy a full day. What would it feel like to hold Joe after the child had been here a year? Two?

What would it feel like to hold a child he and Ellie created together?

Sam shimmied the door to the house open with the hand that was holding Joe's back, then stepped inside. Rather than finding the house peaceful and quiet like he'd left it last night, chaos greeted him. Two of the boys were arguing in the corner, while another two were setting the table. Lynnette and Janey played in another corner, but

Ellie seemed to be missing, with the door to the bedroom shut up tight. Suzanna—if he recalled her name correctly—stood at the stove mixing something in a pot.

The scent hit him. Not eggs, and certainly not steak to go along with them. Not even flapjacks.

Porridge.

He crossed the room to lay Joe down on the empty bottom bunk. Where had Ellie gotten porridge from? Had it been inside the lone trunk he'd unloaded from the wagon yesterday?

At the thought of the thick, globby meal, his stomach twisted.

"Give it back. I don't care if you're big enough to wear it." Martin, the tall boy who wore a constant scowl, still argued with a brother who was only an inch or two shorter than him.

"You borrow Leroy's clothes all the time. Why can't I borrow yours?" The other boy tossed back.

"Because it doesn't belong to you." Martin seethed the words, his hands clenching into fists.

"Hey, now." Sam stepped between them before Martin let one of those fists fly.

"But it matches Mr. Owens's shirt." The younger boy curled his fingers into fists too.

It matched…? Sam looked at the boy, whose name he couldn't remember, then looked down at his own shirt. Sure enough, his had a faded blue and red pattern, while the boy's had a faded blue and orange one. What had made the boy want to dress the same? And how had the boy known what shirt…?

Sam stilled. He'd forgotten to change his shirt in the barn, and he'd told Ellie that was the reason he'd come to the bedroom last night. He whirled around, glancing at the closed bedroom door before striding back toward the front door. He still had time to—

"Sam?"

He froze two steps from the door. Funny how he'd only ever had two conversations with his wife and the house was filled with noise, but he recognized her voice instantly over the chaos.

"I thought I heard you out here."

He needed to turn around and face her. Besides, she'd probably already noticed his shirt from the back.

But what if he turned around and saw tears in her eyes? He scrubbed a hand over his face. *Please, God, anything but tears.*

"Sam?" she said again, and this time uncertainty trembled in her voice.

He turned to face her and forced a smile that felt about as taut as the barbwire fence stretching between his ranch and the Westin's. "Morning, Ellie. Did you…?"

Sleep well. But he wasn't going to ask about that, not seeing how she'd gone all stiff on him when he'd tried kissing her.

She moved toward him now, sending a stern look at the two brothers who had been arguing over the shirt.

She wore a plain green dress that looked right pretty next to her pale skin and bright hair. But the image of her standing in her nightgown last night planted itself in his head, and the house suddenly grew hot. He'd tried to look at her face last night, he had. But there'd been the lamplight, and the thin, fine material of her gown, and he'd seen the outline of every curve and dip and swell of body.

What was a woman thinking wearing a nightdress like that if she didn't want to be kissed?

"Sam?"

He blinked. Ellie stood in front of him, wearing her green dress and not her nightgown. She was also gesturing to the table with a puzzled look on her face.

"Ah…" He scratched the side of his head. Had she asked him something? "What was that?"

"Do you want to eat breakfast with us? It's ready."

He didn't want to eat breakfast, no, because it looked like porridge was the only thing they were having. But something told him he shouldn't go skipping meals on his first day as a married man. "Um… sure."

"Did you want to sit?" The pleasant smile she'd been wearing had dropped from her lips, and her brows were drawn down to reveal faint creases across her forehead.

Had he done something to cause that look? He shifted in the room that still felt entirely too hot.

She spun on her heel, muttering something he couldn't quite hear as she stalked to the table.

The table. Right. That's what he was supposed to be doing, sitting down. All the children were seated, though that meant four of them were sitting cross-legged on the floor. Everyone had bowls that Suzanna had dished out, and a spot waited for him right at the head of the table.

The house was awful quiet too, and not the good kind. No, this was the kind of quiet that made a man want to scratch between his shoulder blades, or better yet, bolt out the door and get started on the day's work.

Instead he moved to the table, sat, and bowed his head. "Dear Father, please bless this food and thank you for the hands that prepared it. Amen."

As soon as he raised his head, the children all grabbed their spoons and started shoving porridge into their mouths.

He looked down at his own bowl of globby, brown mush. Maybe porridge wasn't as bad as he remembered. After all, it had been fifteen years since he'd eaten it. He raised his spoon to his mouth and took a bite.

Definitely not better than he remembered. Mrs. Codwittle had at least attempted to sweeten the mush with a bit of sugar, but it didn't taste as though Ellie or Suzanna had added even a pinch of something to help mask the flavor.

He forced himself to swallow, then looked up to find Suzanna watching him, her bowl almost empty. "Do you like it?"

"I… ah…" Would saying yes count as lying? "I haven't had porridge for a long time. It's… different than I remember." *And not in a good way.*

Suzanna stared at him blankly, and the blob of porridge from her spoon dropped back into the bowl with a splat.

"I can… um… tell you worked hard to make it… Thank you?"

She smiled then, her lightly freckled cheeks scrunching up beneath her eyes. "You're welcome. I made a little extra, so you can have seconds if you're still hungry."

Seconds. Boy howdy, he'd walked himself right into that one.

He scooped up another bite of porridge, but before he raised the spoon to his mouth, his gaze collided with Ellie's across the table. She sat with Lynnette on her lap, spoon-feeding the slop to the little one. Her lips were pressed into a firm line now, and her eyes seemed to be giving him some sort of lecture. But he'd be hanged if he knew what, exactly, she was trying to tell him.

Something about eating his porridge? The hairs on the back of his neck bristled. It was hardly his fault he didn't like porridge. She probably hadn't been fed the mush twice a day for the first thirteen years of her life. If she would have asked before telling Suzanna to make it, he'd have informed her it was just about the only food he wouldn't eat.

"Is there anything you'd like the children or me to do today?" Ellie's question should have sounded polite and considerate, but the clipped tone to her voice warned him otherwise.

"There's a henhouse out past the barn. The eggs need to be

gathered." Maybe that would get her to think about making something other than porridge tomorrow.

"There were five eggs this morning." She nodded toward something behind him.

He turned to see a handful of eggs sitting in a basket near the sink. If she'd already collected them, why hadn't she fried…?

Wait. There were only five eggs, because he only had five laying hens. The hens would have served them well enough if she'd only brought three of her brothers and sisters to Texas, but five eggs would never do for a family of ten.

"I need to go into town here first thing this morning. While I'm there, I'll see if I can buy some hens already laying so we can have more eggs on hand." Should he tell her the main reason he needed to go to town?

Ellie held another spoonful of porridge to Lynnette's mouth, but the babe chose that moment to scrunch her lips together and arch her back. The blob of porridge fell from the spoon.

No, his new wife had enough to worry about without him telling her about the land, especially since the issue would be cleared up with a quick visit to the courthouse.

Ellie wiped the porridge from Lynnette's lap, then looked up at him while bouncing the babe on her knee. "Would you like us to do something else while you're gone?"

"You can send some of the young'uns to gather dried grass. We'll need to make mudbricks for the second room."

She paused, a spoonful of porridge halfway to Lynnette's mouth. "You're planning to add another room? To the house?"

"Of course." The boys couldn't sleep in the barn forever. It stormed nearly every afternoon for the month of July and first half of August, and the family would need better shelter. Not to mention the setup in the barn left it open for all kinds of unsavory critters.

Now that he had a family, he had an obligation to provide for them, even the Bible said so. "I need to get the cattle branded first, and Sunday's church. So we'll start on the mudbricks first thing Monday morning."

The rumble of approaching horses vibrated through the window.

"Excuse me." He stood and walked to the door, which served the handy purpose of getting him away from his porridge.

Two horses trotted into the yard, the beasts instantly familiar, just like the two female forms atop them. But what were Anna Mae Harding and Charlotte Westin doing here, and so early in the morning? He headed outside, reaching the palomino just as Daniel's sister swung down from her saddle in a flurry of petticoats and ruffles.

"Is it true?" Anna Mae peeked around him, her dark brown eyes sparkling. "Tell me it's true."

"Is what true?" He looked past the two ladies. Had Daniel or Wes come with their sisters?

Anna Mae clasped her hands beneath her chin and let out a sound that reminded him of a squealing coon. "That you got married!"

"Of course it's true." Is that why they were here? "Ellie's inside. Come and meet her."

"This is so exciting!" She rushed toward the house, the flounces of her full skirt trailing behind her.

He turned to Wes's younger sister, Charlotte, and extended his arm. "Suppose you want to meet Ellie as well."

"I can't believe you would do such a thing." Rather than rest her hand on his arm, Charlotte took a step back from him, her jaw hard.

Sam scratched the back of his head. So she wasn't excited about meeting Ellie?

Charlotte stared at him, much like Ellie had done before he'd bolted from the breakfast table.

Confounded females. Was she mad at him too? For what?

Charlotte huffed and stalked toward the barn, probably wanting to visit Long Arrow and Bella. He looked back at the house. Should he go inside with Anna Mae and Ellie? If he didn't, Anna Mae just might scare Ellie clear back to Michigan. But he'd known Charlotte since the day she was born, and leaving her mad just didn't sit right.

He followed Charlotte into the barn, where she was stroking Bella's muzzle and holding out a handful of sugar cubes.

"I don't understand what you're upset about." So help him, if Wes had told his sister that Ellie was going to poison him and steal his land, he really would plant his fist in the dunderhead's jaw.

"You're married... to... to a stranger." Charlotte dropped her hand from Bella's muzzle.

She stood uncommonly tall for a woman, and wore one of her familiar split skirts that was the same serviceable tan color as his trousers, and was only a shade lighter than her hair. But her skirt would either be made of some fine imported material or expensive leather that was so thin and butter soft a person could swaddle a baby in it.

"Ellie's not a stranger." Seemed Wes had only told his sister part of the story—not that he was surprised. But he was getting tired of repeating himself. "I've been writing her for over a year. Now why—?"

"And you think that makes things better?" Charlotte's words caught, and she pressed a hand to her mouth, then blinked.

Was she crying? Quiet, poised Charlotte? Sam shifted from one foot to the other on the packed-dirt floor. Why were women suddenly bursting into tears around him?

"Hey... ah, don't cry. Please?" He stepped closer and rested a hand on her upper arm.

Charlotte drew in a breath and looked up, hurt radiating from her soft blue eyes.

"How could you?" The words emerged as a whisper but were laced with an emotion so thick Sam dropped his hand.

How could he *what*? Weren't most women happy about weddings and having a new lady in town? When Millie Cunningham had gotten married last fall, Charlotte and Anna Mae had worked themselves into a tizzy over the style of Millie's dress and type of flowers she'd carried.

Maybe Charlotte was upset not to have been invited to his wedding. It wasn't as though there'd been much to the ceremony, but she'd probably wanted to be there anyway.

"I'm sorry," he said. "I would have let you know about Ellie coming and invited you to the church had I known how important it was to you."

Blue fire ignited in her eyes. "That's not what I'm upset about, and you know it!"

Sam blinked. He couldn't remember the last time Charlotte had acted this way. Wes could throw a right good fit when he was upset, but Charlotte usually kept to herself.

"Actually, I don't have the first clue what's got your dander up. You'd best just go on and spit it out."

"If… if you wanted a wife so much…" She drew in a shaky breath and looked away. "Why didn't you ask…? Why didn't you and I…?" She gave a small shake of her head and pressed her hand back over her mouth.

The breath whooshed out of him with enough force she might have taken one of her fists and planted it smack in his gut. "There's nothing between us, and even if there was, it wouldn't have worked out."

"You don't know that."

He did, and she had to as well, somewhere deep down. Sure, they'd shared a private conversation or two around the campfire over the years he'd worked for her pa, and he'd always been the first cowhand to set aside his work to help Charlotte with her horses, but he'd looked at it as nothing more than being some type of honorary brother. "Does your pa know you're here?"

"I don't see why that matters." She raised her chin in a defiant gesture that would have made Wes proud.

"You know he won't let you marry any man who isn't a rancher."

"You're a rancher."

"With a hundred head of cattle. Your pa will want you hitched to someone who runs fifty thousand head or better."

"But he wants your land. Maybe if—"

"I'm not selling." If he'd said it once, he'd said it a thousand times. "Besides, I'm a married man now, and talking about this won't do us any good. Come inside and meet Ellie."

Charlotte didn't budge. She stood with her shoulders back and chin up, and she looked right impressive too, like she could be painted and hung next to her pa's picture above their fireplace. "I can't believe you chose some stranger over me."

"You were never available for choosing." But even if she had been… "Look, you and Anna Mae are the closest things I have to sisters, and I want you both married to good men. But I can't rightly see myself getting hitched to either one of you." He tried to hide his grimace, but couldn't quite help the edges of his lips from turning down.

"I turn twenty-one this summer."

"All right…?" What did her age have to do with anything?

"Before he left on his trip, Pa said something about how Simon Creed has a son a little younger than Wes." Charlotte wrapped her arms around herself in a lonely hug. "He plans to invite the Creeds down for a visit when he gets back in June. And if the Creeds aren't interested, there's the Mortimers clear over by San Antonio."

So this was the true reason Charlotte had come to visit him. To be fair, Agamemnon Westin had been yammering off and on about finding Charlotte a husband since she'd turned eighteen. But at the same time, he was bound to make good on his promise one of these days. He'd certainly done so with her older sister, Mariah.

"I can find my words around you the way I can't when I'm in a room full of Pa's rich rancher friends and their sons." Charlotte's gaze dropped for a moment, then she brought it back to meet his, her eyes the same pale blue color as her shirt. "And you're... you're... nice. You don't try to control my every action and thought like Pa and Wes do. There's something to be said for being kind, and I won't apologize for wanting to marry a kind man."

"I'm right glad you think me kind. But do you hear yourself? Everything you just said, it's not romance or love. I was simply your most convenient choice for a husband." Though he didn't have a clue how that had happened, and if he'd known Charlotte's thoughts had headed in that direction, he'd have talked her out of them long before now.

"Convenient choice?" Her voice took on a sharp edge. "Let's say you're right, and that's all you are to me, a convenient choice. What kind of choice was this mail-order bride of yours? You can't say paying to bring a woman two thousand miles and taking in her eight siblings is convenient."

No, it was anything but convenient, but it didn't feel like marrying his sister either. He rubbed the back of his neck. People might call him crazy, but he'd been praying for the wife he'd one day marry since the afternoon he and Wes and Daniel had made that pact against Harrison and Cain. When he'd spotted that ad for the mail-order-bride service in the paper last year, he'd felt compelled—and maybe even led of God—to inquire about a bride.

"You know I want to put down roots, to have a family of my own. I've never hidden that from anyone."

"And you somehow thought the best way to put down roots was by sending for a stranger to marry." Charlotte tossed up her hands in a gesture she must have learned from watching Wes work up a temper.

"Ellie and I come from similar situations. We don't have much to our names, not either of us, and we both want to build something special. May as well do it together."

"Let me try to understand. You don't want to build a life with me, but you're willing to build a life with this other woman you don't even know, let alone love?" Charlotte stalked away from the stall, then pivoted and stormed back inside before turning to repeat her path again.

"Love will come in time." If he didn't believe that, he'd not have married Ellie yesterday.

He didn't see Charlotte's fist coming until it struck him in the jaw.

~.~.~.~.~

"Sam did a right good job with this house, don't you think?"

Ellie couldn't stop staring at the woman standing in the middle of the room—the most beautiful woman she'd ever seen. The woman looked to be about the same age as her, but the similarities stopped there. This woman had dark brown hair that contrasted perfectly with her milky skin, and a small face with features so delicate she seemed more like an angel than a human. She wore normal enough clothes, with a ruffled shirtwaist that looked to be made of plain cotton and a dark blue skirt embellished with a ruffle at the very bottom. But the everyday garments only drew more attention to the beauty of her face.

The woman was currently turning in a slow circle around the room. She'd come inside a few minutes ago, introduced herself as

Anna Mae Harding, the sheriff's sister, and started chattering about how happy she was Sam had gotten married and how nice his house looked.

"I saw the house once, when Daniel came out to help Sam, but that was maybe a month ago." Miss Harding didn't seem to mind the noise of the children playing indoors, the squeaky hand pump at the kitchen sink, or the clatter of dishes that Suzanna, Christopher, and Henry were all washing. "I can't believe how quickly Sam finished everything, but it makes sense now if he knew you were coming."

Ellie pulled her gaze away from the small woman with the riveting dark eyes and looked at the plain brown walls of the house. At first, they'd looked like they were made of dirty, uneven plaster. But apparently the bricks supporting the house had been made of earth and straw, then coated with a type of smooth mud mixture that hardened while it dried. She'd never seen anything like it, but the walls were thick and solid, not made with flimsy boards and full of cracks that let the wind in like their home back in Eagle Harbor.

"It seems as though Sam did a lot of work to get this place ready for me." She glanced out the nearest window, which looked out over rolling yellow land toward town. But the view was also empty of people, Sam included. Didn't he want to visit with his friend's sister?

Maybe she shouldn't be surprised he'd up and disappeared given the way he'd scowled at her all through breakfast. It was almost like he hadn't wanted to join them at the table as a family. Either that, or he was mad she hadn't kissed him back last night.

"And eight brothers and sisters." Miss Harding shook her head, her pretty eyes growing wide. "I didn't believe Daniel when he said there were so many, but…"

Janey chose that moment to dart in front of Miss Harding, nearly causing the woman to stumble.

"Give me back that donkey." Joe raced after Janey. "I had it first."

Ellie bent and caught Joe around the stomach before he could race past her. "Go back into the bedroom and play so I can visit." She gestured to the room where Leroy had been watching the twins and Lynnette.

"But she took my donkey," Joe whined.

"He wasn't sharing." Janey fisted her hand around the small wooden toy.

There'd been a whole basket of wooden figures sitting by the corner of the bunkbed on the far side of the room. She'd guessed Sam had carved them for Lynnette before they'd arrived, but Sam hadn't said a word to her about them, and Janey and Joe had taken more of a shine to them than Lynnette.

"Either you two find a way to share without arguing, or I'll put the donkey up for the morning." Ellie set Joe back on the floor and straightened.

"Fine, Janey can have him for now." Joe twisted his lips together and huffed. "But I want him as soon as she's done."

Janey clutched the toy to her chest and raced back inside the bedroom without bothering to thank her brother.

Ellie sighed and plopped her hands on her hips. She'd give the twins about two minutes before they bickered again.

Leroy had come to the doorway with Lynnette on his hip, probably to corral the twins back inside, but as soon as Lynnette saw her, she started squawking and trying to climb out of her brother's arms.

"Oh, how darling." Miss Harding headed straight for Lynnette. "Do you mind if I hold her?"

"Go right ahead." Ellie waved her hand in Lynnette's direction. "She likes being held by just about anyone."

Lynnette went straight for Miss Harding's shiny gold necklace and the large, blue-green pendant hanging just below her collar.

"My, but she's a strong one." Miss Harding smiled down at the child and let her have the pendant. "And she's your sister?"

Ellie stiffened for a moment, but there was nothing sly in the tone of the other woman's voice or calculating in her pretty brown eyes. The question was fair. Had she gotten married at eighteen and found herself pregnant right away, Lynnette could well be her daughter. "My sister, yes. I'm afraid my ma never fully recovered from bearing her. She died last fall."

Something sharp pierced her chest, and a familiar hollowness opened inside her. She turned away, sucking in a deep breath and blinking back the sudden burning sensation behind her eyes. One day she'd be able to speak of her mother without warding off a bout of crying, but probably not anytime soon.

A flash of movement outside the window caught her eye. Sam? She moved closer to the open square in the wall. "Who's Sam with?"

"Hmmm?" Miss Harding muttered from somewhere behind her, then she appeared at her side.

"The woman out there upset with my husband." Ellie jutted her chin toward the lady in the matching brown vest and skirt with a dark red bandana around her neck.

The woman was clearly upset, holding her shoulders and back taut and wildly raising her arms while Sam slumped against one of the horse's stalls.

Miss Harding let out a small sigh. "That would be Charlotte Westin. She'll be in to visit in a minute."

"Westin?" Ellie's back turned as stiff as the woman's outside. "Any relation to the Mr. Westin I met yesterday?"

"Mr. Westin?" Miss Harding's eyebrows rose. "No, he's away right now. You couldn't have met Mr. Westin. Daniel said you only met him and… Oh, are you talking about Wes? He doesn't go by Mr. Westin. That's his pa."

"So she's a relation to…?" Calling the man by such a familiar name plain felt wrong, especially considering how he'd stormed out of the church right before the wedding. "…to Sam's friend?"

"She's Wes's sister, yes."

Evidently sour moods ran in the family.

"Why don't I help you make up some biscuits?" Miss Harding hooked their arms together. "Sam will be wanting some when he rides out to check the herd later."

She would have turned, but Sam stepped up to the woman outside and placed his hands on her shoulders. They stood awfully close, closer than she and Sam had stood during their wedding yesterday.

"Does he love her?" She whispered the words to herself, but Miss Harding grew still beside her.

"That's probably a question for your husband." Her voice came out smooth and gentle, like a ma talking to her newborn babe. "But seeing how he married you yesterday, I reckon not."

"Miss Westin loves him then." She should leave the window, but she couldn't quite force herself to move.

"Charlotte… cares. I assume you know Sam grew up at the old orphanage in town. He left before it closed. I think he was about thirteen when he started working for Mr. Griggs right here on this ranch. When Mr. Griggs moved to Austin a few years later, Sam started working for the Westins. He's been on that ranch for ten years or better. Reckon Sam's more like a brother to Charlotte than anything else, but I'm not quite sure Charlotte sees things that way."

Miss Harding kept their arms hooked together but didn't try moving away from the window. "Charlotte's having a hard time of things right now, for reasons that have everything to do with her pa and nothing to do with Sam. When Charlotte rode up to my house this morning, she said she wanted to meet you, which is why I came along. I'm awfully sorry. Had I known she'd throw a tantrum as soon as she saw Sam, I would have tried to keep her in town.

"Not that I can really change Charlotte's mind once it's made up, but I would have made an attempt." Miss Harding shifted Lynnette higher onto her hip and tugged on Ellie's arm. "Now let's make up that batch of biscuits. Standing here stewing won't do you any good."

Part of Ellie ached to storm outside and demand to know what was going on between her husband and this other woman. But she didn't have a claim to Sam that went back decades like Charlotte Westin did.

In his letters, Sam had told her over and over that he wanted to put down roots and start a family. But it looked like he had roots aplenty—roots that had nothing to do with her.

Chapter Six

Daniel took a sip of coffee and drew in a breath of light, cool air as he surveyed the dusty street. The sun had long ago peeked over the Bofecillos Mountains, painting the land with a bright gold brush. He stood on the porch in front of his office, leaning against the right post as he did just about every morning. The roof overhead cast him in shadow, though there wasn't much need to stand in the shade considering the temperature hadn't yet reached seventy degrees. Summer was taking its sweet time arriving in Twin Rivers this year. The temperature today might not even break ninety degrees, which was downright cold for May.

Oxen bawled, and Daniel ran his eyes down the road toward where the Chihuahuan Trail intersected O'Reilly Street. Sure enough, a group of Mexicans were driving a team of a dozen oxen down the road. The giant cart the oxen pulled was laden with goods purchased in Austin, Texas and headed to Chihuahua, Mexico. Looked like the traders intended to ford the river bright and early. Two dozen or so similar *carretas* would pass through Twin Rivers before nightfall. Some days he'd even seen as many as three dozen. With summer holding off its arrival, there would probably be an influx of travelers all trying to conduct business before the temperatures climbed over a hundred and ten degrees and settled in for a bit.

As sheriff, he made sure no trouble arose while travelers passed through his town, but he had little to do with the goods brought into the country or taken out. The border agents down at the river handled that, at least on the American side of the Rio Grande. Mexico probably had some tariff laws that should apply to American goods being brought into Mexico, but he'd never met a single Mexican border or customs agent, and he'd been living in Twin Rivers his whole life.

A shadow scampered between the buildings across the street, darting from the back of the haberdashery to the courthouse. Daniel frowned. If school were out for the summer, he'd assume children were playing in the shade of the two buildings, but school didn't let out for another month. He set his coffee mug down beside the porch post and headed toward the small space that separated the three-story courthouse from the shop next door.

Hushed voices slithered through the narrow opening, the deep voices telling him grown men were speaking. The cadence of the words revealed the men spoke English, not Spanish, but the words themselves eluded him.

Why would two people meet behind the courthouse like this? Why not simply have a conversation at the front of the courthouse in broad daylight? Two people talking was hardly a crime.

Daniel edged closer to the back of the building, then stopped. Did he show himself or try listening? He still couldn't hear much. Random words like *May*, *cattle*, and *trip* drifted to him, but none of those seemed sinister.

A sudden sting tore through the top of his shoulder, piercing like an Apache arrow with a poisoned tip. He gasped and looked down to see a scorpion on his shirt. He flicked it off before the vixen could land another sting and stomped on it.

The talking ceased.

No point in staying hidden now. Wretched scorpion. The critter had probably been on the wall of the courthouse and climbed onto his shirt when he'd been standing still. Didn't the lousy thing know the sun was up and he was supposed to be under a rock somewhere sleeping?

"What's going on back here?" Daniel strode around the back of the building, jaw set and hand on the butt of his pistol, ignoring the screaming sensation in his shoulder.

"Were you spying on me?" Robbie Ashton, Wes and Charlotte's brother-in-law, turned to face him, his eyes blazing with defiance.

"Who were you talking to?" Daniel scanned the alley.

"None of your business."

Daniel raised an eyebrow. Robbie might only be twenty, but the man had a difficult childhood, first with his wealthy father disappearing on the way back from Austin, then with the man his ma remarried falling into debt and getting the family evicted from the trading post Robbie's father had built. Abigail dying last year hadn't helped anything, but the Ashton family had been having trouble long before then.

"As sheriff of this town, all suspicious activity is my business." He wasn't going to stand here and let the scamp disrespect him, even if the man was Wes's brother-in-law. "Now who were you talking to, and where did they go?"

Either the other person had disappeared around the opposite corner of the building or they'd darted into the back door of the courthouse. But if Robbie had business with someone in the courthouse, why not go inside and speak with them properly?

"Just… uh, someone I ran into back here." Robbie looked around, refusing to focus on any one point for more than half a second. "He already left."

The boy was lying. It was clear from the auburn curls atop his head down to the tips of his cheap, flimsy boots, but if Daniel could keep him talking, then he might end up saying something useful. "What were you doing back here in the first place?"

"I had to go to the courthouse… on an errand for my… uh, my ma."

"On an errand for your ma?" Daniel sent the boy the steely look he reserved for horse thieves and cattle rustlers. "The courthouse doesn't open for another fifteen minutes. And shouldn't you be out at the Westins' ranch, working?"

Wes had hired Robbie last fall when Sam had left to ranch his own spread.

"Yes, sir, I was just headed there…" Robbie repositioned the hat on his head. "Um, after visiting my ma this morning."

No way had Robbie Ashton been to visit his ma, but the man seemed bound and determined to lie.

"I best be off so I'm not late." Robbie tipped his hat and scampered to the far end of the building, then disappeared around the side.

Daniel placed a hand on his shoulder and rubbed where the scorpion sting still screamed at him, then shook his head. He'd be keeping an eye on Robbie from here on out. But hopefully the rest of his day would be filled with nothing more than issuing warnings to Robbie and his ilk. Chasing off loiterers was a heap better than learning rustlers had moved into the area or a thief had stolen from townsfolk and then crossed into Mexico, where he had no ability to bring the culprit to justice.

Daniel walked back through the narrow space along the courthouse and stepped around the front of the courthouse, only to find Sam Owens tethering his horse to the hitching post.

"Howdy, stranger." Daniel tipped his hat.

Sam turned, his mouth set in a firm line.

"Didn't expect to see you in town so early." Or at all today. Sam should be home with his new wife, even if his house was filled with people.

"Came to talk to you about something that happened yesterday and check on something at the courthouse." Sam's lips twitched as he looked back at the building. "Showed up a little too early."

"Let's head over to my office and talk there. None of my deputies are in yet." His deputies usually didn't come in until around supper to help patrol the town at night. He started across the street. "Anna Mae and Charlotte make it out there all right this morning?"

"You knew they were coming?" Sam paused at the bottom of the steps leading up to the porch. "Why didn't you stop them?"

"Ellie's new to town. I was thinking she might like a little company." He winced. That had come out wrong. "Ah, company of the female variety, that is."

Because Sam sure would have provided his own type of company last night.

"So you thought it was good to send Charlotte out to meet Ellie when she was spitting nails?" Sam frowned at him, then climbed the steps to the sheriff's office and opened the door.

"Mad? Charlotte?" Daniel paused to grab his coffee cup from where he'd left it by the post, then trailed his friend inside. "Why would Charlotte be mad?"

Nothing riled that woman, least of all a wedding. "Anna Mae was plumb floating when she learned you got yourself hitched. When Charlotte showed up before breakfast saying she wanted to ride out and visit…" He shrugged. "We figured it was late enough you'd be up and about, especially with all them young'uns."

If he'd had any hope of talking Charlotte into sticking around for breakfast, he would have tried. Not that she'd have paid him any mind if she'd stayed. She would have talked with Anna Mae and maybe his parents and ignored him.

Like she always did.

"Yeah, well, you could have made sure Charlotte was as happy about the wedding as Anna Mae before sending them both to my place." Sam took his hat off and hung it on the peg by the door, revealing deep furrows in his brow.

"Why wouldn't Charlotte be happy?" Daniel hung his hat beside Sam's. "She was plumb giddy last summer at Millie Cunningham's wedding."

Sam stalked toward the desk, but rather than sit in one of the empty chairs, he turned and paced back to the hats on the wall. "Because to Charlotte's way of thinking, I married the wrong person."

"Why does Charlotte think that? She doesn't even know Ellie." Daniel headed to his desk, where he set his coffee cup down beside the plate of bacon and eggs he'd scraped clean.

"Because Ellie isn't, ah… Ellie isn't Charlotte."

"Of course she isn't Charlotte. She's from Michigan and…" Wait. He turned to face Sam. Surely his friend hadn't meant what he'd just said.

But the pained look in Sam's eyes told a different story.

"Do you mean Charlotte… and you?" His throat turned dry, and he had to work at pushing the rest of the words out. "The two of you…? She's upset you married Ellie and not… her?" His voice cracked on the last word.

"It never would have worked."

"No." He sank down into his chair, his heart thumping. Charlotte married. He'd known it would happen, had been telling himself that since the day in church three years ago when he'd looked over and discovered his best friend's little sister had changed from a girl into a woman. But since when did Charlotte want to marry Sam?

Daniel pressed his eyes shut. "Sorry. I didn't realize there were feelings between you two."

"There aren't. At least not on my part. I don't think Charlotte's feelings are genuine either. It's more that she'd rather marry someone she knows over whoever her pa ends up picking."

He couldn't blame Charlotte. But if she thought she had a chance of thwarting her father's wishes, she was mistaken. Oh, he might have realized Charlotte was a woman three years ago, but he'd known long before that day both of the Westin sisters were off-limits. Agamemnon Westin V wouldn't stand for his youngest daughter marrying a plain old sheriff like him or a small rancher like Sam.

"Guess I should have talked to Charlotte before Ellie came," Sam muttered.

"You should have talked to all of us before Ellie came."

"Probably." Sam stalked to the corner of the office, where the cooling kettle sat on a table by the back door, and poured himself a cup of coffee. "I was worried about what Wes would say, and I've never been much for talking about this type of thing. You know that."

Yes, he knew, and part of him could even understand why Sam hadn't said anything to Wes. But why hadn't Sam told him?

Because it wasn't Sam's way, and he should be used to that by now. "In some ways I feel like you and I are family, and in other ways, I feel like you're still the orphan boy Wes and I found trying to catch catfish without a rod or hook or bait. And when Wes tried letting you borrow his rod, you threw a rock at him."

Did Sam plan on changing his independent ways for Ellie? Because if Sam had as much trouble sharing things with Ellie as he did with everyone else, then the newlyweds were going to have a rough time.

"I remember that day." Sam sat in the chair across the desk from him, the edges of his lips curving into a smile, which he covered by taking a swig of coffee. When Sam looked up again, his lips had turned down and a haunted look filled his eyes. "I can't change the fact I don't have parents or that I was raised in the Codwittles' orphanage."

"You think too little of yourself. You took a bullet to your shoulder to save my pa's life. That's the kind of thing a man does for family." His last words emerged as a rough whisper. He didn't need to look in a mirror to know he was now the one wearing the haunted expression.

How many times had he replayed that day in his mind, wishing he would have done something different?

Wishing his childhood friend Cain, now a Texas Ranger, would have done something different.

Wishing even Sam would have done something different and arrived a minute or two earlier.

Then the rustler would have never fired his gun. Then pa's leg would have never taken a bullet in the artery. Then pa would still have both legs…

And his position as sheriff.

Daniel drew in a breath and stared down at the scarred top of his desk. Who was he to criticize Sam for not being able to overcome things from his past? He couldn't put his own past behind him either.

~.~.~.~.~

Why did Daniel have to go bringing up the day his pa lost his leg? Sam shifted in the hard wooden chair across from Daniel's desk.

Sure, he'd forever be glad for that first day at the river when he'd met Wes and Daniel, and he was just as glad that Wes and Daniel hadn't given up on him, seeing how their friendship had lasted twenty years. But that lonely little orphan boy was still somewhere inside him and always would be.

He glanced up in time to see Daniel press his eyes shut, the lines around his eyes and mouth wreathed with grief. Maybe one day Daniel would be able to talk about his pa without losing control of himself, but that day might be a long time in coming.

Then again, if he'd had a pa as good as Hank Harding and that pa had lost a leg, he'd get teary too.

"I meant to say that you don't give yourself enough credit." Daniel's voice had lost its tortured tone, and when he opened his eyes, they were chock-full of the kindness Daniel always carried. "You stood by Wes when he married Abigail. And after he buried her, you were the one to drag him out of the saloon every night for a month straight. When one of us needs something, you act like the best brother a man can have. But when you need something—like a wife—you say your life isn't our business. It's not normal for a man to get himself a sweetheart or propose without his closest friends knowing."

So that's what Daniel had been getting at when he'd started in about his pa, and Daniel was usually right about this kind of situation. Good thing, too, because he didn't have the faintest notion of what "normal" meant for most families.

Ellie was supposed to help with that though. After all, she had eight siblings, she had to know what being part of a family was like.

He still wasn't sure how they'd started talking about families. He only knew that he wanted one something fierce, and now that Ellie was here, the rest should fall into place.

"I need to get on over to the courthouse, but I want you to know I found some men riding across my property yesterday." Sam set his empty coffee cup on the corner of the desk. "I meant to tell you sooner, but then Wes got his dander up about Ellie coming and I plumb forgot."

"Men on your ranch? Did they look like they'd been driving cattle?" Daniel stood from behind his desk and grabbed his hat from the peg, then gestured toward the door. "I'll walk over to the courthouse with you. I need to see if a date has been scheduled for the Lòpez hearing. You can tell me more on the way."

Sam grabbed his hat, settling it on his head before stepping into the bright Texas morning. He told Daniel everything he could remember about the men who'd looked like rustlers but had claimed the railroad owned his land.

"I haven't gotten any reports about cattle being rustled." Daniel paused at the stairs inside the courthouse, his face set in grim concentration. "I'll tell my deputies to keep a lookout, but I need you to give me a description of the two men before you head home."

"Sure thing." Though he really should get back to the ranch to make sure Ellie was getting on all right.

"I need to go check on that date. I'll meet up with you after I've finished." Daniel started down the hall toward the clerk's desk.

Sam took the wide stairs up to the third floor, which was already sweltering despite it being several hours before noon. Dusty sunlight filtered through the long, tall windows set beneath the building's eaves, illuminating the cavernous space filled with records. The room not only functioned as the land office, but also contained the county files for just about everything else a man could imagine.

"Howdy, Manny. You mind pulling up the deed for my ranch? I need to see if it matches something on my own deed."

Manuel Thompson looked up from where he stood at the counter with a crate of papers. His dark eyes and gray-speckled hair told of his Tejano mother, yet his skin was only a shade darker than Sam's own tanned skin.

Manny slid a sheaf of papers into a crate marked "Court Records, A" that was sitting on the counter. "Sure, just let me put this back."

He hefted the crate, which looked overlarge in his wiry arms, and disappeared into a row of shelves filled with similar boxes. His shoes clacked against the plain wood flooring as he moved two aisles over and rummaged through one of the crates at the front of the aisle.

Sam took out his handkerchief and dabbed at the bead of sweat dribbling down his temple. How did Manny stand working up here? But the man had served as Twin Rivers's county clerk for as long as he could remember. The court and sheriff's office also used him as a Spanish interpreter when needed.

Manual looked up, his brow furrowed. "The deed doesn't appear to be here."

"What do you mean?" Sam leaned over the counter.

The clerk shoved his glasses higher on his nose, one hand holding his place in the box of papers. "It, ah, seems to be missing."

Sam turned suddenly cold despite the sweltering air surrounding him. "How can the deed to my property be missing?"

Manny pulled a sheet of paper out of his file and came toward the counter. "Well, the deed to the property isn't exactly missing. Just the one that has your name on it."

Sam's heart thundered against his ribs. Did that mean Manny had a deed *without* his name on it? There had to be some kind of mistake. Yet the words from the men he'd met yesterday echoed in his ears. *You're mistaken, mister. This here land belongs to the Southern Pacific Railroad... If you don't believe us, maybe you should go down to the courthouse and see for yourself.*

"Let me see that." Sam snatched the sheet of paper.

Footsteps pounded on the stairs and Daniel bounded into the room. "You ready to give me those descriptions?"

Sam didn't look up. His mouth had gone dry as he scanned the unmistakable words in front of him. Everything was as the men who'd trespassed on his property yesterday had claimed. The deed stated the Southern Pacific Railroad owned the land, and a note at the bottom added that the land had been awarded by the State of

Texas in exchange for laying railroad line.

"Sam?" Daniel stopped in front of him. "What's wrong?"

He shoved the paper toward Daniel, then balled his hand into a fist and slammed it on the counter with enough force that Manny jumped back. "That land is mine. There's no way the railroad owns it."

Daniel's brow drew down and his eyes took on a dark, serious glint. "We know the land is yours. The whole town knows it, just like the whole town knows the land used to belong to old man Griggs."

True. When the wealthy businessman had, upon his death, awarded twelve thousand acres of land to an orphan who'd once worked his ranch, every paper in West Texas had written an article. Sam hadn't had the slightest inkling he'd been included in the man's will, nor had he seen Griggs in years. The old man had been living up in Austin for the past decade, his ranchland sitting unused. But Sam could still recall sitting around the campfire with the wizened rancher, drinking coffee strong enough to peel the hide off a longhorn and yammering on about how he was going to own a spread one day.

Old Man Griggs had never minded listening, and one night he'd even shared a Bible verse about how a man who didn't provide for his family had denied the faith and was worse than an infidel.

At the time, Sam thought the rancher was feeling sorry for him and meant the person who had left him at the orphanage must be worse than an infidel.

The Western Gulch Ranch and all the property it entails to Sam Owens, so he can make something of his big Texas dreams. That single line of the will that had given him a chance to be a rancher and not just a cowhand for the rest of his life. And that long-ago night had taken on a different meaning. Mr. Griggs hadn't been talking about whoever had abandoned him, but had been promising to provide for him, like he would have if they'd been family. In some ways, he must have been like a son to the man who'd lost both of his own boys in the War Between the States.

"That there deed has to be a fake." Sam nodded toward the paper Daniel still held.

"I remember filing the deed in your name last summer, made your own copy on that very copying press." Manuel pointed to the little iron press with two rollers sitting at the far end of the counter. "And the deed in Mr. Grigg's name sat here untouched for years before that."

"Then where did this other deed come from? And where's the one that says the land belongs to me?"

"I've never seen the railroad deed before." The clerk pushed his glasses higher onto his nose.

"Could somebody else have filed this new one?" Daniel leaned an elbow on the counter and tapped the paper. "Maybe on a day you were sick?"

Manny straightened and puffed out his chest. "Sheriff Harding, in twenty-seven years, I've only missed three days of work. No one else would have filed the deed."

"And even if someone else did file it, that doesn't explain what happened to mine." Sam shifted in the thick heat.

"Do you still have your deed to the property?" Daniel turned to him, his eyes dark beneath the brim of the hat he'd not bothered to take off.

Sam gave a quick nod. "I've got it in one of them fancy safe boxes at the bank."

"I don't know how this happened, Sam, but you bring me in a copy of your deed and I'll switch them out." Manny picked up the railroad deed and looked at it again. "No one's going to argue the land isn't yours."

"Go on and bring the deed in, but Manny here might not be able to switch them so easily." Daniel rubbed a thumb back and forth over his chin. "I don't know how that deed got on file, but now that it is, a judge will probably need to rule on who the land belongs to."

"Even if the papers were put there fraudulently?" Sam rasped. "Can a judge do that? Just give my land to someone else?"

"No, at least not without evidence that another person or entity has a stronger claim on the land than you do. But your situation is different because everyone knows the land belongs to you." Daniel eyed the railroad's deed. "Still, the appearance of that other deed..."

"It has to be a fake." He slammed his fist on the counter a second time.

"I agree, but how did it get here? And you said you had men on your ranch yesterday claiming the land was the railroad's. If those men were to appear in town with one copy of the deed, and Manny here knowingly removed their deed and put yours in, he could get fired for tampering with the records."

"But my deed was there first!" How could Daniel be so calm? How could he insinuate someone else might have a claim to the land?

"Simmer down, Sam." Daniel reached out and settled a hand on his shoulder. "I'm heading back to my office to fill out a report, and when Judge Grenville has a break today, I'll ask if this is a case that needs to be ruled on. In the meantime, you go get your deed so Manny can make another copy, and we'll have both of them on file. There's no question something fraudulent is going on, but I'd like to know why. You won't get any answers by rushing to cover up the fraud."

He didn't want answers. He'd just touched a document that said the land he'd put a house on and bought a hundred head of cattle for wasn't his. As far as he was concerned, they should burn the other deed and lie about ever having seen it.

But Daniel wasn't a liar, and he couldn't ask Manny to do something that might cause the man to lose his job. "I don't have the key to the bank box with me. I have to go home and get it."

"Just get the deed in before the courthouse closes, so we've got two competing deeds on file."

"No one's going to kick me off my land without a fight."

"No one's going to kick you off your land at all. But at the same time, you're going to handle this nice and orderly, not with the smoking end of a pistol. Do you understand?" Daniel's voice had taken on an official-sounding tone, the one that said he was more sheriff than friend at the moment.

"I understand." But he couldn't stop the flicker of fear that ignited in his gut. What if he had to go to court to defend his land? What if he somehow lost the ranch?

No, he'd not let himself think that way, not when he had eight children and a wife to care for.

Chapter Seven

A cold chill swept through Ellie as she stared at the fenced area that had been full of cattle when they'd arrived last night and when she'd woken this morning.

It now sat empty of every last one.

"What have you done?" she rasped at her brother.

"I just wanted to help the baby. It was bawling. I wondered if it was hungry." Martin crossed his arms over his chest and slumped against the fence post. "How was I supposed to know all the cows would run out the second I opened the gate?"

"You should have waited for Sam to return and then asked him about helping." She kept herself from shouting, but barely. Even so, her voice vibrated with enough frustration she could almost feel the ground quiver beneath her feet. "You had no business coming in here."

"Maybe we can get them back." Leroy studied the bright yellow land covered with dry grass and scraggly shrubs. A handful of cattle dotted the hill on which the house and barn sat, but nowhere near the number that had been fenced in.

"How do we go about doing that?" She scanned the paddock again, panic clawing into her chest. She was supposed to be spending the day proving she was an asset to Sam, and here his animals had been let out on her watch.

"We can try using that rope." Leroy walked to the side of the paddock and grabbed the one hung over the fence post. He weighed it in his hand for a moment, then shook his head. "Or maybe we should wait for your husband to get back and tell him we're sorry."

Husband. The word caused the breath to rush from her lungs. Sure, Miss Harding had used it earlier, and the sheriff had said it once or twice after the wedding yesterday. But hearing the word from her own brother's lips nearly doubled her over.

"Sorry. Yes, we'll tell him we're sorry." But the word sounded so very trite considering there'd been two dozen cattle or better in the pen a half hour ago.

How mad would Sam be? She twisted her hands together. Did he have a temper? He'd never said so in his letters, and she'd thought she'd come to know him rather well over their year of writing. But now that she was standing smack in the middle of this hot, barren land Sam loved, everything seemed foreign and strange.

"*If* that husband of hers comes back," Martin muttered. "Could be he's like Pa, got what he wanted from Ellie last night and rode off first thing this morning."

Heat burst onto her face, and it had nothing to do with the glaring sun beating down on them. "Sam Owens is nothing like our father."

"Says who?" Martin rolled his eyes. "You probably got a babe growing inside you right now, and the wastrel you married won't be back until she's a year old, just like Pa."

Ellie clutched a hand over her stomach. She most certainly did *not* have a child growing inside her, but she wasn't about to explain how badly she'd ruined her wedding night to her brothers.

"Sam didn't abandon us. He'll be back shortly." Or so she hoped. But she could also hope he stayed away long enough for them to get the cows back, couldn't she?

Oh, what a wretched rancher's wife she was. First she'd clammed up when she should have been kissing her husband, and now she'd gone and lost his cows. Sam might have mentioned adding on to the house at breakfast this morning, but at this rate, he'd probably decide to ship all her siblings off to an orphanage as soon as he returned.

"When did he say he'd be back?" Leroy looked up at the sun, then over at the cattle on the hill. Two more of them had wandered off, leaving only a ma and her calf in sight.

He hadn't. He'd only poked his head in the door to tell her he was leaving for town. That had been before Anna Mae left, but at least he'd been more considerate than Miss Westin, who had gotten onto her horse and thundered off without ever coming inside.

"What in the blazes happened?" A shout rang over the desert, followed by the vibrating thunder of a horse speeding closer. "Where are my cattle?"

Ellie turned in time to see Sam astride the sleek brown horse that was missing from the barn. He stopped the beast before the open gate and swung down, his neck and cheeks flushed.

She swallowed and took a step closer to Leroy. Hopefully Sam's unnatural shade of red had something to do with how quickly he'd been riding his horse.

"I asked where my cattle are." He stalked toward her.

"I… um… the gate got left open and—"

"The gate got left *open*?" He thrust his hand toward the gate. "How did it get opened? Last I checked, they don't open themselves."

Ellie narrowed her eyes at Martin, but given the way he'd twisted his lips together to sneer at Sam, he wasn't about to own up to his doings.

"It was me, sir." Leroy stepped forward.

Ellie sent him a glare. Nothing good would come of lying, even if Leroy was doing so to protect Martin.

Leroy looked away from her and kept right on talking. "The one calf was upset, so I—"

"No." Ellie nudged Leroy with her elbow. "You see, Sam—"

"I don't believe this. I was gone for two hours. Two hours! Do you know how long it will take me to round them up?" He jabbed a finger at her. "I brought you here to help me, not make more work for me."

"We'll help," she squeaked. "All of us. Won't we, boys? We'll get the cows back."

"And how do you plan to do that?" His voice had gone soft, yet it held a sharp edge that somehow seemed worse than his shouting.

"I… uh… Maybe you can tell us?" She didn't know the first thing about cattle. She'd be lucky to feed and water them, let alone get a beast that weighed five times her own weight into a pen.

"That's what I thought." Sam stalked toward the house and disappeared inside, slamming the door behind him.

Her eyes clouded with tears, and she blew out a trembling breath.

"Aw, don't cry. It could have been worse." Leroy patted her back. "He doesn't seem like the type to take his fists to you, even if he's piping mad."

True. But she wanted a husband who loved her, not one who merely refrained from beating her.

Sam emerged from the house, his face even redder than before. "Whatever you've got in the oven is burning."

The biscuits! She'd left the final batch in the oven when Leroy had come inside to tell her Martin had let out the cows. She rushed toward the door. The entire batch was probably ruined.

"Don't expect me for supper," Sam called over his shoulder. "I'll be lucky to have the cattle rounded up by sundown."

She stopped and turned back to face her husband. "But…"

He'd already swung onto his horse. A moment later he flicked the reins and raced off over the desert, leaving her to crush the fabric of her skirt in her fingers and stare at his back.

~.~.~.~.~

Sam's boots dragged against the packed dirt as he trudged toward the house. His back ached, his head pounded, and his eyelids kept begging to close. The two slices of Mrs. Harding's lemon cake he'd snitched from Daniel's office earlier had long worn off, and his stomach twisted itself into a weary knot of hunger. He was still missing two cows. Hopefully he could round them up before Wes and his hands arrived in the morning. With darkness falling, he'd run out of time to fetch more beasts tonight.

Scents of meat and some other food he couldn't quite name wafted from the kitchen, causing his stomach to growl as he neared the small, square building. Dim lamplight poured from the window, lighting the house against the backdrop of the setting sun and growing darkness. It looked right homey, his house. Like the kind of place a man could go inside, pull off his boots, and relax. Maybe even get a few of the knots in his shoulders rubbed out by a caring wife.

Yet despite the fact he'd been returning cattle to the paddock all afternoon, he'd not ventured into the house once. In fact, he'd ridden around the far side of the paddock and not even approached the yard for the few hours Ellie and Suzanna had been outside doing wash.

Because he didn't have the first clue what to say to Ellie. Should he tell her about the property? That Daniel had informed him he needed to go before a judge and defend his right to the land? He'd found his deed safely stashed in his safety deposit box at the bank and had taken it straight to the courthouse for Manny to make another copy before he returned it to the bank.

But what would happen if he lost the place he'd worked so hard to build? He'd still have his cattle, and there was some open range higher up in the mountains, but a man couldn't be much of a rancher without at least a little spread of his own.

Sam rolled his shoulders, though the action did little to alleviate the knots tightening his muscles. Even if he didn't tell Ellie about the land, he needed to apologize for yelling at her. Hadn't one of her brothers said he'd been the one to let the cattle out? But instead of stopping to listen, he'd gone on ranting. Sure, he'd been half-crazed with worry that he'd not be able to find his bank key or that the deed to his land would be missing from the safety deposit box. But being worried was no excuse to go off yelling at Ellie—or anyone, really.

Sam scrubbed a hand over his face. He couldn't put off facing her any longer. She'd probably cleaned up supper long ago, though the smell of it lingered. Maybe Ellie hadn't even saved him a plate. Given how he'd treated her, he didn't deserve to eat any of her cooking.

But he was hungry enough his stomach just might start eating itself from the inside out. He turned the knob on the door and stepped inside, half expecting to find the table clear. A plate piled with meat, gravy, and potatoes sat in the middle of the table instead.

Then there was Ellie. She lay with her arms folded on the table, her head resting atop them. Her eyes were closed in slumber, and while most of her bright red hair was still swept up onto her head, a few strands had fallen free to shimmer like fire beneath the light of the lantern.

Had she tried to wait up for him? An odd sensation started in his chest. It was strange, really, that bit of tugging. He pressed a hand to his breastbone to quell the feeling, but it didn't stop, only grew stronger the longer he stared at her.

He moved away, which lessened the pulling sensation a bit, then sat down in the chair opposite the table from her. The food radiated a mild warmth, though supper had probably been eaten hours ago. He scarfed down one bite, then another. He felt half-starved, and a man's taste buds could never be trusted in such a situation, but he could swear he'd never tasted anything so good before.

He carried his plate to the sink and ran water over it, but his clattering didn't wake her. A quick glance at the stove told him the top had been scrubbed clean. Hang it all, but the kitchen looked far different than when he'd come in to get the bank key and found flour-coated baking sheets and burning biscuits. A man couldn't ask for a more perfect-looking house.

Ellie shouldn't have gone through so much effort for him, not when the last words he'd spoken to her had been in anger.

He wasn't used to people getting into his things, and especially not mettling with his cattle. But he was a married man now, he'd have to start trying to… to…

What?

Talk to her? Thank her? He turned to face her, still sleeping soundly at the table. He'd been so certain he should marry her, so certain he needed a family. But now that he had one, he felt as lost as a newborn calf without its mama. What was he even supposed to do with Ellie tonight? He couldn't rightly leave her to sleep at the table, but was it appropriate for him to put her to bed? Last night she'd made clear that she wanted nothing to do with the intimacy that most married couples shared.

She looked utterly fragile lying on the table with her hair falling out of its bun to contrast with the pale shade of her skin. Yet her brow was furrowed, the sides of her lips turned down as though peace eluded her even in sleep.

He came around the table to her. The sight of something gold caught the light, and he reached out and pulled a wayward pin from the mass of fiery tresses. A lock of hair fell against her cheek. He removed another pin, this one causing a lock of hair to fall at the back of her neck. She'd stood before him with it down last night, the bright color shining beneath the lantern. His fingers had itched to reach out and touch a lock, to see if it was as smooth and silky as it looked.

He hadn't stroked her hair then, but he did so now, letting the soft tresses fall over his hand until her hair engulfed it, working pins out whenever he came to one.

Her breathing was even, her shoulders rising and falling in an ageless rhythm that calmed his own breaths and caused his eyelids to grow heavy. If Ellie were awake, would she let him touch her hair?

Probably not.

"Ellie, sweetheart. We need to get you to bed." He withdrew his hand and placed it on her shoulder.

Her eyelids didn't even flutter.

"Ellie." He shook her shoulder. "It's time for bed, darlin'."

She still didn't move.

He leaned closer, and faint scents of sugar and flour wafted from her. "Ellie?"

"What…?" She let out a small groan and her eyes blinked open. "Who…?"

"It's me, Sam. You fell asleep at the table, and now it's time to get you in bed."

She blinked again, then looked around, a confused glaze over her eyes. He pulled the chair back from the table and took her elbow to help her stand.

"Sam, I'm so sorry about the cattle, did you get them all back?"

"Shhh…" He put a finger over her lips, but the soft warmth of her breath puffed against his skin, and he jerked his finger away. He nodded toward the bunk beds where Suzanna, Janey, and Lynnette slept, the younger two crowded on the bottom bunk together. "You don't want to wake the girls."

"But your cows, did you find them?" She ended her words on a yawn.

"All but two. I'll look for them in the morning. I'm sorry for yelling at you earlier. I should have realized this is the first time you and your siblings have been around cattle." He kept hold of her elbow as he guided her into the bedroom.

Her hair fell in soft waves over her shoulders, so rich and lush he could barely keep himself from running his fingers through it again. Instead he pulled back the cover on the bed, then stilled. Should he help her out of her dress? Was she wearing something underneath that she could sleep in?

But she lay right down and curled onto her side, as though changing into a nightdress was the furthest thing from her mind. "I'm just so sorry. I never meant for the cows to…"

He laid his fingers over her lips once more. Warmth from them radiated into his hand and traveled up his arm.

"No more about the cattle tonight. I was wrong for shouting at you, and we can talk more in the morning." He pulled the thin blanket up over her shoulders and tucked it around her, leaving her cocooned on the bed. "And thank you for dinner. I've never tasted anything so good before."

"It was just meat and gravy," she spoke on another yawn. "No trouble at all to fix."

She blinked once, then twice, before closing her eyes a final time.

Her position on the side of the bed left plenty of room for him to lie down beside her. Should he? Nothing was wrong with a husband and wife sharing a bed—or any of the other things that went along with marriage.

He lifted a hand to the top button of his shirt, but stopped before he slipped it through the fabric.

Ellie might have been accepting of his touches tonight, but she was barely coherent. What if he crawled into bed and then woke in the morning to find himself lying next to a woman who recoiled at his touch?

He bent down and placed a kiss on her forehead. That would have to do…

For now.

Chapter Eight

Ellie shut her eyes against the light streaming through the window and snuggled deeper under the thin blanket atop her bed. A spot of warmth bloomed on her forehead and spread clear through to her fingers and toes. Had she imagined Sam's kiss on her brow last night? Had she imagined him pulling out her hair pins? Had she imagined…?

She rolled over and opened her eyes, but no form lay in the bed beside her. In fact, the opposite side of the bed was completely undisturbed. Yes, she must have imagined that last bit. But his presence lingered in the room, as though he'd been with her minutes ago rather than hours.

A shout sounded from outside, followed by another.

She sat upright and looked out the window. Just how late had she slept? Much later than usual, given that the sun had already risen clear above the mountains in the east.

Her hair cascaded around her shoulders in wild, bright waves, proving that she hadn't imagined Sam taking the pins from her hair. She still wore the same green dress she'd donned yesterday, yet another testament to most of her memories being accurate, even if they were hazy.

She slipped out of bed, shoved her feet into her shoes, and opened the bedroom door. Suzanna stood at the stove mixing a pot of porridge.

"Where is everyone?" Ellie padded across the packed dirt floor. Were the rest of the children with Sam? Hopefully he'd not be upset that she'd slept so late.

The man who had gently guided her to bed last night didn't seem the type to get upset over her sleeping in. But that same man had also yelled at her when his cattle had gotten out.

Then again, if her memory from last night could be trusted, he'd apologized for yelling. Maybe that's why he'd been so tender when helping her into bed, because he was trying to make up for how he'd treated her.

If only she could remember everything. Had she said something to him before drifting off to sleep? Maybe something about being glad she was in Texas and happy he was providing a home for her siblings? Or had she only thought those things?

"Everyone else is outside." Suzanna gave the pot a final stir, then lifted it off the stove and set it on the table. "I peeked in on you once, but you were sleeping awful hard, so I decided to make breakfast."

"Did you measure the grain before you started cooking?" Ellie frowned at the pot, which contained double the amount of porridge they usually prepared.

"Of course, but I figured Sam's friends would eat a heap of it." Suzanna wiped her hands on her apron.

"Sam's friends?"

"Get them while I set out bowls and spoons. They're just past the cow pen." Suzanna waved a hand absently toward the door and went about setting the table as though she were the one in charge of the kitchen.

Ellie yawned and peered outside, blinking at the light that blazed from the sky above and bounced off the rocky yellow ground. Maybe someday she'd get used to the blinding brightness of the desert, so very different from the dappled light that cascaded through the rich green trees and shrubs surrounding their home in Eagle Harbor.

Sure enough, a group of men huddled on the far side of the cow pen, and the children had gathered there as well, even Martin.

She stepped out the door and started across the yard. She counted six men in all, four of which were holding a calf on the ground while Sam kneeled beside the beast's belly. The last man stood beside a small fire that had been built a few feet from the calf's head.

No, not a man. The person didn't wear trousers but a split skirt. Everything else about her was exactly like the men. She wore a wide-brimmed hat with crimped edges, a bandana, a vest that matched her split skirt, and a dusty shirt beneath. Why, she even had leather boots that looked almost identical to Sam's.

Ellie stiffened. What kind of woman came alongside a group of men to help with cattle? Surely such things weren't proper, not even in Texas.

Wait, the woman from yesterday—Charlotte Westin, the one who had feelings for Sam—had worn a split skirt too. Was this the same person?

Ellie looked away from the other woman, her jaw suddenly tense, and stared at the poor calf being held on the ground.

"What are you…?" But her words were swallowed by the calf's frantic mooing.

Sam looked up at her for a moment, then took a knife from his belt and moved his hand toward the calf's nether regions.

Surely he didn't intend to cut the cow *there*.

The calf bellowed and shrieked. "Sam, stop, you can't…"

The woman chose that moment to take a long rod from the fire at her feet and shove the end of the rod against the calf's right shoulder.

"Stop," she gulped. "You have to stop."

She didn't know whether she spoke loud enough to be heard over the poor beast's bawling, but one of the men untied the rope that bound the calf's front legs, and the animal scrambled up and took off running and squealing.

Sam looked up and scanned the children. "Leroy, go let its mama out of the paddock, then shut the gate."

One glance at the pen told her which cow Sam meant. A light brown beast stood at the entrance, bellowing one moment and snorting the next, all while watching the calf that circled back toward the pen at full speed.

"Ellie?" Sam stood to his feet. "You're awake. Ah… is something wrong?"

Wrong? She sniffled. Of course something was wrong. "You're hurting them! Is this what you made such a big fuss about yesterday? You were mad Martin let your cows out when you were keeping them here just to… to hurt them?" She was shrieking louder than the calf now, but couldn't quite stop herself. "How could you?"

He came toward her, questions flooding his eyes. He reached a hand toward her shoulder, revealing knuckles smeared with blood.

"Don't touch me." She shrank back from him.

"I don't know what you expect. I run a cattle ranch, and this is what ranchers do." He scowled, his look as dark as the one he'd given her yesterday when he'd returned home to find the cattle gone from their pen. "There's enough trouble with rustlers stealing registered brands already. If I don't brand my cattle at all, I won't have a single beast left for market come fall."

She sucked a breath in through her nose. Perhaps that made sense. Sam would need a way to prove he owned his cattle, though surely there was a better way to mark them, one that didn't cause pain.

"And that other part. The part with the…" She waved her hand toward where his knife was now sheathed in his belt. "…the blade."

"Ranchers castrate all male cattle they don't plan to breed." Sam used the bottom of his bandana to wipe a trickle of sweat from his temple. "If we let them roam free for two years with the heifers, just imagine the mess we'd have on our hands."

"No, I can't imagine the mess. As you said, you're a rancher. That means you're trying to breed cows. So why would you castrate the males?"

Sam muttered something beneath his breath that may have pertained to greenhorns and needing patience from God. "Because the cattle I sell for beef has never been bred. It makes for the tenderest, best-tasting meat. The males I castrate, they're called steers. And the females I don't breed are heifers. I'll take them to market when they're full grown but still young, at about a year and a half old. Then I've got about thirty breeding cows, and three bulls—those are the males I haven't castrated. Bulls."

"Oh, well…" Who could have guessed cows were so confusing? Her eyes flitted to the knife still sheathed to Sam's belt. "Can't you give the calves laudanum first? So that that castration doesn't hurt them so much?"

"Laudanum?" His voice took on a high, raspy quality. "Do you know how expensive—?"

"Come on, Sam, rope the next one," a familiar male voice called from somewhere behind Sam. "I don't want to be here all day."

Ellie looked past Sam's shoulder to see Mr. Westin standing with a thumb hooked into the waistband of his trousers and the tip of his boot tapping impatiently on the ground.

She should have realized he'd be involved with something so loathsome.

"Why are you out here with your hair down? And in the same dress as yesterday?" Sam didn't look at his friend but instead ran his eyes down the length of her, concern glinting in his eyes. "Are you feeling ill?"

She drew in a breath and glanced down at herself. Why hadn't she thought to put her hair up or change clothes? "I'm fine. I didn't know what the commotion was in the yard, and I forgot to put myself together before coming outside.

"The porridge is ready." She spoke loudly enough for everyone to hear. "That's what I came here to tell you. Suzanna made enough for all of you, if you want to wash up and come inside."

"Porridge?" The woman stepped away from the branding fire and looked at Sam, a teasing smile tilting her lips. "You're feeding him porridge?"

"Is something wrong with that?" Ellie raised her chin.

"Don't tell me he's eaten any?" This from the insufferable Mr. Westin, who now had a grin plastered across his face.

"Of course he ate some. Yesterday morning he…"

Laughter erupted from the workers.

She pressed her lips together and turned to Sam, whose ears were red.

"Ah, I don't much cotton to porridge." He could barely be heard over the laughter. But he shifted from one foot to the other and looked down. "We ate so much of it at the orphanage that I lost my taste for it."

He hated porridge? So much so that all his friends knew of his aversion? Heat burst onto her cheeks.

"I see," she said. Though she didn't, because how hard was it for him to explain? This must have been why he'd not wanted to come to the table for breakfast yesterday and then barely answered Suzanna's questions about his food.

And here she'd thought he'd been mad at her for not kissing him on their wedding night.

Her back stiff, she turned away from Sam and looked at her siblings. "Come along. It's time to go inside and wash up."

She should probably invite Sam's friends in for porridge again, but at the moment, every last one of them was settling down from their bout of laugher, and that after she'd only mentioned porridge. How would they respond if she actually served them a bowl of it?

"But Ellie," Joe whined. "I want to stay out here with—"

"I said inside. Now." The words came out sharper than intended, but her siblings started for the house, even Martin. She stalked into the house behind them and pointed to the table. "Get seated."

Suzanna went to the door and peeked outside. "Aren't the others—?"

"No." Ellie grabbed the small sack of flour off the shelf by the sink, along with the sugar, salt, and three eggs from the basket. Sam wanted something other than porridge? Then that's what she'd give him. Never mind that she'd used most of the flour and butter for the biscuits yesterday; she could make do.

Scanning the shelf, she searched for a jar of dried apples or blueberries but found nothing to add to the muffins, not even cinnamon. Fine, plain muffins it was, with an extra sprinkle of sugar on the top. She whisked the eggs together while the children ate in silence behind her, then added a bit of milk to the mixture. She was just reaching for the flour when a shadow fell over her.

She looked over her shoulder. Not Sam, thank goodness. She had a mind to chase him away with a broom if he darkened the door of the house. Leroy stood there instead, an empty porridge bowl in his hand.

"Are you all right?"

"Fine, just mixing up some muffins." And making a mess in the process. She should probably stop whipping the whisk around the bowl so quickly if she didn't want flour everywhere. "Help the twins and Lynnette finish up, and if you go back outside, stay away from the men. I don't want you watching that."

"Martin and I are supposed to help with the ranch. Don't you think—?"

"No."

His shoulders slumped. "We should leave."

"And go into town? For what?"

"No. We should leave Texas."

Ellie's hands stilled on the mixing bowl and she glanced up to find hard determination filling her brother's eyes—determination that looked far too old and wise to belong to a fifteen-year-old.

"We can't leave. I'm married." She started mixing again. "Why would you even say a thing like that?"

"Staying here isn't working." Leroy set his bowl in the sink and leaned against it, causing his shadow to fall over her again.

Since when had he grown tall enough to leave her in his shadow? "Everything is fine. We have food, don't we? And a roof over our heads."

"We could have had those things in Eagle Harbor."

Not if she married Sam. Leaving her family hadn't seemed like a bad idea when Ma had been alive and she and Sam had started writing letters. But she couldn't abandon her siblings now that Ma was gone and Pa wanted nothing to do with them. Besides, if the children went back to Eagle Harbor, their mother's secret had a greater chance of getting out—not that Leroy knew of it.

Leroy looked at the table behind her, which was suspiciously quiet considering seven children still ate. Then he leaned close and lowered his voice. "You didn't come for food or a roof, you came because you wanted a man who'd treat you right. The way Mr. Cummings treats his wife."

A vision of Isaac Cummings catching Aileen in his arms and

pressing a kiss to her forehead right on the porch of the sheriff's office for half the town to see rose up in her mind. Then a vision of Elijah Cummings sitting in the pew in front of her at church and pulling Victoria close during one of the songs before bending down and whispering something in her ear that caused her cheeks to flush and love to shine from her eyes.

She should probably ask which Mr. Cummings her brother meant, but both Elijah and Isaac treated their wives with love and kindness.

She'd also wager both of them told their wives if they cooked something they despised.

And that their wives didn't go stiff as fenceposts beneath their kisses.

"There's no changing things now." Ellie drew in a breath, long and slow. "As I said, I'm a married woman, and that means something before God. I can't just up and leave my husband because my marriage is having a difficult start."

"I'm not suggesting you leave..." Leroy looked down. "Just... just the rest of us."

"No." The word exploded from her mouth so forcefully that the clanking of silverware behind her went silent. She turned to her brother and jabbed a finger into his chest but kept her voice low enough the others wouldn't hear. "Not a one of you is leaving. Where would you go? To an orphanage? I can't have that on my hands. Sam said you could stay, so you're staying."

But would Sam change his mind if he knew the truth about them? If he knew she'd not bothered to tell him everything about her family, much like he'd not bothered to tell her he hated porridge?

Except her secret was much bigger than a dislike of porridge.

"I'm not a child anymore. I know what you're doing by insisting we stay. You're trying to make things right for us after losing Ma and

Aunt Maude turning five of us away. But don't you see? You've spent your whole life trying to make things right for us. In Eagle Harbor, you exhausted yourself working at the bakery and taking in Ma's wash and mending, all while trying to care for us. But maybe..." Leroy's voice squeaked and he cleared his throat. "Maybe it's not possible to make things right, at least not for all of us and not all at once. But it might be possible to make things right for you and your new life here. I don't want to watch you sacrifice your happiness for the rest of us."

She should have known something like this was coming. This was what God did to her, after all. He dangled hope in front of her only to yank it away. True, she'd expected Sam to kick them out rather than Leroy to up and leave, or perhaps Leroy and Martin to fall in with the wrong crowd again and this time end up locked behind bars for a spell. But she wasn't about to give her siblings over to be raised by the mercy of strangers' whims.

"What kind of sister would I be if I let you leave?" She tossed the whisk into the sink with a violent clatter. "You might be old enough to make it on your own, but Lynnette is one. Janey and Joe are six. I can't abandon you like... like Pa abandoned us."

"Well maybe you should, because it's awful hard on the rest of us knowing we're the reason you're so unhappy."

"You are not the reason I'm unhappy. Sam Owens is!" All it would have taken was one sentence from the man. *I don't like porridge.*

Leroy's jaw held a determined tilt that told her she just might awake in the morning to find him gone, even if he didn't take the others with him.

"Stay, Leroy. Promise me. I don't know what I'd do if you left. We all need more time." She reached out and gripped his hand. "You ought not make such a serious decision when we've been here less than a week. I'm sure the longer we stay, the easier things will be on everyone."

"Easier on everyone except you. That's my point. You deserve a chance to see how things could be between you and Sam without the rest of us getting in the way."

"No one's getting in the way."

"No? Don't you think Sam might have found a chance to tell you he doesn't like porridge if you hadn't spent yesterday running around helping everyone unpack, washing our travel clothes, and making meals for ten people? Without us, the cattle wouldn't have gotten out either. Do you know how late Sam was out rounding them up last night?

She shook her head. She'd fallen asleep before he'd arrived and hadn't bothered to check the time when he'd moved her to the bedroom.

"You probably wouldn't have fed Sam porridge without the rest of us here, because the handful of eggs you're getting from the henhouse are enough for two people."

Ellie squeezed her eyes shut. What was she to say? Leroy was right, but admitting it would only convince him to leave.

"Give it time. Surely you can do that for me. We'll see where things stand in a month. If our situation isn't improving then… then…" She couldn't bring herself to say he or any of the others should leave. "Then we'll talk about what we should do."

"I'll give it a month, but I want you to write Elijah and Victoria Cummings and see if they'd be willing to take some of us if things don't work out with Sam." Leroy crossed his arms over a chest that seemed to be growing broader and more masculine by the day. "I suppose Martin and I could get a job on one of the ranches around here, but the rest of—"

"I'm not letting Lynnette go anywhere. And I've a mind to keep Janey and Joe too."

Leroy scowled. "Keeping the younger ones will only be harder on you."

"They need to be with family more than Henry or Suzanna or Christopher."

"Elijah and Victoria Cummings would make a right fine family for Janey and Joe."

"Stop." She held up her hand and blinked away the hot moisture pricking the backs of her eyes. "Stop talking like this. Things will work out, you'll see."

"I'm not going to let you throw away your first real chance at happiness on account of us. Write a letter now, today, asking if they can take us, and I promise to wait a few weeks before deciding whether to leave."

She opened her mouth to respond, but Leroy shoved away from the sink and strode toward the door, his strong gait more like a man's than a boy's. Did he realize how much he looked like their older brother Clifford? Leroy would turn sixteen this fall, and that would make him the same age Clifford had been when he'd left home to work as a sailor.

That job had led to his drowning at only nineteen years of age.

Ellie sucked in a breath, sharp and tinged with the pain of lost loved ones. She'd write Victoria to appease Leroy, but she couldn't let him or any of the others leave. They weren't a burden.

They were all she had left in the world.

~.~.~.~.~

Sam shoved his knife back into its sheath while the calf before him shrieked and bellowed.

"It's time for a break." Wes released his hold on the beast and stood, letting the calf run pell-mell away from the branding fire.

Sam wiped the sweat from his brow before looking up at the paddock. Only four more calves left.

"Let's finish and be done with it. You can be home before lunch." His stomach chose that moment to let out a loud growl.

"Hungry after missing breakfast?" Wes chuckled.

"Stow it."

"I still can't believe she yelled at you for branding and castrating the calves." Charlotte repositioned the branding iron in the fire. "I knew marrying her was a mistake."

"It wasn't a mistake." Sam rose from his position on the ground and headed toward Long Arrow.

"It might be if she only cooks porridge." Ailes, one of the hands from the A Bar W, wiped his dust-streaked hands on his thighs and stood.

"Don't know." Dobbs clapped Ailes on the back. "I sure wouldn't complain about having a spread of my own and a wife to come home to at night, even if all she cooked was porridge."

"She cooks more than porridge," Sam gritted. "Last night she made the best-tasting beef and gravy I've ever had." He swung up onto Long Arrow and started for the paddock. He didn't need to tell Wes to move behind him and open the gate. After so many years of working spring roundup together, the two of them had things down pat.

But Ellie and her siblings had never before been around cattle. He probably should have explained what he would be doing this morning before he'd started. But when? She'd been asleep when he'd gotten back to the house last night.

He scanned the simple adobe home. Ellie had disappeared inside over two hours ago. Should he go inside and try talking to her?

"You going to rope the calf sometime today, or can we take that break?" Wes slanted a glance at the house and then looked back at him, an amused expression on his face.

Sam started Long Arrow forward, twirling the lasso over his head and directing his horse toward where the cattle had packed together at the back of the pen. He threw the rope toward one of the calf's legs, then gave the rope a jerk. The calf fell to the dirt, its legs bound together. Sam looped the rope around his saddle's pommel, then pulled on Long Arrow's reins and dug his heels into the horse's side. Long Arrow dragged the calf out of the pen, and Wes slammed the gate shut before the mother cow could follow, though she kicked up a fuss at the front of the paddock.

Ailes grabbed the calf's roped front legs, while Dobbs grabbed a hind leg. Wes appeared a moment later and held down the second hind leg. This calf was a female, so it only needed branding. The workers held down the beast for less than thirty seconds while Charlotte stamped its hide. Sam stayed astride his horse, and the second the newly branded calf was released, he started toward the paddock to get the next one.

Before he reached the gate, the door to the house swung open, and out stepped Ellie. She'd changed into the yellow dress she'd been wearing the day she'd arrived and had put her hair up in a sloppy bun that only made him think of how silky her tresses had felt twining about his fingers the night before. She came straight toward him, her chin up and shoulders back, carrying a basket on one are arm and a blanket and kettle in another.

"I made you and your friends a snack. There's coffee too if anyone wants it." She plopped the basket and kettle down on a patch of ground and spread the blanket beside it.

"Boy howdy, are those muffins?" Ailes stared at the basket. "It's been an age since I had me a muffin."

"They are, thank you. Lunch will be ready around noon." Ellie turned and started back toward the house.

Ailes and Dobbs rushed toward the blanket. Wes and Charlotte approached more slowly, but no one snubbed their nose at the food.

"Ellie, wait." Sam swung off his horse.

She stopped walking but didn't turn.

"Thank you for the muffins." He swiped the hat from his head, mainly because it gave his hands something to crush while he stood in front of her. Words swarmed in his head, but how to know which ones he should say? "I'm… I'm sorry I didn't tell you about the porridge. And the calves. Or rather, what all roundup means. It didn't seem like there was a good time, but I should have made a bigger effort."

"It's fine." But she didn't look like it was fine. She looked like she was ready to bash him over the head with a cast iron pan. Either that or start crying.

And no, he didn't have the slightest notion how a woman could look both ways at once.

"Oh, here. I almost forgot." She reached into her apron pocket and handed him a folded paper.

He opened it and found himself staring at a long list of foodstuffs.

"It's a list for the general store." Her words were sharp and clipped, as though the urge to hit him over the head with a pan was winning out over the urge to get teary. "If you want something other than porridge for breakfast, then I need more food to cook with."

"Fair enough." Except it really didn't seem fair, because as near as he could tell, the items on this list would total three dollars or better, and with the two dollars he planned to spend on laying hens, that meant he'd be through half their money for the month.

Was having a family this expensive for everyone?

He scanned the list a second time. Dried apples? He'd never seen such a thing in the general store. He'd never seen a real apple there either, though he'd eaten one a time or two on one of the longer trail drives that had taken him far enough north for apple trees to grow. "Just how much of this do you need today?"

"All of it, if you want me to make fancy food." She plopped a hand on her narrow hip.

"What are the fresh strawberries for?" He'd only had those a time or two as well. Wild ones grew in eastern Texas or high up in the mountains, no fruit grew down in the river valley save the prickly pears that grew on cacti.

Ellie looked at him as though he'd sprouted a pair of longhorns. "A pie for tonight."

A pie sounded right good, but he'd bet his saddle that Mr. Cunningham at the General Store wouldn't have any strawberries to sell Ellie. The only fruit that made it to the middle of the desert this time of year came in cans. Any kind of fresh fruit would spoil in the summer heat long before it reached Twin Rivers.

He dug in his pocket and pulled out a dollar bill. "Pick out the five or six things you need most and we'll get the rest next week."

Hopefully. If he came up with extra money.

"You want *me* to get the food?" She stared at the dollar, then looked off in the direction of town.

"I need to finish with the calves, then ride out and check the herd." He hadn't had time to ride his land yesterday to make sure the cattle weren't straying, which gave him no choice but to get out on the range today.

"I'll go after lunch and take Martin and Christopher with me." She took the dollar and slipped it into her pocket. "We should be able to carry everything back before dark. Do you mind if Suzanna makes dinner?"

"Carry everything back?" He blinked, and not because the sun was glaring down on him. "Are you thinking of walking?"

"How else am I supposed to get to town?"

"Take the wagon. It's four miles into Twin Rivers. You can't walk there and back."

"I don't know how to drive a wagon. I told you that in my letters."

No, she'd said she knew little of horses in her letters, and he'd promised to teach her to ride once she was here. But she'd never written anything about not knowing how to drive a wagon. Everyone knew how, didn't they?

But the confused way she was looking at the barn told him she didn't have the faintest notion.

"Sam, are you coming? Or has this not been a long enough break for you?" Amusement tinged Wes's voice.

"Be there in a minute." He handed the list back to Ellie. "Figure out what you need most and write it on a separate paper. I'll go into town and get the supplies later." Never mind that he'd be missing dinner for the second night in a row.

"Thank you," she said, but she pressed her lips together as though she was still unhappy about something, then she took the list from his hand and strode away.

Sam settled his hat back atop his head. After writing Ellie for a year, he thought he knew the woman he was marrying. So how come the longer he and Ellie were married, the more confusing his wife became?

Chapter Nine

Ellie shifted beside Sam on the wooden pew, but her movements didn't stop the cloying heat from pressing in around her. Was the church building this hot every Sunday, or was the temperature today more extreme than usual? Of course, some of the heat could be related to the heavy stares people were sending her way.

Not that she could blame them for staring. Twin Rivers was a small town, and a bride arriving with eight siblings in tow couldn't be a normal occurrence. Still, people attempted to be friendly. She'd talked to a dozen or so women who had come up to their pew and asked Sam for introductions. But an awkward silence always followed the introduction, when the women's gaze would drift to her siblings, as though counting to make sure eight children truly sat in the pew with them. Then the women would mumble something about how nice it was to meet them before heading back to their seat.

Sam sat beside her, his back stiff and shoulders straight as he stared ahead at the empty pulpit. Did he always behave this way at church, or had she embarrassed him in some way? She hadn't seen Sam last night because he was out late again with his cattle, something he claimed he couldn't avoid after going into town to get her groceries earlier in the day. Once again she'd woken up in her bed after falling asleep at the table, but she hadn't had the chance to ask what he'd expected of her or the children today.

Did he want the children to make friends at the potluck after church? She sighed. If only she knew how to put a smile on his face rather than a frown.

Of course, she could always start by kissing Sam back the next time he kissed her. But he hadn't attempted another kiss since their wedding night, though he'd certainly been tender when he'd pulled the pins from her hair and put her to bed the past two nights. He'd been kind and attentive when he showed her how to drive the wagon on the way into church earlier too.

Hopefully Leroy had noticed Sam's kindness. Her brother had kept his word and hadn't left, but how was she going to convince him that he and the rest of their siblings were better off staying with her and Sam than going back to Eagle Harbor?

Perhaps if Leroy made some friends at the meal after church today, he'd want to stay in Twin Rivers. And she'd talk to the schoolmarm about sending some of the children to school. Surely once the children settled in and met some young'uns their own age, Leroy would see how foolish his talk of leaving was.

Or so she hoped.

"Move over, you're squishing me." Martin gave Christopher a shove toward Suzanna.

"Don't." Ellie reached over Janey and laid a hand on Suzanna's lap before she could shove Christopher back into Martin. "Mind yourselves."

"Can I sit on Sam's lap?" Joe popped up from the far end of the pew and started clambering over everyone's legs.

"Um..." Ellie looked at Sam. "How about you sit on my—?"

"Sure, cowboy. Come on over." Sam held his arms out for the boy.

Ellie blinked. Since when had Joe taken such a liking to Sam?

Since when had Sam taken such a liking to Joe?

Joe snuggled into Sam's lap and tucked his little head in the crook of Sam's arm as though he'd been sitting there since the day he was born.

"Oh, good. I thought we'd be late."

At the sound of the friendly voice behind her, Ellie looked over her shoulder to see Anna Mae rush into the pew and plop herself down.

Anna Mae then leaned forward, resting her hands on the pew back. "Ellie, how are you settling in?"

Oh, just dandy. One of my brothers let Sam's cows out of the pen on Friday, then yesterday I embarrassed my husband in front of his friends, at which point my other brother decided everyone but me should leave Texas.

"I'm still adjusting to life in the desert." That was about as nice of a way to phrase things as she could manage without lying.

"Does Daniel need help getting your pa inside?" Sam rose and set Joe on the pew bench.

Anna Mae looked toward the back of the church. "I think Wes is out there, but they won't complain about more help."

Sam headed outside before Anna Mae had even finished her sentence, passing the form of another woman on the way—a woman whom Ellie had seen far too much of since arriving in Texas.

Charlotte Westin slipped into the pew beside Anna Mae. She wore a dress that fit her chest and waist snuggly before flaring around her hips. The fabric shimmered in the light and parted halfway down her skirt, revealing a ruffled underskirt. Ellie didn't know much of women's fashion, but something told her she'd see wealthy women in Chicago and Austin wearing similar dresses.

But the color was wretched. Anna Mae would probably look fine in the dark gold shade, but it made Miss Westin's delicate complexion look sickly.

Unlike Anna Mae, who still leaned close to the pew in front of her, Miss Westin sat with her spine perfectly straight and shoulders back, though she gave her nose the slightest wrinkle when she looked at Anna Mae. "Why are we sitting back here?"

"So that Ellie doesn't have to be alone, you dunderhead."

Miss Westin scanned the pew full of children. "She's not."

Anna Mae rolled her eyes. "She is in the ways that matter. Ellie, you and Sam come over and share our picnic blanket after church."

Oh. "Thank you, it's kind of you to offer. We brought our own blanket, but maybe we can put it..."

Her words tapered off as she caught more movement at the back of the church. Sam and Mr. Westin stood beside a man sitting in a chair with giant wheels on either side of it. A woman with dark brown hair streaked with gray stood on the opposite side of the sitting man, and Daniel wheeled the man forward.

Was Anna Mae's father an invalid? Anna Mae was so cheerful and friendly, and Daniel had always appeared so strong and commanding, she'd not imagined either of them having an ailing parent.

Anna Mae tapped Ellie's back, as though she wasn't already looking over her shoulder. "You have to meet my parents after church. I've told them all about you."

Hopefully Anna Mae had told them good things. At least she and Daniel hadn't been at the ranch to witness her argument with Sam yesterday, but what if one of the Westins had mentioned it?

Piano music started, and Ellie turned toward the front of the church. Sam slipped in beside her but stayed standing while the preacher called for the rest of the congregation to rise. Behind her, Daniel and Mr. Westin found places near their sisters, and the dark-headed woman pushed the wheelchair up beside the pew and then slid into the spot on the end next to Anna Mae.

The building only grew hotter as a handful of latecomers filled the empty spaces and the church service progressed, but the pastor's words about God's mercy held her attention despite the stifling heat and Lynnette being passed from Leroy's lap clear down to hers at some point. After church, everyone filed out of the building and headed toward the tables of food that had been set up beneath the one scraggly tree that stood in the churchyard.

Ellie corralled the children outside and handed out plates. "If you see someone your age, go make friends. You don't have to eat at our blanket. Leroy, Martin, I see some boys your age over there." She nodded at the corner of the church.

Martin rolled his eyes, but Leroy turned and headed straight toward them.

Dear God, please let him make friends today.

She filled plates for the younger children and led them over to a blanket Sam had set up in the baking sun. Before she could fill her own plate with food, the preacher's wife and the schoolteacher both approached her, excited to introduce themselves and ask if the children would start school on the morrow.

Ellie said she'd talk to Sam but she was hoping to send five of her siblings to school. By the time she headed back to the blanket with her plate, her cheeks ached from smiling at so many strangers. Hopefully both Sam and Leroy had noticed how friendly she was being. She was fitting in well enough, wasn't she?

She sat down only to find the children had all finished eating and most of them darted off to play. A quick scan of the churchyard told her Leroy and Martin were eating with the group of boys, and Janey and Joe were throwing a ball with two children who appeared to be near six or seven.

Leroy wouldn't be upset at her if she ate without Sam, would he? The two of them eating together would look best in front of everyone, but Sam was deep in conversation with the preacher and Mr. and Mrs. Harding.

Little Lynnette crawled beside her leg and popped her thumb into her mouth, then laid down on the blanket, her eyes drifting closed in slumber.

A quiet, peaceful meal... That just might be better than eating with Sam. She dug her fork into the odd meat covered in red sauce that the teacher had called brisket, then lifted it to her mouth.

I'm not going to let you throw away your first real chance at happiness on account of us. Leroy's words rose in her head, and the tangy meat turned bitter in her mouth. She wasn't throwing away her happiness by tending to her siblings. She was just... eating later than everyone else. Again.

But that didn't mean she was unhappy. Except if she'd come to Texas on her own, like she and Sam had planned before her ma died, she'd probably be standing beside him right now, meeting Mr. and Mrs. Harding, whom she hadn't spoken to yet. And her belly would be full of food to boot.

Was Leroy right about how much she sacrificed her own happiness for the rest of them?

"I thought you were going to put your blanket next to ours." Anna Mae plopped down beside her, a large piece of pie on her plate.

Ellie swallowed her bite of brisket and forced yet another smile to her lips. "Sam set it here before I had a chance to tell him where I wanted it." She'd also assumed Charlotte Westin would be eating with Anna Mae, but only Daniel and Mr. Westin occupied the Harding family's blanket—not that she was eager to eat in Mr. Westin's company either.

Ellie reached over and patted sleeping Lynnette's back. "Besides, I can keep an eye on the little ones better from here."

Anna Mae smiled at Lynnette. "She's so sweet I want to scoop her up and take her home with me."

"Isn't she?" Ellie reached out and stroked a feathery tuft of hair off her sister's forehead.

Across the churchyard, Sam helped Mrs. Harding move the wheelchair toward Daniel and Mr. Westin.

"I didn't realize your father was…" *Unable to walk. Maimed. An invalid.* How did one phrase such a thing?

Anna Mae's brows drew down, and she tilted her head to the side. "Sam didn't tell you?"

"Ah…" Ellie shifted. How to explain that she and Sam hadn't shared much conversation since she'd arrived? She thought back to his letters but didn't recall reading anything about a friend's father being tethered to a wheelchair.

"Sam saved Pa's life seven years ago."

Ellie's fork clattered to her plate. Sam certainly hadn't written anything about that.

"Pa was sheriff then, not Daniel." Anna Mae set down her pie. "We were having trouble with a band of rustlers on the other side of the border, and the Rangers were called in."

"Rangers?"

"They're like the army, maybe. Except they're run out of Austin, by the State of Texas, and their units are smaller. They travel in groups of anywhere from twenty men down to just one or two. Sometimes they work with the army, sometimes they work with local sheriffs, and sometimes they work on their own. Maybe they're more like a sheriff's department that covers the entire state than like the army.

"Cain's a Ranger." Anna Mae spoke the last words softly, a subtle flush stealing over her cheeks.

And who is Cain?

But Anna Mae was already forging ahead with her story, something about how the Rangers had been busy chasing a couple thousand head of rustled cattle over the border. "A posse from town was helping them, but we didn't realize that some of the rustlers—"

"I want some pie." Janey rushed onto the blanket and plopped down, pointing at Anna Mae's half eaten slice.

"I want more beans." Joe ran up beside his sister, his little chest heaving. "Can I have pie too?"

Ellie slanted a glance at the table, then looked back at Anna Mae. What had happened with the Rangers and rustlers? And how did that involve Anna Mae's pa getting maimed and Sam saving him? Given the way Joe was bouncing up onto the balls of his feet, he didn't look willing to wait for Anna Mae to tell the story before he got more food.

"I'll be right back." Ellie set her own plate down, never mind that she'd only gotten five or six bites of food, and headed for the table with Janey and Joe trailing behind her. Halfway there, Suzanna came sauntering over, fanning her bright red cheeks with her hand.

"Are we going to leave soon? I'm hot."

Ellie sighed. Evidently talking to Anna Mae was no different than talking to Sam. She only ever had two minutes of conversation before half her siblings decided they needed something, and all at the same time.

"I want to visit with Anna Mae for a while yet, but come with me to the table. You can help carry Janey's pie back."

"Pie?" Suzanna's face lit up. "I didn't realize there was pie."

"I think it got set out after most of us had been through the line."

"Is it apple pie or strawberry?"

If only. "No. They don't have fruit like that down here." Sam had told her as much when he'd returned from the store yesterday without a single piece of fruit. He'd said sometimes in the winter when food could be transported without spoiling, the general store could get some berries and yams from Hill Country, where there was more water for fruit to grow, but nothing was available in the summer.

"Then what do they make pie out of?" Suzanna scrunched up her nose.

"It looked like Miss Harding had some type of custard pie."

"What's custard?"

"Something not nearly as good as apple or strawberry, at least when it comes to making pies. It's a type of sweetened milk mixed with egg that's cooked down until it thickens." She'd made things with it a handful of times at the bakery in Eagle Harbor, but they had so many berries and apples to use as filling that she'd rarely resorted to custard. Why put milk filling into a pie when she had fruit to choose from?

Unfortunately the only fruit that seemed to grow here was prickly pear, and when that was out of season and the weather was too hot to transport other fruit, people probably had no choice but to use custard in their pies.

Martin ambled toward them, his shoulders slumped and a scowl back on his face. "I'm bored. There's nothing to do. When can we leave?"

Ellie looked back at the corner of the church just in time to see Leroy throw back his head and laugh at something one of the other boys said. At least he was getting on well with the others. "When Sam is ready and I finish speaking with Miss Harding."

"And after we get some pie." Suzanna raised her chin.

Martin's face didn't brighten at the mention of dessert.

"Did you and Leroy make friends?" Ellie reached the food table and headed toward the pot of beans at the end. "Suzanna, please get a piece of pie for Janey too."

"Only if you tell Martin to stop pulling my braid."

"Martin?" Ellie looked over her shoulder, where Martin and Suzanna stood glaring at each other.

"I didn't do it." Martin held his hands up. "It was Joe."

"Was not," Joe retorted.

"Will you all please behave." Ellie turned back to scoop some beans from the pot.

"I saw you, Martin." Suzanna growled.

Scuffling sounded behind her. Ellie set the spoon back in the pot and half turned. "Children—"

Someone slammed into her from behind. She dropped the plate and fell forward, banging her knee on the leg of the table. She pushed her arms in front of her as she fell, but she wasn't quite able to save herself from the bowl of mashed potatoes. She tried to straighten, but Suzanna plowed into her again. They both fell into the table together, causing it to tilt at a precarious angle.

"No." She tried to right both herself and the table, but Suzanna's legs were tangled with hers, and when she attempted to stand, she only crashed into the table again. The beans slid off first, followed by the brisket, cornbread, rice, and the rest of the food, including the two custard pies.

The thunking and splattering of food hitting the ground gave way to an ominous silence. She didn't need to look up to know everyone in the churchyard stared in her direction.

"Are you all right?" she asked Suzanna, who had ended up in a heap on top of her legs.

"I… I think so." Suzanna slowly climbed off her and stood. Splatter from the ruined pot of beans covered Suzanna's dress, and rice clung to her arm and hair.

"What happened?"

At the sound of Sam's voice, she looked away, but that didn't stop his shadow from falling over her.

"Is anyone hurt?" The sheriff asked in an official sounding tone.

"It wasn't my fault."

"We're fine," she said at the same time as Martin.

"Can you stand?" A palm appeared in front of her face.

She took Sam's hand and pulled herself upward. A mistake. Standing only emphasized the colorful mixture of beans, brisket sauce, and mashed potatoes smeared across her dress.

Behind Sam, the sheriff stood with Martin, but her brother's face was a hard, defiant mask. Leroy had left his new friends and now stood on the other side of the sheriff, but he looked as angry as Martin.

More of Leroy's words from yesterday spiraled through her. *"You can't deny we're just messing things up for you."*

No. The thought screamed through her head, causing the word to form on her lips, though no sound emerged.

Unfortunately, the townsfolk didn't seem to have any trouble speaking.

"All that food gone to waste."

"Why, there's not even any left to take to the Eldridges'."

"And the Martinezes'."

Some of the women glared at her, but those ladies were somehow easier to handle than the women with hands pressed to their mouths, disappointment in their eyes.

"Maybe we can save some of it." Anna Mae picked her way forward over the food-strewn ground. "Look, there's a few beans left in the pot."

"Not all the brisket spilled." The pastor's wife picked up the pot of meat.

Another woman groaned. "The pies are completely ruined."

Ellie stared down at the ground, moisture welling in her eyes. Today was supposed to be a good day, a perfect day, a day where she made friends and got to know the people of Twin Rivers. A day where she did her husband proud and proved to Leroy that all of them could have a decent life down here in Texas. How had it gone so wrong?

The pastor's wife approached, the lines around her mouth and eyes wreathed with concern. "Ellie, I'm so sorry. Why don't you come with me, and we'll get you cleaned up? I have a dress you can borrow."

The woman moved to wrap an arm around her shoulders, but Ellie stepped away before the pastor's wife soiled her clothes by brushing them against her own dress. Besides, she didn't want this stranger's kindness or generosity—not when things were going so poorly living off her husband's kindness and generosity.

No. She just wanted to close her eyes and disappear.

She settled for the next best thing.

"Thank you, but we're leaving now." She couldn't even bring herself to look at Sam as she spoke. Was he angry? Embarrassed? Thinking marrying her had been the biggest mistake of his life?

She turned and walked toward the wagon. She'd embarrassed her husband in front of the entire town and just handed Leroy a reason to leave Twin Rivers. How many more mistakes would she make before she learned how to be a blessing to her husband instead of a burden?

And would the rest of her family still be in Twin Rivers by the time she figured it out?

~.~.~.~.~

Martin Spritzer was a troublemaker. Daniel watched as the half-boy, half-man trailed Sam, Ellie, and the rest of the young'uns to the wagon. Martin had shoved his sister straight into Ellie on purpose. He probably hadn't intended to knock the leg out from under the table and send all the food sliding to the ground, but he hadn't exactly owned up to the accident either. If Sam didn't straighten the boy out, he'd be running with bandits soon.

"We can make quick work of this mess if we all help clean up." Preacher Russell's booming voice carried across the churchyard, prompting several of the women standing nearby into motion.

Daniel bent to pick up the pot of mashed potatoes at his feet but couldn't help another glance back over his shoulder. Sam was handing Ellie up into the wagon, the messy stains on her dress prominently displayed as she climbed aboard. Poor woman. What an impression to make on her first Sunday in Twin Rivers.

Both Anna Mae and Ma would be upset if such a thing happened to them, and they'd lived here their entire lives. And if that much food somehow spilled on Charlotte, she'd clam up for a month or better.

Charlotte. Daniel looked around the crowd. Where was she? He hadn't seen her in the churchyard once since the service ended, not even standing in line at the food table.

Had she left? Normally she'd be one of the first people helping to clean up the mess of food.

"Who wants these scraps for their hog?" Preacher Russell's voice rose over the chatter of the townsfolk. "We'll put everything in this here pail."

"I do." Bill Barrow worked his way to where the preacher stood near the table Wes was trying to fix. "And you can bet she'll eat every last bit of this."

Daniel carried the nearly empty pot of potatoes to the preacher and Bill. "Put the scraps in here. It's my ma's pot, so just bring it by sometime this week."

"Thank you, Sheriff. This should work fine." The preacher took the pot from him, then bent his head toward Wes, who was still crouched on the ground studying the table. "Is it broke?"

"Afraid so," Wes answered. "It's going to need two new legs."

"Suppose we can get some cottonwood and fix it later this week." Preacher Russell grimaced and rubbed the back of his neck. "Do you two mind carrying it around back of the church while Bill and I load these scraps in his wagon?"

"Not a problem. And I can help you with the new legs later too." Daniel went around to the good side of the table while Wes bent and hefted the broke end. They moved in tandem, two men who'd been working together all their lives. Neither of them needed to count down to when they both lifted the table off the ground, and neither of them needed to speak before deciding Wes would lead.

"Have you seen Charlotte?" Daniel asked as they moved away from the group of women finishing the cleanup.

"No. She sat beside me in church, but now that I think of it, I haven't seen her since then. Why?"

"Just... ah, wondering."

"I'd say she's off somewhere with your sister, but Anna Mae's right there." Wes dipped his chin in Anna Mae's direction as a frown etched across his brow. "Hopefully she shows up. I was planning to leave soon."

Daniel swallowed. At least Wes hadn't questioned him too much about why he'd noticed Charlotte's absence. After all, it was perfectly normal for a lawman to observe when someone was missing from a crowd, especially his sister's best friend.

And if his sister's best friend just happened to have golden brown hair and sky-blue eyes? If she stood a bit taller than all the other women in town, and carried herself with a quiet sense of dignity? If her face lit up brighter than the sun when she worked with the horse herd she kept at her father's ranch or raced across the desert on the back of her prized mare, Athena... well, who wouldn't notice?

He set the table down behind the church and gave his head a brief shake. He was going to end up in a heap of trouble if he didn't find something else to talk about right quick. "It's about time for my midday patrol. If I see her, I'll send her back here."

He hadn't exactly moved the subject away from Charlotte, but it truly was time for him to do a round. He let his deputies have most of the day on Sundays off and put a note on the door of his office saying he was at church if someone needed him, but it was about time for him to get back to work. Besides, letting Charlotte know her brother was looking for her if he happened to see her was common courtesy, wasn't it?

"Sounds good." Wes repositioned his hat on his head. "I have some business to discuss with James Hall. If she still hasn't shown up by the time I'm finished, I'll search down by the river."

"She might have gone home by herself." The Westin men let Charlotte ride pretty freely through the hills surrounding Twin Rivers.

Wes scanned the dwindling crowd of church folks. "She could have…"

But it didn't seem like something Charlotte would do without mentioning it first.

"I best be off." Daniel turned and strode around the front of the church then down O'Reilly Street. When it came to Charlotte Westin, he needed to get his wandering thoughts under control. She was a family friend, nothing more, and things were going to stay that way.

But truly, if she had her heart set on marrying against her pa's wishes, why had she looked to Sam and not him? Did she not find him attractive? Had he done something to push her away?

The alley that stretched from behind the courthouse to the back of the general store was completely empty, void of even the usual crowd of boys playing kick the can. He strolled to the Chihuahuan Trail where three giant carts pulled by teams of oxen lumbered toward the Rio Grande. A quick jaunt down to the river told him the customs agents were collecting the usual tariffs from merchants both entering and leaving Mexico.

Nothing looked out of the ordinary. Indeed, the afternoon couldn't seem any more mundane. Maybe Charlotte had been in the privy earlier and was already with Wes.

Daniel strode down O'Reilly Street toward his office. The empty porch told him no one waited for him. He'd make a quick stop to ensure no one had left a note while he and his deputies had been at church. Then he'd do one last pass through town on his way back to Wes.

He clomped up the handful of stairs to the porch and stepped into the shade of his office. Just as he'd expected, his note saying he'd gone to church was still tacked to the door, and no other note had been slid beneath the door. He stretched the crick in his neck and rolled his shoulders, then turned to leave.

A giggle sounded from the back of his office, then a man's voice, rough and husky, but too quiet to make out any words.

He scanned the room, his eyes narrowing on the open window in the back corner.

More rumbly, husky words rolled through the air, followed by another giggle.

Daniel pressed his lips together. He didn't need two lovebirds using the back of his building as a rendezvous spot. Pulling the door shut behind him, he walked across the plank flooring of the porch, then ducked around the far side of the building.

He didn't bother to keep his steps quiet as he rounded the corner into the small alley and skidded to a stop.

Robbie Ashton leaned against the wall, speaking in low tones that didn't carry even to the edge of the building. The man obviously hadn't heeded his warning to stop sneaking around. But the sight of the woman trapped between the building and Robbie made his heart come to an abrupt halt.

"Charlotte?"

They must not have heard him, because Robbie leaned closer and whispered something into Charlotte's ear. She smiled up at him and another giggle escaped, light and melodic and fun, unlike any sound he'd ever heard her make.

Daniel strode forward. "What are you two doing back here?"

Charlotte's head whipped toward him and she gasped.

Robbie didn't move from where he'd pinned Charlotte to the wall. No, he kept his attention focused entirely on Charlotte as he growled, "None of your business."

Charlotte's face had grown pale. She shoved at Robbie's chest, trying to push him away, but as gangly as Robbie was, he somehow managed to stand stalwart.

"I believe the lady wants you to move." Daniel yanked the younger man back by the collar.

Robbie made a choking sound, then spun on his heel, which twisted his shirt from Daniel's grip. "We're not doing anything illegal by being back here."

"Robbie," Charlotte pushed herself off the wall and squeezed his arm. "Go, please. I'll talk to you later."

"Fine, I'll go." Robbie scowled at Daniel. "But only because Charlotte asked me, not because you told me to. Being sheriff doesn't mean you have the right to order me around."

"No, but it does give me the responsibility to try finding someone who's been missing from the churchyard for two hours."

Robbie pursed his lips into an even tighter scowl, then turned and stalked off.

"Is Wes looking for me?" Charlotte peered over her shoulder in the direction of the church, though she'd not be able to see it since they were standing behind the building. "I didn't mean to worry him. I guess I just… lost track of time."

"What are you thinking disappearing like that and sneaking around? And with Robbie Ashton, of all people." First Sam, now Robbie. Had the Charlotte he'd known for nigh on twenty-one years gone plumb crazy?

"Don't start telling me who I can and can't spend time with. You heard Robbie, it's not any of your concern."

But it was. She was his sister's best friend. His position as sheriff aside, he still had a duty to look after her. And yet… Robbie Ashton? What could she possibly find appealing about the gangly, freckle-faced redhead? "Robbie's not like Abigail. He's mad at the world and looking for trouble. Stay away from him."

"Oh sure, take Pa and Wes's side. As if I don't already have enough men in my life telling me what I have to do." She settled her hands on her hips.

"Your pa and Wes know about Robbie?" That was about as likely as a skunk spraying someone with rosewater. "There's no way your pa's going to let you marry him, so why—?"

"How do you know I want to marry him?" Her face turned suddenly pale, and her pretty blue eyes grew even rounder than usual. "Wait, Sam told you what I said to him, didn't he?"

"We may have discussed it."

"I never should have said anything to him." She slumped back against the wall and hung her head. "Oh, I'm making a mess of everything, aren't I?"

He wasn't going to argue about the mess part. But could he blame her? He wouldn't want Agamemnon Westin V picking his spouse. Only sheer luck had allowed Mr. Westin to approve of Wes marrying Abigail. Otherwise their father would have sent off to Austin or Houston or San Antonio for a fancy bride with a bank account big enough to match Wes's.

Charlotte stayed against the wall with her head bent, hands covering her eyes. Was she crying? He fished a handkerchief out of his pocket and stepped forward. Anna Mae got teary at the thought of a centipede getting squashed, but he couldn't recall the last time he'd seen Charlotte lose her composure.

"Here." He held out the bit of white cloth that Anna Mae had monogramed for him.

Charlotte looked up to reveal eyes that looked worried, but also dry. "Don't tell Pa and Wes about Robbie. He'll lose his job if they find out."

"If you're so all-fired concerned about Robbie Ashton, then why sneak around with him doing things that you know will get him fired?" The confounded woman made no sense.

"You wouldn't understand." She glanced away.

"Try me."

"If I marry Robbie, then Pa can't marry me off to some rich rancher."

"And being married to a cowhand with a debt-ridden ma and step-pa is somehow better than marrying a rich rancher?"

"Robbie's comfortable to be around. Like Sam, except now he's married, so I can't exactly up and marry him anymore."

He raised his eyebrows.

She clasped a hand over her mouth, then pulled it away a second later. "See, this is why I can't marry some hoity-toity rancher like Pa wants. I'm always saying the wrong thing, or taking a wrong step at a dance, or getting unfashionably dirty." She gripped her skirt, hiked the shimmery, expensive fabric up about two inches, and stared down at her hemline. "See?"

Indeed, so much dust covered the bottom of her gown and lace edging that most people wouldn't know the lace should be white. He only knew the lace's original color himself because he'd inspected her dress a bit more closely than was proper when she'd arrived at church that morning.

He looked up from her skirt, and his line of sight collided with hers. Mistake. Her eyes swam with a silent plea for him to help her.

If all you want is someone comfortable, someone you know, then marry me. I'll do a better job loving you and providing for you than Robbie Ashton ever will. But he couldn't say such a thing. What if Charlotte said yes to his offer? Was he really prepared to go behind Wes's back and marry Charlotte?

God, give me wisdom to know what's right, and the strength to do it. He'd not uttered that prayer on that fateful night seven years ago when Pa had lost his leg, but he'd taken to uttering it at least once a day since.

If Charlotte ran off and secretly married, she'd have a say in her choice of husband, but she'd drive a wedge between herself and her family. Knowing Agamemnon Westin V, that wedge might never dissolve.

And if he were the one to run off with her?

Wes would kill him. Literally. Then he wouldn't be able to provide for his parents or Anna Mae, Wes would end up strung from a noose, and Charlotte would be a widow and in the position to have her pa marry her off again.

"Daniel?" Wes's unmistakable voice rang out from inside his office.

"Come on." Daniel extended his elbow to Charlotte. "Let's go see your brother."

"Only if you promise not to tell him about Robbie," she whispered, not moving from her position by the wall.

"Why? So you can run off and marry him without any of the people who love you knowing what you're about?" He matched her quiet tone, though the frustration smoldering inside him was anything but calm and complacent.

"Again, I don't see why this is any of your concern."

"Because marriage is forever, and I don't want to watch you spend the rest of your life trapped in a mistake. Promise you won't do anything rash, or I'll traipse inside and tell Wes what you've been up to this instant." Which was probably what he should do anyway.

Trouble was, not even Wes could watch Charlotte every moment of the day. If she made up her mind to sneak away and marry Robbie, no one would be able to stop her. And the woman had a point about marrying someone she knew instead of whatever stranger her pa picked.

"You can't tell Wes. Then Robbie will get fired, and he needs his job." She reached out and gripped his arm. "You know how bad his step-pa is with money."

Indeed, the whole town knew how bad James Hall was with money. Wes might not have said what he'd needed to talk to the man about earlier, but he hadn't needed to. James Hall was swimming in debt to the point he'd lost the Ashton's trading post three years ago. Robbie working at the A Bar W wasn't going to make up much of what his step-pa owed, but the money probably put food on his parents' table.

"I'd rather see Robbie get fired than you make a hasty decision you'll regret for the rest of your life." He met her eyes evenly.

Blue fire flashed in her gaze. "As opposed to letting Pa make a decision for me that I'll regret for the rest of my life?"

"Daniel?" Wes called a second time. "Are you here?"

Daniel looked back at the window, then dropped his voice to a softer whisper. "He won't marry you to an ogre. Look how well Mariah's marriage turned out."

Charlotte gave a sharp, bitter laugh. "Don't you see? That's the problem. I'm not Mariah."

No, she wasn't anything close to her social, fun-loving sister that enjoyed being married to an important rancher near Austin, hosting elaborate parties, and chairing organizations like the Austin Beautification Society.

Charlotte would be content to live on Westin land her whole life, care for her herd of horses, and never meet a stranger. He couldn't imagine her living anywhere other than Twin Rivers.

Maybe that's what this was about. Maybe marrying a man she didn't know and moving somewhere new would be too much for her. Maybe if she could stay in Twin Rivers and still find someone her pa would approve of, then things would turn out well enough.

Of course, "well enough" wasn't exactly what God had in mind when it came to marriage.

"Daniel? Charlotte?" Wes rounded the back of the building. "I thought I heard voices back here. Um… is there a reason you're standing behind the office instead of inside it?"

Charlotte gave him a pleading look.

"Not really," Daniel muttered. "I'm just glad I found her."

Though he hadn't found her in time to keep her from canoodling with Robbie Ashton.

He blew out a breath, avoiding Wes's stare. Hopefully he wouldn't regret keeping Charlotte's secret.

Chapter Ten

From her position on the ground, Ellie wrapped her arms around her knees and stared out over the twisting river. On the opposite side of the bank, a yellow, rock-strewn plane gave way to a massive wall of cliffs. That was Mexico? It didn't look any different than the side of the river where she sat. But then, this deserted, hot region of Texas may as well be a whole different country compared to Michigan.

She closed her eyes and drew in a breath of hot air that turned muggy this close to the river. For a moment she could almost taste the clean, crisp breeze whipping over Lake Superior, almost see the towering trees that had surrounded their tiny home in Eagle Harbor and the dim, flimsy walls of the cabin she'd lived in her entire life.

Threadbare curtains hung over the single window that looked toward the woods, the chinks in the wall let in the cruel spring wind, and rust coated the old cookstove. But as she stood in the doorway of the cabin, a sob rose in her chest.

Was she really leaving Eagle Harbor?

"You don't need to go. You know that, don't you?" a gentle feminine voice said from behind her.

A hand landed on her shoulder next, and she stepped away before Victoria Cummings could pull her into a hug, which would only mean more tears.

"The cabin looks so much bigger with everything gone from it." She shouldn't be surprised. Ten people had a way of filling up a space.

"Stay." Victoria moved in front of her, kindness radiating from her soft brown eyes. "We don't know anything about this man you're marrying. You and your siblings can live with Elijah and me if you need to."

Yes. *The word was on the tip of her tongue. But instead of opening her mouth to voice it, she shifted back and swallowed.*

If only staying was as simple as Victoria made it sound. But Victoria Cummings didn't know the truth about her family, and neither did anyone else in town.

Which was why she needed to pack up her siblings and leave—so that no one would ever find out. "I'm excited to go, really. I think... I think good things wait for us in Texas."

"Then why do you look ready to cry?" Victoria's brows drew down in concern.

Ellie sucked in a breath through her nose, long and slow. "I'll miss this place, is all. It's the only home I've ever known." And it was, which made leaving all the harder. But surely it was only the idea of facing something new that caused her heart to clench and her stomach to churn. Surely when she got to Texas, things would look better. After all, she'd finally found someone who wanted her.

Except the man she'd moved here to marry didn't seem at all like the man who'd written her sweet letters for over a year. Did he even want her as his wife?

Ellie drew in a trembling breath. Probably not. No one seemed to want her, except maybe Victoria Cummings.

"Ellie?"

She scrambled to a stand and whirled around.

Sam stood maybe ten feet behind her with both the horses. What did he want? To lecture her for causing a scene at church?

"I..." He sucked in a breath. "Leroy said you came this way, and

I thought maybe… well, in our letters, I said I'd teach you how to ride a horse. I have to check the herd yet today, so I was thinking you could ride with me for a ways."

"I want to go home." The words bubbled up and spilled out before she could stop them.

Sam rubbed his chin. "Do you want to try riding Bella back to the house then, or walk and wait until another day to learn to ride?"

"That's not what I meant." She bit the side of her lip. "I thought marrying you was God's will, but now that the children and I are in Texas…"

"Ellie…" He tied the horses' reins to a shrub and came toward her. "Don't say that."

"It's all such a mess." Tears blurred her eyes, but before she could reach up to wipe them away, strong arms wrapped around her, drawing her against a warm, solid chest. She buried her head in the crook of his shoulder.

~.~.~.~.~

She was crying. Sam gulped in a breath of air. What was he supposed to do? He should have addressed this in one of his letters: no crying once they were married. It seemed like a reasonable request.

Except Ellie chose that moment to start crying harder.

"Hey there." He stroked a hand down her back, then up again. Her slender back dipped in at her waist, and the fabric of her dress was so thin it felt almost as though he was touching her skin. He swallowed and tried patting her shoulder instead. "Don't worry. There's nothing to cry about."

"You don't understand."

No, he didn't. Why would she want to go back to Michigan? Was the house not to her liking? If not, he planned to start the bricks for the addition tomorrow.

Or maybe she wasn't upset about the house, but about her dress getting ruined in front of everyone at church. As soon as he'd gotten home, he'd set Martin to mucking out the barn as punishment for pushing Suzanna into Ellie and the table, but Ellie had been inside washing up and probably didn't know.

Or maybe she was still upset about the branding and learning how a ranch was run.

She sniffled and nuzzled her head against his shoulder, causing stray bits of hair to tickle his neck. A warm sensation spiraled through him, kind of like when he snuggled with Joe at night, but different, because he suddenly had a burning desire to bend his head a little lower and kiss the tears off Ellie's cheeks, or perhaps press his lips to hers.

Maybe a woman's crying wasn't so bad after all. Ellie sure wasn't all stiff in his arms the way she'd been that first night when he tried kissing her. And she didn't have that stubborn tilt to her jaw or fire blazing in her eyes like she'd had yesterday when Charlotte said he didn't like porridge.

She sniffled again, her head still nestled on his shoulder. "Are you sorry you married me? Be honest."

Sorry? About holding a woman like her in his arms? About marrying a woman who spent every minute of her day trying to help either her siblings or him? Sure, the cows had gotten out of the paddock, but that happened to just about every rancher at some point.

"Two are better than one. The Bible says that in Ecclesiastes chapter four." He took her by the shoulders and held her back just far enough to look into her face. "Two are better than one, because if one person falls, the other can help him up; and if one person is cold, the other can lie next to him and give heat; and if one person gets attacked, the other person can come to his aid. I'm glad you're here, because that means I've got someone to stand by my side, to help me. And as your husband, it's my duty to help you too."

Hopelessness and misery shone from her eyes, and something twisted inside his chest, just as painful as that night seven years ago when the rustler's bullet had ripped through his shoulder. Somehow, when he'd imagined his wife coming down to Texas, he'd always seen happiness and joy in her eyes, never sorrow.

He dropped his arms from her, then hung his head. "I'm doing something wrong. I should have realized I'd mess this whole marriage business up. I thought I was going about things right by writing all those letters and letting your brothers and sisters stay on with us. But the truth is… well, I guess I'm not much for talking or explaining things. And I'm sure not much for knowing what's going on inside that pretty little head of yours."

He shifted on the uneven ground. Maybe Wes's pa was right. Maybe he really would lose the bride God had given him, and all because he was an orphan who didn't have the first clue about being part of a family.

"You're not the one who keeps messing things up, I am." Ellie hugged her arms to herself and looked across the river into Mexico. "You never talk to me, and the once or twice a day when we try to talk, the children always interrupt. And since I don't know any better, I then end up making a breakfast you hate or letting the cows escape their pen or doing something else wrong. Nothing is going like I planned. Coming to Texas was supposed to… to be…"

What? Sam rubbed the back of his neck. Was she going to finish? Probably not, given the way she'd pressed her lips together and was staring out over the desert rather than looking at him.

But if all she wanted was to talk, that didn't seem so hard, even if he wasn't as smooth at it as Daniel or Wes. "I'm here now, and there aren't any young'uns about. Sit with me a spell."

He grabbed her hand, then sank to the ground, tugging her down beside him. "What do you want to talk about?"

"I don't know."

All that fuss, and she didn't even have something to talk about?

"Maybe we should talk about Charlotte Westin."

He scratched his head beneath his hat brim. Why would Ellie want to spend their time together talking about someone else?

"If you wanted a wife, how come you didn't marry her?"

Oh, so that's what she wanted to know. But where should he start?

Probably with the simplest part. "Charlotte's pa never would have allowed us to marry."

"So if not for her pa, the two of you would be wed."

He cringed. That didn't sound quite right. "Shucks, Ellie." He loosened the bandana around his neck, which had suddenly grown tight. "Charlotte is more sister to me than anything. Seems awful strange to think about sharing the marriage bed with her, or having us some young'uns."

Ellie stilled beside him, and the breaths coming from her mouth turned small and shallow.

Was she thinking about their own marriage bed and how they hadn't shared it yet? He shifted closer, ducking his head until mere inches separated their foreheads. Maybe she was wondering if he'd stay in the room with her tonight.

Did she want him to?

His gaze dropped to her lips, a pale shade of pink that made them stand out from her white skin and scattered freckles. Her tongue darted out to moisten her lips.

Just the smallest drop of his head, and their mouths would meet.

"Why wouldn't her pa have allowed it?" she asked.

He blinked. "What?"

"Charlotte's pa, you said he wouldn't have let the two of you wed. Why not?"

Oh, that's what she'd been thinking about. Not anything to do with the two of them and the big bed back at the ranch that was only half occupied every night. Not anything about whether she wanted him to lean over and place his lips on—

"Sam?"

Charlotte. Right. She'd asked him about Charlotte. "Because her pa thinks I'm destined to fail, both as a rancher and as a husband."

Wait. Had he just said that? Out loud? He scrubbed a hand over his face. Teach him to blurt the first thing that sprang to mind after thinking about Ellie and the marriage bed.

He glanced at his wife. But she wasn't looking at him with the same loathing that had shone in Mr. Westin's eyes the last time they'd spoken. In fact, her forehead had drawn down, causing a crease to mar the creamy skin between her eyebrows.

"We'll make certain you succeed then." She reached out and patted his arm. "Succeed and prove him wrong."

Was she talking about him succeeding with the ranch, or as a husband? Because if she was talking about the husband part, he sure felt as if he'd already failed. But he could change that, couldn't he? Just because their marriage had gotten off to a rocky start didn't mean they were destined for years of difficulties. Why, even Wes and Abigail had had their share of spats, and they'd been more in love than any two people he'd ever known. Daniel's parents got into arguments every so often too, yet overall they seemed as happy and content as a married couple could be.

"Do you love her?" Ellie's words were a whisper against the rushing of the river and the cawing of a bird above.

Sam looked at her. She was biting her bottom lip, and rather than looking at him, she stared at the ground, where her finger attempted to trace a pattern on one of the larger rocks.

Was she still talking about Charlotte? Probably, seeing how he hadn't told her any of the others he'd been thinking about.

He bit back a groan. How long would it take for him to get better at this talking business? "No, I don't love Charlotte, at least not like that. I already said she's like a sister to me."

"She loves you though." Ellie's finger stilled on the rock.

Sam sighed. "Maybe, or maybe I'm like a brother to her, and I was just the easiest way she could get out from under her pa's thumb. If I were a little better at explaining things, Charlotte and I could've talked about this whole business before you came. But sometimes it's hard to get all the words jumbled inside my head out of my mouth."

"I think your words are coming out just fine." She rested a hand on his forearm and smiled up at him. "Now that we're actually talking, that is."

He grinned back down at her. That was a right sweet thing for her to say, but then, he still had an awful lot of thoughts he'd not shared with her.

"I want you to know that talking with Charlotte or knowing that she wanted us to marry wouldn't have changed me writing that mail-order-bride service." He captured the hand on his arm with his free one and scooted around to face her. "And it wouldn't have changed me asking you down here to be my wife."

"How can you say that?" Her jaw trembled, but she kept her eyes on his, as though searching them would give her a desperately sought answer to a question she hadn't voiced. "I brought eight siblings with me. No man bargains for that when he finds himself a bride. And then I served you food that you hated, and I didn't stop Martin from letting the cattle out of the pen. I embarrassed you in front of your friends yesterday, and today after church, I embarrassed both myself and you in front of the whole—"

He pressed a finger to her lips. "So you spilled a little food on your dress, and a table got knocked over. I can guarantee it's not the first time in the history of Twin Rivers that some young'uns knocked over a table."

She tried to speak beneath his finger, but he pressed it more firmly to her mouth.

"Cattle get out of paddocks every so often. And as for serving me mush for breakfast, well, now you know not to. It's as easy as that."

She drew in a shuttering breath and pressed her eyes shut.

She wasn't going to cry again, was she? The woman had to have used up all her tears by now. He withdrew his finger from her mouth, but when she opened her eyes, they were void of tears, yet filled with something so soft he nearly leaned forward to kiss her.

"Thank you." Her breath fanned against his face as she whispered the word.

He shifted closer, but she sniffled and looked down, fiddling with the fabric of her dress. Did she not want to kiss him then? Did she think they sat too close?

"I'm glad you came out here to talk." She leaned her head back against his shoulder and gave a soft little sigh. "I'd like to do it again sometime, if that's all right with you."

"Fine with me. I'm sure we'll find lots to talk about." Like his court date and how the railroad was claiming ownership of his land. It seemed like the kind of thing a man should talk over with his wife.

But not right now. Ellie was looking up at him with all that tenderness in her eyes again, and a soft smile had spread across her face. For the first time since arriving in Texas, she looked downright content… and maybe even happy.

And he'd been the one to put that look on her face.

He couldn't bear to tell her about the land and risk wiping away all that contentment.

Chapter Eleven

Sam set the mudbrick atop the low wall with a grunt and rubbed his shoulder. His old bullet wound had bothered him the entire time he'd built his house. Now that he was adding two more rooms, his shoulder screamed at him when he hefted too much weight and ached throughout the rest of the day.

He turned and headed back to the wagon stacked with adobe bricks that had spent the past week drying in the sun. Making the bricks himself meant the addition wouldn't cost him anything, at least not if he could build everything from adobe and cottonwood. If he put glass in his windows, stone on the floor, and tile on his roof, then he'd not be able to afford to build on for a few more years. But he wasn't looking to have a place as fancy as the Westins'. No, he needed something sturdy and strong and serviceable. Something that would protect the family he'd wanted for as long as he could remember, and adobe would serve them fine.

"Make sure you stack those bricks straight." He nodded to where Leroy and Martin moved bricks into place. "Otherwise we'll have ourselves a crooked wall."

Martin rolled his eyes and muttered something under his breath but went back to the wagon for another brick. Did that boy ever smile? Seemed like he'd had a penchant for trouble since he'd arrived two weeks ago.

Maybe Martin would be better off in school with his younger siblings. He and Ellie had decided to keep Leroy and Martin home, seeing how the boys were both old enough to work on the ranch. But Martin put so much effort into avoiding work, and was so careless about the work he did do, that it was almost easier to do the work alone or with just Leroy for help.

"I keep telling him to stack the bricks straight." Leroy grabbed a canteen from where it sat on the wall and took a gulp of water. "But he won't listen."

"It's hot." Martin had walked back to the wagon but didn't reach for another brick. "I'm ready for a break."

"Sure you are." Though Martin had a point this time. It wasn't even noon, yet the air was already hot as blazes.

Sam wiped his forehead with his bandana. They'd only started building yesterday, but between the three of them, they'd gotten two whole rows of bricks completed. If they kept working at this pace, the addition would be done by the end of May, a whole month before rainy season started.

"Let's finish this row of bricks." Sam tapped his foot on the new wall. "Then we can have a break."

The rumble of approaching horses echoed in the distance. Sam frowned. Ellie was due back from town any time, but the wagon and Bella didn't thunder across the desert like that.

He headed around the side of the house, which gave him a clear view of the road. Nope, not Ellie. Not even Daniel or Wes. A group of three men rushed toward him, but he'd never seen a one of them before in his life.

He started down the road, and the men slowed their horses as they neared, meeting him a little distance from the house. "Can I help you?"

"You sure can." A thin rider with weathered skin and a gray

mustache thrust a piece of paper toward him. "You can get off my land."

His land? Sam set his jaw and reached for the paper. A deed. His heart skittered to a stop and the breath clogged in his throat.

"You're mistaken." He could barely manage the words over his thick, lumbering tongue. "This is my land. There's a deed on file at the courthouse."

The corner of the man's mustache twitched. Though his clothes were dust-covered and cut in the same style that every cowhand wore, they had the look of being made of the same butter-soft leather the Westin family used—the kind of fancy material that cost more money than most cowpunchers made in a year. "That's what they told me when I went to file this earlier. Said there were two claims to the property."

"There are." Sam hooked a thumb in his gun belt, positioning his palm only a few inches from the butt of his pistol. "But the second claim belongs to the railroad."

"That's who I just bought this land from. Paid two thousand dollars for it."

Sam had never seen ice before in his life. Ellie had described it in her letters though, said it was thick and hard and cold, that it formed on the harbor every December. He could swear a chunk of the cold stuff had planted itself in his heart and was now spreading to his limbs.

"If I were you, I'd go back to the railroad and ask for my money back." Sam kept his voice even. "This land doesn't belong to them."

"And if I were you, I'd pack up and leave. I don't take kindly to trespassers on my land."

"It's not your land," Sam's hand inched closer to his pistol.

"We'll see what the judge has to say about that next week." This from one of the other riders. Sam had barely paid them any mind, seeing how the first rider had shoved a deed in his face right away.

The mustached man leaned down, getting as close as he could without dismounting from his horse. "Next week. Count on it."

The man turned his horse around and spurred it back in the direction it had come, the other two riders following closely behind.

"We sure will," Sam muttered to himself. But what if the judge ruled in the railroad's favor? Or maybe it wasn't in the railroad's favor anymore, but in favor of the man he'd just met. No, he'd not let himself think that way. He'd win the case. Everyone knew that the land had belonged to old man Griggs, and everyone knew Griggs had left the land to him upon his death.

But maybe he should hire a lawyer, just to make sure he won.

Except where would he get the money for a lawyer when he barely had money to feed his family?

A cloud of dust appeared on the horizon. Ellie? Sam drew in a breath. He'd told her he had to clear up a few details about his ownership of the land but hadn't given any specifics. She had so much else to worry about with keeping house and washing clothes and tending the little ones that he didn't want to worry her more. Besides, the two of them had been getting on better. He'd spent a week teaching her how to drive the wagon while they took the children to school, they'd gone riding on horseback twice last week, and they spent a half hour or so talking every night before bed, getting to know each other in a way they hadn't been able to do through letters.

She hadn't asked him for more details about the land either, just squeezed his hand, smiled up at him, and told him to let her know if he needed help.

If he told her that he might lose his land after bringing her all the way down here and marrying her so she could help with the ranch, what would she think of him?

You're going to fail. Agamemnon Westin's voice came back to him, and it wasn't so different from the voices of Mr. and Mrs. Codwittle on the day he'd told them he was leaving the orphanage. *You're an orphan, boy. You're never going to make something of yourself.*

But he *was* making something of himself, and he would succeed...

As long as he could keep his land.

The cloud of dust materialized into the familiar form of the sheriff atop his white and brown appaloosa. Sam waited at the side of the road until Daniel reined to a stop beside him.

"Bad news." Daniel's face was red beneath the wide brim of his hat, and his horse, Charger, huffed out a breath, the beast's sides heaving from running at a full gallop. "I just saw Manny. Looks like rather than face you in court, the railroad decided to sell your property to a rancher from Montana. The rancher came to the courthouse to file his deed this morning."

"You passed him and his riders on your way out. They were just here." Sam nodded toward the road.

"What did they say?" Daniel swung down from his horse.

"About the same as you, except that I need to get off this land now because the man who thinks he owns it doesn't take kindly to trespassers. That, plus I'll see him in court next week." Sam repositioned his hat on his head, the next words burning before he even forced them from his mouth. "He... he looked rich enough to hire a lawyer."

Another cloud of dust appeared on the horizon, moving far slower than any of the men on horseback had. Ellie. "Can the railroad sell a piece of property if there are two claims on it?"

Daniel shook his head. "I don't know. That's a question for Harrison."

"As if I can go to Austin and ask." Their childhood friend had been living in Austin for almost a decade, where he'd studied law and now had his own practice. Harrison's pa still spent most of his time in Twin Rivers, so Harrison visited every so often—unlike Cain, who hadn't been back to town since the day after Daniel's father had been shot.

He could try writing Harrison a letter, but with only a week until court, he wouldn't have a response back by then. And if he wanted to pay for a lawyer's help, he'd have to go clear to Fort Davis to find one. There wasn't a single lawyer practicing in all of Brewster County.

Bella's clomping grew louder, and Sam looked over his shoulder to see Ellie almost upon them. She sat holding Bella's reins so confidently she might have been driving a wagon since she was a child. The pretty green color of her dress and bright shade of her hair stood out against the muted yellow and brown shades of the desert, making her look as bright and cheery as a flower.

A smile spread across her face as she pulled the wagon to a stop beside them.

"Mr. Cunningham got my dried apples in!" She held up a sack that was bigger than the bag of sugar currently sitting on the shelf near the stove.

How much had that sack cost?

"You're going to have the best pie you've ever tasted in your life tonight." Her eyes danced with happiness. "Just you wait."

"Can I come for supper?" Daniel asked.

"Sure! Or I'll bake one for you and the deputies and drop it off when I take everyone to school tomorrow. Whichever you want."

"Can I pick both?"

Sam jabbed his elbow into Daniel's side. He had ten mouths to feed, no money coming until fall, and a rancher trying to take his land. He couldn't start feeding dessert to an extra mouth every day.

"Don't you have sheriff work to do?"

"Too much of it." Daniel tipped his hat toward Ellie. "Pleasure seeing you, ma'am."

Sam turned back to Ellie. He should really ask how much the apples had cost, but her eyes were still alight with happiness and her smile had grown even bigger.

"I'm... uh, looking forward to trying this pie of yours." And he was. He just didn't have money to pay for dried apples—especially not if he was going to Fort Davis to find himself a lawyer.

~.~.~.~.~

Martin was getting himself into trouble again.

Ellie stood beneath the shade of the barn watching Lynnette scratch at the ground with a stick. At least that's who she was supposed to be watching, but her eyes kept drifting to the new addition where her four older brothers all worked alongside Sam. Leroy and Martin stacked bricks while Christopher and Henry teamed up to carry the bricks from the wagon. They'd only started the walls this week, but the one they were working on was already as high as Sam's shoulders. After this row was completed, Leroy and Martin would have to move to one of the lower walls and start stacking there. All of the boys worked with energy and smiles, except for Martin, who kept yawning and rubbing his eyes, stacking bricks at only half the rate of Leroy.

He'd disappeared for two hours last night. He may have told her he'd been down by the river, but after fourteen years of living with her brother, she could sense a lie.

Last summer both Leroy and Martin had said they'd been hired for a job that made good money, but the job had also required them to be gone at odd hours of the day and night. They hadn't realized who'd hired them, but they had well understood they shouldn't be breaking windows and putting dead mice on doorsteps. Yet they did it anyway. A deputy had awakened her in the middle of the night to let her know a band of criminals had been using Leroy and Martin to distract the sheriff from bigger crimes being committed in Eagle Harbor.

When Leroy and Martin got caught, they'd been quick to repent, not even balking at the community service hours the sheriff had given them. Indeed, after that incident, both boys had straightened up.

Until Ma died.

Leroy had responded to their mother's death by becoming more responsible, more mature, but Martin had grown quiet and sullen. Still, he hadn't gotten himself into any more trouble in Eagle Harbor. But of all her siblings, he'd put up the biggest fuss about moving to Texas. And now that he was here, he'd started disappearing again.

She worried the fabric of her skirt in her hands.

She needed to tell Sam. She'd written to him of the trouble her brothers had gotten into last year, of course. But she'd also told him how well both boys had done over the winter. Had Sam noticed how Martin had disappeared last night and likely lied about where he'd been?

Sam set another brick atop the wall, then paused and wiped his forehead with the end of the bandana tied about his neck. It wasn't even lunchtime yet, but the sun was already merciless. Indeed, his normally loose shirt stuck to his chest, making every bunch and pull of his muscles visible.

She swallowed. It seemed wrong, a woman as plain as herself being married to someone so handsome, but Sam didn't seem to mind her plainness. She swore he'd been ready to kiss her last night before he'd headed to the barn to bed down with the boys. There'd been something about the softness in his voice when he'd told her goodnight, about the longing in his eyes when he'd looked at her, about the way his jaw had worked back and forth before he turned away and lumbered outside.

She'd almost leaned forward and planted her lips on his, almost invited him into the bedroom with her. But she hadn't yet shared their secret. Becoming his wife in the truest sense seemed wrong when he didn't know the full truth about her. Just like letting him work so hard on the house seemed wrong when he didn't know their secret.

Would he turn her siblings away once he found out? Surely not. She might have believed so right after their wedding, but after two weeks of him working hard while still managing to set time aside to spend with her siblings, two weeks of teaching her and her siblings how to live on a ranch, two weeks of sharing quiet talks in the kitchen after everyone else had gone to bed, she couldn't see Sam turning his back on her or the children, even if he did know the truth.

So why was she so antsy?

Life in Texas was going along well. Too well. Martin had to be getting himself into trouble again. Or maybe Leroy was still planning to leave. All she knew was that life never went smoothly for the Spritzer family. As soon as things seemed to fall into place, God would send another insurmountable—

"Ellie! Ellie!"

She stepped out of the barn and scanned the desert.

Janey raced over the hill, skittering around shrubs and cacti. "It's Joe! He fell into a crack in the ground and can't get out."

Ellie's throat turned dry and blood rushed in her veins. She looked past Janey toward the disappearing slope the girl had just run up. "Where's Suzanna?"

The older girl had taken the twins for a walk while everyone else helped with the house.

"She's with Joe. She said to bring some rope. The crack is so deep we can barely see him."

"Christopher, come watch Lynnette!" Ellie rushed to the coiled rope hanging on the barn wall. Just how far had Joe fallen? Had he been hurt, or was he simply stuck?

A banging sounded behind her, and she looked over to find Sam throwing open the gates to Long Arrow and Bella's stalls, then moving toward the saddles. "I'll take Janey with me on Long Arrow. You follow on Bella."

"All right." She wasn't a fast rider yet, but she'd do her best to keep up. And if Sam rode ahead, Joe would get help faster.

She'd never seen her husband saddle horses so quickly. His fingers barely paused for a second as he tightened the cinches around both horses' bellies. He helped her mount Bella, then took the rope from her and draped it over Long Arrow's pommel.

"Is Joe hurt?" Ellie tried to keep the worry from her voice as she took in her sister's flushed and panicked face.

"He's crying and says his arm hurts."

Ellie stifled her gasp. *Dear God, please keep him safe.*

But what if God didn't protect Joe? God hadn't kept Clifford safe on the day he'd drowned, and God hadn't kept Ma safe after she'd borne Lynnette. Why would God keep Joe safe now?

"You're going to ride in front of me in the saddle, all right?" Sam picked Janey up and hefted her onto the horse.

Janey bit the side of her lip and stared down from her towering position on Long Arrow. "It's too high."

"I won't let you fall." Sam swung up behind Janey and dug his heels into Long Arrow's sides. The horse bolted from the barn like its tail was afire.

Ellie did her best to keep up, but Sam raced ahead, as fast as the rocky terrain would allow. The horse's hooves kicked up a violent storm of dust as it weaved between mesquite and cacti. By the time he finally reined in Long Arrow and dismounted on the top of a rounded hill, his form had become a mere shadow in the distance.

Ellie spurred Bella forward, going as fast as she dared over the uneven terrain. She dismounted on a large slab of rock that formed the top of the hill.

"Can you get him out?" Tears streaked Suzanna's face as she stared at a dark gap that cut through the rock, going deep into the ground.

Ellie hadn't been sure what Janey meant by a crack in the ground, but now the explanation was all too apparent. It looked as though the ground had opened up and split in two one day, leaving a narrow but jagged crevice through the middle of the desert. The fissure didn't extend very far, not considering she could see where it ended maybe a quarter mile away, but it looked entirely too deep.

She hurried to the edge. "Joe? Are you down there?"

A faint whimpering reached her, but the crack was so dark she couldn't make out his form.

"Don't worry. I'm coming." Sam had tied the rope to Long Arrow's pommel and was backing the horse toward the giant fissure. "Ellie, stand next to Long Arrow and keep him steady. When I give the word, start moving him away from the crack. "I'll need his weight to pull us up."

Her heart started racing anew. "You're… you're going down there?"

It was a stupid question. Of course he was going down there. Joe was only six and had to be terrified. Even if he wasn't hurt, he wouldn't be able to make it up the rocks on his own. And if Sam weren't here, she'd gladly climb down there to get her brother.

For some reason that seemed preferable to Sam disappearing into the dark earth. She eyed the ominous crack and couldn't stop a fresh burst of fear from igniting in her belly.

"Be safe." She rested a hand on Sam's arm and blinked back the moisture pricking her eyes. What if Sam got injured while climbing down? What if God took both her husband and her brother on the same day?

"Hey." Sam looked down at her, his eyes filled with such tenderness that her heart squeezed even tighter around its erratic thumping. "Don't worry, sweetheart. I'll be safe."

Was it her imagination, or had his voice gone deep and raspy? She swallowed back the lump of fear that kept rising in her throat, then stretched onto her tiptoes and planted a kiss on his cheek.

His eyes held hers for the briefest of instants, and then he turned without a word and walked to the crack. A few moments later, the darkness swallowed him.

God, please bring them both back alive.

But no matter how desperately her heart might cry the words, they wouldn't reach God's ears. Or if her prayer did reach God, He'd only turn His back on them—just like He'd already done time and again.

~.~.~.~.~

Sam gasped at the pain. His shoulder, already sore from four straight days of stacking mud bricks, cried out at holding his weight. He sucked in a sharp breath and found footing on the craggy wall, taking some of the weight off his injury before working his way deeper into the earth.

The whimpering at the bottom of the crevice grew louder, and something low tugged in his belly, almost as painful as the tearing sensation in his shoulder.

"Don't worry, cowboy. I'm coming."

"It hurts," Joe wailed.

"What hurts?" Sam struggled to keep his voice calm as he reached the ground and let go of the rope. Panicking would do him little good. He'd strapped a lantern and flint steel to his belt, but enough light filtered from above to allow him to make out Joe's small form lying about ten feet ahead.

"My arm."

Dear God, please let it be only that and nothing worse.

Joe was talking, which was a good sign. At the very least, he'd not hit his head hard enough to knock himself out. But what about his innards?

Sam picked his way through the rocks littering the crevice floor. He'd worked with a cowboy once whose horse had stumbled going up a slope. The horse had fallen, taking the cowhand with it. But in the fall the pommel somehow pierced the man's gut. The man's death had been slow while he, Wes, and another cowpoke, Ailes, all tried to staunch the endless flow of blood from the cowhand's midsection.

One of the sharp rocks littering the ground could do the same to Joe. Sam's chest twisted itself into a hard, tight knot. Losing a brother would be hard on Ellie, who'd already buried too many family members. But losing the little guy who snuggled up to him every night?

The knot in his chest tightened even more.

"It's all right, buddy. I'm here now." He took the last few steps and crouched beside Joe, surveying him for blood while almost afraid to glance at his midsection. The boy was curled on his side with an arm cradled against his chest, but nothing dark and wet stained his stomach.

"Can you stand? I'm going to get you out of here." He rested a hand on Joe's cheek, where wetness streaked the child's skin, and brushed away a tear with his thumb. "It'll be all right. Don't cry. I need you to be brave for me."

"My arm hurts real bad, and I don't like the dark." Joe sniffled but pushed himself up on one arm until he sat on the ground. "But I knew you'd rescue me."

Sam blinked. How had the boy known that?

Joe reached out and wrapped him in a one-armed hug. He held Joe as tight as he dared, keeping the child pressed against his chest, the boy's soft hair tucked beneath his chin.

"Sam?" Ellie's voice echoed from above. "Do you see Joe? Is he all right?"

"I think he has a broken arm." He looked up at the crack. "I'll be ready to come up in another minute."

Sam took off his bandana, then fished a second bandana out of his pocket. He tied the two together and rolled them into a long band before tying them across Joe's chest to secure his arm. When he stood and hefted the boy in his arms, his shoulder protested the weight, but he picked his way back to the rope. Joe clung to him the entire time, wrapping his good arm about his neck with complete faith.

When Sam reached the rope, he stared at it. Coming down with just himself and two arms had been painful enough, but now he had to go back up carrying not just his own weight, but Joe's too.

He moved Joe to his left side, but his shoulder screamed at him. It would be better by far to let his left arm bear the weight of only Joe, rather than the weight of both of them. But he'd never forgive himself if his arm grew weak on the way up and he dropped the boy. He shifted Joe to his right arm, which didn't even flinch at the weight.

"Hang on tight," he whispered. Then he gripped the rope with his left arm and shouted toward the sky, "Bring me up!"

And dear God, let me keep my grip on the rope.

~.~.~.~.~

There would be no lawyer. Sam stood in the corner of the sickroom at the doctor's house, staying out of the way the best he could while

Dr. Mullins tied the sling firmly into place around Joe's neck.

Pain knifed through his shoulder anew, but he shifted against the wall, easing the piercing sensation a tad, and looked at the bed.

He was happy to pay the doc for his services, especially if it meant Joe would have full use of his arm again. But the extra bill also meant that even if he had time to go to Fort Davis and find himself a lawyer, he didn't have a spare cent to pay the man.

"It should take about six weeks to heal fully, but I want to see you next week, just to make sure the bone is healing straight." Dr. Mullins stood back from the bed and surveyed the sling holding Joe's arm against his chest.

"Yes, sir." Joe looked down at his injured arm. His crying and sniffling had stopped under the older doctor's ministrations, though pain lines still creased Joe's brow.

"And no running or horseplay, do you hear?" The doctor reached out and ruffled Joe's hair. "Nothing can jostle that bone while its healing."

Ellie moved to sit beside Joe on the bed, giving him a sideways hug. Each time Joe had whimpered since coming out of the crevice, Ellie had given him a gentle hug. If he sniffled, she'd given him a tender look. If he cried, she had a special way of patting his back.

The woman was utterly amazing.

So Sam had stuck to the corner, staying out of the way of the two people who so clearly knew what they were doing around Joe. That, and his shoulder was still screaming with pain. He didn't know what he'd done to it in the crevice, but it hurt almost as bad as the night the rustler's bullet had torn through him.

As though sensing his pain, the doctor looked up at Sam, a gentle frown creasing his forehead. "You all right?"

"Right as rain," he gritted, never mind the fresh stabbing sensation just beneath his collar bone. He'd be using every spare penny to pay the doc for tending to Joe's broken arm. He wasn't about to let the man look at his own shoulder.

He just hoped the pain was better by Monday, when he needed to set more bricks.

Chapter Twelve

"I still don't think we should have left Joe." Ellie shifted on the wagon bench beside Sam and looked over her shoulder. "Maybe we should go back."

The desert spread behind her, yellow rolling hills dotted with scrubby brush that grew in varying shades of brown. The sun had begun its westward descent but hadn't yet sunk far enough to paint the landscape with the shade of dusty pink that signaled the end of the day. This forgotten section of Texas might not have the same vibrant colors as sunset over Lake Superior, but the land held its own sort of barren beauty. If she ever left, she'd miss the open vistas and muted hues.

"Joe will be fine." Sam reached over and settled a hand on her knee. Had he noticed she couldn't keep from bouncing it? "Leroy, Suzanna, and Christopher are all capable of caring for him."

Ellie turned back around and stared at the buildings of Twin Rivers, growing ever larger with each clomp of Bella's hooves. Sam was right. In the three days since Joe had broken his arm, the children had all gone out of their way to help both her and Joe. Even Martin had seemed truly sorry for his brother's injuries.

But if she didn't go back to the ranch, that meant...

"Really, something might come up." The overly bright sound of her voice bounced across the desert. "The children might need me."

"Ellie..." Sam's voice held a combination of warmth and warning. "This is important to Anna Mae. She'll be hurt if you skip her birthday for no reason."

If only Anna Mae were the problem.

"Is this a big party?" Maybe if there were a lot of people, she'd be able to avoid Charlotte, much like she had at church for the past two Sundays.

"Why don't you want to go to Anna Mae's birthday?" Sam glanced her way, worry furrowing his brow.

She cringed. "It's not Anna Mae, I promise."

"Is this about Charlotte?" His jaw tightened so subtly most people wouldn't have noticed.

She tore her gaze from her husband's face, only to find herself looking at the town they approached much too quickly. "Perhaps."

"Has she done anything to you? Said anything to you?"

Ellie shook her head.

"Then what's the problem with seeing her at the Hardings'?"

Ellie shifted. Had the desert air turned suddenly hotter? "Charlotte Westin still has feelings for you."

"Not those kinds of feelings." Sam flicked the reins, urging Bella into a faster trot. "I've already told you. She's trying to escape her pa's fist, and trust me, his grip is made of iron."

"Maybe." That didn't mean she wanted to spend an evening in Charlotte's company. But as for Anna Mae? The two of them were getting to be fast friends. Anna Mae had even visited her on Monday, bringing some cookies for Joe with his broken arm. Feeling welcomed was nice, as was starting to feel like she belonged in the small town that meant so much to her husband.

Unfortunately, Anna Mae's party consisted of a small number of people. Mr. and Mrs. Harding were present, along with Anna Mae,

Daniel, Wes, and Charlotte. They dined on a spicy kind of beef and tortillas, both of which were smothered in a red sauce. Mrs. Harding called them enchiladas and said they were a Mexican dish.

Somehow Ellie ended up seated directly across from Charlotte, which turned into a game of neither of them looking directly at the other, but Charlotte was unfailingly polite and didn't act untoward to Sam in any way. Laughter and giggles filled the table, and Mr. Harding told them a story or ten of some of the more bizarre situations he'd dealt with as a sheriff.

"And now it's time for the birthday treat." Mrs. Harding set a warm, dried-apple pie on the table.

"What's this?" Anna Mae blinked.

"It's one of Ellie's pies." Daniel leaned back and patted his belly. "And boy howdy, are they good."

Anna Mae's deep brown eyes found Ellie's, and a smile lit her face. "You made me a pie?"

Ellie squirmed. Did everyone at the table really need to look at her? "Actually, I made two. There's another set aside in the kitchen."

"It'll be the best pie you've ever had in your life." Sam reached out and nudged the dish closer to Anna Mae.

Mrs. Harding leaned over the table with a knife and began cutting the pie and putting slices onto plates.

"Thank you." Sam reached for his plate, then hissed in a breath and rolled his shoulder.

"Is your shoulder bothering you?" Charlotte accepted her own piece of pie. "Did you reinjure it somehow?"

"It's been giving me trouble since—"

"Reinjure it?" Ellie straightened. "Since when do you have a shoulder injury?"

Charlotte's face reddened. "Sorry, I just meant the gunshot wound, but—"

"Gunshot wound?" Ellie's voice emerged loud and high.

"Surely you've seen the scarring, even if he hasn't told you the story." Charlotte looked back and forth between them.

Ellie shook her head, her lips turned down. "I had no idea."

But clearly Charlotte had known.

Sam shifted beside her, and quietness settled over the table. She glanced up to find everyone sitting with their perfectly cut pieces of pie in front of them, but no one scooted their plates closer or reached for a fork, and no one looked directly at her or Sam.

Sam's neck and ears had turned a deep shade of red, but he kept his head bent, refusing to look her direction, just like everyone else. The silence lingered, so heavy and weighted that the ceiling above them just might fall onto the table. What was wrong? Had it been something she'd said?

Yes. The realization crashed down on her. She'd told everyone she hadn't seen the gunshot wound on Sam's shoulder, but in doing so, she'd also told everyone that she'd never seen her husband's shoulder. Or back. Or chest. Or wherever else scarring might have occurred.

And here they'd been living together as man and wife for three weeks.

She shot up from the table. "Excuse me, I think I need to..."

She didn't finish her sentence, just rushed out the door. She needed air, cool air, like the wind that constantly whipped over Lake Superior, the kind that would sting her cheeks and clear the brimming moisture from her eyes.

But all she found was the hot, stifling air of the desert. She blinked her eyes against the moisture and crossed the yard, then headed down the narrow space between the sheriff's office and the post office.

"Ellie, wait," Sam called from behind her.

She kept going, crossing O'Reilly Street toward the big, sturdy building towering higher than any other in the town. She didn't know where she wanted to go, exactly, just as long as she was alone.

She'd already reached the shadowed side of the courthouse when a hand grabbed her shoulder and spun her around. She found herself staring at a broad, muscular chest—a chest that had a gunshot wound somewhere near one of its shoulders.

She curled her hand into a fist and pounded the end of it smack into Sam's breastbone. "Why didn't you tell me?"

"Ellie…"

"Why didn't you at least stop me from saying I'd never seen your injury?" She pounded his chest again.

He withstood her assault, as firm and unyielding as a rock. "What was I supposed to—?"

"Now all your friends know. About you… about me… that we haven't…" Her fist loosened, and tears filled her eyes anew, but she refused to release them. "It's not any of their business if we don't act as man and wife behind the closed doors of our bedroom."

"I'm sorry. I wasn't trying to hide my injured shoulder from you. The story just never came up. And I had no way of knowing Charlotte would ask the question she did, or what that question would lead to for us."

"For me, you mean. I'm the one that looked like the fool, not you."

He reached down and captured her hands, then drew them to his chest, where he held them fast. "We both looked like fools, darlin'."

Maybe. But if he'd never thought to tell her about his shoulder, how many other things had he never thought to tell her? Who was this man that she'd married, truly? She'd felt like she was starting to know the man behind the sweet letters she'd received in Eagle Harbor, but maybe she didn't know anything at all.

"What else haven't you told me?" she croaked.

~.~.~.~.~

Sam stuck a finger in the collar of his shirt and tugged. *What hadn't he told her?* "About what? My scars? The one on my shoulder is it. I promise."

"About anything! What does the rest of the town know that I don't? What important information have you not shared with me?" Ellie was furious, her words bouncing from the courthouse on one side of them to the haberdashery on the other, filling the space between the two buildings with a chorus of echoes. "First about you hating porridge, then about branding and castrating the cattle, now your scar, what else does everyone who's lived in Twin Rivers their entire life know that you somehow forgot to tell me?"

Oh, curse his inability to communicate. He dropped Ellie's hands, not that holding them to his chest was doing much good when they were as stiff as dried adobe and her eyes were shooting fire at him.

Why hadn't he told her about the night he'd saved Hank Harding's life? They were spending time talking every night. He could have told her.

Sam rubbed the back of his neck. Probably because the story made him look like too much of a hero. Any other person would have done what he did. His deeds weren't all that commendable, not really.

"Again, I never meant to make you look like a fool. And I think you know just as much as the rest of the townsfolk do about me now, but…" The rest of his words turned to sawdust in his mouth.

"But what?" She narrowed her eyes at him. "So help me, Sam, if you're keeping more from me, I'll—"

"The ranchland." The words wrenched from somewhere deep inside him.

"What?"

He pressed his eyes shut for a moment, then opened them and met Ellie's blazing green eyes. "I have to go to court to defend the ranchland."

"You already told me about that." A small wrinkle creased the skin between her eyebrows. "You said it was a small issue, something that would easily be cleared up."

"The railroad sold my land—or rather, what they claim to be their land—to a rancher from Montana. He showed up last Friday, saying I needed to get off the ranch." He scrubbed a hand over his face. "The court hearing was supposed to be simple, but now that a third party is involved, I don't know what to think."

She sank back against the wall of the haberdashery and wrapped her arms around herself. "Why didn't you tell me?"

Because I don't want to look like a failure in front of you. He blew out a breath. Why bother hiding the truth from her any longer? "All I've ever wanted was to own a ranch and have a family. I brought you down here with the understanding that I had twelve thousand acres of ranchland. If that gets taken away, then it makes me a… a…" *A freeloader, a wastrel, a vagrant.* "…a shell of a man with nothing to offer you."

"You still have something to offer." She dropped her arms from around herself and pushed off the wall.

"No. I can't even go back to being the foreman on Wes's ranch. They moved Jeb up to that position after I left last fall." And even if he could go back to work for the A Bar W, the one room foreman's cabin wasn't big enough to fit Ellie's siblings. It was a step up from the bunkhouse, sure, but the simple house didn't offer much beyond a separate place to sleep and cook a meal or two.

That confused look was back on her brow, making his fingers itch to reach out and wipe away the tiny wrinkle between her eyebrows. "I have no clue what a ranch foreman does, but it's probably not what I'm talking about."

"What can I possibly offer you if I lose the ranch?" He raised his hands, only to let them fall helplessly back to his sides.

"Whatever is between us, as husband and wife, that is. You have that to give me."

Whatever is between them? Something was probably supposed to be there. He'd felt it whenever he'd read one of her letters. There'd certainly been something special between Wes and Abigail, and something special between Wes's parents before his ma died. Mr. and Mrs. Harding shared a special sort of connection too, even though Mr. Harding was an invalid.

But he and Ellie were a far cry from being able to live on whatever was supposed to be between them. And he might not know all that much about having a family, but that mysterious thing she was talking about probably had a name—love.

What made one person love another so much that little else mattered? And how did a man end up in love in the first place? Was it a kind of pit someone fell into? A trap one somehow got snared in? Probably for Charlotte, because her pa was dead set on trapping her into a marriage that would benefit the A Bar W.

But what about Mr. and Mrs. Harding? Or Preacher Russell and his wife, Emmaline? Had love been like a pit or snare for them, or had it been different? Gentler, maybe, something they both purposely walked into and were still happy about years later.

Sometimes with Ellie, when they spent time talking before bed or he took her riding, they shared a special kind of connection. Was it the beginning of love? How could a man tell for certain, especially when the connection disappeared as soon as they were surrounded by others?

"You told him no, right?"

He blinked. "What?"

"The rancher from Montana. You told him you weren't getting off your land, didn't you? That it's your land, not his."

"Ah..." Was that what they'd been talking about? If so, then how had he gotten so sidetracked thinking about him and Ellie and… and… and falling in love? Sam cleared his throat. "I told him no. But it looks like I'll be facing him in court too, not just the railroad."

She reached out and rested a hand on his upper arm. "Do you think there's a chance you might lose the ranch?"

His heart thumped against his ribs and sweat broke out along his forehead, but in all truthfulness… "Not really. Mr. Grigg's ownership of that land was well established, and I have a copy of the will where he left me the land. If I thought this was more than a nuisance, I wouldn't have started building onto the house."

That, plus he needed the addition finished before the thunderstorms came in July. If he'd waited until the middle of May to start making mudbricks, he might not get things completed in time.

"But I still worry." How could he not with so much at stake? "I also expect both the railroad and the new rancher to show up with lawyers, and I don't have one."

She rubbed his arm gently where her hand still rested and stared up at him. Her wide green eyes looked almost golden in the dying sunlight. "So get one."

"There isn't time. I go to court tomorrow at eleven."

"Tomorrow?" She withdrew her hand. "And you weren't planning to tell me any of this?"

"Not more than I already had." He winced as soon as the words were out. "I'm sorry. I see now that I should have."

"Yes, you should have." She only took a single step back from him, yet it felt as though she'd ridden clear back to the ranch on her own.

But he needed to tell her the whole of it, seeing how the handful of things he'd kept back were causing so much trouble. "Even if there was time left to find a lawyer, I don't have the money to pay for one. I barely have money to feed all of us."

The air grew still beside him. A glance Ellie's direction told him that crease was back on her brow and her shoulders were slumped.

His own shoulders rose and fell on a sigh. Here he was admitting yet another way he was about to fail the wife he'd promised he would care for. And she thought they could live on love if he lost the ranch?

He wasn't worthy of her love. "I had money set aside to get us through to fall and the cattle drive, but that was money enough for five people to live on, you and me, and three of your siblings. When you showed up with all of them, everything changed. I couldn't rightly send half your siblings to an orphanage, and I certainly wasn't going to turn the whole lot of you away. But we only have about ten dollars a month to live on, and it seems we need twice that just for food."

"Oh, Sam." A tear streaked down her cheek, catching the fading beams of sunlight in a glistening drop of orange and yellow. "Why didn't you say something?"

"I remember the letters I was getting from you a year ago." He hung his head. "You were living on nothing up in Eagle Harbor. I promised that if you came down to marry me, I'd take care of you. But here I am running out of money and treating you no better than your pa did."

Her entire body stiffened, her jaw tightening like a sprung beaver trap down by the river. "You're a far better man than my pa. Don't you worry about that."

But he did worry, and he had the sickening sensation he was still going about this marriage business all wrong despite his best efforts. After all, he was spending a half hour or better talking to her each night, and he couldn't manage to tell his wife the right things.

"I have something to tell you too." Ellie looked down, her words quiet in the small space between them. "It's only fair, now that you've told me about the land and lack of money."

She'd been hiding something from him? His sweet wife? "What is it?"

She swiped at her cheeks with her hand and sniffled.

And now she was crying. Again. Sam shifted from one foot to the other. About what she had to tell him, or about how she thought he'd respond?

"I didn't know." A tremble shook her voice. "Not about me or any of us. Not until Pa came back."

"I thought your pa was dead."

"Not dead… just gone. Always gone."

Yep, those had been the words she'd used in her letters. *My pa is gone, and my older brother Clifford drowned last year. It's just my ma and me raising the children now.*

But he'd taken "gone" to mean dead.

"If your pa returned, then why do you have all of your siblings?" Not that he was complaining about Joe curling up next to him at night or Suzanna smiling when he complimented her on something she cooked. But wouldn't the children rather be with their father back in Michigan than living in a strange town so far away?

Ellie sniffled again, the noise louder than last time. "Pa doesn't want us… be-because… we're illegitimate."

Illegitimate. The word spiraled through him like a twister tearing over the desert.

But she had an absent father and a mother left to raise children on her own. How had he not seen this?

Because there were nine children.

No, Ellie's older brother who'd died made it ten children. Were they all illegitimate? He could understand one child being born out of wedlock, like Cain. He could maybe see two illegitimate children. But ten?

"You probably want nothing to do with me now, nothing to do

with any of us." She'd bent her head to stare at the ground at some point, and loose tendrils of her hair hung down to hide most of her face. "Here I am, upset you didn't tell me about an old shoulder injury or going to court or not having much money, but I'm the one with the bigger secret. I'm sorry. I guess part of me was hoping…"

Her words trailed off, and she drew in a shuddering breath.

"Come here." He closed the space between them and wrapped his arms around her. He half expected her to pull away or mutter something about leaving her alone, but she turned her face into his chest. The tears that had been brimming in her eyes ever since they'd left Anna Mae's coursed down her cheeks in waves.

He didn't know how long he held her, her shoulders trembling with sobs that rarely escaped her mouth. The faint scent of her hair wafted up to him, a lemony sort of smell that mixed with the traces of sugar and flour that always clung to her after she'd baked a dessert.

Should he say something to soothe her? If only he knew what words to use.

He waited until her sobs turned back to sniffles and her hands loosened on his shirt, then he took her shoulders and shifted her back just far enough to look into her eyes. "This doesn't change anything between us."

She blinked, causing another tear to escape and trickle down her cheek. "I feel like everything about me is a lie. At the very least, you deserve a wholesome wife, someone who wasn't born in sin. Had I known Charlotte had her eye on you, I never would have come to Texas."

"I don't know who my parents are." He smoothed a strand of hair away from her brow and tucked it behind her ear. "I might have been born to an unwed ma, just the same as you. But I see the dedication you have to your brothers and sisters, the way you work hard for all of them, and for me too. I see how gentle you are even when Martin deliberately bothers you, and how patient you are when Joe wants to go off on an adventure. I don't know what kind of relationship your ma had with your pa, but you are a wonderful person, and I… I…"

I'm proud to have you as my wife. But his throat closed off, which was just as well, since Ellie chose that moment to burst into tears a second time.

"I should have told you sooner, before you married me, before you agreed to take everyone in." The words poured from her in a torrent of tears and mumblings. "Aunt Maude was supposed to take Christopher, Suzanna, Henry, Janey, and Joe, you see. Except I think she learned the truth about us somehow. That was why I had to leave Eagle Harbor, in case the secret came out. I don't know how Ma managed to keep the truth hidden all those years, but everything changed after she died. I was hoping to tell you about all this before we married, hoping that you'd want to adopt everyone too, but I wasn't planning on marrying you the same day I arrived. And when I realized you only expected me to have Lynnette, Martin, and Leroy with me, I just went ahead with the wedding before you changed your mind about wanting everyone."

Sam settled his arms around her and drew her back against his chest. Something about the way she nestled against him caused a surge of protectiveness to swirl through him. "Of course I can adopt everyone. What's involved in that? Filling out some papers at the courthouse?"

"Yes. There might be a fee of a few cents to file the papers, but we mainly just need to go to the courthouse and have you fill out some forms."

"We'll do that after the court hearing tomorrow. It'll make me right proud to have everything be official." And it would. God was finally giving him the family that he'd wanted for so long. "But I'm having trouble understanding your pa. What kind of man has ten children and leaves them to fend for themselves?"

"One who already has a wife and children."

"Ellie, no." She may as well have taken a brick and slammed it into his chest. Such news must have devastated her, and so soon after she'd lost her ma. "Where is he? I'm due for a trip to Michigan."

"Shipping season has started." She reached up to wipe a trail of wetness from her cheek. "He'll be all over the Great Lakes until November. He has a home in Chicago though, and other children. A wife he actually married."

Her words seared his heart like a fiery knife, and he wasn't even the one that had been wronged.

How many times had he wondered about his parents, who they were and what they were doing, if they were still alive and why they'd sent him to an orphanage? Ellie could answer all of those questions, but he'd never dreamed the answers might only make things harder.

"And your mother?" he rasped. "How did she and your father, uh… come to know each other?"

"Pa is a captain with his own ship. Not many men can say that. Usually ships are owned by big shipping companies, like Great Northern or Mellar Shipping." Her voice emerged dull and flat, as though she were a clerk discussing shipping charts rather than the man who had helped give her life. "Ma and Pa met in another port. But when Ma got pregnant with my older brother Clifford, she followed him up to Eagle Harbor and told everyone she was married. She said Pa was a backwoodsman, not a captain, but even so, the story took root. I grew up believing it, and so did everyone else in town. Pa would come through a couple times a year and visit, stay for a week or so. I think now his ship was probably making a run to Duluth or some other nearby port. He would get dropped off on the way there and picked up on the way back. After Ma died, I tried contacting Pa to see if he could take us in."

She swallowed, her muscles going tense beneath his arms. "I found an address for him in Chicago and sent a letter. His wife opened it. I don't think she knew about us until I sent that letter. Ma must have known not to contact Pa in Chicago, but I didn't have the faintest notion. When Pa arrived in Eagle Harbor, he was furious. But that's not the worst of it… His wife arrived in town the next day."

"His wife?" Sam's face turned cold.

"She'd followed him. Pa managed to keep her from telling the entire town about us, but just barely. You should have heard the shrieking, seen the anger in her eyes. She never even knew we existed. She must have written to Aunt Maude and told her Pa had never married Ma. It was her way at getting back at us, as though my siblings or I had a choice in the matter. Pa's wife, Alice, she said if she ever caught Pa coming back to Eagle Harbor, or if I ever tried to contact Pa again, she'd write a letter to the newspaper up there, telling all of Copper Country the truth about us. That was when I wrote you to ask if all of us could come. I never dreamed you didn't receive the letter."

Sam tightened his hold on her, rubbing a hand up and down her arm. "I'm right happy to have all of you together with me."

"But we're loud and busy. There's so many of us that things are always in a state of chaos. I bet everything was peaceful and quiet before we came."

"There's such a thing as too much quiet." No question having a house full of people took some getting used to, but what would he do with himself if the ranch house was empty again? He'd barely been able to stand all that quiet when he'd been single. And that didn't account for the times Christopher wanted their shirts to match or Lynnette giggled when he swung her into the air or Leroy puffed out his chest in pride over something he'd accomplished around the ranch.

"You're glad to have us? Truly?"

"Of course I am." He wrapped his arms tighter around her and buried his nose in her hair, drawing in the scent of her lemon soap.

"Even though we're all illegitimate?"

"I told you, that doesn't matter, at least not to an orphan like me. I might be every bit as illegitimate as you are. The only difference is that I'll never know."

"Pa thinks Janey and Joe and Henry aren't his. He says he didn't visit Ma at the right time for them to be born. I never knew of Ma seeing any men besides Pa, but what if Pa's right?"

"I don't see why it matters."

She pushed back just far enough to look into his eyes. "You're probably the only man in Texas who'd say such a thing."

Was he? "I don't care about what kind of family you came from. I care about the family I can make with you going forward, right here in Twin Rivers."

Her gaze latched onto his, deep and searching, then she pressed up onto her tiptoes and placed a kiss on his jaw. "Thank you."

The simple contact sent warmth flooding through him. She stayed where she was for a second, her breath puffing against his face.

He lowered his head, brushing his lips against hers for the briefest of instants. Sweet. She tasted sweet, but salty too, like candy and tears mixed together.

He pulled back, and she drew in a breath, her eyes wide in the dying sunlight. If she kept looking at him that way, he'd have no choice but to pull her into his arms and kiss her right and proper, the way he'd watched the preacher kiss his fiancée all those years ago.

Instead, he took her hand. "Come on, let's go home."

Chapter Thirteen

Ellie shifted on the wagon bench and blinked at the road in front of her and Sam. Darkness had fallen swiftly across the desert. Something told her that Sam had intended to be home before now. But then she'd stormed out of the Hardings', which had somehow led to them talking about Sam's court date and lack of money, and her parents never being married.

And then he'd kissed her.

She twisted her hands in her skirt. She'd expected him to need time to adjust to what she'd told him, except not only had he said her parentage didn't matter, but he'd also proved it by pressing his lips to hers.

Ellie untangled a hand from her skirt and held it to her lips, savoring the feel of Sam's mouth against hers. The kiss had been sweet, nothing like the awkward one he'd attempted the night they'd been married. But just when she was ready to lean in to kiss him back, he'd raised his head and said they needed to go.

Had he not liked kissing her? She eyed her husband. He sat with his shoulders straight and chin up as he guided Bella to a stop in the yard near the house. He'd commended her for taking care of her siblings and working hard around the ranch. But if he thought so highly of her, then when were they going to become husband and wife in the fullest sense?

Perhaps something else held him back. Did he not find her pleasing to look at? Was she too thin for his liking? Or maybe he thought her bright hair and freckles revolting.

"Are you coming?" Sam had climbed down from the wagon and now stood with a hand extended, waiting to help her down.

She rested her hand in his, and a warm shiver spiraled through her. But he helped her step down without putting his hands around her waist, his movements brisk and efficient. As soon as she stood on the ground beside him, he took a step back from her.

Do you think I'm attractive? The words vibrated on her tongue, but she clamped her mouth shut as Sam climbed back into the wagon. He'd already said her parentage didn't matter, already said he was glad she and her siblings were with him in Texas. His willingness to give them a home was more important than whatever he thought about her looks.

"Are you going to head inside?" Sam stood beside Bella's head, gripping the mare's bridle.

"Yes, I was just… ah, looking at the stars."

He frowned, probably because he'd been watching her closely enough to know her face hadn't been tilted up to the heavens.

She started to turn toward the house, but a shadow moved at the side of the barn. She narrowed her eyes at the familiar form. "Martin? What are you doing up?"

The darkness cloaking the barn and single lamp inside the house told her the rest of the children had already gone to bed, just as they should have at this hour.

"Just had to relieve myself." Martin straightened where he stood a few steps away from the opening to the barn. "Don't get huffy."

She strode toward him. "You're breathing awful hard for just going to the privy and back."

"My breathing ain't none of your business."

"Isn't. It *isn't* any of my business, and you're wrong. Where were you? Meeting friends? Did you go into town? Who did you meet?" She raised a hand up to touch his cheek, and sure enough, it burned hot from exertion. *Using the privy?* Did he think her a fool?

"Ellie, Martin?" Sam walked toward them, leading Bella and the wagon. "What's going on?"

Martin's jaw hardened in the moonlight. "Nothing more than my sister sticking her nose where it doesn't belong." He turned and stalked into the barn.

She would have gone after him, but Sam gripped her upper arm. "Let him go, sweetheart. He's in no mood to talk to you right now."

"He's getting into trouble again."

"I'll ask him where he was. Could be he's more willing to talk to me about this kind of thing."

"Why? Because you're a man?" She hurled the words like an arrow from a tightly-strung bow.

"All boys who grow up without a pa find themselves in a hard place round about Martin's age."

"But you know what happened last summer." Surely he remembered the letters she'd written about the trouble Leroy and Martin had landed in. "What if he's gotten tangled up in something illegal again?"

"Then we'll deal with it. Together." He rested a hand on her cheek, his calloused palm cupping her skin with such tenderness she nearly closed her eyes and leaned into the touch.

"Now go on inside." His voice turned deep and rough in the darkness. "You've already had a long night."

Her shoulders rose and fell on a sigh. "All right."

The rooms inside the house stood dark with the exception of the single lamp burning on the table. Suzanna and Janey lay sleeping in the top bunk while Joe and Lynnette snuggled together on the bottom bed. She took the lamp with her into the bedroom, hung her dress on a peg, and donned her nightgown. Not the lacy one she'd tried wearing before, no. She'd not touched that since the night Sam had left her standing alone in front of the bed.

She paused at the window, but darkness shrouded the barn outside. Were Martin and Sam still talking, or had Martin shrugged Sam off just as easily as he'd ignored her?

She reached for the Bible on the nightstand, the one that had rested unopened for too long. She'd finally told Sam her secret, and just when that situation seemed to be resolved, Martin was likely getting himself into trouble. God had to be punishing her family for being conceived in sin. How else could she explain her family going from one hardship to another to another so quickly?

The Bible probably had an answer for what she should do about Martin, but would God bother to show it to someone like her? Maybe He wanted Martin to go to prison for the rest of his life, maybe that was another part of God's punishment.

A creak sounded near the door.

Ellie raised her head to find Sam standing in the doorway, his tall form outlined by the dim lantern. "Where did Martin go?"

Sam stepped inside the room and closed the door behind him. "He says he was at the Westins' ranch."

"Doing what?"

Sam rubbed the back of his neck.

"Did he tell you? "

"Not entirely, but I don't think he was causing trouble."

She slapped the Bible closed. "How do you know that if he won't tell you what he was doing?"

Sam shrugged. "Just a sense I have."

"Well, I have a sense too. And it says the opposite of what your feelings are telling you."

"And you might be right. Could be your brother is getting himself neck deep into trouble and he just bamboozled me. But I think we need to give him some time, maybe a bit of space. Losing your ma wasn't easy on him, neither was moving from Michigan to Texas. He seems to know what's right and genuinely feels remorse when he does something wrong, like pushing Suzanna into you after church and having the table full of food fall. You might not have noticed, but he acted sorry after that happened even if he didn't admit it was his fault. I'd be more worried if he hadn't cared about the trouble he'd caused."

"Maybe," she muttered. "I suppose time will tell."

"Suppose it will." Instead of turning to leave, Sam moved deeper into the room, his steps confident and shoulders back, as though he came here every night while she was dressed in her nightclothes. "I know we got to talking about other things tonight, but Charlotte had a point."

"She did?" Ellie slid the Bible off her lap and onto the bed beside her.

Sam reached up and untied the bandana around his neck, then loosened the first button on his shirt.

Heat burst onto her cheeks, and she twisted the folds of her nightgown in her hands. What was he doing?

"You should know about my scar."

"Oh." So he wasn't planning to stay long—which meant she had no reason to be nervous about what might happen next.

"The town had some trouble with rustlers a few years back, and one night..."

His lips kept moving, saying something about the Mexican border and rustlers and the sheriff. The trouble was, his hands were moving down his shirt at the same time, making quick work of the buttons and leaving a narrow trail of golden skin down the center. How was she to make sense of his words and pay attention to his fingers at the same time? Then he slid his arms from his shirt, revealing a chest and torso edged with muscular lines and toned from a life of hard work.

Her throat suddenly felt as though she'd swallowed a pail of desert dust.

He'd stopped talking at some point and now stood looking at her, as though waiting for some type of response. But what was she supposed to say? That he was handsomer without a shirt on than with one? That she wondered how it would feel to press her check against the warm skin just below his neck?

"So now you've seen the scar."

The scar, right. She took a step closer to study the small patch of puckered skin high on his shoulder, but the moment she started examining it, he turned and showed her his back.

Oh dear. Who knew a man's bare back could be so appealing? Or that a man's shoulders could have so many muscles?

He turned back around to face her and started talking again, saying something about the bullet going straight through, and his shoulder usually not paining him so much. But the words floated above her, vague and slippery things she couldn't quite grasp. Had there been a scar on his back she should have looked at?

He gestured to the bed. "You may as well climb in. No sense in you standing there getting cold."

Climb in? Was he here to do more than show her his scar after all?

She couldn't find her voice to ask. She couldn't even find her voice to tell him that the desert in May would never feel cold to someone who'd grown up on Lake Superior, not even after the sun went down. And she certainly couldn't move her feet, which seemed to have grown roots and burrowed down into the packed dirt beneath them.

Oh, what a dunderhead she was. A quarter hour ago, she'd sat in the wagon wondering when Sam planned to make her his wife in all ways. But now that he was here, her heart pounded against her ribs and sweat slicked her hands.

Perhaps she just wanted to have everything done and over with more than to actually, well… do any of it. She didn't know the first thing about keeping a man happy in a physical sense. Her friends in Eagle Harbor made holding hands and hugging and kissing seem so easy, but nothing was easy with Sam.

"There have been times where I thought about sleeping in here, but I was worried about Joe being too young to stay out there without an adult." Sam undid the top button of his trousers. "Now that Joe's inside because of his arm, the others should be fine by themselves. That, and… well, you're my wife, Ellie. The two of us didn't know each other very much at first, but we're coming to know each other more every day. And hang it all, but it's my bed too. I have every right to sleep in it, don't I?"

"Um…" She glanced at the bed and tried to shift her weight, but her feet were still rooted to the floor.

"And maybe I want to hold you sometimes, like I did in town tonight when you were upset about your pa."

Something warm swept through her, something that didn't make the notion of getting into bed with him quite so terrifying. "You want me to get into bed so you can hold me?"

"Right."

She blew out a breath. No, that didn't seem terrifying. If anything, it sounded rather pleasant. "You're sure you don't want more?"

"Not tonight. But maybe eventually." His voice emerged low and raspy, and his eyes held hers with a burning intensity. "Eventually I want you to be my wife in every way. And I want young'uns too. I know we have your siblings to look after, but I want at least a couple babes that come from my own seed."

She slid a hand over her flat belly as though she could almost feel his seed growing there, never mind the impossibility of that at the moment.

Sam moved his trousers down his hips, leaving him in nothing but his drawers.

Oh dear. Ellie looked at the ground, at the wall, at the ceiling, at anything other than at her husband. She'd just find something else to focus on while he put his nightclothes on.

A rustling sounded, and footsteps padded toward the bed. "Are you coming?"

She looked up to find Sam moving the quilt back—and still wearing his drawers and nothing else. Did he always sleep in so little? Surely he'd noticed she was covered from her neck to her ankles. Didn't he intend to don a robe or nightshirt, or better yet, pull on a fresh set of clothes?

He slid beneath the covers, then patted the bed beside him. "Come lie down. I won't kiss you, but it's time we start sharing a room."

She forced her feet forward, then climbed onto the bed. The actions were normal, familiar, things she'd done every night since she'd arrived. Except tonight she lay as straight and stiff as the new wall Sam was building on the other side of the house.

He reached over and extinguished the lamp on the bedside table, and the room plunged into darkness.

Again, another thing that happened every night, yet rather than roll onto her side like usual, she stared straight up at the ceiling, not moving a finger lest she accidentally brush him.

"This isn't quite what I had in mind." Sam's deep voice vibrated beside her, and then an arm draped across her waist and pulled her closer.

She sucked in a breath and tensed even more, but true to his word, he only held her, just as he'd done earlier that evening.

She drew in another breath, slower this time. The warmth from his chest emanated into her side, and the strength of his muscled arm wrapped around her tighter than a blanket ever could. She rolled onto her side and settled her head deeper into her pillow. Maybe sleeping beside him wasn't so alarming after all.

"It's nerves, isn't it?"

Her eyelids flew open. "What?"

"You grow stiff when you're nervous. It's not that you dislike me so much as that you're frightened." The words sent a puff of breath whispering over her neck and tickling her ear.

She turned her head back to face the wall and settled into her pillow once more. "I don't like trying new things, and I always freeze when I'm uncertain. It's been that way for as long as I can remember."

"Good."

Good? What was good about being unable to function when she was nervous or scared?

He didn't seem inclined to tell her, just nestled his chin against her hair and pulled them closer together.

She drew in a breath and closed her eyes, letting her body melt into Sam's.

No, this wasn't bad at all, and she'd little reason to be so nervous. His chest settled into an even rhythm, in and out, in and out, much like it had earlier that night when he'd held her against him while she cried.

When he'd lowered his lips to touch hers.

He'd been so sweet and gentle when they stood beside the courthouse, just like he was being now. A sudden ache welled up inside her, but unlike the hollowness that had filled her after Ma's death or after Pa turned her away, she knew how to soothe this ache.

She only needed to turn around and find Sam's mouth with her own.

"Sam?" she breathed.

"What?" His breath whispered across her hair and tickled her neck in a way that made her want to squirm.

"I know you said you wouldn't kiss me, but… but what if I want you to?"

He raised himself up on an elbow and turned her onto her back. The intensity in his eyes burned through the darkness surrounding them. "Are you sure?"

Yes. No. Oh, how was she to know? She fisted her hands in the covers.

He lay back down and tucked her against him. "We'll wait, sweetheart. I want to be sure you're ready."

Did that mean he was ready now, and she was the one keeping more from happening? She wasn't sure whether to thank him or cry.

Chapter Fourteen

"It wasn't me. You got the wrong man."

"Really?" Daniel slammed the door to the jailcell shut behind Bo Thompson and turned his key in the lock. "You were found riding one of Rutherford's horses out of town, and you think you're the wrong man?"

"I was taking the horse back. Found it roaming the desert near where I was passing through." Bo swallowed so loud the sound echoed through the jail. "I recognized it as belonging to Old Man Rutherford and thought I'd do him a favor."

"Uh-huh." Did Bo think he was a fool? No one did Old Man Rutherford any favors. He'd probably shoot a person for trying. "And I'm sure you've got a good explanation for why you were traveling toward Mexico rather than toward Rutherford's on his horse?"

Bo licked his lips, his eyes skittering to the side. "I sometimes get my directions mixed up, is all. I would have realized I was going the wrong way when I reached the river and turned around then."

"Uh-huh." Daniel turned and walked back toward his office. "Best save the rest of your story for the judge. Maybe he'll be inclined to believe you again."

Though hopefully not. This entire scenario wouldn't have happened had Judge Grenville allowed Bo to go to court three months ago, when Milton Faver found him rustling cattle north of Twin Rivers. But somehow Bo had scrounged up enough money to get a highfalutin lawyer who filed a motion to dismiss the case for lack of evidence. Judge Grenville had agreed with the lawyer and dismissed it for some reason that must have made sense only to him. No one else in town could make hide nor hair of the judge's decision, and half the townsfolk thought Bo should have been swinging from the end of a noose weeks ago.

Daniel pushed through the door that separated the jailhouse from his office. Maybe Bo had spent all his money on a lawyer the last time around, and this time he'd be forced to sit behind bars long enough to learn he needed to leave other people's livestock alone.

"I filled out the report already, boss." Abe Melford, the deputy who had arrested Bo, drained his cup of coffee. "You need anything more from me here, or should I go back out on patrol?"

The clock hanging on the wall read quarter to eleven, which meant it was nearly time for Sam's court hearing. "I'm headed over to the courthouse now. Stay in the office in case someone stops by while I'm gone."

Abe gave a quick dip of his head, then studied the jailhouse door. "You don't think the judge will let him off again, do you?"

"Hopefully not. I'm just glad you caught him before he made it to Mexico. That there is one of Rutherford's best horses. The man's probably already noticed it was gone."

"Probably." Abe headed around the desk and stretched out in the chair.

"I'll be back in an hour." Rather than walk out the front door and cross the street to the courthouse, Daniel headed out the back. A narrow alley separated the sheriff's office from the house he'd grown up in, which was downright handy when he needed to get to the office in a hurry, and frustrating when someone tracked him down in the middle of the night over a lost cat.

Sam hadn't wanted anyone to know about the court hearing, but Anna Mae would have throttled him if he'd kept silent about the rancher from Montana. She'd also threatened to throttle him if he didn't tell her when the hearing was scheduled.

Daniel climbed the steps to the house, then let himself inside the empty kitchen. His boots clacked against the cool stone flooring as he moved toward the parlor and reached for the door handle.

"I think it's strange."

He stilled at the sound of Charlotte's clear yet quiet voice. Had she come to visit Anna Mae?

"I think it's sweet." Anna Mae's words floated through the door. "If you'd never met your husband, wouldn't you want to wait a bit? Get to know him first?"

Husband? Daniel frowned at the slab of cottonwood separating him from the womenfolk. What were they talking about? Neither one of them had a suitor, let alone a husband.

Charlotte laughed, but it carried derision, not the tinkling, delicate sound that always made his own lips curve upward in response. "If Pa has his way, I won't know my husband well on my wedding night either. But something tells me I won't have a choice about joining him in the marriage bed."

His face turned cold despite the sweat beaded at his temple. What was Charlotte doing talking about her wedding night, about being forced to a marriage bed she had no desire to visit?

But no, the conversation was more than that. His sister and Charlotte must be talking about Sam and Ellie and the information they'd all accidentally happened upon last night.

Sam was doing things right by moving slowly with Ellie—not that Sam had asked him. But both Sam and Ellie had willingly agreed to the union, even if it hadn't entirely been a love match. If Charlotte didn't want to get married in the first place, and her stranger of a husband expected wifely duties from her right away…

He stifled a groan. He ought not to be thinking of Charlotte's marriage bed. It wasn't as though he'd ever be the other person in it.

"That's why Sam would have made a good husband." Charlotte spoke again, softer this time, nearly wistful. "He's the only man around who wouldn't force his wife into marital relations before she was ready."

Not the only one. Daniel held himself as stiff as a rockface to keep from barging into the room and blurting the words.

"Sam *is* making a good husband, Charlotte." Anna Mae's voice had turned gentle. "Just not to you."

Daniel opened the door before the conversation went any further. Charlotte sat with her back stiff and jaw tight, clearly not happy with Anna Mae pointing out Sam would never be her husband. Anna Mae wasn't wearing her usual smile either, but sat with her shoulders slumped and her lips curved slightly down as she watched Charlotte.

"It's about time for court to start," he announced. "Do either of you want to go to the hearing?"

"Court? Why would I go to a court hearing?" Charlotte frowned.

"Because you don't want Sam to lose his land." Anna Mae nudged Charlotte with her elbow.

Charlotte's blue-eyed gaze flitted up to meet his. "What land is Anna Mae talking about?"

Daniel cleared his throat. "Sam's ranchland."

"Sam can't be in danger of losing his land. Mr. Griggs left it to him in his will."

"Apparently the State of Texas awarded the railroad that tract of land as compensation for some of the track they're laying to the north." Daniel gave her a quick rundown of the details, but the more he spoke, the more confused lines etched themselves across Charlotte's face. "With the land now sold to a rancher from Montana, Sam, the rancher, and the railroad have to—"

"Sam never mentioned a word about any of this." Charlotte's voice held a slight tremble. "We haven't talked much since Ellie arrived, but still, we used to… One would think he'd… Is it too much to expect that…?"

"Sam's a married man now." Anna Mae rested a hand on Charlotte's shoulder. "It wouldn't be proper for him to tell you his troubles the way he used to when he was working for your pa."

"I see." Charlotte drew in a breath and straightened her shoulders, then stood. "I can't go to court. I have somewhere else I need to be."

"Where?" The word slipped from his mouth before he could call it back. He'd not seen her with Robbie Ashton over the past few weeks, but he couldn't quite scrub the encounter he'd stumbled across from his mind either.

"Since when are you my keeper?" Charlotte's chin came up a notch.

"Since I'm the sheriff of Twin Rivers County, and you're a resident."

"It's true." Anna Mae rolled her eyes. "He fancies himself the entire county's keeper."

"Well, I'm afraid this meeting doesn't concern you. Now if you'll excuse me." Charlotte moved around him, her posture still painfully stiff, and marched off without so much as a glance over her shoulder.

Which was how she always left him. Without ever looking back. As though he wasn't worthy of extra thought as soon as he was out of her sight.

Daniel drew in a long breath. If he'd realized how difficult women could be when he'd been younger, he never would have made that pact with Sam and Wes to get married. Cain and Harrison had the right of it, he should have sworn to never get hitched at all.

~.~.~.~.~

The judge will rule in my favor. The judge will rule in my favor. The judge will rule in my favor.

Sam stood in front of the wooden chair and blew out a shaky breath. The raised bench in the center of the courtroom remained empty of Judge Grenville. But the rancher who had come to his property last week sat across the aisle from him, his scruffy, gray-brown beard singling him out among a trio of three clean-shaven, official-looking men in suits.

As if one lawyer wasn't bad enough. Did one of them work for the railroad, or were they all three in Mr. Eckler's employ?

And why did it matter? He had a cut and dry case. He could prove Mr. Griggs had left him the disputed land. So why was he nervous?

"Sorry." Ellie rushed up to him, then slid between him and the wooden table he'd been told to sit behind. "I didn't think it would take so long, but I wanted you to have this. I thought it might cheer you up before court."

She reached for his hand, which was clenched tightly at his side, and tucked some bills and a few coins into it.

He blinked. "What's this?"

Her lips curved into a gentle smile, and she leaned just close enough to be inappropriate for such a public place. "It's money, silly."

"I know it's money, but where did it come from?"

"It's from the mercantile. I took them the pies I baked this morning."

That's why she'd been up at dawn baking pies? She was trying to earn them more money?

Her eyes searched his for a moment, and the corners of her lips turned down. "I suppose I should have told you first. I wanted it to be a surprise, but I should have been open about it instead."

"No," he choked, then looked back down at the money in his

hand. Three dollars and fifty cents. Enough to get them through the rest of this week and into next week. "You can give me surprises like this any time."

"I would have baked pies sooner. I made them all the time at the bakery in Eagle Harbor. I just wish you would have told me we needed extra money."

"Me too." He reached down and gripped her hand in his, then bent his head and whispered into her ear. "Just like I wish I'd started sharing a room with you sooner."

The prettiest flush stole up her neck and across her cheeks, and he leaned closer. Would Eckler and his team of lawyers notice if he planted a kiss on his wife's brow?

A hand clapped him on the back. "I see the lovebirds decided to show up this morning."

Sam jerked away from Ellie and glanced over his shoulder. Daniel had slid into the bench behind him and was grinning wider than a rattler who had just found a nest of mice.

"I brought reinforcements." Daniel jutted a thumb toward Anna Mae and Wes beside him.

"Reinforcements that didn't even know you had a court appointment today." Wes scowled at him. "Since when is the railroad claiming they own your land?"

Since about two weeks after Wes's pa had offered him a handsome sum for the land, then told him he'd fail as a rancher. Maybe he was being a chicken liver, but he'd not wanted word about the second deed to get back to Agamemnon, or to anyone else around town.

"Don't worry." Daniel drew off his hat. "Sam has proof of his claim to the land. This case should take all of fifteen minutes."

Except it didn't. After Judge Grenville entered the chamber, the bailiff swore everyone in, and one of the rancher's lawyers plus the railroad's lawyer had each given elaborate diatribes, the judge took his time examining the deeds from both the railroad and Sam. At some point Daniel went upstairs to get Manny, who testified that he remembered Mr. Griggs's original deed being on file, and that the deed Sam had submitted last year matched Griggs's deed perfectly. But when Sam approached the bench and handed Judge Grenville a copy of Mr. Grigg's will along with several newspaper articles about him inheriting the land, the judge only frowned.

"There's no question here that Mr. Griggs left you land he thought was his, but was that land truly his to begin with?" The judge stared down at him, flat, milky-brown eyes looking out from behind round spectacles held up by his bulbus nose.

"It belonged to him since Texas separated from Mexico." Sam shifted from one foot to the other in the hot courtroom.

"Perhaps." The judge scratched the side of his balding head and turned his flat gaze back to Sam's deed. "Or perhaps he simply paid to have a false deed drawn up and claimed the land for himself at a time when land clerks were in no position to pay attention to records."

"But..."

"The railroad here has evidence that the State of Texas awarded this land to them." Judge Grenville held up a piece of paper. "If the State of Texas is awarding land, then that means Austin has no record of Mr. Griggs ever owning this land, let alone you."

"But there is evidence." Sam took a step closer to the bench. "A copy of my deed was—"

The judge banged his gavel. "I rule that the parcel in question rightfully belonged to the railroad, and seeing how a bill of sale between the railroad and Mr. Eckler has been presented, that sale is lawful. The land belongs to Mr. Eckler, effective immediately."

Sweat broke out on Sam's forehead. He couldn't have heard right. No one had ever questioned Mr. Grigg's ownership of the land, not once in all the twenty-eight years he'd lived in Twin Rivers.

Wasn't it possible Austin could have made a mistake? One misfiled deed, one tired clerk working late at night, and Texas had come to give land to the railroad that the state didn't own.

The judge rose from his bench. Across the aisle, the trio of men in suits all shook Mr. Eckler's hand, wide smiles on their faces.

"Your Honor." Daniel stood, his voice ringing out over the courtroom. "Surely there's been some mistake."

The judge banged the gavel again. "Sheriff Harding, you do realize that I can't rule in Mr. Owens's favor simply because he's your friend, correct?"

Sam winced. He and Daniel might be friends, but no one had ever accused Daniel of giving him special treatment. Daniel would probably come down harder on him or Wes for breaking a law than he would on anyone else in town.

"Correct, your Honor." Red had climbed up the back of Daniel's neck, and his shoulders drooped. "I was… ah, merely inquiring as to when the Owenses need to be off the land. You said ownership was effective immediately, but Sam has to find a house to let and a family of ten to move off the property. Plus he's got over a hundred head of cattle to round up and move to open grazing. You can't mean Sam has to completely vacate the land by sundown tonight."

The judge twisted his lips together in a scowl and plopped back into the seat behind his bench. "Very well, he has until the fifteenth of June to have all his possessions off the land. Anything remaining at that time will become the property of Mr. Eckler."

The fifteenth of June. The breath clogged in Sam's throat. What did that give him? Three weeks? Three and a half? Would that be long enough to find a place to live, round up his cattle, and move ten people? How was he going to afford a place to live? Sure, he could graze his cattle on open rangeland, but he may as well deliver fancy, handwritten invitations to rustlers telling them to take his cattle, especially if he wasn't living close enough to ride his herd every day.

"Your Honor." Wes shot to his feet beside Daniel. "Sam should also be due compensation for the house and barn he built. The deeds and the ruling you made all deal with vacant land. The bunkhouse that Mr. Griggs once maintained on the property has long since collapsed, but Sam put his own labor into his house and barn. Even if the state owned the land and signed it over to the railroad, they're not entitled to the buildings without compensation."

The judge's face turned a deathly pallor of gray. His eyes slid to the lawyers sitting with Mr. Eckler, then dabbed his lips with his handkerchief. "Very well. I order Mr. Eckler to pay a sum of fifty dollars to this court by the end of the month, to be given over to Sam Owens in exchange for the structures he built on the property."

The lawyers all turned toward the judge, and one of them took a step forward. "Your Honor—"

"This court is adjourned." The judge banged his gavel, then stood and exited the room.

Sam felt the thud of the door closing behind the judge somewhere deep inside—in the same place where the door to his dreams had just slammed shut.

Chapter Fifteen

"Something's wrong."

Sam raised his head only long enough to glance at Daniel pacing across the Harding family's kitchen.

"You mean besides the fact I just got kicked out of my home?" Sam dropped his head to his hands again and stared back down at the table.

"Don't worry." From her position in the chair next to him, Ellie leaned close and rubbed his back. "We'll get some new ranchland. It might take us a few years longer than you planned, but you'll have a ranch of your own again one day."

Why? So a judge could take everything he'd worked for away from him a second time? A nauseous sensation roiled through his belly. He'd dreamed of having his own ranch for years, and he'd dreamed of having a family on that ranch for just as long.

And he'd lost everything in the thirty-second span it had taken for Judge Grenville to issue his ruling.

Not only that, but for some reason, the land dispute hadn't arisen until after he and Ellie had been married—after he'd said Ellie's eight siblings could stay. What was he going to do with so many young'uns to care for and nowhere to live? He couldn't send them to an orphanage to be raised the way he had. But what if he didn't have a choice?

But if any provide not for his own, and specially for those of his own house, he hath denied the faith, and is worse than an infidel.

That wouldn't be him, would it? Surely God knew he was trying to provide for his family.

Trying and failing, just like Agamemnon Westin had predicted. A thick, hot ball of guilt formed in his stomach.

"No, something's wrong with the judge's ruling." Daniel's bold voice filled the kitchen, where everyone had gathered as soon as court adjourned.

Even Charlotte had shown up, though she'd not been present earlier. Sam didn't need to look up to know that the movement in the kitchen came from Mrs. Harding, who was probably bustling around filling the platter in the center of the table with more of the cookies no one was eating.

"Why didn't Grenville send to Austin for word about who owned the land and postpone the case until he heard back?" Daniel's voice again. The man was having more trouble than him accepting the judge's ruling. "I've seen him send to Austin for similar things. Why was he so eager to make a ruling today? He seemed almost happy to award the land to Eckler."

"And why did he give you so little for your house and barn?" Ellie's hand paused on his back for a moment, then took up its stroking again. "Surely they're worth twice that."

"More like three to four times the price Grenville gave," Wes gritted. "Confound it, Sam! Why didn't you tell me about this dispute? I could have hired a lawyer so you at least had representation. I could have even sent a man to Austin to see firsthand what the state had to say about who owned that parcel."

Sam shook his head atop his arms, not daring to meet Wes's gaze, which was sure to be just as hard as the sound of his voice. Yes, he should have told Wes about the court date, should have asked for help, should have done a lot of things differently.

If only he'd recognized his mistakes in time to save his ranch.

"Well?" Wes slapped the table, his voice echoing through the room. "Is there a reason, or are you just that all-fired determined to do everything yourself, hang the friends that want to help you?"

A chair scraped against the floor, then footsteps clomped away from him, louder than the sound of Mrs. Harding's constantly scurrying feet. But the sound of a door slamming didn't resonate through the room. Instead the footsteps started again and grew louder, until he could sense the large, vibrating body beside him.

"I swear, Sam." Wes's voice was calmer now, but that was almost worse, because it had a raw, jagged quality that brought back memories of the weeks after Abigail died. "Sometimes I think you're like a brother to me, and other times it's like you're still that same boy Daniel and I found fishing on the side of the Rio Grande, determined to catch a fish on a rusty hook and with no bait."

Was he really that difficult of a friend? Sam blew out a breath and raised his head off the table. "Your pa told me I'd fail at ranching. I didn't want word getting back to him that I might lose my land. That's why I didn't tell you."

"That man!" Wes raised his arms into the air with a jerk, then dropped them back by his sides. "Is there nothing he doesn't try to control?"

Sam shook his head and fixed his eyes on a blank spot on the wall opposite him. "Your pa might be controlling, even mean, but he also took a modest cattle outfit and grew it into one of the biggest ranches in Texas. If he says I'll fail, then there's a reason."

"Yeah, because he wants you to sell him your land so we can have your water rights."

"Too late for that. I should have taken the money he offered. Then when this business with the railroad came up, he would have been the one needing to defend ownership, not me."

"You turned him down last October." Charlotte's calm voice permeated the kitchen, the quietness in her tone a stark contrast to Wes's loud declarations. "There's no way you could have known what would be happening now."

"He offered me more money." Sam reached for his cup of milk, but rather than lift it, he traced an S on the moisture that had gathered on the outside of the glass. "Triple what he said he'd give me last summer."

Charlotte stilled, a cookie halfway to her mouth. "When?"

"A few weeks before Ellie came," he mumbled.

"And when you didn't do his bidding, he said you'd fail." This from Wes, who had backed up from the table and now leaned against the hutch with a dark look in his eyes.

"Something like that." Sam squeezed the wet milk glass so tightly it might shatter.

"If you still had that land, I'd tell you to reach a compromise." Mr. Harding leaned back in his wheelchair and crossed his arms.

Sam blinked. "A what?"

"You have twelve thousand acres, but you don't need even a quarter of it for your herd. Why not sell the Westins, say, two thousand acres? Enough so they have access to the water on the Rio Grande and can continue to grow their cattle, maybe even divert some of the water farther into their property. Then you've got a little extra money in your pocket to buy more stock and care for your family. Everyone would have won."

Of course Mr. Harding would come up with the best idea. The man had always been able to see through to the heart of a matter—a trait he'd also given Daniel.

Sam looked at Wes, who had lost the dark glower on his face and seemed to be contemplating Mr. Harding's idea. It really was a perfect plan…

If he still owned his land.

"This Mr. Eckler from Montana, is he the one who followed you out of the courthouse?" Charlotte broke off a piece of cookie but seemed more interested in crumbling it than taking a bite. "The one with the brown and gray beard?"

"Yes," Anna Mae answered.

Charlotte's brows drew down. "I've seen him before, with one of his lawyers—and Judge Grenville."

Sam stilled. "You have?"

"I'm sure of it."

"Where were they?" Daniel stepped to the table and rested his hands on it, leaning across the familiar wood until only a few feet separated his head from Charlotte's. "How long ago did you see them? What were they doing?"

"Three or four days ago, and as far as I could tell, they were talking and nothing more."

"Could Eckler have paid the judge to decide in his favor?" Ellie asked.

Sam clenched his teeth. That would be just his luck. One person gave him ranchland free and clear, and another turned around and swindled it away from him.

"That's a pretty heavy accusation, and you have nothing but speculation to base it on." But Daniel's forehead had drawn down into a look of concentration. "Charlotte, when you saw the judge, Eckler, and the lawyer together, did you hear what they were talking about?"

"No." Charlotte crumbled more of her cookie onto the plate before her, still not taking a bite. "I wasn't very close, and I only saw them for a moment before I had to leave."

"And where, exactly, was this?"

Charlotte looked away. "Around."

Wes pushed off the wall and came closer to the table. "Around where? Because if the judge met with Eckler and his lawyer after this hearing had already been scheduled, I doubt they would have held the meeting in broad daylight right in front of the courthouse."

"Was anyone else with you?" Daniel had pulled a small notepad out of his breast pocket and now stood with a pencil nub poised above it. "Might there be another witness?"

"Robbie Ashton." She mumbled the name so softly Sam had to strain to hear it.

"What were you doing with Robbie Ashton?" Wes narrowed eyes that were hot enough to shoot flames at his sister.

Charlotte looked down. "It's not your concern."

"It is, and you know it."

"Lay off her." Sam shoved a piece of cookie in his mouth and pressed on before Wes decided Charlotte wasn't allowed to leave the house for the next six months. "Robbie works for you and was related to Abigail. Charlotte would have as much reason to be with him as she had to be with me at any point in the past ten years."

Daniel made an odd, strangled sound in his throat.

"But getting back to my land…" Sam drew in a deep breath. "I need to go to Austin."

"What?" Ellie dropped the remaining piece of her cookie onto the table.

"Huh?" Wes scratched the back of his head.

Everyone else just looked at him, questions written in each set of eyes, except for Mr. Harding's. The man already seemed to be a step ahead of him.

"Austin." Sam stood. "Maybe there's nothing wrong with my deed. Maybe Judge Grenville was bought off, and that's why he didn't delay the case and send to Austin for more information. Or maybe the judge is right, there's nothing dastardly going on, and Mr.

Griggs never truly owned the land. But the only way I'll know for sure is by going to Austin and seeing what deed the state has on record."

"Then I'm going with you." Ellie reached for his hand and locked their fingers together.

"No, you can't." Sam plopped back down in his chair. "I can't. I don't know what I was thinking. I have twenty-four days to find a place for us to live and round up my cattle."

"You have to go." Anna Mae leaned forward over the table. "Your land is at stake, and you don't have time to lose. We'll watch the children, won't we, Pa?"

"We won't mind having some young'uns around, as long as they don't mind being a bit crowded," Mr. Harding said.

"We're rather used to being crowded, sir." Ellie smiled at him.

"It will be nice to have some little ones here." Mrs. Harding rested a hand on her husband's shoulder, then leaned down and gave him a peck on the cheek.

"No, we'll take them." Charlotte scooted her chair back from the table. "We have plenty of room, and Consuela will be thrilled to have some children to dote on. It's the least we can do to help."

"Thanks, Charlie." A slow smile spread across Sam's lips. This was the Charlotte he remembered, the one who was always willing to help someone else. The one who sent him friendly smiles and poked fun at things while they worked together around the ranch. The sullen, withdrawn woman who'd been parading around since Ellie arrived had seemed like a stranger.

"Pa will be furious." Wes tapped his fingers on his crossed arms.

Charlotte let her shoulders rise and fall in a shrug. "Good thing he's not here to complain then."

"And if he comes home before Sam gets back?"

Charlotte shrugged again. "If he's busy fuming about the

children, then he won't notice when you and some of the hands are gone rounding up Sam's cattle."

"He'd still notice, but you're right." Wes rubbed his chin and looked around the kitchen. "We should watch the young'uns. We've got room enough and a cook on staff."

"You don't have to, truly. Ellie can stay and watch them." Sam stood again. His friends offered too much help for him to accept. The children were his and Ellie's responsibility, the cattle were his responsibility alone. His friends shouldn't put themselves out for his sake.

"I want to help, Sam. We all do." Wes clapped a hand on his shoulder. "Are you listening to me when I say that? We all want a chance to help you the way you've helped us in the past."

"But..."

"No. We're your friends, and we want to help. Now let us."

Sam looked around the room. Hope radiated from seven different pairs of eyes. Part of him still wanted to say this wasn't their problem, that it was his ranch and he could handle everything himself. But he couldn't. He'd already tried to deal with the disputed deed on his own, and that had gone terribly wrong.

"Thank you," he whispered.

Wes grinned and gave him a thump on the back. "You're welcome, friend."

Chapter Sixteen

Ellie reached for the skirt hanging on the peg beside the door, then paused. The breadth of everything happening seemed surreal, as though she were reading events that unfolded in a story book.

But the hard truth remained. She, Sam, and the children all needed to leave the ranch.

Dear God, please help us to figure out a way to get the land back.

Because if Sam truly had to hand his ranch over in twenty-four days, what would happen to the children? Would she have to send them back to Eagle Harbor? She'd not yet received a reply from Victoria Cummings saying whether the Cummingses could take in any of her siblings. Did that mean they would go to an orphanage?

Ellie closed her eyes. For the first time in her life, things had seemed like they might work out. She was trusting Sam with her secrets and coming to care about him… maybe even love him. Sam was sharing his burdens with her, wrapping his arms around her at night, and starting to care for her as well.

She didn't wonder where their next meal was coming from, nor did she worry about the cruel wind off Lake Superior tearing through the cracks in their small shack. She and her siblings had food, clothes, and a sturdy house that would last for years. The children were making friends at school, and Sam truly seemed to enjoy having everyone about. Now that she was baking pies to earn a little more money, the situation seemed nearly perfect.

And then a judge had gone and ruined everything with a handful of words.

Ellie fisted her hands in the skirt she was supposed to be packing for the trip to Austin. Why did everything always have to fall apart on her? Was this God's way of punishing her and her siblings for their parents' sin?

Please God, not Sam's land. Find some other way to take vengeance on our family if You must, but don't punish Sam. He only ever tried to care for us.

"Ellie?" She turned to find Leroy standing in the doorway behind her and forced a smile onto her face.

"Sam wanted me to make sure everything's packed for Lynnette and the twins." Leroy nodded toward the window that faced the barn, where Bella and Long Arrow were both hitched to the wagon. "He's ready to take us to the Westins'."

"Yes, their things are ready." Though she'd probably missed something. Her brain had been numb earlier when she'd thrown the little ones' clothes into the trunk she'd brought from Eagle Harbor. "I figured I'd ride along to the Westins' with you. I want a chance to say goodbye to everyone."

"You know the rest of us can't stay in Twin Rivers much longer, right? Not with Sam losing the land today." Leroy took a step closer.

Goodness, but when had he gotten so tall he could meet her gaze without looking up? "We'll get the land back." She had to believe it. She wouldn't let God punish Sam for helping them.

"But if you don't—"

"Please, Leroy, not right now. I have to pack." And she couldn't talk about the judge's ruling anymore without shattering into pieces.

"You can't possibly keep us if he loses this house." Leroy crossed his arms over his chest.

If. But God hadn't taken the land from them quite yet, and she wasn't giving up until she'd exhausted every last option.

"Perhaps we can let a house in town, one even bigger than this one." The idea seemed nearly impossible, but if God truly did take the land, maybe He'd at least still allow everyone to stay together.

"And how will Sam pay for it without land on which he can raise his cattle?"

She could hardly argue, not when her brother's thoughts so closely matched her own. "That's why we'll get the land back."

"If you don't, we can't stay." Leroy's eyes held a determination that seemed too old for his fifteen years. "Not any of us."

"Enough!" She made a slashing motion with her hand. "You said you'd stay if Sam and I could work things out between us, and we are. Why are you so anxious to up and leave every time something goes wrong? Is staying with your family that much of a…?"

Movement beyond the door caught her eye, and she clamped her mouth shut a fraction of a second before Charlotte appeared in the doorway.

"It seems I'm interrupting." The other woman looked between her and Leroy. "I can wait."

"No, we're finished." Ellie put a finality in her voice that Leroy wouldn't argue with, at least not in front of another person.

Indeed, her younger brother pursed his lips together and stalked outside, slamming the door to the house behind him.

Charlotte looked over her shoulder for a moment before turning back and coming a few steps closer. A worried furrow knit her brow, but she blew out a breath and spoke. "I'm sorry about Sam losing the land. I just wanted to let you know. He's a good man, and he doesn't deserve to have it taken from him like this."

This was what Charlotte had come to tell her? She'd all but said as much after the court hearing. "Thank you. I agree that he didn't deserve to lose it. But I owe you a true debt for taking the children while we're gone."

"It's no bother. I'm happy to help Sam… and…" Charlotte swallowed. "And I'm happy to help you too. I'm sorry we got off to such a poor start. I should have welcomed you to Twin Rivers that first day with Anna Mae instead of storming off like I did. Sam obviously cares for you, and it's nice to see him happy."

Ellie's hand cramped around the shirtwaist she was supposed to be packing. How could Charlotte tell Sam cared for her? He'd not breathed a word of his feelings to her, only said that he'd wait to kiss her. And was she really the cause for his happiness? He hadn't exactly seemed unhappy with her, but she couldn't take credit for all his happiness either. Only for the times when he smiled softly at her and planted a kiss on her temple, or took her riding just before sunset to see the shadows fall over the distant mountains, or packed a picnic lunch for the two of them and took her wading in the river during the heat of the afternoon.

But would he still care for her after he realized he'd lost his land because he'd married her?

Charlotte raised an eyebrow as though she expected some kind of answer.

What had the other woman asked again? "Ah… thank you?"

Charlotte gave a brief nod. "I also wanted to…" She snapped her mouth shut and shifted from one foot to the other. "That is, I… I want you to take Athena on the trip."

Charlotte's words came out on a rush, and she fiddled with the edge of her vest. Her straight back and perfectly relaxed shoulders spoke of years spent at a finishing school somewhere, but she certainly wouldn't have learned to toy with her vest at a fancy school for girls.

Maybe she truly was as shy and awkward around people as Sam and Anna Mae said.

"Thank you." Ellie gave her a soft smile, though that didn't stop Charlotte's nervous fidgeting. "But who's Athena?"

"My horse. She's the finest of my herd, and she'll serve you better than Bella on the trip."

Ellie sucked in a breath. She might not know much about Charlotte Westin, but the woman was renowned for her horses. If Charlotte claimed the horse was her finest, then Athena had to be a good animal—and also worth hundreds, if not thousands, of dollars.

"You don't have to do that. Bella will serve fine."

The side of Charlotte's mouth quirked up into a small smirk. "Bella is charming, truly she is. But she's not the same quality of horseflesh as Athena. The only reason Bella's alive is because Sam insisted he could heal her leg. She injured it as a colt, and we all figured she'd need to be put down, but Sam…" Charlotte shook her head, and a soft sort of moisture filled her eyes. "Well, let's just say he's always had a heart for animals in need of a home."

For people in need of a home too. Which explained why he'd been so willing to take in all of her siblings without having a moment's extra notice. Sam hadn't told her how he'd come to own Bella, but she could well imagine him insisting on trying to save a young horse that everyone else had given up on.

"Thank you." Her voice emerged rough and gritty, and she cleared her throat. "It would be my honor to ride Athena."

Charlotte offered her another smile, tentative but genuine. "You're welcome. I've got a couple white shirtwaists to lend you for the trip too. Cotton and long sleeves to keep the sun off your arms. You've not been out on the desert for any length of time before, and you'll need to protect your skin and keep cool."

"I appreciate your kindness." Ellie tilted her head and studied the other woman. This hardly seemed like the same person who'd argued with Sam the day after their wedding, but she'd easily take the new, friendly Charlotte over the snooty one. "Whatever you think I'll need for the journey, I'll gladly bring. You know far more of traveling through the desert than I do."

"Ellie?" Sam called from the yard. "Charlotte? You ladies coming?"

"We better go, but if there's anything else you need, just ask." Charlotte turned and walked outside with quick, strong steps that belied the shy and almost frightened woman who had just spoke with her.

Ellie stuffed an extra skirt into the sack that would go inside her saddle bag. She wasn't quite ready to start calling Wes a friend, but she might have judged Charlotte wrongly after all. If nothing else, she could be grateful that Sam had a group of friends willing to come to his aid when life fell apart on him.

~.~.~.~.~

The desert was hotter than she'd realized. Oh, she'd known it was hot from the first day she'd ridden the stage out of San Antonio with her siblings. But on the ranch, she'd always been able to go into the house or barn and find shade, or walk down to the river where she could sit beneath a cottonwood tree and dip her toes in the cool water.

But not on the trail. The sun beat mercilessly down on her, baking her skin despite the wide straw hat Sam had insisted she wear and the long-sleeved, white shirtwaist Charlotte had sent her off in that morning.

Sam had said it would take ten days, possibly even eleven, to reach Austin. She'd been sitting on Athena for four hours, and already her legs ached from being stretched across the saddle, and her stomach churned with hunger.

She reached down and grabbed the canteen from where she'd

looped it around her pommel. Would she be wasteful to dump some down the front of her shirt after she drank? Perhaps then she wouldn't feel so hot.

In front of her, Sam rode astride Long Arrow, his body swaying in a natural rhythm with the horse that made her own movements atop Athena feel awkward and stilted.

Didn't his legs ache from being in the saddle for so long? Was he not hot enough to fall off his mount and melt into the ground?

She wouldn't ask him to stop, not when they only had such a short period of time to reach Austin and return. But surely he'd have to water the horses soon, wouldn't he?

She followed him up two more hills before she saw a telltale strip of green in the valley below.

Sam turned back on his horse and pointed. "We'll stop at the creek, give our horses some water and rest."

Water and rest for the horses. No mention of water and rest for them. Hopefully he wouldn't mind if she waded out into the stream and collapsed.

Their horses probably spent ten minutes ambling down the hill until they reached the stream, but traveling that little stretch of trail seemed to take hours. When they finally reached the wild tangle of grass and cottonwoods lining the water, Sam slid off his mount and moved to her.

"There's a bit of privacy behind that tree there, if you need to use the bush." He fit his wide hands on either side of her waist and helped her down.

"Thank you. I believe I'll…" But the second he released his hold, her legs melted and she stumbled into him.

He chuckled and looped an arm around her back, supporting her weight. "A bit saddle sore, are you?"

"Just a tad."

"Walk around as much as possible to keep your muscles stretched. You'll get used to the feel of the saddle after another day or so."

A day or so? She wouldn't last another hour on the hard leather that Charlotte Westin had claimed was "right comfortable."

But she did need to find a bit of privacy, so she pushed herself away from Sam. This time her legs held her weight, and she wandered toward the tree he'd pointed out with only a slight limp and a few winces.

She returned to find a blanket spread beside the creek, their canteens refilled, and jerky and biscuits laid out.

"I'm going to dip my toes in the water." She peeled off her boots and stockings, then plunged her toes into the creek without waiting for an answer. The water from the meager desert stream wasn't nearly as chilly as that of Lake Superior, but she'd take anything that would help cool her.

Sam scooted closer and handed her a piece of jerky, then took a bite of his own. The heat from his body emanated into hers, but he didn't talk as he sat there, just scanned the desert. For what, she couldn't say.

He hadn't said anything to her about losing the land because God had cursed her for being illegitimate. Had he figured out the connection? Was he angry with her? Or was he simply tired? Either way, he'd put things together sooner or later, which meant she'd better say something.

"I want you to know how sorry I am, Sam." She dragged in a breath of hot desert air and forced the rest of the words out before she could stop herself. "I'm aware everything is my fault. I haven't figured out a way to fix it yet, but I will. That's why I was so determined to go to Austin with you."

His brows drew down beneath the brim of his hat, and a slight frown etched the lines around his mouth. "What are you talking about?"

"You losing the land. It's because I'm illegitimate. I'm used to life being difficult for me and my family, though I didn't realize it was God punishing us until a few months ago. But still, I never thought… that is, I didn't realize… oh, I just can't bear the thought of you suffering because you married me." She twisted her hands together and stared into the distance, where blue-shadowed mountains rose out of the rocky golden earth. "Losing Clifford should have been enough. You'd think God would be satisfied with that, but then He had to go and take Ma too. And even that isn't enough, because now He's taking your land."

"Ellie, no." Sam's throat bobbed as he swallowed his last bite of jerky. "This didn't happen because of your parents' sin. This is something else entirely."

She shook her head. "You can't know that."

"I can." He reached out and clasped her palm in his, surrounding her fingers with the strength of his hand. "Look at Joseph in the Bible. His pa had two different wives, and his brothers hated him so much that they sold him into slavery. None of that was Joseph's fault. The sin belonged to his brothers. My land is the same way. I don't know who's trying to take it, but it has nothing to do with your parents.

"And when I look at you, I see someone like Joseph." Sam's voice rumbled low in his chest. "Someone who doesn't let her family's actions stop her from doing right. If most people were put in Joseph's place, they would curl up like a yellowbelly and whine about how they weren't supposed to be a slave. But Joseph became the most trusted man in Potiphar's house. And even when he lost his position with Potiphar and was thrown into prison, he still honored God, so much so that he became Pharaoh's right-hand man. When I see you caring for your siblings, bringing them all the way to Texas so you can stay together, working day in and day out to provide a good life for them, I see a modern-day version of Joseph. It's an honor to have someone so hardworking and upstanding for a wife."

He counted marriage to her as an honor? Something warm spread inside her, warm and hopeful and content. "I see what you're saying, but…"

She tugged her hand away from him and looked down. She was getting ahead of herself. Sam's words might sound pretty and promising, but she had twenty years of experience that refuted Sam's claims. "You don't understand. God has a way of doing things like this to me… to my siblings."

"My deed to the ranch disappearing isn't some kind of judgment from God because you're illegitimate." His voice took on a firm edge, and he reached out and gripped her shoulders, forcing her to look at him. "God loves you, Ellie Owens, and He promises to have good things in store for you. That doesn't include punishing you because of your parents' sin."

"My whole life has been a giant punishment." She searched his face, imploring him to understand, to hear. He hadn't been with her in Eagle Harbor. He didn't know how bad things could be for her family, but she'd never forget. "We're cursed. Don't you see? I'd hoped the trouble would go away once we left Eagle Harbor and all the lies my parents had been slowly weaving, but we only ended up bringing our trouble to you."

"God might be trying your faith, like He did Joseph, but He's not bringing these things into your life out of some sense of revenge." Sam's grip on her shoulders turned into a caress, then he slid an arm beneath her legs and swept her onto his lap, cradling her against his chest. "'Who shall separate us from the love of Christ? Shall tribulation, or distress, or persecution, or famine, or nakedness, or peril, or sword?… Nay, in all these things we are more than conquerors through him that loved us. For I am persuaded, that neither death, nor life, nor angels, nor principalities, nor powers, nor things present, nor things to come, Nor height, nor depth, nor any other creature, shall be able to separate us from the love of God, which is in Christ Jesus our Lord.'"

The Bible verses soaked into her, soothing a place deep inside that had never quite felt still or content.

But could those verses really be true? Did God love her in spite of all the bad things that had happened to her?

Sam leaned down to place a kiss on her brow. "Those verses mean your parents' sin can't separate you from God's love either. Your pa is the one who messed up, and not just because of how he treated your ma. He has a duty to God to provide for you and your siblings, whether he wants to admit it or not. But you are nothing like your pa. You found a way to move all of your siblings down here so that you could care for them. If I had an older sister like you, maybe I never would have ended up in the Codwittles' orphanage."

"You mean that?" She shifted against him, turning so she could meet his eyes.

"I do. Psalm 34:8 says, 'O taste and see that the LORD is good: blessed is the man that trusteth in him.'" He tilted his head to the side, his brow drawn down beneath the brim of his hat. "Maybe your problem isn't your parentage, but that as soon as God allows a trial into your life, you automatically assume it's some kind of divine retribution. Your trouble is that you're afraid to trust God through the hard times along with the good."

"What good times?" The man still didn't comprehend a thing she'd said. She'd tried explaining, but he just didn't see how difficult her life had been—and still was, now that Sam had lost his land.

Sam opened his mouth as though he had more to say, but instead of speaking, he leaned down and pressed his mouth to hers.

She sucked in a breath and stiffened, but he nibbled at the corner of her mouth and toyed with her bottom lip until she found her mouth opening to his.

His body surrounded her, solid chest, strong arms, but all sheathed in the gentleness of his hold and the tenderness of his mouth against hers. This was what she'd imagined, when she'd dreamed of one day being in love, when she'd hoped for having a husband and a home and all the other things in life that seemed to come easily to everyone but her. She'd imagined being held as though she were a lifeline, kissed until she panted for breath, and overwhelmed until all thoughts left her head save for those of the man who cradled her in his arms.

Sam drew back, his chest heaving as he pressed his forehead to hers. "You wouldn't call this good, Ellie? What we have between us?"

Good? She blinked up at him. What was he talking about?

The memories flooded back then, their conversation about God punishing her—or maybe not punishing her, but her assuming every bad thing that happened in her life came about as a result of God's punishment. "Yes, there's good between us. But aren't you worried about the land?"

"Of course. I'll do everything in my power to get it back, which is why we're headed to Austin. But if the Lord takes it from me, then we'll find another way to move forward together. And God will still be good, whether we have that land or not."

She tried to see it. Tried to understand. But if God took Sam's land from him, Leroy would leave, and probably Martin, maybe even Christopher and Suzanna and Henry too. How could any of that be good?

"I need to pack things up." Sam placed another kiss on her forehead, then shifted her off his lap. "We have to hit the trail. Sit here in the shade for a few more minutes and rest. I'll let you know when it's time to leave."

"All right." She hugged her knees to her chest as he gathered the blanket and food. *Taste and see that the Lord is good.*

Was God truly good, and her troubles boiled down to a failure to trust Him?

The idea seemed too simple to be right.

But what if she was in the wrong, and God really did love her the same way he'd loved Joseph of old?

Chapter Seventeen

His wife was miserable. Sam didn't need to look over his shoulder again to know that Ellie's face would be flushed from the heat of being outside all day, that her eyes would be half closed with drowsiness, or that she would wince each time the horse trotted over a patch of uneven ground.

In the four days since they'd left Twin Rivers, she hadn't uttered a word of complaint. But her silence somehow made things worse. Did she think he couldn't tell she was saddle sore and overheated? Did she think he didn't care she was hurting?

He guided Long Arrow away from the trail toward a small stream surrounded by cottonwood trees. The shade and water would make a good spot to bed down for the night. If Ellie were feeling better, he'd push on for a couple more hours, see if he could put another five miles behind them, but not when his wife needed a rest. He slowed Long Arrow to a stop and swung out of his saddle, then turned toward Ellie.

She led her mare to a stop but didn't dismount, just looked down from her and blinked her heavy eyes. "Why are we stopping? I thought you wanted to ride until sundown."

Because you need a break. He shrugged and surveyed the leafy canopy that covered the strip of land by the creek. "Looks like a right purty spot to camp for the night."

She made a sound in the back of her throat. It could have been an agreement, or it could have been a groan. "I'll get down in a minute."

She was probably too sore to dismount. He walked over to the horse and reached up. Her waist, which was damp with sweat, felt too thin beneath his hands, something that hadn't changed since she'd come to Texas. He lifted her off the horse and slid her to the ground.

She looked up at him from beneath the wide-brimmed hat that shielded her face and neck from the relentless sun. Exhaustion clouded her eyes, and sweat beaded her brow to the point it dripped down the side of her face.

"Thank you. I'm not sure I could have…" Her eyes rolled back in her head, and she started to fall.

"Ellie?" He wrapped an arm around her and pulled her against his chest.

Her eyes sprang back open, and she looked at him in confusion. "Sorry. I just… Did I faint?"

"Not quite." Moisture seeped through the chest of his shirt and sleeve where he held her. Was her back as wet as her waist? If her shirt was getting him wet, then it had to be soaked. "Did you get hot and dump your canteen over your head?"

She gave her head a small shake and mumbled something unintelligible.

That meant all this moisture was sweat, except she shouldn't be sweating this much, not from merely sitting atop a horse. He glanced at her flushed face, at her eyes, which were still clouded and confused, and his heart gave a single, heavy thump. Heat sickness.

"You need shade, now." He kept his arm wrapped around her and attempted to guide her toward the river, but she stumbled over the terrain as though she were drunk.

"Ellie..." He spoke her name as a warning, but it sounded more like a panicked plea. "I'm going to carry you."

He swept her into his arms before she could object, not that she had the ability to protest. She managed to tuck her head against the crook of his shoulder, but otherwise lay boneless as he carried her toward the shade and grass beneath a large cottonwood.

He set her down, but the grass surrounding her only made her look more flushed and ill. He rocked back on his knees. "You should have told me you were overheated."

"You wanted to get farther down the trail." Her eyelids fluttered open, and she met his gaze for a moment before nestling deeper into the cool grass. "Don't worry, I'll be fine."

Yes, she probably would be fine after she cooled off and rested, but overheating in the desert was nothing to take lightly. If someone with heat sickness didn't get their body cooled down, they could die. "How much water have you been drinking?"

She gave a listless shrug, not bothering to open her eyes.

"Does your head hurt?" He grabbed the canteen that was slung over his shoulder, propped her shoulders up against his knees, and held the canister to her lips.

She pushed the water away. "It's pounding, and I have been drinking. My canteen is empty."

"How long have you been without water?" His hand tightened around his canteen. "Why didn't you tell me you needed to stop?"

Again, she shrugged, her eyelids closing. "Just let me rest."

"Drink first." He moved his bottle back to her lips.

"No, I feel sick."

Nausea too? Just how ill was she? "Your head hurts and you feel sick. Is anything else wrong?"

"I ache."

"Your legs, from sitting in a saddle? Or do other places hurt too?"

"I ache all over."

How could she have gotten so sick without him realizing it? He pressed a hand to her heart, but it didn't race beneath his palm. Her breathing was deep and even too, and she hadn't reached the deathly point where her body stopped sweating. She was ill, yes, but not dangerously so yet.

"I'll be right back. Your stomach might be upset, but you need to eat something and drink more water, lots and lots of water." He headed back to where he'd left Long Arrow and Athena tied to some mesquite, everything he'd ever learned about heat sickness swimming through his mind. Ellie should have been drinking more water. But now that she was dehydrated, she needed salt to help her body absorb the water. He dug in his saddle bag for the jerky and a couple extra bandanas, then returned to where Ellie lay in the grass, her eyes closed in slumber.

He coaxed her back into a sitting position and slowly fed her jerky and water, water and jerky, until she refused to eat more and slumped to the ground. Then he went to the creek, dipped the bandanas in water, and returned to wrap one of the cool cloths around her neck and lay another on her forehead.

She moaned softly and turned her head but didn't open her eyes.

"I'm just trying to cool you down," he whispered. Had the creek been bigger, he would have deposited her into the middle of it to cool her faster, but the shallow trickle was only a few inches deep.

But if he truly wanted to cool her down…

He scanned the row of buttons trailing down the front of her shirt, buttons that would give him easy access to a corset that could be loosened. The trouble was, those buttons would also give him access to skin that she always kept well hidden beneath a dress or shirtwaist or nightgown—except for the nightgown she'd worn the night of their wedding.

Even so, she'd cool down faster and breathe easier with her corset loosened. He undid the buttons slowly, one by one, his fingers trembling each time he slipped a little wooden nub through its hole. He may have imagined unbuttoning his wife's clothing a time or two before, but he'd always imagined her being awake and smiling at him when he did so, always imagined soft whispers and gentle kisses accompanying undressing her.

But she wasn't even awake to ask if he could loosen her corset in order to help cool her.

Once her shirtwaist lay open, he worked her corset strings until the undergarment was so loose he could have pulled it off her. Then he stood. Best to let her rest now. Besides, nothing good would come of sitting on the grass staring at his wife's open shirt.

He ate jerky of his own and refilled the canteens. When he went back to check on Ellie, her face was no longer flushed and her breathing was deep and even. He dipped the tepid feeling bandanas back in the cool stream, then laid them across her brow and around her neck again.

Next he led the horses to the creek to drink and laid out the bedrolls, and when he'd finished that, he sat against a tree trunk and stared out over the desert for a spell, watching as the sun tracked slowly west, turning the plains to the east a dusty blue.

"You shouldn't have let me come."

He turned to find Ellie propped up on one elbow, her skin a healthy mixture of cream and pink. His eyes drifted to her gaping shirt, to the patch of skin between her collarbone and corset, and he swallowed.

She looked down, then pressed a hand to her shirt, holding it shut.

"You were hot, and I thought loosening your corset would cool you down faster. I would have asked, but you were sleeping."

"It's fine." She pushed herself to a sitting position and did up two buttons in the middle of her shirt. "I knew I wasn't feeling well, but didn't realize quite how ill I was. I just didn't want to slow you down any more than I already had."

He shook his head, then scanned the horizon. Dry, arid land and rocky dirt surrounded them, true, but the desert grass grew thicker and greener here than in Twin Rivers. They were gradually traveling into the moister climate of eastern Texas.

"We've managed forty miles a day. That's not slow."

"You know what I mean." She dropped her head back to the ground but kept her gaze on him. "You'd still be riding today if not for me."

He'd travelled to Austin by himself before on an errand for Wes's pa. The desert might look pretty under the hues of twilight and dawn, but it was also a barren, lonely place. He'd no desire to make a five-hundred-mile trip by himself.

"Two are better than one, and I mean that. I don't regret bringing you with me. Just think, if I get heat sickness, then you can come alongside and help me. Same if I get a rattler bite." He pushed to his feet, walked the small distance that separated them, and then stretched out on his side, his head propped on his elbow so he could see every last bit of the woman he'd married. "I'm just sorry you got so sick. Next time your canteen gets empty, tell me. And thank you for coming along."

A soft smile crept across her freckled face. "It's my pleasure."

"Now you're lying. There's nothing pleasurable about this for you." He reached out and tapped her nose. "But you are still sweet to come with me."

And loyal, constant, faithful.

He should probably drop his hand from her face, but instead he reached out to smooth a wayward strand of hair away from her brow.

Then he touched her cheek, just to make sure she wasn't overheated. Not because her skin felt silky soft beneath his hand.

An ache started in his chest. This woman had stood by his side, gripping his hand in the courtroom five days ago, then insisted on coming with him to Austin when doing so meant leaving her siblings for three weeks or better. God hadn't given him a wife. God had given him an angel.

"I love you, Ellie Owens." The words flowed out of him like water down a swift river.

"You what?" She drew in a deep breath, and the air between them stilled as she searched his eyes.

"I said I love you." The words came out bolder this time.

"But…"

He didn't wait to hear what she had to say, but dropped his head to hers and kissed her. She tasted of sweetness and desert dust, of life and breath and promises of tomorrow.

He broke his lips from hers and moved his elbow so that he lay flat on the grass, then hooked an arm around her shoulders and brought her to the ground with him. He found her lips again almost instantly, and a soft sigh escaped her.

A sense of rightness and peace filled him. For years he'd dreamed of having a loyal, helpful wife. But he wasn't dreaming now. His wife was here, in the flesh, and he intended to lay like this all night, with his arms wrapped around her and the warmth from her body seeping into his.

~.~.~.~.~

She must be dreaming. Had her husband just said he loved her? She'd imagined hearing those words for as long as she could remember, dreamed of having a man look at her the way Sam had a few minutes ago, then gathering her into his arms and pressing his lips to hers and kissing her so thoroughly she forgot her name.

But did he truly love her? After only living with her for a few weeks?

Sam stroked the side of her jaw with his thumb in a way that nearly made her groan. She somehow found her mouth opening wider in response, then he kissed her even deeper, which shouldn't have been possible. He'd already kissed her so thoroughly she struggled to suck breath into her lungs.

He wrapped his arms around her back and drew her fully against him, causing her aches and pains to fall away until the soreness in her legs vanished and her cracked lips lost their sting.

If only Leroy could see her now, he'd realize how close she and Sam were growing even with all the children about. The moment she returned to Twin Rivers she'd tell Leroy how this trip had brought her and Sam together.

But if Sam didn't get his land back, where would they all go? Could Sam afford to house and feed all of them without his ranchland?

A sick knot formed in her belly, and she pulled away from the kiss.

Sam groaned and drew her back against him. "Ellie, you undo a man. Let me love you tonight, the way a husband is supposed to love his wife."

She froze, the breath clogging in her chest and her lungs refusing to work.

"You're turning stiff again."

"Yes." She could barely hear herself speak the word over the thundering in her heart and rushing in her ears.

"Why?"

"Because I… I…" She didn't know.

"Do you like laying here with me like this?" His finger toyed absently with the strand of hair hanging beside her ear, and his breath puffed hot against her lips.

"Yes. No." She blew out a breath. "I don't know. Maybe a little… or a lot."

The weathered lines around his eyes creased, and the corners of his lips tilted up.

He was laughing at her, the lout!

"I'm going to kiss you now. I know you like kissing, so there's nothing to get nervous and stiff over, all right? Just trust me."

She pulled far enough back to look into his eyes, into the dark brown hue that held her still with their deepness, their intensity, their love. She reached her hand up to rest against his cheek, scruffy from not shaving that morning.

She'd committed herself to Sam on her first day in Texas. And if she could somehow go back to that day and relive it, she wouldn't change marrying him. He protected her, he cared for her, and for some reason she couldn't fully understand, he even loved her.

She was growing to love him too, this man who had taken in not just her, but all of her siblings. This man who had climbed down into a crevice to rescue Joe and added two extra rooms onto their house to fit all her siblings. This man who had never once spoken of how many cattle he'd not be able to buy now that he needed to use any extra money to feed their family.

Yes, she was growing to love him. Even if he never got his ranchland back, her place would still be by his side… and in his bed.

She leaned in and pressed her lips to his, tasting a bit of salt, but sweetness too, and the care and love he spoke of so freely.

"I already trust you," she whispered. "And I want you to love me tonight."

Chapter Eighteen

Ellie wrapped her arms around herself and stared out at the landscape. Green surrounded her. Not the deep emerald shades from the grass and trees that grew around Eagle Harbor, no. Brown cracked and speckled this duller green, but it was still a shade of green, and it came from grass and trees that spread out over the landscape. In the desert, green could only be found at the river, and yellow rock made up the rest of the earth, interspersed with an occasional streak of white or rust-colored clay.

A brush of wind teased the ends of her hair. From her position atop a small hill, the land stretched out before her. She couldn't see all the way to Austin, at least not yet, but Sam had said they'd reach town sometime around midday.

She bit her lip and looked back over her shoulder to where he still slept on the bedroll they'd been sharing for the past seven nights.

O taste and see that the LORD is good: blessed is the man that trusteth in him.

Was it as Sam said? Was God truly good to her? He'd seemed to be good on this trip, giving them speed on their journey and allowing them to know each other in the way a husband and wife should.

Perhaps Sam was right, and her trouble could be summed up by not trusting God. Maybe instead of worrying about what lay in store for them in Austin today, she needed to trust God had her best end in view.

Sam had packed a Bible in his saddlebag, and last night she'd flipped it open and read a passage in Jeremiah about God thinking good thoughts of peace toward His children and giving them a good end.

But how could she trust that God had peace and good things in store for her when He had already taken so much from her family?

"You're up early."

She jerked and spun around, only to find herself caught in Sam's arms.

"Good morning." He smiled down at her. "Beautiful view, huh?"

She looked back over her shoulder. The green might not be lush and full, but at least it was there. "It is."

"I wasn't talking about the trees and grass, darlin'." He burrowed his face into the side of her neck, nuzzling into the bright hair she'd not yet put up for the day.

She wrapped her arms around him, holding tight while he raised his head enough for his lips to graze hers.

He groaned and pulled back, then traced her lips with his thumb. "If only we didn't have to get moving. This is a right purty spot for some loving."

"It is," she spoke despite the rush of heat that burst onto her cheeks, then she pulled away from him and headed toward the bedroll that needed packing. "Are you nervous about today?"

Sam dug biscuits out of the saddle bag. "Austin has to hold some clues. What happened in Twin Rivers doesn't make sense. I hope we'll have some answers about the land by nightfall."

So did she, because if Austin didn't provide answers, then she might have to say goodbye to her siblings.

They rode through lunch, opting to eat more jerky on horseback in order to reach the state capitol sooner, and ended up plodding through the city in the early afternoon. Dust from horse hooves and wagon wheels choked the air, while a constant stream of traffic kept movement slow. Women and children passed by on the walkways lining the edges of the streets, and men in suits crossed from building to building. The only difference between the streets of Chicago and the streets of Austin was most of the men wore cowboy hats like Sam's rather than top hats. That, and the extraordinary amount of dust.

Sam led the horses down a series of roads, winding into the heart of the city before he pulled Long Arrow to the side of the street and tethered him to a hitching post.

Sam reached up to help her down, but she couldn't keep her gaze from drifting up, up, up, to the very top of the building.

"This one?" She'd never seen a building so tall, except for maybe glimpsing one in Chicago when she and her siblings made their way from the docks to the train station. "Are you sure?"

"I told you Harrison's done well for himself."

"And you expect me to go all the way up to the top?" Was such a building even safe?

Sam wrapped his arms around her waist and swung her down before she could manage another question, then tucked her hand into his arm and led her up the steps of the towering stone building.

The doorman frowned at Sam. "Do you have an appointment, sir?"

"Not particularly, but Mr. Rutherford has issued me a standing invitation to stop by whenever I'm in town."

The older man pressed his lips together and grunted but held the door open and ushered them inside the lobby toward a booth with another attendant. "Mr. Dittmore can ring Mr. Rutherford's office for you."

Sam clasped his hand over hers on his arm, his grip warm and strong, then led her inside and toward the attendant wearing a stiff suit and standing behind a counter. "Sam Owens here to see Harrison Rutherford, please. I don't have an appointment, but Mr. Rutherford will want to see me anyway."

The attendant turned and began speaking into an odd looking device with two cones, one of which the man held to his ear. A moment later he put the cone back in some sort of holder and gestured toward the side of the lobby. "Take the elevator to the top floor, and he should be with you shortly."

"Elevator?" Ellie whispered as Sam led her across the polished tile lobby. "What's an elevator?"

"A machine that will hoist us up to the top floor without us needing to climb a single stair."

Her steps slowed. "Hoist us? How does that work?"

Surely the machine wouldn't leave them dangling above the lobby for everyone to gawk at, not in such a fine building. But the image of a crane hoisting heavy beams high above the Chicago docks sprang into her mind and stuck.

Sam stopped next to a man standing beside at a shiny metal gate attached directly to the wall. "The top floor, please."

"Yes, sir." The man pushed the gate toward the wall, allowing the crisscrossing metal bars to fold into themselves and leave them space to walk into a small, box-like room without any windows.

"Sam, what are we…?"

The man stepped into the room along with them, shut the first gate, and then shut a second gate that attached to the room itself, locking them inside. He pulled a lever, and the room began moving up at a slow rate while a humming sound filled the air. They passed through the ceiling of the first floor, where a large number one was painted on the wall before they passed another metal gate for what had to be the second floor. Then they went up again into the walls of the building, passing a two this time.

"It's a shaft in the building," Sam explained. "It runs from the bottom clear up through the top, and there's a pulley system down below that will either raise or lower the elevator."

"It's… ah… quite lovely." At least the notion of not walking up seven flights of stairs was lovely, but not the confined room and gate locking her inside.

"Don't forget the emergency brake," the man beside the lever said. "If something goes wrong with the pulley or machinery below, the elevator has an automatic brake to keep it from… well…" He gestured to the floor. "You know."

Something could go wrong with the pulley? She tightened her grip on Sam's arm. Walking up seven flights of stairs suddenly didn't seem so bad.

"And here we are." The man pulled the lever on the elevator, and it slid to a smooth stop. "The seventh floor."

He opened the gate that had shut them inside the small room, then opened the gate that would close off the shaft while the elevator was on a different floor.

"Thank you." Sam flipped the man a coin and led her out of the contraption to where a dark-haired man in a pinstriped suit waited with a smile stretching across his face.

"Sam!" The man barely gave Sam time to release her arm before clobbering him with a hug. "It's been too long, my friend. So good to see you."

"You should visit Twin Rivers more often." Sam clapped the man on the back.

"Twin Rivers." The man shook his head, causing a wayward thatch of blond hair to fall across his brow. "The trip would be dreadful in this heat."

"But the company at the end of the journey would be worth it."

"That it would." The man, who had to be Mr. Rutherford, studied her. "And who have you brought with you?"

Sam turned and put his hand on the small of her back, gently pushing her forward. "Ellie, this is Harrison Rutherford. His father owns Fort Ashton, the trading post just west of Twin Rivers."

"Call me Harrison, please." Harrison took her hand and bowed low over it.

"Harrison, this is my wife, Ellie Owens."

"Your wife?" Another grin spread across Harrison's face, larger than the one he'd been wearing when Sam had first stepped off the elevator. "Well, I'll be. You actually did it, went and got yourself hitched, and before you turned thirty."

"Don't look so surprised." Sam rolled his eyes.

Harrison slung an arm over Sam's shoulders, which looked a bit ridiculous given the crisp suit he wore, then he turned his attention back to her. "It's lovely to meet you, Mrs. Owens. Now tell me, how much did this scoundrel have to pay you to get you to marry him?"

Pay her? But Ellie met the man's warm eyes and found herself grinning at him. "Nothing much, he only had to pay for my passage from Michigan."

She wouldn't tell him that Sam had purchased three additional passages besides hers so that she could bring three of her siblings with her.

"Michigan, you say? How interesting." Harrison dropped his arm, but he gave Sam a sly look. "Seems like you won't be getting your head shaved after all."

"Head shaved?" Ellie blinked. "Why would my husband be shaving his head?"

Harrison threw back his head and laughed. "He hasn't told you about the pact, I see."

"What pact?"

Sam opened his mouth, but Harrison spoke first. "A pact we made as boys about when each of us would get married. Sam here opted for marriage before thirty, or his head got shaved."

Sam's eyes narrowed. "I didn't come here for you to harass me about my wife. Did you get the letter I sent? The one asking about the deed to my property?"

"I did." The grin dropped from Harrison's face. "I was in Houston for the better part of a month and only received it upon my return here a few days ago. I sent you a letter in response, but you would have been nearly here by the time I posted it. Come into my office and I'll explain."

Harrison ushered them past where a clerk sat working and into a fancy office with a polished desk made of some kind of red wood she'd never seen before. Behind the desk stood a series of windows, and she couldn't stop her feet from moving toward them.

The view stole her breath. Not in the kind of way that climbing the bluffs above Eagle Harbor sucked the air from her lungs, no. Those bluffs stood taller and afforded the person standing atop them an endless view of wide blue lake and sky.

But this view afforded her a direct look into the street below, at the wagons and horses and streetcars and pedestrians. At so many people and so much movement she grew slightly dizzy. And since the building she stood in towered above most of the others, she could look out over an endless number of rooftops and church steeples.

"It's a bit addicting, isn't it?"

She turned to find Harrison watching her from where he stood next to the grand chair behind his desk. On the other side of the desk, Sam stood by a pair of empty chairs, probably waiting for her to come and sit down.

"Sorry." She hurried back to Sam, who helped her into a chair and sat beside her. “I’ve never seen anything quite like that before. Now I understand why you have your office on the top floor.”

“I’ve been looking out those same windows for five years, and I never tire of it.” Harrison sat behind the massive desk. With his tall form and impeccable suit and perfectly combed hair, he looked commanding enough to govern the entire state of Texas.

“You must have left Twin Rivers what? Twelve days ago?” Harrison asked.

“Eleven,” Sam answered.

“Yes.” Harrison looked at his desk with a frown and moved a few papers around before stopping at one with Sam’s familiar handwriting. “The court date had already passed by the time I returned from Houston and read your letter.”

“I knew there wouldn’t be enough time for you to respond.” Sam’s fingers tapped a rhythm on the arm of his chair. “But when I learned the railroad had sold the land to another rancher, I felt like I had to try seeking your advice. Before that, I truly thought everything was a mix-up, and the problem would easily be solved in my favor.”

“Since you’re here, I assume the court case didn’t go your way?”

Sam gave Harrison a single, jerky nod.

“I went to the state land office as soon as I read your letter.” Harrison pulled open a drawer and hefted out a stack of papers, then began sifting through them. “The State of Texas never awarded your land to the railroad.”

Ellie stilled, the breath catching in her lungs. Was Harrison right? If so, then every one of their troubles had just been solved. She sank back in her chair. Sam could keep his land, and she could keep her siblings. *Thank you, Father.*

“Then what happened?” Sam leaned forward, the stern lines of his face showing none of the relief sweeping through her. “How could there be two deeds?”

"The railroad one is fraudulent, probably because someone is trying to steal your land." Harrison's hazel eyes took on a cold, hard glint.

"Why would someone do that?" Ellie reached over and gripped her husband's hand, which was clenching the wooden arm of the chair so tightly his nails would leave marks.

Harrison shook his head. "You would know better than me. I haven't been to Twin Rivers in three years. Has something there changed to make Mr. Grigg's old ranch suddenly valuable?"

"Nothing." Sam gripped her fingers so hard she had to bite back a wince. "If anything, our land is supposed to become less valuable with the railroad going in north of us. Everyone says travelers will stop using the Chihuahuan Trail and trek straight north to the nearest railroad stop."

"Here are copies of everything I sent in that letter." Harrison slid several papers across the desk to Sam. "I also had a notarized letter from the state saying they never awarded the Southern Pacific Railroad your tract of land. Furthermore, the railroad itself has no record of your land being given to it."

"What does that mean?" A look of confusion settled over Sam's face, probably a mirror image of the confusion on her own face.

"It means that whoever falsified that deed also impersonated the railroad in court. The railroad knows nothing of the land and is receiving land much closer to where the track lies as compensation for putting down more railroad line."

"So all I need to do is take this new evidence to Judge Grenville and have the case go back to trial?" Sam flipped through the papers.

"No, I'm afraid your case is already closed, especially since this evidence was available before the trial but you failed to procure it. However, the information here suggests criminal activity on behalf of whoever falsified the deed. If you can prove the other deed fraudulent and that a crime has been committed, then your land will be given back to you, possibly along with a sum of money to repay you for your troubles."

Ellie straightened. Hadn't Charlotte said something about seeing Mr. Eckler and lawyers together with Judge Grenville before the court date? "What if the judge who decided the case was paid off? Can the case go back to trial then?"

Harrison narrowed his eyes and studied the two of them. "If you weren't treated fairly during the judicial process, then you can launch an appeal. But in my opinion, you've been fighting this case from a civil litigation perspective, yet you're better off to approach everything from the criminal side. Someone has obviously committed a series of crimes, such as creating a fraudulent deed and impersonating a lawyer from the railroad. That's probably why the supposed 'railroad' sold your land to this rancher fellow from Montana. As soon as the fraudsters realized the deed would be scrutinized in court, the criminals pretended to sell the land to someone who could maintain a presence in court easier than the false railroad lawyer."

Harrison sat back in his chair and gestured to the papers in Sam's hand. "You're already good friends with the law in Twin Rivers. Take this information back to Daniel and find out who's trying to steal your land and why. Everything will be awarded back to you as soon as you uncover the perpetrators of the crime."

"What if we get back to Twin Rivers and find that rancher from Montana has sold the land again?" Ellie twisted her hands together. Harrison made everything sound so easy, but if they couldn't find who was behind the fraud, would Sam lose his land forever?

No, surely not. Hadn't she decided to start trusting in God's goodness? There had to be a way forward, a way for Sam to get his land back. They just needed to figure out what steps to take next.

"How are we supposed to discover who created the fraudulent deed or impersonated the railroad's lawyer if the land keeps changing owners?"

"The farther away you get from the original fraud, the more difficult getting your land back will be. That's true."

"We need to hit the trail." Sam sprang up from his seat, his hands clenched into fists. "I have to find out who's trying to take my land."

"Now?" She nearly whimpered. Of course they needed to return to Twin Rivers, but couldn't she spend at least one night sleeping in a real bed, one hour soaking in a real tub, before turning back and heading through the blistering desert?

"Have you considered the possibility there might be precious metal on your property?" Harrison steepled his fingers beneath his chin. "There's a new quicksilver mine going in near Terlingua. That would provide incentive for someone to swindle you."

Sam just shook his head and kept muttering, as though Harrison hadn't even spoken. "I should have asked for help earlier. Then I would have known all of this, but I truly thought the judge would rule in my favor. And the money for hiring a lawyer…"

"I don't expect to be paid for this. You shouldn't even need to ask." Harrison rose from his chair and came around his desk, a grim set to the faint lines etching the corners of his mouth.

"No, not you. I knew you'd be happy to help." Sam sighed and scrubbed a hand over his face. "I was talking about a lawyer in Twin Rivers County. I only had three weeks between discovering both deeds and the court date, that wasn't enough time for you and me to even exchange letters."

Sam took the sheaf of papers off the desk, his shoulders rising and falling in a deep sigh. "Thank you for your help, truly. But Ellie and I best start for home."

"I know you're anxious to get back and set things right, but stay at least one night. I've spare rooms aplenty." Harrison looked between the two of them, then his gaze settled on her. "Give your woman a rest from the desert and eat food cooked in a real kitchen instead of over a campfire."

"Please, Sam." Ellie couldn't help the pleading in her voice. The offer sounded too wonderful to refuse. "One night won't set us back too much."

Sam turned and ran his eyes down her form and back up again. She wasn't quite sure what he saw, only that a bit of the determination leached from his gaze. "One night. We leave at dawn tomorrow."

Harrison clapped a hand on Sam's shoulder. "Great."

~.~.~.~.~

They didn't belong here. Sam glanced at Ellie seated beside him, then looked around the opulent dining room with its polished wood table and elaborate chandelier hanging overhead. Massive drapes adorned long, floor-to-ceiling windows while a giant, gilt-trimmed mirror on the next wall reflected the dinner party seated at the table.

He'd stayed in Harrison's house many a time when in Austin on cattle business, but Harrison had never before opened his dining room. The small parlor where he, Harrison, and Wes normally ate always had a comfortable, welcoming feel.

Seated at the head of the table, Harrison acted as kind and friendly as ever, even dressed in a highfalutin three-piece suit that had probably been made just for him by some fancy tailor. But between the expensive china that was probably worth as much as Sam's ranchland and house, and the company Harrison had invited for dinner, he couldn't help but feel like a dusty tumbleweed that had somehow rolled into an elegant mansion.

"So in two more years, you'll be looking at the next governor of

Texas." Mariah Sheffield, Wes and Charlotte's married sister, finished whatever she'd been rambling about and took a sip of water. The trio of deep green jewels around her neck caught in the light from the chandelier above and glittered, as did the matching jewels in the two gold combs poised in her perfectly coiffed hair.

Was this really the same woman who had once ridden across the dusty desert on horseback, trailing him and Wes and the others to see what they were up to? He couldn't imagine her on a horse now—more like in an enclosed buggy that had been specially made to keep out dust.

No wonder Charlotte wanted to marry on her own without her father's approval. She'd wither away if her pa married her to a stuffy, proper social climber.

"And you'll also be looking at the first lady of Texas." Across the table from him, William Sheffield took Mariah's hand and sent his wife a sickeningly sweet smile.

Did the two think they were at a campaign speech instead of attending dinner with friends Mariah had known her entire life?

"But I am concerned about Charlotte." Mariah drew her lips that had been stained a perfect shade of red into a pout. "Normally I can see Father's perspective on things, but his choice for Charlotte's husband... Well, let's just say we've heard some things that could make family relations uncomfortable."

"Your father's picked someone?" Sam's half-eaten leg of lamb curdled in his stomach. Charlotte had said her father was trying to find her a husband, but she hadn't said anything about him settling on a certain man yet. "Your pa's been gone from Twin Rivers for six weeks or better. Doesn't he have better things to worry about than who Charlotte marries?"

He knew firsthand that marriages could be arranged via letter. But part of him had been hoping the old codger would grow a heart and let his daughter choose whom she wanted to wed.

"We received a letter two days ago with the name of Charlotte's new intended." William took a sip of water. "Unfortunately, we're not sure the union will be a good match."

"Yes, in some ways the match suits." Mariah slid William a glance, the jewels in her hair still spiraling blinks of light around the room. "But in other ways we could see the marriage being something of a disaster."

"Something of a disaster for William's political aspirations, I assume?" Harrison spoke for the first time since Mariah had started in on William's plan to become governor. "You don't actually feel as though this man would hurt Charlotte in some way."

"Oh no, not hurt her, at least not in the physical sense. He doesn't have that type of a reputation, just one for being a little… ah… undiscerning with some of the company he keeps."

"Why not let Charlotte choose who she marries?" Ellie blurted. She'd barely said a word during the meal, though she'd eaten every last bit of lamb, potatoes, and green beans off her plate.

Mariah gave a light, tinkling laugh. "You obviously don't know my sister well. If left to her own devices, Charlotte would marry just about anyone and claim she was content."

"And there's something wrong with that?" Ellie's words came out low and fierce, her gaze intense enough to challenge Mariah.

"Well, not for some people." Mariah merely shrugged at Ellie's glower and gave off another perfectly false laugh. "But Charlotte is used to being kept in a certain sort of style, you see. She might say she doesn't care about the kind of clothes she wears or how big her house is, but put her in a three-bedroom house and a gingham dress, and she'll quickly realize that all aspects of a potential mate should be considered before marriage, not just matters of the heart."

Matters of the heart. Mariah had spoken the words carelessly, as though they were no more significant than the day's weather.

William took another bite of lamb, evidently not the least bit upset by Mariah's statement. Maybe he didn't mind being married to a woman who valued him only for the dresses and jewels he could buy her.

"Perhaps," Harrison spoke quietly, "'matters of the heart' are more important to Charlotte than they are to you, Mariah."

"Your pa let Wes marry Abigail." Sam snuck his hand under the table and found Ellie's, then gave it a squeeze. "If Wes can marry for love, then why not Charlotte?"

"That was before Abigail's family lost Fort Ashton." Mariah's shoulders tightened, and she raised her chin a notch. "Her family at least appeared to have some means back then, though none of us knew their true state. If Father had, he never would have allowed Wes and Abigail to wed. And do keep in mind that Abigail's father and stepfather were both traders. A trader isn't the same as a rancher, of course, but the match still had some advantages. Charlotte would marry a cowhand if Father let her."

It was almost as though Mariah knew of the conversation he and Charlotte had the day after he'd married Ellie. Sam pressed his lips together into a hard line. Poor Charlotte. With both her father and her sister set against her, she had little hope of finding a happy future.

"Harrison, I thought your father owned Fort Ashton? I'm confused." Ellie's brow creased.

Harrison shifted, the muscles in his face going tight, though the small movements meant most people wouldn't be able to read his subtle signs of discomfort. "He does now. After Ben Ashton's death, Mrs. Ashton married James Hall, a man who wasn't nearly as savvy in business as Ben Ashton or my father. My father kept lending Hall money until Hall had so many debts my father acquired the fort." Harrison's voice held a dark, chilling tone that silenced everyone at the table.

Sam prodded an uneaten bite of potato with his fork. If the town of Twin Rivers took a vote on who should be occupying Fort Ashton, the Ashton family would win, hands down. Old Man Rutherford might have had legal grounds to claim the fort, but that didn't exactly mean it was right.

Either way, nothing good would come of retelling the misfortune that had befallen the Ashton family after their pa's mysterious death. Rutherford had owned the fort for three years, and Harrison hadn't been to Twin Rivers once since, nor had he discussed it on any of Sam's trips to Austin.

"So tell me, Harry." Sam leaned back in his chair and stretched his arms, then grinned when Harrison sent him a glower. He hated being called that. "Any fancy Austin ladies catching your eye these days?"

"Not a one. Don't see that happening for two years or better." A sly smile turned the corner of Harrison's lips, though the coldness didn't quite leave his eyes. "I'm more curious to know if Daniel is wooing anyone."

Sam winced. Daniel was the oldest of the lot, turning thirty in another nine months. The faint laugh lines around Harrison's mouth said he'd gladly travel all the way back to Twin Rivers for the sole purpose of shaving Daniel's head.

"Truly, Harrison, you ought to consider Melanie Krough." This from Mariah, who used her fork to pick at the leg of lamb she'd barely touched. "She's lovely to look upon and comes from a good family."

"Perhaps I shall consider her—in a few more years." Harrison sent Sam a pointed look. "I have no plans to marry in the short term. If ever."

So Harrison still hadn't changed in that regard. When he was a boy, he'd decided women were more trouble than they were worth, and even now that he'd made a name for himself as a lawyer, he didn't seem apt to change his opinion of the fairer sex. Of course, things might change the day he turned thirty and didn't need to worry about his head getting shaved if he married.

Sam sent Ellie a wink. Foolish as that blood oath had been, he'd been right to swear with Wes and Daniel about getting married before thirty all those years ago. Harrison didn't know what he was missing.

William used the lapse in conversation to steer the discussion back to his political goals and start dropping hints to Harrison about how much money he would need to run a campaign for governor. But the darkness that had appeared in Harrison's eyes from discussing his father never quite dissipated.

They ate their dessert to Harrison's noncommittal sounds of boredom while William and Mariah tried several different tactics to get Harrison to make a campaign donation. When it came time to leave the table and head to the drawing room, Sam excused himself and Ellie, claiming they needed a full night's sleep before leaving at dawn the next day.

Harrison shot him a frustrated look as he followed the Sheffields down the hall, but Sam merely grinned back. If Harrison couldn't hold off a couple of social climbers for another hour, then he probably deserved to lose some of his money.

"So what did you think of my friends?" Rather than offer Ellie his elbow as was proper, Sam laced his fingers with hers and led her up the stairway of dark, gleaming wood and down a hallway covered in ornate rugs.

"Mariah seems…" She gave her head a little shake. "Hard. I almost feel sorry for her, though it feels wrong to say such a thing when she's wearing a silk dress and emeralds, and I'm sitting across from her in cotton with a single ribbon in my hair. Do you think she's happy?"

"Yes. Or rather, I think she has what she wants. A wealthy husband, fine dresses, jewels to glitter at her neck, a last name that's recognized throughout all of Austin." He opened the door to their room and led Ellie inside.

"And Charlotte doesn't want that."

He couldn't imagine Charlotte hosting weekly parties—or even happily attending them. No, Charlotte wanted her horses and her friends. And a man she at least felt comfortable with, even if she didn't love him.

"I feel sorry for her." Ellie raised her eyes to his, disquiet etching the lines of her brow.

"For Mariah or Charlotte?"

"Both." She cocked her head to the side, her somber expression turning into a small smile. "But do you know what else I feel?"

"What?"

Her lips widened into a bigger smile, and she leaned up on her tiptoes to place a kiss on his jaw. "Blessed, because while I might not have silk and jewels, I have a man who loves me."

He looked down into her face, so sincere while her eyes brimmed with growing love.

If only he could smile at her as brightly as she smiled at him, but he just couldn't bring his lips to curve that much. "I wish you also had a place to call home."

A worried look flashed across her face, there and gone in an instant. "We'll get your land back, the two of us together. Two are better than one, remember? And I aim to stand by your side and help you every step of the way. Just you wait and see. I know we'll get it back. We have to."

She was right, of course.

But what if he failed anyway?

Chapter Nineteen

Ellie couldn't let Lynnette out of her arms. The little one had long grown tired of being held on her lap and kept trying to squirm free, especially given the playful noises Janey and Joe made from the other room. But try as she might, Ellie just couldn't get her arms to release the child.

She'd held every last one of her siblings to her chest when she and Sam had returned to the Westins' ranch an hour ago. It seemed as though all the children had grown an inch during the time she'd been gone. Joe still wore his splint, but he hadn't winced in pain once, not even when she'd hugged him. According to Charlotte, the doctor might remove his splint as early as next week.

If given a choice, she'd have taken all the children outside to play or up to the bluffs above the ranch house for a picnic before plotting ways to get Sam's land back, but her husband had other ideas.

Conversation swirled around the dining room table, where Daniel, Wes, Sam, Charlotte, and Anna Mae had all assembled, every last one of them ignoring the platter of lemon cake and pitcher of milk in the middle of the table. Unfortunately, Sam's friends hadn't told them much of use so far, and they had to turn the land over to Eckler the day after tomorrow.

"What do you mean Eckler left town?" The frown already marring Sam's face deepened.

"He left the day after you did, him and all three of those fancy lawyers." Daniel's face looked just as grim as Sam's.

"Why didn't you stop him?" Sam's hands curled into fists on the table.

"There's nothing illegal about leaving town. I know something doesn't feel right about the situation, but I can't exactly stop people from leaving unless they're either wanted for a crime or they've got an upcoming trial."

"Eckler and the others are wanted for a crime now, so go find them." Sam thrust a hand toward the legal documents they'd gotten from Harrison, which he'd spread across the table for everyone to see.

"Settle down." Wes gave Sam a thump on the shoulder. "Eckler and his slimy lawyers will return at the end of the thirty days to make sure he gets that land, and when they do, Daniel will question them."

"I will, but just to be clear, they're not wanted for a crime at this point." Daniel shifted the papers around on the table, then paused when he reached a certain document. "We have to be able to prove their involvement before things get to that stage. Right now, they are considered persons of interest, not wanted criminals."

"But if they don't say something that gives them away while you talk to them, then what happens? Are you left without someone to charge for falsifying the deed? Am I still left without my ranch?" Sam gritted his last words through clenched teeth.

"It will be all right." Still holding Lynnette, Ellie reached for Sam's hand and pried his tightly clenched fingers open to lace hers with his. "We'll get the land back eventually. Daniel will keep looking for who did this, and someone, somewhere is bound to make a mistake that gives everything away."

But the words sounded hollow to her. Just how long would it take to seek justice? Just how long would she and Sam be out of a home? How long was it reasonable to keep the children with them if Sam had nowhere to run his cattle? She'd been trusting in God's goodness the whole way back from Austin, so why wasn't God giving them a hint on how to get Sam's land back?

A muscle twitched at the side of Sam's jaw as he looked back at Daniel. "Did you ever question Judge Grenville? Ask why he was seen meeting with people who were scheduled for court later in the week?"

Red crept up the back of Daniel's neck. "I'm afraid the conversation didn't get very far. The judge wasn't particularly pleased with the insinuation he'd been paid off, and he had some rather uncharitable insinuations to throw back at me."

"Can you check Judge Grenville's bank records and see if he received an unusual sum of money sometime this month?" Charlotte broke off a piece of lemon cake but dropped the chunk back to her plate rather than put it in her mouth.

"Not without a warrant, and do you know how hard it is to get a warrant on a judge?" Daniel rubbed his chin. "I'd have to ride to the next county to even apply for one."

"Then ride to the next county. It might be the only chance we have." Sam shoved himself up from the table and stalked toward the door.

"Where are you going?" Ellie rose, still cradling Lynnette in her arms, though drowsiness pulled at her sister's eyelids.

"Into town. Someone needs to find a place for us to stay, since it doesn't look like I'll be getting my land back anytime soon."

Ellie winced, not that Sam could see it as he trudged through the door and out of the house.

"I'm sorry." Daniel pressed his eyes shut and slumped in his chair. "I know it seems like I did nothing while you and Sam were gone, but I swear I interviewed every last person I could think of. No one knows anything, except maybe the judge, who accused me of meddling with the law in order to help my friend and said he'd let the town know what I was up to if I didn't stop."

"Which he could have said because he was guilty." Anna Mae crossed her arms over her chest with a huff.

"He also could have said that because he's not guilty." Wes snagged a piece of lemon cake from the center of the table. "Given Daniel's friendship with all of us, it could easily appear he's using his position to meddle on Sam's behalf."

"No one can accuse me of that now." Daniel picked up the legal papers and began sliding them back into their thick yellow envelope. "We've got proof of fraud right here in front of us."

But would that proof lead to any arrests? Ellie released a shuddering breath. She'd been so certain everything with the land would fall into place once she and Sam returned to Twin Rivers.

"I'd best get back to my office and look at these closer, probably see what Pa has to say." Daniel tucked the papers under his arm. "Maybe there's something new I can try. And if I have enough evidence here, I'll send one of my deputies to Brewster County tomorrow to see if I can get a warrant for Judge Grenville's bank records."

"I'll hire an investigator to look into this Eckler character." Wes spoke around the piece of cake he'd inhaled in two bites. "I don't know why I didn't think of the idea right after court. If the man doesn't return to Twin Rivers for some reason, then maybe we can track him down in Montana."

Ellie forced a smile and small "thank you," but the words tasted like curdled milk in her mouth. How long would it take to hear from an investigator? One month? Two? Six?

Sam had two days to be off that land.

And she had two days to decide what would happen to her siblings if they didn't get it back.

~.~.~.~.~

Ellie wrapped her arms around herself and stared out over the landscape. Dying orange and pink touched the plains to the west, while a deep, hazy blue slowly inched across the mountains to the east. From her position on the Westins' stone terrace, she could just make out the dip in the land and the trail of lush green that surrounded the Rio Grande before a wall of cliffs sprang up on the Mexican side of the river.

The children were all abed, but Sam had yet to return from town. Maybe his long absence hinted at something good. Perhaps he'd found them all a place to live and was making the final arrangements.

But if so, how did he plan to pay for rent? He might be able to sell off his cattle now, even though it was only June, but doing so would ruin his chances of having a good herd next year.

If he even owned a herd next year.

"Ellie?"

She jolted, then pressed a hand to her heart and spun around to face Leroy, who should have been abed like the others. "What's wrong?"

The solemn look in his eyes told her all she needed to know.

"I was in the other room earlier, listening while you and Sam were talking to the sheriff. You're not getting the land back, are you?"

"We will… eventually." But getting it back within the next two days seemed about as likely as snow falling in the one-hundred-degree heat they were having.

"Where will you and Sam stay while you're trying to catch the people who did this?"

She and Sam. He hadn't said *we*. "I don't know. Sam's in town working on that now."

"This came while you were gone." Leroy handed her a letter with handwriting she recognized even before her gaze landed on the return address of Eagle Harbor. The back flap had already been broken. She raised an eyebrow at her brother as she pulled the letter from the envelope.

"You were gone, and I wanted to know what it said." His shoulders rose and fell in a shrug.

She unfolded the letter and glanced at the first paragraph. Victoria would take the children. All of them, or however many couldn't stay in Texas. Victoria and her sister-in-law Aileen had even offered to travel here to collect everyone.

Something hot and sharp pierced her chest, and she dropped the letter to her side. "Sam and I are getting on better. He even…"

She pressed her eyes shut only to find memories of Sam stroking the hair back from her face, bending in for a kiss, holding her against his bare chest while the starry Texas sky spread out above them.

"He loves me. And I love him too." Though she'd not told him yet, not with the weight of their lost land pulling at them. "Don't you see, Leroy? Everything you said Sam and I could never have with you and the others around, we have that anyway. Love. Family. A…"

Home.

Had she nearly said that? Tears flooded her eyes, hot and fierce, and they refused to be blinked back into submission.

"Things will turn out all right, Ellie. You'll see." Leroy's arms wrapped around her, arms that had put on some muscle since he'd started working the ranch. He drew her against a chest that seemed fuller and stronger than it had three months ago too. "We'll go back to Eagle Harbor with the Cummings women, and you and Sam will find a way to settle in by yourselves right quick. Did you read the whole letter? Gilbert Sinclair has offered to pay our passage back to Eagle Harbor, just like he paid for the extra tickets on the way down."

She should probably say something kind about the wealthy industrialist's generosity, but the words refused to come.

Had she made it this far only to lose the things that mattered most? Her hands fisted in Leroy's shirt. *God, this isn't fair! My family shouldn't have to leave. Sam shouldn't lose his land!*

The silent plea wrenched from a place deep inside her, shaking her body with the force of the unspoken words.

But even as her sobs subsided, she knew the truth. Without the land, keeping the children would be too much to ask of Sam. Oh, he'd probably tell her he could keep them, but doing so would ruin any chance Sam had of scraping a ranch back together. She couldn't ask her husband to give up his lifetime dream for a bunch of children he had no obligation to.

"It'll be all right, Ellie." Leroy patted her back. "You don't need to cry. We're going somewhere safe."

She drew back only to find her brother's eyes moist with tears as well, though he held his jaw in a hard line.

"Leaving you will never be all right, but unless some miracle happens, you're right. I can't keep all of you here. I'll talk to Sam about letting Lynnette stay though."

And sending the children back to Eagle Harbor brought up another problem. Should she tell Leroy and the rest of the family their secret? Knowing the truth would only discourage them, just as it had her. But if Pa's wife learned most of the children were still in Eagle Harbor, would she tell everyone they were illegitimate?

Maybe Sam would know what to do, just like he'd known what to tell her. She'd talk to him before mentioning anything to Leroy.

"You look troubled and exhausted." Leroy dropped his arms from around her. "You should get to bed."

"As though I'll be able to sleep."

But she allowed her younger brother to lead her inside and down the hall to the room Wes had given her and Sam. She sank onto the bed and stared at the closed door for one moment, then another, before curling up beneath the covers, wrapping her arms around herself and waiting for sleep to claim her.

But the solace she hoped to find eluded her even in her dreams.

~.~.~.~.~

Sam groaned and rolled over, shifting his weight on the bed for probably the third time in the last two minutes. Beside him, Ellie snuggled close enough that the warmth of her body leached into his. He wrapped an arm around her and nestled her back against his chest, then peeked an eye open. Streaks of pink and orange sunlight filtered through the window.

Was it dawn already? He released Ellie and sat up, scrubbing a hand over his face. He should have slept well, especially considering last night had been his first time in a real bed after ten nights on the trail. But how was a man expected to sleep when someone had swindled away his land?

How was he supposed to sleep when the cost of housing his family would eradicate his savings in two months' time?

He needed to find another job—one that paid once a week rather than once a year when he took his cattle to market. But Twin Rivers didn't have all that many jobs to offer. Either a man worked for himself, worked as a trader on the Chihuahuan Trail, or worked as a cowhand and slept in a bunkhouse with all the other cowhands. A trader was never home to spend time with his family, and a cowpuncher's salary wasn't enough to provide for a family of ten.

"You're back." Ellie shifted beside him, her eyes blinking open. "Sorry I fell asleep last night. I tried to wait up for you."

"Don't be sorry." He rested a hand on her shoulder, the fabric of her cotton nightgown so thin he nearly touched the warmth of her bare skin. "You deserved a good night's sleep after our trip back from Austin."

She grimaced and pushed herself into a sitting position. "I think I slept better on the trail."

That made two of them. Here they were, in what was probably the fanciest house in the county, and neither of them could manage a decent night's rest. "Go back to bed, sweetheart. It's still early."

"Actually, there's a reason I was waiting up for you last night."

Something about the way she spoke had worry climbing into his chest. "What's wrong?"

Her shoulders slumped and she looked down at the coverlet. "I'm going to send the children back to Eagle Harbor."

"What…?" The breath whooshed from his lungs in a giant rush. He couldn't have heard right. "What do you mean?"

"Read this. It explains everything." She reached for a letter on the bedside table, chancing a look in his direction before bending her head.

He took the paper, his eyes barely able to focus on the words in the dim morning light, but he skimmed the loopy, elegant handwriting nonetheless. "You asked one of your friends from Michigan to take the children? But I thought…"

How could she, and without telling him? Hadn't she wanted everyone to stay together?

Yes, of course she had. She'd pleaded for that very thing the day she'd arrived on the stage.

"I don't understand," he rasped. "Why do you suddenly want to send your brothers and sisters away?"

"Haven't you figured it out?" She moved her hand to cover his on the bed, tears welling in her eyes. "We can't keep them, Sam, not without your ranch."

Something hard and tight clamped around his chest, which was still having trouble sucking in air. "You said just yesterday afternoon that we'd get the ranch back."

"And we will, but I don't know how long it will take, and neither do you." Her hand fisted around his, her grip so tight he was sure to have nail imprints in his skin. "I can't ask you to keep the children in the meantime. It's too much."

Too much to have Joe snuggle against his chest or Lynnette reach her stubby arms toward him when she wanted to be picked up? Too much to listen to Janey and Joe's quiet chatter as they played with the wagon and horse figurines he'd whittled, or see Leroy's look of contentment as they rode across the ranch together looking for stray cattle?

But he didn't have a ranch to ride across with Leroy, or places for Janey and Joe to sleep. Not anymore.

Ellie had started babbling, a long stream of words that included something about Leroy feeling so many young'uns underfoot was ruining her chance for happiness with him and wanting the children to leave long before now. She also mentioned something about how both of them had grown closer together on the trail without anyone else around.

He blew out a breath. She was right. They had grown closer on the trail, and she was also right that he couldn't afford to care for them until he got his land back—whenever that might be.

But her siblings had become part of his family. He couldn't just allow eight members of the only family he'd ever known to leave because things turned difficult.

If a man provide not for his own, he is worse than an infidel.

But he wasn't an infidel, and he wasn't going to let the children walk out of his life.

"Don't I get a say in any of this?" The edges of the paper crinkled in his grip.

Ellie glanced up at him, then away. "No."

"You're wrong. We're husband and wife, which means I have as much a say as you, and I say no. You never should have written your friend about taking the children without first talking to me about it."

"You don't have any claim to them. They're my siblings, not yours, which makes this my decision."

"Don't tell me I don't have claim." His voice thundered through the room. "I'll go to the courthouse today and file adoption papers for each and every one of them."

He should have done so before he left for Austin, but he'd had so little time to go and return before he needed to hand over his ranch to Eckler. Still, if he would have filed those papers as Ellie asked the night before court, they wouldn't be having this conversation now.

"I don't want them to go either. But don't you see?" She rested a hand on his arm, her grip calm and gentle atop the trembling in his own muscles. "They can't stay because you're too good. You'd ruin us trying to provide for all of them, unable to send any of them away but unable to ever save money for more land. We have to let them go. It's not to an orphanage, but to a loving home where—"

"If you have such a wonderful place for them to stay in Eagle Harbor, then why didn't you leave them there to begin with?" He shoved her hand away from his arm.

"Because I was too selfish to see the mistake I was making." One of the tears shimmering in her eyes crested and trailed down her cheek. "After Ma passed, I just wanted us to all be together, but I never considered how much of a burden that would place on you."

"Your siblings aren't a burden."

"No," she sniffled. "They're rather wonderful, aren't they? But I was selfish, and I wasn't thinking. And now that I've come to love you, I see what a terrible position I've put you in."

Now that she'd come to love him? His body turned hot, then cold. He'd confessed his love for her two weeks ago on the way to Austin. He'd not pushed her to say the same, wanting to be sure she truly meant the words when she spoke them for the first time.

But none of his dreams of having his wife tell him she loved him had ever involved tears streaking Ellie's face or rage coursing through his own body. "How dare you tell me you love me after you've gone behind my back about your siblings. That's not what love looks like."

"I can't ask you to sacrifice your dream of a ranch because your wife came saddled with eight brothers and sisters." She sniffled again, her gaze seeking his, imploring him to understand.

He understood nothing. "I dreamed of a family too. Not just a ranch. You brought me that."

"We'll have our own family one day, maybe even eight children of our own. But adding them to the family one by one, year by year, is a heap different than having you take in eight children all at once."

She was being unfair. Utterly, completely unfair. If she loved him, she would have talked to him about her siblings, asked his opinion, included him from the very beginning.

He stood from the bed and pulled on his trousers, then slipped his shirt over his head. "How long?"

"What?"

"Until they leave? How long?"

"Oh." She bit the bottom of her lip and studied the letter. "Probably two months or better. It will take some time to answer Victoria and then get the money for their return passage sent here."

Two months. He strode out the door, ignoring Ellie's question about where he was headed. He had two months to save his ranch—or lose his family.

He stalked down the hall and rounded the corner into the parlor.

"Owens."

Sam stilled. He didn't need to turn and seek out the speaker to recognize the grizzled sound of Agamemnon Westin's voice. The man must have returned from wherever he'd been sometime late last night.

"You here to pay me rent for grazing your cattle on my land?"

Of course that would be the first thing Mr. Westin wanted to know. No asking how he'd been, how many calves he'd ended up adding to the herd that spring, or how many cows he'd impregnated recently. No hint that he was a good rancher, even if his land was being swindled from him.

Had he truly ever thought the man would look at him and see value in him as a person and not just the money he'd made the A Bar W during the decade he'd worked at the ranch?

"How much do you want?" Sam spun to face the richest man in the county.

Except Mr. Westin didn't look as intimidating as he remembered. His body seemed thinner, his skin a frail gray shade.

"Bet you're wishing you sold me that land two months ago." The aging man still managed to sound as hale and hearty as he ever had, even if he'd lost weight over the past couple months. "I told you that you would fail."

"You should be glad I didn't sell you that land. You'd have lost it just the same as I did. Someone falsified a deed that made it look as though the railroad owned the land."

The man blinked and sat back in his cushioned chair. Sam didn't know how Westin had heard about the lost ranchland in the first place, but he must not have spoken to Wes since returning, or he'd know the rest. "I still want rent for grazing your cattle."

"He's not paying you anything." Wes entered the room, a cup of coffee in his hand. "Someone swindled his land from him. This is the least we can do."

Mr. Westin humphed. "We don't owe him any help, not when he should have sold that land to me."

"Had you been in his shoes, you would have made the same choice. And he'll get the land back, though that might take some time." Wes took a swig of coffee and looked at Sam. "Which is why

I want to offer you your old foreman position."

Agamemnon choked, though he didn't have a coffee cup to drink from like Wes. "He gave up that position. He can't have it back."

"He's a better foreman than Jeb, and you know it. Besides, it comes with a house." Wes spoke without looking at his father, his dark eyes taking on a gentle quality that came out far too little since Abigail's death. "Sam, I know it's not much of a house considering the size of your family. But we can add on a room or two. Won't hurt any to fix that place up a bit. I might be able to work out a pay increase too. Say you'll take it."

"Clearly, I can't leave home for more than a day or two," Mr. Westin muttered, "without my son losing all his business sense in my absence. And just when I thought he was ready to take over the ranch."

"Sam's a friend, and we have the means to help him. There's nothing senseless about it," Wes snapped before turning back to him. "So? What do you say?"

A friend. The words should bring comfort. If he'd learned one thing over the past months, it was that there was nothing wrong with taking help from a friend. Nothing wrong with telling others his problems or leaning on them a little. The Bible even had verses about bearing one another's burdens.

But did taking help mean he had to feel like such a failure? As a man of twenty-eight, shouldn't he be able to keep his family together without depending on others?

Still, Wes's offer provided a way forward without sending the children back to Michigan.

"What will happen to Jeb? Doesn't his ailing ma live with him in the foreman's house?"

"Woman is plumb crazy. Should be in an insane asylum." Mr. Westin barked.

Wes shook his head at his father. "Lots of people lose their memory as they get older. It doesn't mean they need to be locked away."

"She's not just losing her memory." The words shot from Mr. Westin's mouth with enough venom to ward off a rattlesnake. "She's lost every last one of her senses."

Wes winced at that, then took a swig of coffee. "Well, Sam, what will it be? You want to be foreman again until you get your ranch back?"

Maybe, if it didn't mean kicking Jeb and his ma out of their home. Jeb's ma could hardly live with him in the bunkhouse. Sam looked out the window, over the harsh, craggy landscape still covered in the pink hues of dawn.

"Ellie wants to send the kids away," he whispered.

"All of them?" Wes's eyebrows rose.

"Don't look at me like that. You thought I was a fool for taking them in to begin with."

"I was wrong."

Sam swallowed. The words might sound simple, but coming from Wes, they were akin to lassoing a prize bull while blindfolded.

"I'm glad you took them in, glad you gave them a home. I may have thought you were crazy at the beginning, but the truth is, every child should have a family, and you gave eight young'uns one when you didn't have to. And I know those kids have come to mean something to you. Did I tell you Leroy helped around the ranch while you were gone? That boy's got a natural way with cattle. I'd gladly hire him too until you get your ranch back. Reckon then you'll need him around your place."

"Thank you for the offer of foreman. Maybe now we can keep the kids with us." If he could manage to forgive himself for kicking Jeb and his ailing ma out of their house. "I'll let Ellie know of the offer and we'll talk it over."

Which was more than she'd done with him.

Out the window, yellow crept over the landscape, chasing away the dull pink hues of dawn and indicating the sun had crested the mountains to the east.

Sam repositioned his hat on his head and turned for the door. The day was already a-wasting.

"Where are you going?" Wes called after him.

"To my ranch."

"Why? We rounded up all the cattle and moved the last of your belongings out. It's all set to turn over to Eckler come sundown… providing the man shows up back in town first."

What could he say? He had a need to visit his land again, to look around for anything that might have been left behind, see if he'd missed any clues as to why someone was so all-fired determined to swindle his ranch from him. He still had one day before the land officially belonged to Eckler.

He'd spend every minute of it fighting to keep his ranch.

Chapter Twenty

By the time Sam reached his house, the sun's golden rays engulfed the land. The addition taunted him from the side of the main house, mostly finished, but not entirely, seeing how he'd up and left for Austin so suddenly. Would the new owner bother to finish the final wall and put a roof on? If not, the summer rains would begin to wash away his hard work. Mud houses could last for generations, or for only a few years depending on how well they were kept. If Eckler didn't put a roof on it, coat the mudbricks, and repair the coating from time to time, then the structure would slowly return back to the land.

The friends that had cleaned out his house had left nothing inside, not even a spare blanket. The barn stood just as empty, all of his tack and other supplies now probably stored somewhere on the A Bar W.

Sam swung back onto Long Arrow and started for the northern border of his property. He'd ride a circle around the whole thing looking for stray cattle—or anything else he might find out of place.

But everything seemed normal. The lay of the land, the random piles of rocks, the layers of clay streaking the ground in certain places, the growing hills as he trekked closer and closer to the Bofecillos Mountains. He led Long Arrow over a dry creek bed, then down another gully and up a steep mountainside.

Where did his property end? He didn't know the back few thousand acres well. His cattle didn't even use a thousand acres of his land, and the far eastern portion held so many mountains he'd never be able to graze more than a handful of cattle on it. Still, when he got his land back, he'd pay to have it surveyed straight off and put up some boundary stones.

Sam crested a ridge, the height of which allowed him to see the towering cliffs of the Sierra Madre Mountains across the river and the growing peaks of the Bofecillos Range near his own property. Should he go farther? Was he even on his land anymore?

A little more riding wouldn't hurt. If anything, it kept him from going back to the ranch and facing Ellie. He should probably tell her of Wes's offer to be a foreman.

But how was he supposed to forge a future with his wife when she made decisions without him? Two were supposed to be better than one, but what happened when one person went behind the other's back and made a terrible decision?

Long Arrow picked his way down another slope and then back up the next. Sam surveyed the landscape, more mountain now than rolling hills.

He almost missed the hoofprints in a section of powdery clay. They had to belong to a cow. One of his? But where was the beast, and how had a cow strayed so far into the mountains? He followed the tracks to where the patch of clay ended and yellow rocks once again consumed the landscape and obscured any cattle tracks. The hill above ended in a towering rockface, making it impossible to go straight up the slope like he'd done with the other hills. He slowly picked his way around the base of the mountain, then stopped.

More cattle tracks, thousands of them, lying in a soft section of the valley between two towering cliffs.

His heart thudded in his chest. The trail continued as far as he could see, filling the narrow space between two mountains until the tracks disappeared around the base of the cliff. And the tracks were fresh too, as though the cattle had been brought through at dawn. The river couldn't be more than a half mile from here. Did any of the cattle belong to him? Perhaps a few, the rest could well belong to the Westins.

He spurred Long Arrow forward. "Come on, boy. Giddyap."

Maybe he could reach the cattle before they crossed into Mexico.

But a herd of cattle this big would have too many rustlers for him to take on by himself. Still, if he could sneak up on them, he could get information. Those cattle belonged to a rancher somewhere. He didn't have time to go to Twin Rivers, get Daniel and his deputies, wait for whatever posse Daniel put together, and then come back out here. If he rode now, he might be able to reach the cattle before they crossed the river.

Two are better than one.

Sam frowned. Where had that verse come from? His and Ellie's relationship had nothing to do with catching rustlers and saving cattle. At the moment, speed and stealth mattered more than anything else.

~.~.~.~.~

Ellie leaned forward on the mount Charlotte had lent her as the horse headed up a rocky hillside. She should probably be looking out over the desert, like Charlotte and Anna Mae were ahead of her, but instead she stared at the little plumes of dust rising from the hooves of Anna Mae's mount.

Had she really told Sam that he didn't have any claim to her siblings? She pressed her eyes shut, letting the horse guide her over the uneven trail, but doing so only caused the hurt look on Sam's face from that morning to spring to her mind. She may as well have taken one of his knives and shoved it into his heart. In fact, a stab wound probably would have caused him less pain.

She twisted the horse's reins in her hand. For as long as she could remember, she'd wanted a husband to love her. And now that God had finally given her that man, she hadn't clung to him or talked to him or treated him as she should. She'd gone and made a choice without ever once speaking to him.

The choice had seemed wise. She couldn't allow her husband to ruin himself financially because of her siblings.

So why did deciding to send the children away without first talking to him suddenly seem so horrible? She'd only been trying to protect him.

Because she wasn't acting as a married woman should. When she'd said her vows at the front of the church, she'd committed her future to Sam. But then she'd gone and acted as though she was single, as though the children were her responsibility alone. She never stopped to consider Sam had fed and clothed and sheltered all of them for the past two months, that her siblings had come to matter to him. Who was she to rip the children away from him without having so much as a discussion first?

Two are better than one; because they have a good reward for their labour. For if they fall, the one will lift up his fellow: but woe to him that is alone when he falleth; for he hath not another to help him up. Again, if two lie together, then they have heat: but how can one be warm alone? And if one prevail against him, two shall withstand him; and a threefold cord is not quickly broken.

The verses came back to her, verses Sam had first shared with her down by the river, after she'd knocked over the potluck table at church and made a fool of herself in front of the entire town. She'd gone back to the house and looked those verses up.

"So? What do you think?" Charlotte's voice speared into her thoughts.

Ellie ripped her gaze away from the hooves of Anna Mae's horse and looked at Charlotte. The other woman had already stopped and swung down from Athena, and she now stood surveying the land in the bit of shade given off from a small rockface jutting up behind them.

"I never tire of coming here." Anna Mae dismounted. "It's one of my favorite views."

Ellie reined her horse to a stop and climbed down. From where they stood on a little outcropping, the mountains to the east looked close enough to touch. The first peak rose in the foreground, a mixture of bright yellow rocks and shadowy blue. Then another peak rose up beside it, and another behind those two, and on and on the mountains rolled, obstructing everything but the small valley immediately before them.

"It's lovely." Almost lovely enough to wipe the devastated look on Sam's face from her mind. She'd apologize the moment he returned to the Westins'. Hopefully he'd give her another chance.

Maybe she'd been too hasty to doubt God's goodness too. After all, standing here, in the shadow of mountains she could nearly touch, she should be able to rest in God's goodness. To reach out and touch it like she could the rocks at her feet, to wrap herself in it, to taste it. God had created the grand landscape before her, and God had given her a husband who loved her.

Why hadn't she seen God's goodness in that? Why had she gone and made decisions without him knowing?

Sam had told her she was too quick to see the bad in every situation, but not the good. The children coming to Texas and knowing Sam had been good, even if Sam couldn't keep his land in the end. She might not be able to see much good in Clifford's or their mother's deaths, but diphtheria had moved through Eagle Harbor two years ago, and God had kept every single person in their family safe, even though many townsfolk lost loved ones.

God, forgive me for doubting Your goodness. She closed her eyes and tilted her face up to the sky, letting the sun's gentle morning rays touch her skin. *Forgive me for seeing only the bad. Forgive me for allowing my fears to hurt my relationship with my husband. I'd said I would trust Your goodness, but as soon as things grew difficult, I abandoned that plan.*

Peace settled over her, deep and fulfilling, as though that small, aching, restless place inside her had finally found contentment.

"Ellie, you better drink some water." Charlotte's voice interrupted her thoughts again, but not the peace swelling inside her. "It's easy to get dehydrated out here."

"That's one of the things I love about this place, at least at this time of day." Anna Mae took a swig of water from her canteen. "There's shade by the rockface, and you can't say that about many places in the desert."

"Do you come here often, Charlotte?" Ellie headed toward where the other women stood in the rockface's shadow.

"Several times a week." Charlotte stood with her brow knit and a slight frown on her face, as though she'd found something to criticize about the grand mountains before them. "It's my thinking place. So if a week has been particularly hard, I might come every day."

"Thank you for bringing me." If she lived on the A Bar W, she'd come every day.

"Considering everything that's going on with Sam's land, I'm glad I could offer you a distraction." Charlotte spoke the words almost absently, her brow still furrowed. But she wasn't looking at the stunning mountain peaks that rose like a wall straight from the earth. She stared at the valley below them instead.

"What's wrong?" Anna Mae handed Charlotte the canteen.

"The cattle. There were a couple hundred head scattered below when I rode out yesterday, and now there are none."

Ellie surveyed the empty stretch of land with a narrow strip of green from a small creek running through it. "Could they have gone somewhere else?"

"All of them? And so quickly?" Anna Mae chewed the side of her lip. "I might not know as much about ranching as Charlotte and Wes, but it doesn't seem likely."

"Especially not with the stream running through there. Our land doesn't have many water sources, and this time of year the cattle like to cluster in this valley." Charlotte scratched the side of her head beneath her wide-brimmed hat. "Come to think of it, I didn't see a single cow on our ride out here, at least not once we passed Sister Rocks."

Anna Mae's jaw turned firm and she scanned the valley, her eyes taking on the same narrowed, assessing glint that Daniel's had when they'd talked of the rancher from Montana disappearing yesterday. "I don't cotton to the notion of so many cattle disappearing, at least not so quick-like. We better ride back to the ranch for Wes and keep watch for anything suspicious."

"No. You'll stay exactly where you are…" a low voice said from behind them.

Ellie jolted then turned just enough to see a shadowy figure emerge from the pile of boulders rimming the side of the rockface.

"…or I'll shoot." The grizzled man trained a pistol on them, its silver barrel glinting in the sunlight.

Blood rushed in her ears and sweat slicked her forehead and hands. Where had this man come from? Who was he? Dressed in a cowboy hat and dust-covered trousers with a bandana pulled up to cover his nose and mouth, he could have passed for any number of cowhands she'd seen since coming to Texas.

"I mean it." The man cocked his gun and trained it directly on

Anna Mae. "Another step, and I'll blow your pretty little head right off your neck."

Ellie glanced at Anna Mae. Had her friend tried moving? Three unarmed women had no hope of defeating a man with a gun.

"You there." The man pointed his gun at her. "Take this here rope and tie your friends' hands behind their backs."

Holding his gun steady with one hand, he tossed her a rope that had been looped on his belt. It landed with a thud a few feet in front of her, spewing a little plume of dust into the air.

Ellie stared at the thick cord while her feet rooted themselves to the ground. She couldn't tie her friends, especially not when she had no idea what the man intended to do with them.

"Come on," the man growled. "Get the rope and start tying. I don't have all day."

"What are you going to do with them once they're tied?" Ellie took a small step forward, trying to shove down the panic that clawed at her chest.

"Tie you up as well, darling." A sneer formed on the man's lips. "Now move faster."

"I don't understand." She took another baby step toward the rope, just big enough to keep him from pulling the trigger on his gun. Or so she hoped. "We haven't done anything."

"He stole cattle, and we discovered it before he had time to get away." Anna Mae's voice held a sharp edge. "That's enough for a man like him to want us out of the way."

"Stop yacking and pick up that rope." The man aimed the gun directly at her head.

"Aimes, we got trouble." A male voice called from somewhere behind the pile of boulders, then two more shadows rounded the rockface. "Found the boy here spying on—"

At the sight of them, the first man skittered to a stop, as did the familiar form of the boy walking behind him—a boy who had a gag stuffed into his mouth and his hands bound behind his back.

"Martin?" Ellie's breath turned to ice in her chest.

"Robbie?" Charlotte's voice emerged as a small, high-pitched rasp, and she stared at the man who had Martin bound and gagged. "What are you doing here?"

And what was Martin doing here? A heavy feeling settled in her chest. She'd suspected he was involved in something illegal again, but cattle rustling?

"Now you've gone and ruined everything!" The older man thundered at the younger one called Robbie, but he pointed the barrel of his pistol toward Charlotte in such a flippant manner that Ellie could well imagine it going off accidentally. "I can't leave them tied up here with her recognizing you."

"You couldn't have left them tied up here anyway, just like I couldn't have left the spy behind, not unless you want the law to discover the trail. You think they won't search all over these mountains if three women and a boy go missing?" Robbie shoved Martin toward them.

Martin stumbled over the rocky ground and went sprawling forward.

"Martin, no!" Ellie cried.

Without being able to use his hands to break his fall, his face hit the ground first, sliding against the jagged rocks.

She rushed toward him, tearing the bottom hem of her petticoat to staunch the blood oozing from his jaw and cheek.

"I can't believe you're helping rustlers, Robbie." Charlotte's quivering voice rang out over the arguing men. "How could you?"

"We'll have to abandon this trail and use another now." The first man—Aimes?—used his pistol to point again. "It wouldn't have been that hard had you just stayed hidden."

Ellie dabbed more blood from her brother's face, then bent her head close and whispered. "Are you hurt anywhere else?"

He gave a small shake of his head, but his eyes held a panicked glint.

She looked over her shoulder at where Robbie and Aimes stood arguing. Would they notice if she undid her brother's gag? At least then she could learn how he'd ended up here.

She raised his head just enough to fumble with the knot holding the gag in place and worked her fingers into the tight fabric.

A moment later the material loosened and she pulled it away. "What have you done?"

"It's not what you think. I promise." Martin kept his gaze pinned over her shoulder, watching the men as he spoke in a soft voice. "Robbie asked if I was interested in working a job a few weeks back. Told me I could make good money but I needed to think about it some and make certain I knew how to keep my mouth shut."

"You didn't." The boy had learned nothing from the trouble he'd gotten into last year in Eagle Harbor.

"No. I didn't."

She stilled. "What do you mean?"

Martin winced and shifted on the rough ground, his hands still bound. "I remembered what Sheriff Cummings said back in Eagle Harbor. How if a man ever offers to pay us money for something we shouldn't be doing, we need to say no. But Robbie never told me what he was up to, and I was curious. Figured it was illegal, but I didn't have any proof to take to the sheriff neither. So when we moved to the Westins' ranch, I started following him."

Her brother had done right this time? She wrapped her hand around Martin's bound one and squeezed. "When did you learn he was rustling cattle?"

"About ten seconds before he caught me."

"Best get that rope and tie them up. Be quick about it." Aimes's raised voice cut through Martin's words.

Ellie looked over her shoulder to find Robbie headed toward the rope.

Maybe she should have taken it and tied her friends after all. At least then she could have tried leaving the knots lose enough for Charlotte and Anna Mae to slip free.

"Where'd the women come from?" Robbie scooped up the rope and started toward Charlotte.

"Where do you think?" Aimes spat. "Came to look at the view, they did. But then they noticed the missing cattle and were about to ride back for help. I was going to leave them tied up here, figuring we had time to get across the border, but that was before they recognized—"

"Aimes, Robbie, what's keeping you? We still got a thousand head of cattle to get across the river." Another man rounded the large boulder at the side of the rockface. He swept them over with a single glance, not bothering to slow his pace until he stopped beside Aimes. "Best take them to the canyon and tie them up. We got enough time to get across the border before anyone will find them."

"Won't work." Aimes jutted his chin toward Charlotte. "The lady there knows who he is."

"Not only that, but the pretty one's the sheriff's sister," Robbie gritted.

The new man let out a single, low curse, his gaze lingering on them for longer this time. "Shoot them. Hide the bodies somewhere they won't be found."

Shoot them. The words echoed through Ellie's head. He couldn't kill them. She had siblings to care for and a husband to help—a husband to whom she owed an apology.

"We kill them, and we'll have the law on our tails for months," Aimes growled.

"Better than leaving someone behind to snitch." The newcomer rubbed his jaw, still studying them. "Take them to the canyon first. Easier to shoot them where you plan to hide the…"

Bang!

A gunshot echoed across the barren landscape. Ellie jolted with the sound, then turned to see if Anna Mae or Charlotte had been shot. But the newcomer was the one who stumbled backward. A dark red splotch appeared on his chest, spreading rapidly to cover the top half of his vest and shirt.

The gunshot hadn't come from the rustlers… but from somewhere behind the rocks?

Aimes swung his pistol toward the boulders, and Robbie drew his own pistol from his holster.

Both men fired, one right after the other.

"Run!" Anna Mae shouted as she raced for cover behind the horses.

Ellie reached down to undo the rope around Martin's hands, but before she could loosen it, Aimes snagged her by the shoulder and jerked her up.

A warm circle of metal pressed against her temple.

"Let me go," she rasped.

"Put down your gun and show yourself or I kill the woman," he shouted at the pile of boulders.

Silence.

Ellie swallowed the lump of fear lodged in her throat, but it sprang right back up to choke her. Would Aimes kill her if the shooter failed to appear? No, she couldn't die, not without apologizing to Sam first. *Dear God, please save me. Please give me a chance to make things right with Sam.*

She had no choice but to trust God now.

Movement flickered at the side of the rock, then a man

emerged—a man who stood at too familiar a height, wearing a too familiar hat and bandana.

"Sam!" The breath rushed from her lungs in a giant whoosh.

"Kill him, Robbie." The man holding her shouted, the barrel of his gun still pressed to her temple.

"No!" she screamed.

Another gunshot rang out, but not from Robbie's pistol. The shot had come from somewhere behind her. The man holding her lurched, then fell forward, taking her with him as he crashed to the ground and dropped the gun from his hand. His weight trapped her against the biting, rocky earth, and she lay still, waiting for another gunshot or for the man to roll off of her and press his pistol to her temple once more. But he didn't move, not even an inch. Was he… could he be… dead?

"Robbie, drop the gun and put your hands in the air." Anna Mae's voice echoed through the valley.

Ellie rolled, shifting part of Aimes's weight off her and twisting herself enough to see lifeless brown eyes staring back at her and a gaping wound at the back of his head. She wriggled out from beneath the rest of him. A quick scan of the area told her Anna Mae stood behind her horse with her rifle trained on Robbie.

Ellie clambered to her feet and raced to Sam.

"Ellie." His voice cracked on her name, and he swept her up, his arms so tight they nearly crushed the breath from her lungs. "Are you all right? Did you get shot? Did he hurt you in any way?"

"I'm fine. And you? Are you all right?"

"I'm not hurt, just terrified." He crushed her even harder against him, then sucked in a shaky breath. "I could have picked them all off from behind the rock, but then he grabbed you, and I thought…"

He pressed his forehead to hers, his eyes falling closed.

"I felt the same when you emerged from behind that rock." She still hadn't stopped trembling from the horror of seeing a gun pointed at the man she loved, of hearing Aimes tell Robbie to shoot him.

"I'm so glad you're safe," she whispered against his neck. "And I'm so sorry about the children. Forgive me? Please? I should have talked to you. I should have treated you as my husband. Instead I did what seemed right to me without asking you, without even praying to God. It seemed like the only choice, but I was so terribly wrong to make it on my own."

"I forgive you." He stroked a strand of hair away from her face and tucked it behind her ear. "Just don't do it again, all right? I deserve to be talked to first. And there's no way I'm letting you send the children away, not even if keeping them puts us in the poorhouse. We're a family now, all of us."

"But Sam…"

He put a finger over her mouth. "Don't. God's already making provision for all of us to stay together. Wes offered me my old foreman job back. It comes with a house, not a big one, but he says we can add on to it. The house plus the pay will be enough to get by on until we can get my land back."

His old foreman job. Tears filled her eyes. Yes, she'd been far too quick to doubt God's goodness. He'd clearly had everything worked out.

"I love you." She tightened her grip around Sam's back and pressed her face into his chest. "Love you, but don't deserve you."

"Hey, love birds," Anna Mae's voice echoed off the rockface. "Not to interrupt or anything, but we've got a man who needs to be hauled away, two bodies to bury, and a sheriff to find."

Right, of course. They had work to do and questions needing answers, like what Sam was even doing here when he'd said he was going to check his land.

She sniffled and tried to pull away from Sam, but he still held her tight.

"Give me another minute," he whispered. "I've got a fierce need to hold you right about now."

She flung her arms back around him and nestled her head in the crook of his neck. "That's fine with me."

And it was.

Chapter Twenty-One

A dim lamp flickered against the wall of the windowless storage closet crammed with brooms, buckets, rags, a mop, and spare handcuffs. Daniel scooted his chair closer to Robbie Ashton's and glowered at the young man who sat with both wrists handcuffed behind his back.

Outside the thin wooden door, scuffling, shouts, and an occasional curse sounded as his deputies took down the names and descriptions of the rustlers they'd captured and led the men to their jailcells.

"Tell me about the man in charge of this rustling ring." Usually he questioned suspects in the office, but when other men filled it, he'd little choice but to use the sweltering storage closet, much as his pa had done before him.

Robbie sat with his shoulders slumped and head down, but he stayed just as silent as the three men questioned before him. Seemed no one wanted to share anything about their leader.

"What does he look like?" Daniel tried again.

"Like a man," Robbie muttered, his head still down.

"Black hair? Brown? Gray?"

Again, nothing. Just like he'd gleaned no information from the other rustlers. Daniel bit back a growl. "Is he Mexican or American?"

"I'm not saying nothing about the boss, all right? If I do, and you go lock me in one of those cells with everyone else, I'll be dead come morning." Robbie jutted his chin toward the door. "Besides, you're asking the wrong person. I never even talked to him. I glimpsed him maybe twice in my whole time working for him, and that was from a distance. If you wanted to know more, you should have asked Saul before Sam shot him. He knew the boss best, and he would have been the first one to kill me for snitching."

"So Saul had killed before on order from your boss?" Saul must be one of the two dead men Sam and Anna Mae had brought into town earlier.

"I'm not saying nothing."

Of course he wasn't. Daniel sighed and raked a hand through his hair. First he had rustlers set up an operation under his nose. Then when he'd learned of them and gathered a posse to chase them down in Mexico, he'd only managed to catch a handful of the rustlers and a few hundred head of cattle. And finally, once he got the rustlers to the jail, every one of them refused to talk.

He may have caught half a dozen men that morning, but he still had no clue where in Mexico the massive rustling operation was based, who was behind it, how many rustlers were involved, and how many cattle had been stolen over the past few years.

Sweat beaded along his forehead, and a drop rolled down his temple. The closet was always sweltering, but on a summer day like this one, the heat became nearly unbearable. He shifted in his chair, but his shoulder bumped the broom leaning against the wall, which crashed onto his lap. He righted the broom and blew out a breath, narrowing his eyes at Robbie once more.

"Explain how Sam Owens's land is connected to the rustling." Perhaps he could still glean useful information, even if the man wouldn't answer questions about his boss.

A hint of shame crossed the younger man's face, there and gone in an instant, but the man still kept his mouth clamped shut.

"The other men I questioned might not be willing to tell me about their boss, but they've told me everything I wanted to know about you." That was the only information he'd been able to get out of all three of them, but Robbie didn't need to know that. "You've been working with the rustlers for about nine months, which means your complicity helped move at least ten thousand cattle over the border."

Daniel tapped the end of his pencil against Robbie's knee and lowered his voice. "You're looking at a hanging offence, even if you weren't the one rounding up the cattle north of here." The words rumbled out from a place deep inside him, a place that ached. This was Wes's brother-in-law, and he was so young to be tangled up with rustlers. But every word he spoke was true. A jury might well rule that Robbie and the rest of the rustlers should all swing from the end of a noose. "If you have any useful information, you best start sharing it."

"Hanging?" Robbie's voice squeaked and worry knit the young man's brow. "It can't be bad as that. My ma needs me."

"Then cooperate."

"The land always belonged to Sam Owens." Robbie grimaced. "The railroad never owned it, but when the boss realized someone wanted to try ranching Mr. Grigg's tract of land, he was worried about the hidden trail being discovered and he wanted something done."

The answer made sense. The trail had been too well used for the cattle to have come solely from Twin Rivers County, especially not when there'd barely been any reports of rustling over the past few years. If he had to guess, he'd say the trail at the edge of Sam's property had seen fifteen to twenty thousand head of cattle on it during the past twelve months.

"Where are the rustled cattle coming from?" Daniel positioned his pencil over his paper pad.

"Not any one place in particular. You target a specific place too heavily, and the Rangers will be called in."

That explained how the ring had been able to move so many cattle over the border while evading detection. If only he had found the trail last year, or even the year before that, numerous ranchers to their north would all still have their cattle. "Where have you personally rustled cattle from?"

"The A Bar W was the first."

Daniel narrowed his eyes.

"I'm telling the truth." Robbie fidgeted in his chair, though the handcuffs behind his back prevented him from moving overmuch. "I signed on last fall to help drive the cattle across the border, but I never stole them off a rancher's land before the Westins."

"No?"

"No."

He might be half-crazy to believe the likes of Robbie Ashton, but the man's wary gaze held the truth of his statement. Every rustler got his start somewhere, and it made sense that Robbie would start close to him, with a ranch he already had access to and a family that wouldn't look at him suspiciously. "You sure you don't want to tell me more about your boss?"

Robbie hung his head. "A judge might hang me, but hanging would be right merciful compared to what would happen if I told."

"Then tell me where you were driving the cattle to in Mexico."

"Not saying that either."

Despite the heavy heat, a chill skittered down Daniel's spine. He might not know this boss character's name, but if the man could inspire this kind of fear from a jailed man in a different country, then this boss was obviously violent and powerful. "Any other information you want to tell me? Keep in mind that cooperating now could lead to a lighter sentence."

"Um..." Robbie tilted his face up to the ceiling for a moment. "Boss paid the judge to rule in his favor. You know, when Sam Owens took the railroad to court?"

He'd figured as much when Robbie had told him about the false deed, but he scrawled the information down for Robbie to sign later.

"What about Charlotte Westin? You and her were close. Did she know about the rustling?" He knew the answer before Robbie gave it. No way had Charlotte understood what Robbie was up to. But if Robbie had been involved in rustling the whole time he'd been working for the Westins, then why had he been pursuing Charlotte?

Robbie rolled his eyes. "She didn't have a clue. That was the way it was supposed to be."

"And the day I caught you kissing behind my office?" He couldn't stop the words from falling out, nor could he keep the low growl from his voice. Never mind those kisses would have nothing to do with the rustling.

"Look, I don't even like her. She doesn't gussy herself up, and she only ever wants to talk about her horses or the ranch. Most men like a woman who wears a few ruffles and bothers to put on perfume. I swear she uses the same soap as her brother and pa. Smells like a man.

"But she needed to be distracted somehow." Robbie tried to shift in the cramped space, but only ended up banging his knee against the metal mop bucket. "She does a better job roaming the land than any of the cowhands, and she knows that ranch like the back of her hand. If anyone was going to notice me pulling fifty cattle from someplace one day and fifty more from somewhere else the next, she would. When Charlotte and I made plans to meet up, I'd always ask her to ride somewhere away from where I'd been rustling."

Daniel's hand involuntarily fisted around the pencil he held. "How many times?"

"What do you mean?" Robbie frowned at him.

"How many times did you meet her?"

"How should I know? However many times it took. I was going to have to change things though. The crazy woman was talking marriage. As if I could marry her without her pa coming back and killing me."

Oh, Charlotte. She was going to be heartbroken, again. Not that she'd bother to confide in him.

"I hope she learned her lesson." Daniel muttered the words to himself, but Robbie snorted.

"Probably not. She's bound and determine to marry before her pa can pick her husband."

Daniel glared at the criminal in front of him.

Robbie's lips curled. "I know you're sitting there thinking all sorts of terrible things about me for joining the rustlers, but I needed the money last fall. You have no idea how poorly my step-pa treats my ma, and how good he is at wasting money."

"That still doesn't absolve you for stealing cattle." Daniel rose from his chair and grabbed Robbie by the shoulder, hefting him up. Wes was probably devastated knowing his own brother-in-law had been stealing from him. And Abigail'd roll over in her grave if she knew.

Daniel opened the door to the closet and shoved Robbie out in front of him. "Perkins, show him to a cell."

The deputy standing at the coffee kettle looked up, then set his mug down and came toward them.

"My pleasure, Sheriff." Perkins grabbed Robbie by the shoulder and led him toward the door to the jailhouse.

Daniel drew in a breath of cooler, fresher air, but rather than step into his office, he closed the closet door again. He would have sat in his chair, but the tip of his boot hit the mop bucket, which crashed into the mop, causing both of them to fall onto the chair Robbie had vacated.

Figured. He pressed his lips together and smacked the broom leaning against the opposite wall. It fell, knocking into the rack that held the spare handcuffs. Both tumbled to the ground, and handcuffs clattered against the floor. He gave the mop bucket a kick for good measure.

"Sheriff?" A knock sounded on the door. "You okay in there?"

"Dandy," he called. "Just dandy."

He slumped onto his chair.

A massive smuggling operation in his backyard, and not one that had just started, but that had been going on for years. How many thousands of cattle had been driven down that trail and sold in Mexico? Twenty thousand? Thirty? Fifty?

How could he not have known?

But the rustlers had never shown themselves in town. They never had any contact with anyone in Twin Rivers until they'd shown up on Sam's property. Robbie Ashton had been the exception, but being a local, no one suspected a man who had grown up in Twin Rivers and sat in the second church pew on the left every Sunday to be aiding a rustling operation.

Daniel buried his face in his hands. He had to notify the Texas Rangers. They'd sent men to Twin Rivers before, and that was when only a few thousand head of cattle were being rustled over the border. For an operation this large, half the Rangers in Texas just might be called in.

But last time the Rangers had been in town…

Memories rose up. A dark night, a wild chase through the Mexican desert, a triumphant return to town with fifteen hundred head of cattle and seven rustlers in tow.

He'd strode through the door of the sheriff's office, a smile on his face, ready to tell his pa about the chase and declare his intention to join the Rangers. But the smile dropped from his lips at the sight of his father lying unconscious on a makeshift table while the doctor amputated his leg.

Daniel blew out a long breath, but his action didn't stop the face of one of his childhood friends from flashing through his mind, or the sting of his betrayal, or the pointless words of apology his friend had tried offering for abandoning his order to guard the town.

The entirety of the Texas Rangers could come to Twin Rivers and track the rustlers for all he cared—as long as Cain Ramos stayed away.

~.~.~.~.~

"Come on, Long Arrow. Giddyap." Sam dug his heels into Long Arrow's side, but his efforts did little to convince the animal to pull ahead of the other horses and their riders trotting to the A Bar W. Not that he could blame the beast. After tracking two hundred cattle through the Mexican desert, surrounding the five rustlers driving them, and hauling both the cattle and the men back to Twin Rivers, he was ready for a hot bath and a long nap, and his horse needed water, food, and a good brush down.

He pulled out his pocket watch. Three-thirty in the afternoon, yet he felt like it was eleven at night. Maybe once he got back to the Westins', he'd crawl into bed and not wake up until morning.

But he'd see Ellie first. See her, wrap his arms around her, and hold her so tightly he'd be able to feel her heart beating against his.

"What're you grinning about?" Wes asked from beside him.

Sam glanced at his friend, who rode at the front of the group of cowhands. Every able-bodied man on the A Bar W had ridden out with Daniel's posse that morning.

"Ain't it obvious? He's got himself a pretty woman back at home," Dobbs called.

A chorus of guffaws erupted.

"Y'all are just jealous." But heat filled in his cheeks nonetheless.

The familiar gateposts of the A Bar W rose ahead, and higher up on the mountain, the hacienda-style house sat like a sentinel guarding the valley.

Sam dug his heels into Long Arrow again, and the beast must have found a final bit of energy, because this time he moved into a brisk trot, and they pulled ahead of the others.

"You look like you got into a fight with a dust devil," one of the men shouted. "She won't want anything to do with you."

Sam looked down. The cowhand was right. Maybe he should bathe before he sought Ellie out. He ducked his head closer to Long Arrow's neck and spurred the stallion forward over the terrain until he galloped into the yard well ahead of the others.

"You're back!" Ellie's voice sounded from the direction of the terrace, then a flurry of red hair and yellow gingham raced toward him.

He swung off Long Arrow just in time to catch her around the waist and heft her up, spinning her in a circle while she clung to his neck.

"Are you all right? Were there any more gunfights? Was anyone else injured?" She pushed back from him far enough to peer into his eyes, then threw her arms around his neck again and buried her face in its crook. "I was so worried."

So much for her not wanting anything to do with him until he cleaned up.

"Hey look, Sam's back." Suzanna's voice echoed over the desert, followed by more shouts.

He barely had time to set Ellie on her feet before eight young'uns surrounded them.

Joe tugged on his shirt. "Did you shoot some bad guys?"

"Did you get the cattle back?"

"Did you get to shoot your gun?"

"Did you kill anyone?"

The questions came faster than he could answer.

"I'll take care of Long Arrow." Leroy grabbed the horse's reins. "Looks like he needs a good brush down."

"And food and water." Sam hefted Joe into his arms.

"Up. Up." Lynnette reached for Ellie while trying to climb out of Suzanna's arms.

The rest of the men rode into the yard, stirring up a cloud of dust so thick the children all ducked their heads until it faded.

Sam slung his arm around Ellie's waist and tugged her into his side, each of them still balancing a child on the opposite hip. Just like a regular family. He grinned at the men.

"You got yourself some woman, Owens." Dobbs let out a hoot.

Wes jumped off his horse and rolled his eyes, but a smile tilted the edges of his mouth.

"Mr. Westin, did you catch the rustlers?" Christopher raced up to Wes with Henry on his heels. "Did they have guns?"

More voices filled the yard. Voices, people, horses, and utter chaos. He gave Joe a squeeze, then set him down and leaned closer to Ellie. "Give Lynnette to Suzanna. I want to talk to you. Alone."

Ellie frowned up at him. "Is something wrong? Did Wes change his mind about hiring you as foreman?" She handed Lynnette to Suzanna.

"Not that, no. I just want to… talk." He paused for a moment. Him, wanting to talk. Who'd have ever guessed he'd say such a thing?

But the words burned inside of him, hot and sincere and needing to be spilled out so that his wife knew the whole of what had happened earlier, of how he'd almost failed her.

No one noticed as he grabbed Ellie's hand and they slipped away to the terrace on the side of the house.

As soon as they rounded the corner, Ellie turned and clung to him, burying her face in the fabric of his dusty vest.

"Don't cry, love. All is well." He stroked a hand down her back.

"You don't understand. Watching you ride out with Daniel and Wes and the posse earlier was one of the most difficult things I've ever done, especially after you almost got shot this morning. But I trusted God's goodness this time. Truly I did." She squeezed him tighter and rested the side of her head against his shirt. "And here He brought you back to me, safe and sound."

He smoothed a wayward strand of hair from her face, then dropped his hold from around her and looked out over the desert.

"Sam? What's wrong?"

He pressed his eyes shut. How did he explain how close he'd come to failing her earlier? The fear of nearly losing her to his own mistake?

"Is it something with the rustlers? I thought you said you caught them."

He opened his eyes. "Not all of them. There will be more work to do. Daniel thinks Austin will send a team of Rangers down to figure out where their camp is."

"Is that what has you troubled?"

"No, though Daniel didn't look too happy about notifying the Rangers." Considering what had happened to his pa the last time Rangers were in town, Sam couldn't blame the man.

"Then what?" The small patch of skin between her eyebrows creased with concern.

He forced out a breath and drew her back into his arms. How did he explain the fear that had coursed through him when Aimes had grabbed Ellie and pressed his pistol to her head? The certainty in his gut that he was about to watch his wife be murdered? The helpless feeling that carved a hole in his chest when he'd set his rifle down and had come around the side of the boulder weaponless? He'd thought sure they'd all end up dead. Then who would have been left to care for the children?

"I almost didn't turn around." His jaw trembled as he spoke the words.

"What?" She blinked up at him.

"When I spotted the trail on my property and could tell cattle had been through less than an hour ago, I wanted to ride straight for the border to see if I could stop the rustlers from driving the cattle into Mexico."

"Sam, no." She reached up and placed a hand on his cheek. "There were too many men for you to go alone. They'd have killed you on the spot."

"I know that now, but my first thought was to try keeping the cattle on this side of the border."

"What changed your mind?"

"That verse about two being better than one. It doesn't apply just to husbands and wives, you know, but to friends. I had no idea you, Charlotte, and Anna Mae were out riding, or that you'd stumbled upon rustlers. But had I not listed to the disquiet inside me, had I kept riding for the border instead of turning around, you might all be..." He couldn't bear to speak the words aloud.

He'd left the ranch house that morning mad that Ellie had made a decision about her siblings without him. But who was he to judge her when he'd been near to making a decision on his own that would have cost the lives of four other people?

"But you did turn around." Ellie slipped her fingers into his. "I don't deserve a man like you, Samuel Owens."

"I wouldn't say that. I'm the one that's undeserving of the spouse God gave me."

She squeezed his hand, a grin splaying across her mouth. "All right, we'll call it a tie and say neither of us deserves the other."

"Things will be different from here on out. We're going to decide everything together, the two of us. We'll sit and talk every evening and share what's happened in our day. We'll make ourselves into the best family West Texas has ever seen, I don't care where we end up living or what I do for work."

She pressed up onto her tiptoes and kissed him, letting her lips linger on his. She tasted sweet. Of hopes and dreams and a bright future. She tilted her head to deepen the kiss and laced her arms around his neck, bringing herself flush against him.

When had his wife become such a good kisser? Her actions were almost enough to drive every other thought from his head. He could stand here kissing her until the sun went down. Or better yet, pull her into the bedroom, lock the door, and stay with her until morning.

Except he needed to do something else first. Groaning, he pulled away.

She let out her own moan and opened her eyes halfway, then tried following his lips with hers.

Rather than take her back into his arms, he slid the watch from his pocket and glanced at it. "Come on. We've still got time to make it into town."

"Town?" She stared up at him through glassy eyes. "For what?"

"To fill out adoption papers."

"For my siblings?" The glaze left her eyes, and wide green circles gazed back at him. "You really want to? We don't have the land back yet, and adoption is awful permanent."

"We're a family, you, me, and the whole pile of young'uns you brought with you, for richer or for poorer, for better or for worse." He took her hand and laced their fingers together. "I don't want anyone to question that in the future."

"I love you, Samuel Owens."

This time when she spoke the words, a sense of peace and warmth rushed through him. His wife loved him, the little orphan boy that no one was supposed to love.

"I love you too." He leaned in and brushed his lips against hers for the briefest of moments, then still holding her hand, he started for the barn.

"Where are you two lovebirds headed?" A familiar male voice called from behind them.

Sam turned to find Daniel striding across the terrace. Weary lines rimmed his mouth, and shadows haunted the space beneath his eyes.

"I have something for you." Daniel held out a small stack of official-looking papers.

Sam bit back a groan. Had something else gone wrong?

"Well? Aren't you going to take them?" Daniel raised an eyebrow.

"What are they?" Sam reached for the papers.

"A copy of Robbie Ashton's signed confession. You'll find the first paragraph on the second page rather interesting."

Sam moved the first page to the back of the stack and held the second page low enough for Ellie to read it with him. She sucked in a sharp breath a moment before he jerked his head up.

"They admit the deed was fake? That easily?" Hope unfurled in his chest.

"That easily." Daniel hooked a thumb on his gun belt. "Seems the whole reason they wanted your land was because their secret trail ran along the back section of it. Since you intended to run a ranch rather than leave the land be like Griggs did, they figured you'd find the trail."

Sam looked out over the desert in the direction of the trail he'd found that morning. "It'll be a decade before I have enough cattle to start using the far east tract, especially considering how rugged it is.

Probably won't ever be able to graze cattle where some sections of the trail run."

"Seems like the brains behind the rustling ring didn't want to take any chances."

"It says here that this boss character paid off Judge Grenville?" Ellie pointed to the middle of the page.

"I already sent a deputy over to Brewster County. By this time tomorrow, I should have a warrant to look into Judge Grenville's bank record to verify the payment."

"So this means I'm getting my land back." Sam tightened his grip on the papers until they crinkled.

"You'll have to wait until the rustlers have their trials for everything to be official, but yes." Daniel slapped him on the back, a grin splitting the serious lines of his face. "You're getting your land back."

His feet rooted to the ground as he stared at his friend. He couldn't have gotten his land back without Daniel's work today, and he and Ellie never could have gone to Austin to visit Harrison without Wes and Charlotte watching the children.

And he wouldn't have gotten the family he'd always wanted if Ellie hadn't brought the children with her.

He'd started off his ranching endeavors certain he could handle everything on his own. But the truth was, he'd needed help, and not just a little of it. God might not have given him a ma and pa to raise him as a boy, but maybe God had given him something just as good. God had given him people who loved him and cared for him and helped him. God had given him everything he needed to succeed.

A slow smile spread across his lips, then he reached down and grabbed Ellie, picking her up to spin in the air. She squealed and wrapped her arms about his neck, and he drew in the feminine scent of her.

Yes, God had given him everything he needed to succeed—and every last one of his dreams.

Epilogue

Nine Months Later

"Ellie, come quick."

From her position at the table, Ellie looked over her shoulder at where Henry stood in the door of the house, bouncing up and down on his toes.

"What's happened?" She set down the whisk she'd been using to make custard and wiped her hands on her apron.

"It's a calf, a little bitty one that was just born. Sam says we get to keep it in the barn and feed it with a bottle!"

"Just a minute. I need to check on Madeline and then I can go out." She padded over to her and Sam's bedroom and peered into the cradle. Something low and soft tugged at her heart, much as it did every time she looked at the babe. Her own child. Sam's own child. Not even a week old. And much as she expected, the tiny bundle she'd put to rest a half hour ago still slept nestled in her swaddling.

"Ellie, are you coming?"

Coming? She looked back at the door and rubbed a hand over her breastbone.

"Yes, of course." She left the room and followed Henry out of the house and across the familiar yard.

She and Sam owned a little less land now than they had when she'd arrived last May. In July, after Sam had been declared rightful owner of the ranch, they'd sold two thousand acres to the Westins, which had given the A Bar W some permanent water rights. They'd also signed another contract to let the Westins graze cattle on their property for three years, and the barbwire fences on the north boundary had come down.

The result had meant more money for Sam to purchase cattle last fall, and more money in the bank in case unexpected expenses arose—like the midwife's bill for Madeline's birth.

Ellie reached the barn only to find every last one of her siblings crowded around a single stall.

"What's going on?" She rested a hand on Janey's back and peered over the seven-year-old's shoulder. "Henry said we need to bottle feed one of the calves?"

"What are you doing out here?" Sam left the center of the stall and shouldered past Christopher and Suzanna before stopping next to her. "You should be resting."

She shook her head. His concern was sweet, truly, even if it felt a bit stifling at times. "I won't shatter if I come outside for a few minutes."

He twisted his lips together and scratched the back of his head. "Pretty sure I heard someone say a woman should spend a week abed after giving birth."

"Birthing is a natural process. It doesn't automatically turn me into an invalid."

"It's also dangerous."

She couldn't blame him for the concern etched across his face, not considering her own mother had never recovered after birthing Lynnette, and Abigail had died birthing Wes a stillborn daughter.

"A few minutes outside won't hurt me." She pushed up on her

tiptoes and planted a soft kiss on his cheek. "But thank you for caring so much."

He bent his head until their foreheads touched. "If anything happened to you, Ellie, I'd be lost."

"Aw, come on." Christopher's voice rang through the barn. "No more kissing."

"You two kiss enough for the entire town." That from Suzanna.

Sam pulled back and turned to face the others. "I didn't kiss your sister, but from the sound of things, maybe I should."

"No!" The children shouted in near unison.

"Tell me about this calf, love." Ellie squeezed his hand.

"Step aside for your sister." Sam gave Christopher a little nudge, and the rest of the children parted. With her hand still in his, Sam led her into the stall, where a tiny newborn calf lay curled on the straw. Martin sat beside it, feeding it milk from a large glass bottle.

That soft, familiar sensation pulled at her heart again. If only she had a way to freeze this moment in time and capture it, savor it for future years.

Leroy crouched nearby, eyes alert as he took in every last detail about the creature. As soon as he'd learned Sam could keep his land, Leroy declared that he would be staying in Twin Rivers. The obvious love that she and Sam felt for each other, and shortly afterward, the news that she was with child had probably aided in his decision to stay. Wes kept trying to steal him away, offering to pay him a ranch hand's salary if he'd work on the A Bar W. But Leroy had declared more than once that he wanted be with his family.

Ellie sat, her legs curled beneath her, and stroked a hand over the calf's slender back before looking up at Sam. "Where is the mother?"

"She doesn't want him."

"She doesn't…? But how could…?" She pressed a hand to her breastbone again. "What kind of mother abandons its child?"

"This is the mother's first calf, and it was a long birth. The calf was breach and needed to be pulled out. Martin found her riding rounds this morning. I don't know how long she'd been in labor before that."

"I still don't understand."

Sam came over and helped her back to her feet. "Cows aren't like people, darlin'. If a mama cow has a hard time with a birth, she might decide she wants nothing to do with her calf. This is especially true the first time a cow gives birth."

"Will the calf be all right?"

"It should be fine. We'll keep it in the barn and bottle feed it until it's old enough to be weaned."

"Can I feed the cow next time?" Suzanna burst out.

"We should give it a name." Leroy studied the calf from his position in the straw.

"How about Murphy?" That from Joe.

"It's a girl, you dolt." Suzanna scowled at her brother. "I like Lena."

Ellie watched the calf, so tender and fragile as it lay curled in the straw. Yet the animal licking greedily from the bottle Martin held possessed a certain strength. "What about Hope?"

"Hope?" Sam twined his fingers with hers.

"Yes. She could have ended up dead, but now she has a second chance. We'll have to feed her for a bit, but she'll eventually become like all the other cows and go on to bear her own calves, never mind that she had a difficult start."

"Ellie." Sam shifted closer and stared down into her eyes, the heat of his breath brushing her face. "Are you still talking about the calf?"

"Yes. No. Oh, I don't know. I'm just a mess right now." She sniffled, moisture springing to her eyes. Why was she crying, and over a cow, no less?

She didn't know, and evidently neither did Sam, because he pulled away and scratched the side of his head.

"Don't mind her none," Christopher muttered. "Ma always cried a lot right after she had a baby."

"She did?"

"I'm sorry." Ellie used her palm to swipe at her cheek. "I don't know what's gotten into me. It's just seeing this baby calf have another chance, it's like us and the ranch."

He gave her a lopsided grin, and his shoulders shook with a silent laugh. "We are not like a baby calf, darlin'. But we are blessed. We're here, together, on our own ranch, watching both our herd of cattle and our family grow by the day. What more could a man ask for?"

Blessed, that was the perfect word. She sniffled back the last of her tears and leaned against him. At this time a year ago, she'd been full of confusion and worry as she'd left Eagle Harbor to marry a man she'd never met. So many things could have gone wrong. And at first, many things did go wrong. But with God's help, she and Sam had righted them.

Two are better than one, and a threefold cord is not quickly broken. Sam was right, a person couldn't ask for more than what God had already given them.

Want to read more Texas Promise books?

Don't miss Daniel Harding and Charlotte Westin's story in Tomorrow's Shining Dream.
Keep reading for a sneak peek on the next page...

To be notified when *Tomorrow's Shining Dream* releases sign up for my author newsletter.
http://geni.us/AqsHv

Tomorrow's Shining Dream

Chapter One

How hard could attracting a man's attention be?

From her position against the wall, Charlotte Westin looked across her family's crowded ballroom toward the punch table. Three men stood there in suits: her father, his friend Charles Mortimer, and Mr. Mortimer's son, Andrew—the man her father wanted her to marry.

If only she could get him to look at her.

At the moment, a beautiful woman in a creamy lace dress had latched herself onto Andrew Mortimer's arm and leaned close to the circle of men, a wide smile on her face.

Charlotte didn't need to hear the woman's laugh from across the ballroom to know how it would sound. Light, tinkling, perfect. Just like the laughs of all the other unmarried women who had come to visit her family's ranch these past two weeks.

The woman probably didn't have a splotch of punch on her dress from earlier in the evening either, or mud around the white lace at her hem.

Tomorrow. Charlotte sucked in a breath through her nose, then blew it out through her mouth. This would all be over tomorrow.

For two weeks every July, her father opened their ranch to his wealthy friends and business associates who wanted to come and visit.

And people came in droves. It seemed everyone wanted to see the expansive A Bar W cattle ranch at least once in their lifetime, and a good number of those first-time guests then decided to return every year. People usually started arriving just before Independence Day, turning their mostly empty hacienda into something that felt more like an overstuffed hotel than a home.

But on the morning of July 15, everyone started to leave, and by this time tomorrow, the house would be back to normal, blissfully empty but for her, Pa, and her brother, Wes.

She just had to survive tonight's ball first.

Charlotte sighed and leaned her head back against the piece of marble wall she'd claimed for the past quarter hour. She should try going over to the table and presenting herself to Andrew Mortimer again. Surely her father and his friend could manage to reintroduce her to the man they both thought she should marry.

But once the introductions had been made again, what would she say? She couldn't exactly ask him to dance, ask him if he wanted punch, or ask him if he needed any of the other half dozen practical things skittering through her mind. Men were supposed to ask women those questions, not the other way around. And he'd asked her none of those since the ball started two hours ago—hadn't even smiled at her once.

Charlotte pushed herself off the wall, her shoulders slumped. She needed to go over there and at least try to… well, she didn't know. Keep her father happy, she supposed. Now if only she could think of something worthwhile to say on her way across the room.

Maybe some of her trouble was because Andrew had only arrived last night, and if she understood right, his stop at the A Bar W was a brief rest before he and his father both continued on to El Paso for business negotiations. She'd met him that morning but hadn't had time to go riding with him or show him the ranch or do anything else that might tell her whether he enjoyed normal, everyday things like the feel of a horse flying over the desert or the wet nose of a calf nuzzling his cheek. Because if he always walked around with perfect posture and wearing an impeccable suit, how could she—?

"Is something wrong?"

At the sound of the rich masculine voice, her entire body went stiff. She dragged her gaze away from the punch table to find herself staring at Twin Rivers's sheriff, Daniel Harding.

She slammed her eyes shut. Why would Daniel bother talking to her here? They may have known each other their entire lives, and he might also be her best friend's older brother, but he was also the only person in town who knew how badly she'd failed her family.

She kept her eyelids pressed firmly together. Maybe if she ignored him long enough, he'd disappear back into the crowd.

"Charlotte?"

The question in his voice told her he wasn't about to move away. In fact, he stepped nearer, and somehow she hadn't needed to open her eyes to know that, which was rather alarming. How could she sense his presence without even looking at him?

"You look pale. Is there something I can help with?"

He could help by leaving her alone and never talking to her again so her shame could fade away with time—which couldn't happen if he kept showing up, reminding her of what she'd done. Either that, or he could forget everything that had happened this spring.

She huffed out a breath and opened her eyes. "I'm fine, thank you. I think there's a woman over by the hors d'oeuvre table waiting to dance with you."

A lie, but she'd use it if it meant he'd leave her alone.

He didn't even look over his shoulder. Instead he took another step nearer, bringing him close enough she could see the dark ring of blue that rimmed the lighter blue in his eyes. "Did you see something suspicious while you were out riding the ranch today? Did rustler's take more cattle? Have you found sign of where they might be camping?"

She blew out a breath. At least he was asking about the ranch and not interrogating her about Robbie Ashton. But did the man realize how formidable he could be when he narrowed his eyes and started spouting official-sounding questions?

"You two should dance."

Charlotte whipped her head around to find her brother, Wes, had come up beside them. He stood as uncomfortably stiff in his tuxedo as she did in her yards of billowing green silk. But unlike her, he hadn't spent most of his evening standing against the wall avoiding marriage prospects. She'd seen him earlier with no less than three women.

Wes tilted his head toward her. "Go on, Charlie. I haven't seen you out on the dance floor once tonight."

Not with Daniel. Anyone but him.

"Actually, I need to get back to town." Daniel pulled his timepiece from the pocket in his vest and checked the time. "Someone still needs to make rounds even though we're down two deputies."

Wes shoved him in the shoulder and gave his head a small shake. "You're just as bad as Charlie. I only saw you on the floor once, and that was with your sister, so it doesn't count."

Daniel glanced over his shoulder at the couples floating to the music. "Someone needs to save Anna Mae from the vultures, at least I did for one dance."

Indeed, Anna Mae Harding was just finishing up a dance with a banker's son from Austin, a wide smile spread across her face. Two other men stood at the edge of the dance floor, both watching Anna Mae as though they expected to dance with her next.

Charlotte sighed. How did Anna Mae make all this business with men and dancing seem so easy?

"Well, are you going to dance?" Wes placed his palm in the small of her back and gave her a gentle push forward.

No. Her mind screamed the word, but what excuse could she give without Wes growing suspicious? Her brother didn't have the first clue what had happened between her and Robbie Ashton, but if he realized Daniel knew something, Wes would wring the truth from him in under a minute. Besides, maybe if she could control her nerves enough to dance with Daniel, she'd be able to control her nerves later when she danced with Andrew.

Provided she could get Andrew to ask for a dance in the first place.

A quick glance over her shoulder told her that Andrew had left the punch table and was now surrounded by three—no wait, four—women in sparkling jewels and shimmering ball gowns. Two of them looked suspiciously familiar, as though they may have spent the past hour bothering Wes.

"Reckon I've got time for one dance." Daniel took her arm and threaded it through his. "Then I really have to leave."

She was well and truly trapped. She had no way of ducking out of the dance without causing a scene. She straightened her shoulders and raised her chin. Oh well. If she could survive visiting the man who'd once said he'd loved her while he sat behind bars after being caught rustling cattle from her family, then she could survive a dance with Daniel Harding.

They reached the floor just as the music started, but rather than place his hand at her waist, Daniel studied her for a moment, his clear blue eyes traveling down her dress before settling back on her face. "Are you sure nothing's wrong?"

Other than the fact her family had lost three thousand head of cattle because she'd naively fallen for a pair of warm brown eyes and a promise of unending love? Other than the fact Daniel knew everything that had happened and could tell her family at any moment?

Or maybe Daniel was referring to how she was trussed up in some fancy silk creation that made it difficult to move without tripping.

"I already told you, I'm fine." She placed one hand on his broad shoulder, then nearly pulled her hand away at the contact. A warm sensation travelled up her arm, followed by an even warmer feeling that bloomed on her cheeks.

Daniel grabbed her other hand in his. Thank goodness she was wearing her long white gloves, so she didn't have to endure the feeling of his skin against hers.

He settled his palm on her back, splaying it against her ribs. She suddenly wished she was standing by the punch table with her father, if for no other reason than to ease the dryness that had just climbed into her throat.

The quartet played the opening bars of music, and she forced a breath out of a chest that felt too tight to hold air. What was wrong with her? Their position was perfectly normal for a waltz, so why did her skin burn beneath the patch of her dress that Daniel touched?

It had to be shame, pure and simple.

Her muscles stretched tighter than the barbed wire lining parts of the A Bar W as Daniel moved her in time to the music, her chest rising and falling in quick, strained breaths.

She pressed her eyes shut. *Just pretend the room is nearly empty. Pretend you're dancing with Wes while Anna Mae plays the piano. Pretend…*

But she couldn't pretend anything with the way the scents of sunshine and leather and wind twined around her, so different from the warring aromas of perfume and cologne that everyone else had seemingly doused themselves in for the ball.

She stepped on something large and lumpy.

The lump jerked away from her, and Daniel sucked in a breath.

She opened her eyes. "I'm sorry," she breathed, her stomach cramping. "I didn't mean to step on your foot."

Oh, why had she let Wes prod her into this?

Daniel gave her a weak smile. "My foot will recover."

He moved her in step to the triple-time music, one, two, three; one, two three; one, two three. But she still couldn't keep herself from growing stiffer as the dance progressed.

"You can relax, Charlotte. I'm not going to hurt you."

"Why not?" The words exploded from her mouth before she thought to hold them back.

Daniel's brow furrowed, a V appearing between his eyebrows, and his steps slowed. "I don't understand. Do you think I'm going to hurt you for some reason?"

She swallowed and glanced away. "Not physically. I just… why haven't you told my family what happened with Robbie Ashton, with the cattle?"

Daniel studied her for a moment, his eyes all blue and intense and sheriff-like. "Reckon that's not my story to share, but I think you should tell them, if you're asking my opinion."

"I'm not." Her body went stiff again, and she stepped on another lump.

Daniel sucked in another breath, a grimace spreading across his face this time, though he still managed to step in time to the music.

"I'm sorry. I don't know why I agreed to this. Truly. I'm a terrible dancer."

"You wouldn't be if you just relaxed."

"But relaxing while dancing is impossible." As was relaxing while being in the presence of Daniel Harding.

Because he knew about Robbie, of course. Not because he smelled like the desert at dawn or looked handsome in a brown three-piece suit with his hair combed to the side rather than hiding beneath his cowboy hat.

Somehow she managed not to step on his foot again as the music slowed, then ended, but she couldn't force her muscles to relax either.

Daniel unclasped her hand and stepped back. "Thank you for the dance. I really do need to get back into town. Do you have a partner for—?"

"A word, Charlotte."

Charlotte turned to find her father had come up beside her, his form lean and sinewy compared to Daniel's wide shoulders and broad chest. He pressed his lips into a displeased line and glowered at Daniel.

"Good evening, Mr. Westin. I was just taking my leave." Daniel dipped his head at her father.

Father let out a short humph.

"Reckon I'll be on my way then." Daniel turned and headed for the door, his strong gait and broad shoulders causing people to naturally move aside for him.

Did he realize the way he commanded a room when he walked into it? That everyone present paid at least a bit of attention to him, even in a room as large and crowded as this?

"Charlotte."

She blinked, then turned back to her father. "What's wrong, Pa?"

Her father caught her newly freed hand and wrapped it over his arm. The hold would look proper and gentlemanly to any onlookers, but no one else could feel the way his hand clamped atop hers like an iron fetter.

He half led, half dragged her down the same path Daniel had followed to the door of the ballroom and down the stairs. But his steps were slower than usual and his breathing a bit labored.

Had he participated in the last dance? She'd thought he'd been at the punch table talking to Mr. Mortimer. Who had he danced with? The Widow Abernathy, perhaps? Or maybe Miss Sims, a wealthy spinster only a few years younger than her father?

"Where are we going?" she asked when they reached the bottom of the stairs.

"Somewhere we won't be overheard." He steered her toward his office. She stepped through the door into the cool darkness of the adobe room.

Her father lit the lamp by the table just inside the door, then jabbed a finger at her. "You're not making enough of an effort with Andrew."

She rolled her eyes. "I spent the first hour after he arrived hanging onto his every word, like you said. He doesn't want anything to do with me."

Which was fine with her, because she didn't want to marry a rich stranger who would engage her in an endless string of social events. Nor did she want to live on the outskirts of San Antonio in a mansion built with the sole purpose of impressing San Antonio's elite.

"Well, Andrew has agreed to escort you into dinner." Pa straightened the lapels of his tailored three-piece suit, not that they were crooked enough to need straightening. "Try to put on a little charm for him."

As though she had any charm with which to impress Andrew—or anyone else.

Pa turned as though to go, then stopped and stepped closer, his foggy eyes narrowing on her shoulder. "Is that straw on your dress?"

Was it? She looked down at the same time her father reached out and plucked the strand from where it had been stuck along her neckline.

Had she gone through that entire dance with Daniel with straw stuck to her? Another bout of heat burst onto her face. Why hadn't he or Wes said anything?

"Turn around."

She did, and the jerky way her father plucked her back told her more had gotten caught in the silly lace flounces he'd insisted she wear.

"What were you doing in the stable?" he thundered loudly enough the dancers could surely hear him upstairs.

"Calypso is in labor."

A curse exploded from his lips.

She whirled back around and planted a hand on her hip. "Don't be that way. You know how difficult foaling can be on a first-time mother. Someone needed to check on her."

"We have cowhands for that."

"Cowhands that know what to do with birthing cattle. Not horses."

"There's not that much difference."

"There is, and you know it. Calypso is getting along fine at the moment, not that you seem to care. But her labor isn't progressing very rapidly. I expect the foal will be born sometime around dawn."

Father muttered something under his breath that may have pertained to stubbornness and women.

"And I also peeked in at the horse Andrew Mortimer brought here while I was in the stable, so you can't say my being out there had nothing to do with the ball."

Pa set his jaw.

"What? You want me to marry him, don't you?" She threw up her hands. "It's fair that I know at least some of what his horse stock looks like before committing my life to him."

"Such things don't concern you." Pa pressed his lips back into that thin line of displeasure, an expression he wore all too often around her.

"Then what concerns me? How much land he's set to inherit after his father dies? How many cattle they run on their ranch?" She'd visited the Mortimers with her father in January. Their outfit outside of San Antonio was modest, nothing compared to the ranch her father owned. Cattle alone couldn't be what was enticing her father to forge a marriage between their families. "Perhaps I need to find out how well the portion of the railroad they own is doing?"

"None of it concerns you." Pa made a slashing motion with his hands, the movement so forceful the snowy white hair atop his head quivered. "The only think you should be thinking about is going back upstairs and impressing Andrew, charming him, wooing him. You're young and beautiful. Men's gazes follow you when you step into a room, yet you never try to impress any of the men I pick."

"Because I don't want to marry any of them!" Now she was the one shouting loudly enough to be heard in the ballroom. "And men's gazes don't follow me because I'm beautiful—that's Anna Mae. Men watch me because I'm a Westin and everyone knows we're drowning in more money and cattle than we know what to do with."

A sickening sensation roiled through her stomach. The truth was, she had to marry one of Pa's choices, whether she wanted to or not. She'd tried choosing her own husband not once but twice, and the results the second time around had been disastrous.

Daniel might be correct in that she needed to tell her family the full story about the rustlers, but she couldn't just yet, with memories of Robbie Ashton still burning through her like a branding iron to a calf's hide.

"I'll try my best to charm Andrew, Pa, truly." Charlotte fingered the shimmering fabric of the dress she'd donned for the ball, so very different from the leather split skirts and plain linen shirts she usually wore. "But charm doesn't come easy to me."

"I don't care whether it comes easy or hard." Father's voice held a low, flat tone, one that hinted at the business calculations and shrewd thinking that had allowed her father to grow the A Bar W into one of the largest ranches in Texas. "Just go upstairs and show some."

Charlotte straightened her back and swallowed the lump that had worked its way into her throat. Charm. Right. She'd have to do it, because she wouldn't put another three thousand head of cattle at risk by getting led astray by the wrong man a second time around.

~.~.~.~.~

Dancing with Charlotte had been a mistake.

Daniel Harding scanned the desert as he strode through the stone-tiled entrance to the Westin's hacienda and into the darkness. Watching her from across the ballroom had been hard, but what had he been thinking to actually walk over to her and strike up a conversation?

He'd been thinking she looked miserable standing against the wall by herself, and he'd wanted to replace the frown on her face with a smile. And maybe he'd been thinking he wanted a closer look at that dress which shimmered hues of jeweled green beneath the light of the chandeliers or at the hair piled atop her head in a riot of soft curls.

And that's where he'd made his mistake, because she'd been even more beautiful up close than he'd realized.

"You're not making enough of an effort with Andrew."

Daniel paused as a gust of wind blew over the desert. He recognized Agamemnon Westin V's voice, but where was it coming from?

"I am." Charlotte's voice this time, soft yet somehow defiant. "I spent the first hour after he arrived hanging onto his every word, like you said. He doesn't want anything to do with me."

Daniel turned in the direction of the voices. A dim lamp flickered through the open window of Mr. Westin's study.

"Well, Andrew has agreed to escort you to dinner. Try to put on a little charm for him."

Charm for Andrew? Daniel clenched his teeth together. Wes had introduced him to someone named Andrew. He'd been so busy watching the duo of women by his side that he'd barely managed to mutter a greeting. Why was Mr. Westin trying to marry Charlotte to such a man?

But he knew the answer. Agamemnon Westin V had spent years of work growing his ranch from a modest operation into one of the largest cattle companies in Texas, and he intended to use his wealth and fame to secure his children in marriages to similarly wealthy and famous families.

The trouble was, Charlotte wanted wide open spaces and mountain vistas and big, starry skies, not wealth or fame.

And none of this had anything to do with him. It didn't matter that he'd known Charlotte since the day she'd been born. His family didn't have enough money or prestige for Mr. Westin to even consider him as potential husband material for Charlotte.

Charlotte's conversation with her father continued in clipped tones. She'd snuck out to the barn to visit one of her laboring horses at some point in the evening. Not a surprise to anyone who knew Charlotte. She also wanted to know what kind of horse stock the Mortimers kept, how big their ranch was, how lucrative their shares in the Southern Pacific Railroad were. Again, none of this was surprising.

What was he even doing standing here, listening in on this conversation? He had a town to patrol and no deputies to help him tonight.

But if Charlotte she didn't want to marry this Mortimer fellow, then her father shouldn't make her. Did Wes realize how strongly his father was pushing for this wedding? Surely Wes wouldn't stand for such a thing.

And again, none of this was his concern.

He'd known Charlotte would one day marry a man of her father's choosing. The entire town of Twin Rivers knew it. And he'd been reminding himself of that fact since the day in church three years ago when he'd looked down the pew and realized Wes's little sister had somehow grown from a girl into a woman.

The trouble was, he could still feel Charlotte in his arms as he'd led her across the dance floor. Still remember the stiff way she'd held herself, still see the mesmerizing way the lighting had bounced against her honey brown hair. Still recall the way he'd almost gotten her to smile. Almost.

"Did you give Anna Mae one of your dresses to wear tonight?"

At the sound of his sister's name, Daniel straightened. What did Anna Mae have to do with anything?

"What if I did?" Charlotte's voice was short and clipped.

Daniel could almost imagine her standing in front of her father, her chin high and nostril's flared.

"You can't go giving her your clothes."

"Of course I can. I never wear that dress. Even with my horrible fashion sense, I could tell that shade of yellow clashes with my hair but would look gorgeous on Anna Mae. I gave it to her a month or so ago and she altered it."

"Yes, well now Andrew won't take his eyes off her."

"Of course he wouldn't. What man would? She's beautiful." Charlotte didn't speak her words with envy, but as though they were simple fact.

They were the oddest pair, Charlotte and Anna Mae. He would have never lumped them together, but they'd been friends since just about their first day of school. Most women felt threatened by Anna Mae's beauty, and if not that, they couldn't tolerate her constant chatter and never-ending energy. But Charlotte just blinked at her, shrugged, and went on with her quiet, structured life, taking whatever ideas Anna Mae concocted in stride.

"Andrew is supposed to be paying attention to you." Frustration dripped from Mr. Westin's voice. "Not the daughter of an invalid and a half-blood Mexican."

Daniel stiffened.

"Don't you ever refer to my friend that way again." Charlotte's voice slashed out the window and into the night. "If she can find happiness with a wealthy banker from Austin or even with Andrew Mortimer, then I'll be glad for her. After all, happiness is certainly more than you want for me and my future."

The muted clomping of boots on tile told him Charlotte was leaving the room, as did the sound of the door slamming.

Daughter of an invalid and a half-blood Mexican. Daniel stared into the night, his body still rigid. Did Mr. Westin think the same of him too? The man would have to, seeing as he and Anna Mae were full-blooded siblings.

Daniel shoved away from the wall and stalked toward where he'd left his horse, Charger, in one of the paddocks. He grabbed Charger's reins and led him away from the other horses before swinging into the saddle and turning his steed toward town.

If he were to be of any use on patrol once he got back to Twin Rivers, he'd need to scrub the image of Charlotte, dancing beneath the light of chandeliers, aglow in that emerald dress, from his memory.

Why had he even agreed to the dance in the first place? Forgetting the way she'd felt in his arms would take more effort than most anything else he'd ever tried to do in this life.

But he had to find a way to forget, because with him being the son of "an invalid and a half-blood Mexican," Charlotte Westin would never be his.

Order your copy of *Tomorrow's Shining Dream* on Amazon.
http://geni.us/TPAmazon2

Is this your first book by Naomi Rawlings? Want go back to the very beginning, read about the rugged town where Ellie grew up, and meet some of her friends? If so, I want to offer you a free Eagle Harbor novel to try. All you need to do is vist http://geni.us/BFunnelTFLfreeLUL and fill out the information.

Thank You

Thank you for reading *Tomorrow's First Light.* I sincerely hope you enjoyed Sam and Ellie's story. I'm so very excited to be starting a new series set in Texas, and I hope you come to love the rugged town of Twin Rivers as much as I have. The next full-length novel in the Texas Promise Series is Daniel and Charlotte's story, *Tomorrow's Shining Dream.* Click here to purchase.

Want to be notified when *Tomorrow's Shining Dream* releases? Sign up for my author newsletter. Subscribers also get a free novella in the Eagle Harbor Series. Sign Up Here.

Be sure to add author@naomirawlings.com to your safe email list so that the emails go through. I keep all subscriber information confidential.

Also, if you enjoyed reading *Tomorrow's First Light,* please take a moment to tell others about the novel. You can do this by posting an honest review on Amazon or GoodReads. Please note that to leave a review on Amazon, you need to go directly to Amazon's website. Your e-reader may ask you to rank stars at the end of this novel, but that ranking does not show up on Amazon as a review. I read every one of my reviews, and reviews help readers like yourself decide whether to purchase a novel. You might also consider mentioning *Tomorrow's First Light* to your friends on Facebook, Twitter, or Pinterest.

Other Novels by Naomi Rawlings

Texas Promise Series

Book 1—*Tomorrow's First Light* (Sam and Ellie)

Book 2—*Tomorrow's Shining Dream* (Daniel and Charlotte: releasing 2020)

Book 3—*Tomorrow's Constant Hope* (Wes and Keely: releasing 2020)

Book 4—*Tomorrow's Steadfast Prayer* (Harrison and Alejandra)

Book 5—*Tomorrow's Lasting Joy* (Cain and Anna Mae)

Eagle Harbor Series

Book 1—*Love's Unfading Light* (Mac and Tressa)

Book 2—*Love's Every Whisper* (Elijah and Victoria)

Book 3—*Love's Sure Dawn* (Gilbert and Rebekah)

Book 4—*Love's Eternal Breath* (Seth and Lindy)

Book 5—Love's Christmas Hope (Thomas and Jessalyn)

Book 6—*Love's Bright Tomorrow* (Isaac and Aileen)

Short Story—*Love's Beginning* (Elijah, Gilbert, Mac, Victoria, Rebekah)

Prequel—*Love's Violet Sunrise* (Hiram and Mabel)

Author's Note

I hope you enjoyed the start to the Texas Promise Series. I'm super excited to bring you this new series and I was also thrilled to add a bit of Eagle Harbor to the dusty Texan desert.

I hope you're intrigued by the marriage pact at the beginning of the novel, because in the coming books, that pact is going to come back to haunt each and every one of the boys who made it.

As both Sam and Ellie discover in this novel, there's no harm in asking for help when you need it. Oftentimes when we have trouble, help is the last thing we seek, even if it's only a phone call, email, or visit away. Like Sam, we might feel like we've somehow failed if we get to the point of asking for help. But the truth is, everyone needs help now and again, and other people may very well be blessed by getting to help you. I know that *Tomorrow's First Light* is a work of fiction, but I hope and pray this story illustrates the importance of cultivating meaningful relationships and leaning on others when life gives you problems.

While writing this book, I had the wonderful opportunity to go to Texas (for the first time ever). If you ever have the chance to visit Big Bend National Park or take the scenic drive that winds through Big Bend Ranch State Park, do it. The vast beauty of the region is unforgettable. If you're feeling more adventurous, I also recommend canoeing down the Rio Grande. (Yes, for real!)

The fictional town of Twin Rivers is set in what's known as "The Big Bend." It is based on a combination of the towns of Presidio, Lajitas, and Terligua, Texas. The Chihuahuan Trail is a real historical trail that ran from Chihuahua, Mexico to San Antonio, Texas, and the U.S. port of entry for the trail was Presidio.

After Mexico lost the Mexican-American War and ceded Texas (along with parts of present-day New Mexico, Arizona, and California) to the United States, the national Mexican government had a very difficult time maintaining order in its northern regions. Mexico City was far away from the Rio Grande Valley and didn't have a strong enough presence there to enforce laws. Bandits roamed the barren landscape, and many times local Mexican officials were in league with the bandits and paid to look the other way for crimes such as robberies and cattle rustling. The remoteness, mountainous terrain, and small population of the region gave Mexico little incentive to even try maintaining order. Simply put, it would cost too much money and manpower and only a small portion of the Mexican population would reap the benefits.

This arrangement didn't work out too well for the United States, and particularly for those living along the border. The cavalry soldiers stationed on the frontier and the Texas Rangers might not have had permission to cross into Mexico to apprehend criminals for crimes committed in the U.S., but the officers, soldiers, and lawmen living in that region soon found crossing the border to catch criminals necessary if they had any hope of controlling crime.

Eventually the U.S. government pressured the Mexican government enough that they sent troops to the Rio Grande, though this only lasted until the Mexican Revolution, when the government was thrown into chaos and once again and no longer had the resources it needed to control its northern territories.

Thank you for visiting Twin Rivers with me in this novel. I hope that you'll return to this forgotten corner of the Chihuahuan Desert to read Daniel and Charlotte's story, *Tomorrow's Shining Dream*, when it releases in 2020.

Acknowledgments

Thank you first and foremost to my Lord and Savior, Jesus Christ, for giving me both the ability and opportunity to write novels for His glory.

As with any novel, an author might come up with a story idea and sit at his or her computer to type the initial words, but it takes an army of people to bring you the book you have today. I'd especially like to thank my editors, Natalie Hanemann and Melissa Jagears, for pointing out ways to make this book stronger. Also, thank you to Judy at Judicious Revisions, Roseanna White, and Victoria Naegele for helping with the finer details of this novel.

Many thanks to my family for working with my writing schedule and giving me a chance to do two things I love: be a mommy and a writer. Also, thank you to Casey Wagner for watching my youngest child so I could have one day a week to focus only on my writing.

And finally, many thanks to the hospitable people of Terlingua, Texas and the staff at Fort Leaton for answering my numerous questions and helping me make the Texas landscape come alive. Thank you to Janelle at Lajitas and Big Bend Stables (https://www.lajitasstables.com/) both for the tour on horseback and for answering my many questions. Thank you to James at Big Bend River Tours (http://bigbendrivertours.com/) for a memorable trip down the Rio Grande. My only complaint was that the trip was too short. Thank you to the wonderful park ranger at Fort Leaton who answered my numerous questions on two separate occasions. I'm so sorry I don't remember your name. I thought about calling Fort Leaton to see if I could learn it, but figured that might seem rather stalker-like.

And finally, thank you to Curt Swafford of Tarantula Ranch for hosting me and my travelling companions in your guest cabins. Your stories and detailed explanations brought my Texas experience to life and gave me a deeper understanding of the Big Bend. Also, you win the award for hot tub with the best view ever. Seriously, I'm talking mountain vistas at sunset. How many people with hot tubs can claim that view? You also win the award for having the most memorable driveway ever. I never knew it could take fifteen minutes to drive a half mile. Fortunately, the spectacular hot tub views and quintessential stories made up for the driveway. If any of my readers have a desire to go to the Big Bend and stay at Tarantula Ranch, contact me and I'll pass on Curt's information. It will save you some money in booking fees.

About the Author

Naomi Rawlings is the author of numerous historical Christian novels, including the Amazon bestselling Eagle Harbor Series. While she'd love to claim she spends her days huddled in front of her computer vigorously typing, in reality she spends her time cleaning, picking up, and pretending like her house isn't in a constant state of chaos. She lives with her husband and three children in Michigan's rugged Upper Peninsula, along the southern shore of Lake Superior where they get 200 inches of snow every year, and where people still grow their own vegetables and cut down their own firewood—just like in the historical novels she writes.

For more information about Naomi, please visit her at www.naomirawlings.com or find her on Facebook at www.facebook.com/author.naomirawlings. If you'd like a free novella, sign up for her author newsletter.

Made in the USA
Middletown, DE
04 December 2023